SHAVLAN

# SHAVLAN

EUNICE E. BLECKER

# SHAVLAN

A NOVEL

EUNICE E. BLECKER

Newbridge Press, Inc.

Copyright © 2017 by Eunice E. Blecker

All rights reserved. No part of this publication may be reproduced, stored in a retrieval system, distributed, or transmitted in any form or by any means, including photocopying, recording, or other electronic or mechanical methods, without the prior written permission of the author, except in the case of brief quotations embodied in critical reviews and certain other noncommercial uses permitted by copyright law.

While specific characters in this novel are historical figures and certain events did occur, this is a work of fiction. All incidents and dialogue are products of the author's imagination and are not to be construed as real. Where real-life historical or public figures appear, the situations, incidents, and dialogues concerning those persons are entirely fictional and are not intended to change the entirely fictional nature of the work. In all other respects, any resemblance to persons living or dead is entirely coincidental.

Cover Design: Cynde Weinstein

Photographs: Eunice E. Blecker

ISBN-13: 978-1546966166
ISBN-10: 1546966161

Published by

Newbridge Press, Inc.

www.NewbridgePress.com

FIRST EDITION
19 01 18 17 38

*Dedicated*

*to the*

*memory*

*of*

*Sarah Taube Grazutis*

# SHAVLAN

# Contents

# SHAVLAN

Grazutis family photograph taken in Shavlan on the 21st of September 1909. From left to right: Sarah Taube, Ruchel, Avram, Gitka, Charles and Chaya.

# Chapter 1 – Cossacks

## May 1919 – Ekaterinoslav, Ukraine, Soviet Russia

Sarah Taube lay frightened in the dimly lit cellar surrounded by her three precious children. Thank goodness they were asleep, she thought. Her daughter Chaya was well aware of what was happening, but the two younger children were still so very innocent and untouched by the cruel realities of war.

The sound of galloping horses, troops marching, the firing of rifles, and the piercing cries of men, women and children could be heard nearby.

"How could this be happening?" she asked herself.

Where was Dimitri who promised to be there for her and the children if she ever needed him? She was again isolated and alone, with only her wits to help her think calmly and clearly.

It seemed to her as if a curse had been placed upon nearly all of the males in her life.

It first began with her father who was killed during a pogrom, attempting to save the life of a woman he did not even know. Then there was her husband, stuck in a faraway land unable to rescue her in her time of need. Losing her sweet, innocent, young son Avram so tragically still overpowered her with sorrow. And the thought of not knowing whether her eldest son Yankel was alive or dead overwhelmed her with grief. So why shouldn't she think a curse had been placed on those males so closely connected to her? Why indeed.

She was determined to be strong for her children's sake, though there were times when she felt the strain of it was too much for her to bear. But somehow she would always find the strength to carry on, regardless of all the obstacles she had to face.

Sarah Taube could not have known how events on the world stage and people, some of which she did not even know, could have wield so much power over her and her family.

Had fate brought her to this predicament?

To understand how this all came about, we have to go back in time to a small village called Mozir in the Ukraine.

# Chapter 2 – Brother and Sister

## September 1871 – Mozir, Ukraine, Russian Empire

Faivush had been asleep for less than an hour, when his sister, Gesya entered his room.

"Wake up," she whispered in his ear. "Please, wake up. It's almost ten o'clock, and I have to tell you something very important."

Faivush Gelfman, a blond-haired boy of twelve, opened his eyes and saw his sister standing over him.

"I'm leaving this dreadful place," she said. "I can't stand it anymore. If I don't leave now, it will be too late for me."

"Try to stick it out a little longer. Besides, where will you go?"

"Anywhere is better than here."

Gesya, a tall, slender young girl, who recently turned sixteen, lived with her brother, father, and stepmother in a small shtetl not too far from Kiev.

The children's father, Lef Gelfman, a well-to-do Orthodox Jew who ran an inn at the outskirts of town, had remarried soon after the death of his first wife. His new wife, Olga, strong and domineering, took charge of the household as soon as she stepped into the Gelfman home.

"I've learned," Gesya said, with tears streaming down her face, "that I'm to be promised to some strange man almost three times my age who, according to Mrs. Greenstern, the butcher's wife, used to beat his first wife until she killed herself. And I have our stepmother to blame for arranging this marriage for me."

"Why don't you say you refuse to marry him?" Faivush asked.

"That's impossible, my dear brother. You know I have no say in the matter, and within a few weeks I'll be handed over to this barbarian as if I were a slab of meat hanging from the hook in the butcher's ice house.

"I can't let that happen, so I've made up my mind. I'm leaving this place for good. I wanted to tell you so you wouldn't worry or wonder where I've gone, and as soon as I get settled, I'll write you with my new address. But I can't send the letter here. I don't want my whereabouts to be known by *Tateh*"—father.

Her brother thought for a moment.

"I know," he said with a hint of mischief in his eyes. "You can send it to my friend Isak. That way *Tateh* will never find out."

He jotted down Isak's address and handed it to her.

"I wish you weren't going," he said, "but I understand. Some day, I hope to leave this place like you."

After his sister threw some clothing into a small, worn out suitcase, she bent over her brother's bed and gave him a kiss. He breathed in the familiar scent of rose water on her hair as she lingered close to him and, with tears in his eyes, sadly watched as she went out the door, disappearing into the cool September night.

The following morning, when Faivush's father learned his daughter had run away, he no longer considered her a member of the family and banished her from his life.

Faivush felt his father acted cruelly toward his sister, and it opened an emotional chasm between him and his father, which could never be breached.

After a month, Faivush's friend, Isak received a letter from Gesya. The letter stated she had moved to Kiev, an industrial city on the Dnieper River and found employment, working as a seamstress in a clothing factory. From then on, whenever Isak received a letter from her, he would immediately notify Faivush.

Isak had befriended Faivush only a year ago. In fact, he owed his life to him. Last year, on a shivery, Sunday afternoon in the dead of winter, while Faivush was ice-skating at a nearby frozen lake, he heard a young boy yelling, "Help me! Someone, help me!"

Faivush recognized the boy as being his neighbor's son, Isak. He had fallen through a weak patch of ice close to the edge of the pond, and he was screaming for assistance.

Faivush, although frightened, immediately took off his wooden skates and ran to the ground near the hole where Isak had fallen. He grabbed a long branch lying beside an oak tree and held it out for Isak to grab. Isak, pale with exhaustion, managed to pull himself out.

Without hesitating, Faivush, who was wearing a wool sweater underneath his winter coat, removed his outer garment and wrapped it around Isak's body to keep him warm and, with great difficulty, helped him struggle along the snow-covered pathway that led back to his house.

Isak related the story to his parents and word quickly spread that Faivush had saved their son's life.

Shortly afterward, the entire village came out to honor the young man's heroic act.

Faivush's father was extremely proud of his son's courageous behavior. Realizing Faivush could have died in that frozen lake trying to rescue Isak, he was determined to bring about a much closer relationship between the two of them. The boys quickly recovered from their harrowing experience that cold and foreboding winter day and from that time on, became close friends.

Almost six years had passed but Gesya never stopped writing her brother. He was pleased she did not forget him, and although they were separated by distance, they grew even closer as the years went by.

Today was Faivush's eighteenth birthday, and shortly he would be eligible to enter the university. Late in the afternoon, his father called him to his study to wish him a happy birthday and to discuss his plans for the future.

"Faivush, have you given any thought to what university you wish to attend?"

"Yes," Faivush replied. "I'd like to go to the Saint Vladimir University in Kiev."

"Saint Vladimir University in Kiev," his father cried out. "I'm curious to know what made you pick that university?"

Of course, Faivush did not want to tell him Gesya lived in Kiev and since his father never asked about his daughter, Faivush did not think it necessary to share that information.

"I'm interested in studying about the theories and attitudes held by people that act as a guiding principle for behavior," Faivush replied. "Vladimir University has a Faculty of Philosophy. I've heard they accept Jews but they have a quota, so I have to hurry and fill out an application in order to take the entrance exam."

"I'm very pleased you wish to continue with your studies my son, and as long as you get good grades, I'll be willing to fund your education."

"Thank you for all your support throughout my schooling," Faivush replied, "and for giving me the encouragement to continue on. I'll try to make you proud."

"Proud! I've always been proud of you. Never forget what I've been telling you all these years. Do you recall what it was?"

Faivush put his finger to his chin.

"Ah, now I remember. You would always say, "Life without an education is like having a good mind but nothing to use it for."

"Yes, my son. Remember well those words. It's short but meaningful and conveys a great deal of truth."

Faivush's father, as an innkeeper, was invisible to many of the travelers staying at his inn and by listening in on their conversations, he had developed a keen understanding of what was going on politically, so he offered his son some fatherly advise.

"There are many people who say they want political and social reform in the country. I've heard that many radical agitators go to cities and towns to spread their unconventional beliefs and revolutionary ideas. Beware of such people and do not get involved with them."

In Kiev, Gesya was happy to be managing her life and working at the clothing factory. Faivush was fortunate to be accepted into the university, and Gesya would invite him over for dinner whenever he had free time.

One afternoon, while the owners of the factory were away on a buying trip, two women who were political revolutionaries came into the establishment to give a talk. Both women were in their early twenties and were dressed in a similar fashion, wearing ankle-length, black dresses and gray knitted shawls draped around their shoulders.

"Good afternoon," one of the women said with a serious expression on her face. "My name is Alana Konstantinov and this is Anna Borenstein. We're here today to tell you about a political and economic system we truly believe in. It's called socialism. We believe in social democracy. This means the products you make and the profits from the sales of these products should be owned by you, the workers and not the owners of this establishment."

Alana and her friend continued to present and explain, systematically, the policies and practices of socialism and how it would affect the workers.

Gesya was an uneducated woman and could not understand what these women were saying, but still she felt respect and admiration for them. To her, they were completely liberated, both in their ideas and in their actions—something she could relate to in her own life. She was independent and earning her own living.

While Alana and Anna continued to speak, Gesya became even more impressed with them, and after they finished their talk, she chatted with them for a time and then invited them to have their meetings in her small apartment.

Every Sunday, these two women met with Gesya, accompanied by other revolutionaries. Gesya, ignorant as she was, did not have a clue that these meetings were unlawful. Even though she was a victim of ignorance, it did not matter. After a short time, the authorities located and arrested the entire cell, including Gesya.

Not hearing from his sister for some time, Faivush attempted to see her but when he arrived at her apartment, the landlord told him a group of men had taken her away, and he hadn't seen or heard from her since.

Several days later, the news of the arrests had made the local newspaper, and Faivush had learned his sister was accused of being a revolutionary and had been sentenced to two years imprisonment at the Kiev Fortress.

Faivush wanted to visit and see if he could help but when he consulted with one of his friends, it was suggested he stay as far away from his sister as possible.

He was told it was likely she was being watched by the secret police, and he would be under suspicion of being involved with the revolutionary movement if it were made known he was her brother. His friend convinced him to wait until she was released and hope she would contact him.

Faivush was extremely upset about his sister's arrest and put into prison for a crime he believed she did not knowingly commit. He felt sorry for her and was certain she knew nothing about revolutionaries and what they stood for.

He, early on at the university, had grown more antagonistic toward the Tsarist regime and thought he needed to show a more active opposition toward the present government.

As part of his studies, he took a Russian history class from Professor Markov Vladimerskii, an outstanding Ukrainian political thinker. Several weeks into the course, the professor began to take an interest in him because he was one of his more promising students.

One day, after class, Faivush was called to the professor's office and was invited to his home that evening to attend a private discussion group. When Faivush arrived that night, he noticed there were men and women there from various walks of life.

In attendance were students, recent graduates, physicians, and what seemed to be ordinary working-class people. Many subjects were discussed, which centered on the different opinions of those in attendance.

The professor spoke very seriously about socialism and how it could be put into practice for the good of the people.

While attending the meeting, Faivush noticed a young man taking notes and asking a number of questions, and he seemed to be completely engrossed in what the professor was saying.

The young man saw Faivush staring at him and after the meeting, approached him.

"I see you too are interested in the professor's ideas. Let me introduce myself. I'm Anatoly Medvedeva."

"I'm Faivush Gelfman and yes, what the professor said sounded very interesting."

"If you're really interested in the professor's ideas and are willing to do something about it, I'll give you my address. You can meet me there tomorrow evening at seven, and we can discuss it further."

The next evening, Faivush, intrigued by Anatoly, arrived exactly on time.

"Welcome," Anatoly said as he opened the door and led him into a small bedroom.

He picked up a chair for Faivush to sit in and placed it next to a small desk off to the side of his bed.

"What year are you in at the university?" he asked, pulling up a chair for himself.

"I'm in my first year."

"Then I take it, you haven't had time to involve yourself with any interesting groups?"

"No, but I'm interested in hearing what groups are available."

"I understand you're enrolled in several classes with topics pertaining to philosophy. I'm curious. Why have you chosen that particular subject?"

"I've always been interested in learning about ethics, morality, and philosophy," Faivush replied. "I thought I would take a course in Russian history and that's how I came to attend Professor Vladimerskii's lectures. What he said last night made perfectly good sense to me."

Anatoly smiled. "Good. I'm glad to hear it." He moved his chair close to Faivush and began to speak in a low voice so no one outside the room could hear him.

"I belong to a group called, *Students for Change*. They meet every Sunday evening at different locations. We are active in every struggle possible for social justice. We believe in running our organization in a democratic way because we think it's necessary to hear all of our members' experiences and ideas.

"Yes, it is true," Anatoly said, raising his fist in the air. "We are Socialists. We believe the workers should share in the fruits of their labor. We need to change society to benefit the workers and not the capitalists.

"We have weekly meetings where we talk about the politics of making over the world and all mankind. Join us. I promise you won't regret it. Are you in?"

Faivush was speechless. This was exactly the group he was searching for.

"I'm in," he replied, patting Anatoly on the back several times.

Anatoly reached into the drawer of his desk and pulled out two small glasses and a bottle of vodka.

"I wish to make a toast," he announced as his eyes shone with excitement.

Faivush and Anatoly got up from their chairs and raised their glasses high.

"To a long and lasting friendship," Anatoly said.

"And long live socialism," Faivush replied, thinking to himself, I have found something worth believing in.

So after a few months in university, with no previous work experience and with little understanding of the ways of the world, Faivush embraced, along with many other students, a philosophy that sounded fair. Society and future events had not yet molded him into the man he would become.

# Chapter 3 – Death in the Family

## June 1877 – Shavlan, Kovne Guberniya, Russian Empire

Shavlan, a small town located on a hill in western Lithuania, had approximately 2,000 inhabitants, half of which were Jews. It had no paved roads, and the livelihood of its people revolved around a large marketplace in the center of town.

In a small house near the marketplace, Sarah Taube, a nine-year-old, oval faced girl with green eyes and long brown hair, lay sleeping. As the warm summer rays shone through the half open shutter over her bed, she awoke.

Where were the smells of freshly baked bread in the old brick oven, the patter of feet hustling about on the old wood floor, and the clanging of pots and pans in preparation for the day's meals?

While she lay under the covers, she heard soft whispers of prayers coming from her mother's room. Quickly, she threw off the quilt, leaped to her feet, and pulled away the curtain that partitioned her sleeping space.

When she looked in, she could hear her mother murmuring as if with her last breath, "*myne kinder, myne kinder*"—my children, my children.

A loud gasp was heard and then silence like the sudden stillness in the woods after a storm.

She could see Aunt Lena, Uncle Morris, and her brother, Aaron hovering over her mother, with their hands held closely over their faces.

As they began reciting a prayer, Sarah Taube glanced at Aaron. A deathly hush fell over the room. Her mother's body lay motionless. Her face was white, and her skin had taken on a grayish cast.

Aunt Lena, a small, brown-haired woman who looked a lot like

Sarah Taube's mother, called out, "*myne shvester is toit. Myne shvester is toit*"—my sister is dead. My sister is dead.

"Now Lena, you must be brave, especially for the children," Uncle Morris said.

Sarah Taube looked at her mother's body with disbelief. "No, no, it can't be true," she cried. "Aaron, shake her and make her wake up."

"*Mammeh* has gone, dear sister, and there's nothing anyone can do for her." Aaron put his arm around her and placed a kiss on her forehead.

"*Mammeh, Mammeh*" Sarah Taube again cried. "You promised you would never leave me. Wake up. Wake up."

Aunt Lena grabbed Sarah Taube and shook her as if she were trying to shake the reality of what had happened into her body, knowing her mind was not yet ready to accept her mother's passing.

Breaking away from her aunt's firm grip, Sarah Taube threw herself on her mother's chest, still not willing to face the fact that the soul of her mother had already left its body.

"Your mother's days on earth have ended, my child," Aunt Lena said, her voice conveying sadness.

To prove to her niece her mother had indeed left this world, she instructed Aaron to go and get "the feather."

Remembering his mother had plucked a chicken for the previous week's Sabbath meal, he ran into the kitchen, reached deep into the cupboard, and pulled out a single, reddish-brown plume.

How strange it was, he thought, that this one lonely feather laid waiting as if his mother had been saving it for some special purpose.

Holding his breath with anticipation, he placed the feather under his mother's nostrils. The feather did not move.

"Blessed be the True Judge. It is the will of G-d," uttered Aunt Lena.

All realized at that moment the person lying on the bed was never going to regain consciousness.

A torrent of tears began to flow down Sarah Taube's cheeks. Her mother was gone, and she would never again hear her say, "*myne kind, myne kind*"—my child, my child.

No one spoke. Aunt Lena broke the silence.

"Aaron, run and tell the rabbi and the *Chevra Kadisha*, the burial society, of your mother's passing."

Jumping slightly at the sound of her voice, Aaron threw open the front door and hurried across the unpaved street.

The news of death's new purchase traveled swiftly, and when Aaron arrived, he saw the elderly matrons sitting in a circle, sewing a shroud. They spent most of their spare time preparing the plain linen shrouds so that their stockpile would be ready for each life's eventuality.

Gossiping as they stitched, each shroud took on a special quality. With every story told, the seams and hems would change, so no two shrouds were exactly the same. Somehow, they never felt their stockpile was large enough. G-d forbid, they would not have enough shrouds if a pogrom or epidemic were to strike the shtetl.

Years of experience gave these women second sight to foretell when someone's time was drawing near. Sarah Taube's mother had been ill for several weeks, and the progression of her illness kept almost perfect time to the ticking of the matrons' clock in expectation of her death.

"We must make the house ready for "sitting" *shivah*," Aunt Lena said, when Aaron returned.

*Shivah* was the mourning period, and everyone knew quite well what it meant. All the mirrors needed to be covered and would remain covered from the moment of death until the end of the seven days of grieving.

There was one particular superstition regarding the mirrors, and it was if the mirror was not covered, the deceased spirit might get trapped and remain there forever.

After thoroughly searching the house, Aunt Lena found three white pieces of cloth neatly folded and stored in the bottom of an old chest of drawers. This was the same cloth used to cover the mirrors when Sarah Taube's father so tragically passed away two short years ago.

By the time all the mirrors were covered, it was late morning and preparations had to be made because the body needed to be cleaned, purified, and buried before the next sunset.

Early that afternoon, the completed shroud was brought to the mourners' house. The body was undressed, washed, and wrapped in cloth and then placed on the floor, with a lit candle at the head to symbolize the soul and the feet pointing toward the door.

Sarah Taube tugged at a matron's skirt crying, "Don't touch my *Mammeh*. Take your hands off of her and let her be."

"My child, you must let them prepare your mother for her long journey," Aunt Lena said when she entered the room.

Before Sarah Taube could respond, the front door opened and the room filled with relatives, friends, and neighbors who came, as was the custom, to ask forgiveness of the deceased for any insults or offenses they may have inflicted on her during her life.

Night was about to fall as the shadows of the sun crossed the room and signaled it would soon cease its travels, leaving darkness as its legacy of the day.

Aunt Lena and Uncle Morris had no time to think about the future. Only the events of the next day were of concern. They would have plenty of time after the mourning period to discuss the arrangements, which needed to be made for the children.

"Good night," Aunt Lena said just before she blew out the candles. "Tomorrow we have to bury your mother so her soul may enter paradise."

Sarah Taube's mother came to her in a dream while she lay sleeping. Her large brown eyes shone with affection. She wore the Sabbath dress and around her neck hung a single strand of pearls.

Reaching for the three brass candlesticks, she lit them, saying, "Blessed art Thou, oh Lord our G-d, King of the Universe, who hast hallowed us by His Commandments and commanded us to kindle the Sabbath light." And in the flickering glow of the flames, she covered her eyes with her hands and began to say her own prayer, dictated by her heart.

"Oh Lord my G-d, protect Sarah Taube and Aaron from all evil. May they grow up to be good and righteous Jews and honor Thy Commandments, and may you bestow upon them the blessings I could not."

Sarah Taube tried to hold on to the dream but, after a few moments, her mother's image disappeared.

Early the next morning, the sun rose, and the bright yellow rays could be seen through the cracks in the front door. Sarah Taube awoke and looked around.

"Cleanse yourself and say your morning prayers," a voice from the kitchen spoke.

Sarah Taube jumped out of bed and pushed open the curtain, hoping to see her mother standing there preparing breakfast but seeing Aunt Lena, Uncle Morris, and Aaron sitting at the table, soon brought back the sad truth. But because of the dream she had had the night before, she knew the memory of her mother would never leave her.

In the middle of reciting the morning prayers, Sarah Taube pushed herself away from the table, stood up, and shouted, "What kind of G-d are you? You have taken *Mammeh* away. You have taken *Tateh* away. Why have you done this to me?"

"You must not take the Lord's name in vain," Aunt Lena scolded. "*Gott vet shtrofn*—G-d will punish. We're not allowed to question *der oybershter in himl*—the highest one in heaven. Come, sit down beside your brother. Eat your breakfast. Let's not speak of such things."

Aunt Lena poured a glass of hot tea and placed a warm, sweet roll, oozing with plum jam, on a plate before her niece. Aaron lifted her glass and began cooling the tea with his breath.

"Here," he said. "You can sip it now. It will not burn you."

A few hours later, the men from the burial society arrived, lifting the body and placing it on a horse-drawn wagon. Sarah Taube, Aaron, Aunt Lena, Uncle Morris, and several relatives walked behind the wagon, followed by friends and neighbors.

The entire Jewish community attended the funeral. According to custom, the more people accompany the body, the more angels will greet the soul and therefore it was considered a duty to attend.

In a small shtetl like Shavlan, not attending a life event such as a circumcision, bar mitzvah, wedding, or funeral was regarded as an insult and could lead to total rejection of the offender's social and economic life.

The cemetery was located less than a mile from the center of town. The procession marched along the purposely-winding road, so it would take more time to get there.

This was the community's way of showing the departed its reluctance to separate from one of its members. It also satisfied the superstitious, since it helped prevent the dead from finding their way back, perhaps with the help of demons, to torment former acquaintances and pay back the debts of former hurts.

When they approached the cemetery gate, two gentile gravediggers, wearing overalls caked with dried brown dirt, came out of their hut and led the procession, weaving in and out of narrow pathways, toward the grave of Sarah Taube's father. As they neared the gravesite, they could read the inscription on the headstone:

*Yankel Fineberg*
*Son of Abraham*
*Born: 10 February 1828 Died: 28 June 1875*
*Beloved Husband; Loving Father*

And deeply incised in the stone were the words:

*A Fallen Hero, May He Rest in Peace.*

A freshly dug grave lay to the right of the stone and after a bit of earth from Palestine was placed under the head of the deceased, the body was lowered, uncoffined, into its final resting place.

Friends and relatives gathered and paid their last respects, while a gray-haired old man, an official of the burial society, cut a gash in the clothing of Sarah Taube and her family. The clothes of those closest to the deceased were torn to indicate grief.

The grave was covered with earth, and the rabbi, a short, black-bearded man, wearing a tallis that caught the noonday rays in its gold strands, said the appropriate prayers.

"Life was for the living, and there must be a division between life and death," he said, "but as long as we can remember our departed ones, they will live in our hearts for all time."

Aaron took a long, deep breath, and, as the closest male relative, recited the Kaddish, the prayer for the dead, and before the next sundown, as was mandated under Jewish law, the body had been buried.

Just before leaving the cemetery, to symbolize their nearness, Sarah Taube and her family dug deeply into the brown, gritty soil. Each pulled up a small rounded stone and placed it on the grave.

The funeral services had come to an end. People began to leave the grounds, while some wandered off to pay their respects to their own dead.

As Sarah Taube walked with her relatives through the winding pathway, she turned and looked over her shoulder, taking one last glance.

The seven days of intensive mourning known as "sitting" *shivah* was about to begin.

Aunt Lena motioned for Sarah Taube and Aaron to sit on low boxes brought in by the *Chevra Kadisha*. It was customary for the mourners to sit on low chairs or boxes during the *shivah* period, which may have resulted in the expression "sitting" *shivah*.

The house quickly filled with visitors, each carrying a covered container of food. According to Jewish practice, it was prohibited for the grievers to partake in any physical or pleasurable activities until the mourning period was over.

One after another, the dishes kept coming—a basket full of hot bagels—a pot of warm lentils—a bowl of freshly picked peas—all round or circular food to symbolize the circle of life.

Mrs. Bleekman, the local matchmaker, a short, dumpy woman decked out in a black, silk dress and lace head covering, entered the room, carrying a tray of hardboiled eggs.

"Come, eat, Sarah Taube," she said, pointing her fingers at the table.

Sarah Taube got up from the hard box and greeted her.

"Come, eat," Mrs. Bleekman said again. "It's a simple but nourishing meal."

Responding to Mrs. Bleekman's urging, Aunt Lena, Uncle Morris, and Aaron got up and made themselves a plate of food and returned to their seats.

The room was packed by now, and when Sarah Taube looked around, she noticed a tall, bearded young man standing next to her aunt. His eyes were deep brown, and he wore a black suit.

"Aaron, Sarah Taube, come here," Aunt Lena called. "You remember your cousin Charles. He's your late father's sister's son and has come from Shidleve to pay his respects."

"My mother and I were very sorry to hear of your dear mother's passing," the young man said. "She sends her condolences and asks your forgiveness for not being here, but she was not feeling well and could not make the trip."

"I remember you," Aaron said, staring at Charles' face. "You came here with your mother for my father's funeral. Don't you remember him, Sarah Taube?"

"No, Aaron. I'm afraid I do not."

"Well, perhaps you were too young."

Charles went over to the table, placed two hardboiled eggs and a bagel on a plate and handed it to Sarah Taube.

"Would you like a glass of hot tea, Sarala?" he asked.

She was taken by surprise. How strange she thought. Only her father called her Sarala. How much like her father he sounded—forceful, yet gentle at the same time. She took the glass of hot tea and the plate of food from his outstretched arms and began to eat.

While he spoke, she could not take her eyes off of him. Every word he said presented itself as a sweet voice entering her heart. And when the night grew near and people began to depart, she did not want to see this handsome, gentle man leave.

The cloudless summer sky began to darken and the evening stars formed their patterns across the horizon. Dusk had fallen and a new day was about to begin.

Aunt Lena and her husband, Morris Levitt, lived in the center of town, close to the marketplace in a two-story house. There was a bakery shop, a kitchen, and dining area on the first level with a living room and two bedrooms upstairs.

Although they loved children, they were not fortunate to have had any of their own. When Aunt Lena's sister, Ruchel passed away, she and her husband took Sarah Taube and her brother, Aaron into their home. The children were expected to work in the bakery and help Aunt Lena with the daily chores.

Today, marked five months since Sarah Taube and Aaron had moved into their aunt and uncle's house. Aaron was almost fourteen

**and growing restless with life in Shavlan, so Aunt Lena and Uncle Morris decided it was best that he go to America and live with Uncle Morris's brother, Harry.**

**Aaron was very happy to hear the news. He had always dreamed of moving to America, but Sarah Taube wanted to go too.**

**Aaron promised when he got settled he would send for her, and she had to be patient, but soon they would be together again. Final arrangements were made, and Aaron was off to America within the month.**

**"Letter from Aaron! Letter from Aaron!" Aunt Lena shouted one cold winter morning.**

**Grabbing the cotton towel from the counter, Sarah Taube wiped the powdered sugar from her long lean fingers, sat down on a bench near the window, and opened Aaron's letter.**

*2 December 1877*
*Dear Sarah Taube, Aunt Lena, and Uncle Morris,*

*I know it's been a while since I left and you have not heard from me. I had to stay in Hamburg for six days until our ship pulled in. Before boarding, I had to wait in line to be examined by a doctor. Thank G-d I was healthy. They moved me through in a very short time, and I was allowed to board the ship and begin the long journey across the Atlantic.*

*People were huddled together in dark, filthy compartments in the steerage of the ship. There was an empty wooden cot, so I threw my parcel down quickly to claim it. Thank G-d Aunt Lena packed salami, sweet rolls, and breads for me or else I would have starved halfway through the voyage.*

*That first night I couldn't sleep, so I went up on the rear deck. I began to wonder about my future in America. Without knowing the language and having very little education, how would I survive? I felt encouraged somehow, thinking of Uncle Morris sending me to live with his brother.*

*After nine days at sea, the ship landed at Castle Garden, a massive structure built almost one hundred years ago as a fort on a small island close to the west side of Manhattan. After another medical examination, I was given my papers for clearance.*

*Uncle Morris's brother, Harry met me in a special waiting room and took me to live with him in his apartment in the Lower East Side of the city. I go to school in the morning to learn to read and write English and, in the afternoon, I work in a bakery to make money, so I can save for a ticket for you, myne tay'er shvester—my dear sister.*

While Sarah Taube sat, enjoying Aaron's first letter from America, she stopped for a moment and reread part of the sentence.

*"I work in a bakery to make money, so I can save for a ticket for you..."*

She thought to herself, I hope he earns enough money quickly, so I can join him soon.

Then she picked up where she left off and continued to read.

*Life here is wonderful. I have never seen so many people and so many of them are rich. I can tell by their fine clothing. There is plenty of food, plenty of jobs, and plenty of friendly people. I have not forgotten my promise to you. Some day soon I will send for you, and you too will come here to begin a new life. Write me soon.*

*Regards to all,*
*Love,*
*Aaron*

Sarah Taube put down the letter and asked her aunt, "Why does everyone want to go to America? I thought this was our home."

Aunt Lena took off her apron and sat down beside her niece.

"This is not our home, my child. It was never our home and will never be our home. Our families have lived here for many generations and, in most cases, we've been left alone to conduct our lives as we see fit. But we are not real citizens of this country and are tolerated by the gentiles, and if we all left, they would not care. They would just say, "good riddance." We are Jews. We have no country. The Zionists believe we should go to Palestine and build a homeland, but I don't know. And then there are the pogroms.

"Remember your father and how he was killed? He was passing through a town, seeking new customers in order to sell his goods, when a pogrom broke out. Had he not thrown himself in front of a mother and her child, he probably would be alive today. It must have been *bashert.*" It was meant to be.

"Then why don't you and Uncle Morris leave?" Sarah Taube questioned.

"Because Uncle Morris has a fine business here, and he would have to start over in America. I would like to go, but my place is with your uncle. Perhaps someday he will change his mind. Who can tell what the future holds for us?

"When Aaron saves up enough money to send for you, my child, then you will have to make up your mind about what you want to do. Anyway, I'm happy Aaron got to America safely.

"It was just the other day," Aunt Lena continued, "when Mrs. Bleekman told me her cousin was robbed and beaten while en route to Hamburg. Unfortunately, he had to come back because all his money was gone, and he could not pay for his passage."

"He was unlucky," Sarah Taube said, folding Aaron's letter and placing it back into its envelope. "But our Aaron is smart. He knew enough to stay away from any bad people. I'm sure he hid his money under his clothing as Uncle Morris's brother told him to do in his letter. Don't you remember?"

"Yes, I do," replied Aunt Lena, glancing at the clock on the wall. "But enough talk about Aaron. We must finish laying out the challahs in the display case. The customers will be arriving soon, and the store will be crowded with *Erev Shabbos Layt*"—Sabbath eve customers.

Sarah Taube and her family worked very hard getting out their products in time for the shoppers and within minutes, the women began to form a line outside the door.

Mrs. Zimmer, the shoemaker's wife, a short, plump woman, who looked as if she had eaten one or two pastries too many, appeared, wearing a dreary, brown overcoat with a gray-stripped *babushka* wrapped around her head. She was the first to place her order.

"I would like four rolls, four sweet buns, and one large challah," she said, pointing her short, crooked fingers toward the case.

Sarah Taube and Aunt Lena were very busy the rest of the morning. Since it was *Erev Shabbos,* the bakery was open only until noon in order to give Aunt Lena and Sarah Taube enough time to rush upstairs to their living quarters and make their own house ready for the Sabbath.

Four months had passed, and it was a week before Passover. Sarah Taube had finished waiting on the last customer of the day. She had a strange expression on her face and a crinkle formed on her forehead.

"What is a blood libel?" she asked her aunt.

"Why are you asking me this?"

"This morning, I heard Mrs. Bleekman talking about blood libels to Mrs. Levitan, and she said she hoped nothing like that would ever happen in our shtetl. What did she mean?"

Aunt Lena took off her apron, placed it on the counter, and sat Sarah Taube down near the window.

"I guess it's time for you to learn about those hateful words, my dear," she said.

Sarah Taube was now very curious and gave her aunt her undivided attention.

"The term blood libel," her aunt began, "I believe, goes back to the Middle Ages. It is a false accusation placed on Jews, stating they kidnap and murder Christian children in order to use their blood as part of their religious rituals."

Sarah Taube sat deep in thought.

"That could never happen."

"Of course not, my child. It's another form of persecution against us. But whenever we celebrate a holiday and especially if there's a death of a young Christian child in the community, an accusation of murder could be placed on us."

Aunt Lena reached for Sarah Taube's hand and said, "Luckily, it does not occur often, and we should be thankful. But we still have to be on special alert while celebrating our holidays because these kinds of accusations can occur at any time."

As the days and months passed, Sarah Taube anxiously waited for that special letter from Aaron, telling her he had arranged for her to come live with him in America. She received many letters from him but not that special letter she had prayed for. "My G-d, will he ever send for me?" she would ask herself. And so Sarah Taube, a young, naïve girl, settled into a small, quiet shtetl where every day was the same as every other day. The only excitement in the drab monotony in her life to look forward to were the rumors and gossip spread by the town's yentas.

# Chapter 4 – Narodnaya Volya

## November 1877 – Kiev Fortress, Kiev, Ukraine, Russian Empire

Prison life was hell on earth for Gesya. She was locked up in one of many cells with women from all walks of life. The beds were placed so close that one could hardly breathe. The odor of sweat and unwashed bodies permeated the air and remained constant day after day. The men were housed in another area completely out of sight from the women's cells.

One day, during the exercise period in the prison yard, Gesya was approached by a woman who was serving a three-year sentence for belonging to a group advocating forcible overthrow of the Tsarist Government.

She had a very muscular body for someone slight in build. Her eyes were olive green and her hair was pale yellow that reminded Gesya of straw.

"Can we speak for a moment?" she asked, attempting to engage Gesya in conversation. "My name is Katya Chernikova."

Gesya observed her for a few moments and then introduced herself.

"How can you stand it here?" she said, giving a quick glance at the others nearby. "I've only been here a week, and I'm already going out of my mind."

"It will be two years for me," Katya replied, motioning for Gesya to follow her to the side of the yard. "I only have one year to go. Life here gets easier as the days go by. You'll see. Why were you arrested, if you don't mind me asking?"

"No, I don't mind at all," Gesya answered, feeling as though she had made an important contact. "I was accused of belonging to a revolutionary group, but I was an innocent bystander. Look what the

Tsarist government did to me. They threw me into this hellhole.

"I guess you could have called me naïve but not anymore. Sending me to prison has only enraged me, and when I get out, I'll do everything in my power to help overthrow this evil regime."

"Listen to me, Gesya. If you're serious about wanting to become active in overthrowing the Tsar, and if you want to come out of here alive, you will have to join a group like I did. That's the only way you'll be able to survive in this place."

Gesya covered her mouth with her hands.

"What's the name of this group?" she asked in a whisper.

"The name does not matter," Katya replied, shaking her head. "What you have to do is hook up with the leader. All I'll tell you about him is he was the head of a group of revolutionaries until he was found out and thrown in here. Come, I want you to meet him."

Slowly, to avoid arousing suspicion, Katya led Gesya over to a tall, strange-looking man who was standing behind a thick-wired fence that separated the men's exercise yard from the women's.

"I'd like you to meet Gesya Gelfman," Katya said, moving her directly in front of the fence and as close to the man as possible. "I believe she's interested in joining our group."

Egor Borovsky, a giant of a man with a thick neck and muscular arms, greeted Gesya as a small grin spread at the corners of his mouth.

He explained that it would be to her advantage to join his group. He would provide protection from dangerous inmates, and she could engage secretly in political discussions.

This sounded good to Gesya, especially the part about her being protected. She was also eager to learn as much as she could about the group's anti-Tsarist beliefs and so she joined.

◄O►

Faivush was now beginning his second year at the university. After his sister's imprisonment, he became more involved in student protests and revolutionary propaganda efforts. He continued to attend secret meetings and helped with the printing and distribution of various leaflets relating to the cause.

Anatoly, with whom he had developed a close relationship, would often catch him staring into space as if he were miles away. Of course, he was thinking about his sister, Gesya, wondering how she was surviving her incarceration. He had not heard from her in two years. Was she even alive, he wondered?

At the end of her two-year sentence, Gesya was released from prison but was not allowed to return to Kiev. Instead, she was exiled to Novgorod. Novgorod was one of Russia's oldest cities, located in northwestern Russia, between Moscow and St. Petersburg.

Within a few months of living in Novgorod, Gesya escaped from the city, with the help of revolutionary friends she had met in prison, taking up residence in St. Petersburg. There, she joined the notorious Russian left-wing terrorist organization *Narodnaya Volya.* They had attempted to assassinate the Tsar several times but each time the attempt had failed.

The *Narodnaya Volya* supported the idea that the people should control the means of production, distribution, and trade. And they upheld a policy of physical force in the pursuit of political aims and believed a social revolution was not attainable without a political one.

Gesya, still naïve, thought she was finally being accepted into the group when, in reality, they were using her in a cruel and pathetic way. They used her as a cook, messenger, and even as a sexual object, filling her head with strange talk about revolutionary free love.

One Sunday afternoon, Gesya, at a meeting of the *Narodnaya Volya*, met Sophia Perovskaya, an attractive woman who had recently joined *Narodnaya Volya* and was eager to be part of their revolutionary activities.

A committee member attending the meeting recommended that she and Gesya move in together. Two women sharing an apartment, it was thought, would provide camouflage to allow the group to continue holding their meetings without suspicion.

Sophia's background was quite different from Gesya's. She came from an upper-class family whose father and grandfather held highly influential positions with the Tsarist Government.

Since she got along well with Gesya, they agreed to share a place and in a short time, found a two-bedroom apartment in one of the poorer boroughs of the city.

This area was mainly inhabited by former peasants who were given their full rights as free citizens by Tsar Alexander II, who abolished serfdom throughout the Russian Empire.

It didn't take Sophia long to be recognized, and after being with *Narodnaya Volya* for a short time, she was elected to several high level positions, involving a conspiracy to kill the Tsar.

The plan was to blow up the Imperial Train while it was on its way from St. Petersburg to Moscow, but an error was made and the wrong train was blown up.

"So tell me what did you do before you came to us," Gesya asked, while she and Sophia sat at the kitchen table enjoying a glass of tea.

Without giving Gesya too much information, Sophia told her a little about herself and briefly some of the escapades she was involved in.

Gesya was so enthralled upon hearing Sophia's adventures that she could hardly contain herself and wished she could be more like her, a woman who was strong, independent and above all, courageous.

Gesya reached for the teapot, refilled her glass of tea and took a swallow.

"I heard the men talking at our last meeting about the botched up attempt to kill the Tsar," she said. "What happened?"

Sophia gave Gesya a look but did not answer and immediately changed the subject. She could not tell how trustworthy Gesya was and did not want to implicate herself until she knew her better.

"A meeting is to be held at seven o'clock this evening in our apartment," she announced. "This will be a very important meeting." Then a smile lit her face. "Andrei Zhelyabov will be here. You do know who he is, don't you?"

"I know he's a very influential man in the *Narodnaya Volya*," Gesya replied, watching Sophia's reaction to her answer. "But since they have me doing menial jobs during the meetings, I rarely have time to sit in and listen to what's going on, let alone meet the members."

"Well, Gesya, we'll have to change that, won't we? I'm well aware of how the women are treated by the men. They believe they are the intelligentsia, the intellectuals, and the thinkers. We will have to show them we can be as effective as they are. Perhaps even more so."

Gesya was reluctant to ask the next question but decided to go ahead and ask it anyway.

"When and where did you meet Andrei?"

"Andrei and I met three years ago during the "Trial of the 193". Do you remember reading about it?"

"No. What was it about?"

Sophia paused and refilled her glass with tea before going on.

"The "Trial of the 193" was a series of trials, involving 193 students and other revolutionaries. Both Andrei and I were among those arrested. We were charged with spreading slanderous information against the Russian Empire and sent to the Petropavlovskaya Fortress where we were held for trial."

"You mean you were locked up in prison?" Gesya asked, raising her eyebrows slightly.

Sophia nodded. "Yes but most of us were acquitted, including Andrei. Afterward, Andrei was one of the main organizers of *Narodnaya Volya*, and he's now a member of its Executive Committee. I've already received instructions from him, so we have no time to waste. It will soon be dark."

Gesya had arranged six wooden chairs around a large rectangular table in the dining room. Her job was to make sure there was seating for everyone, plenty of tablets and pens, refreshments and, of course, bottles of vodka.

Sharply at seven, Sophia and Gesya heard soft knocking at the door.

"I'll get it," Gesya said, quickly walking across the room.

"Hello, my name is Stepan Khalturin," offered a handsome young man with a nicely trimmed mustache and a goatee.

"My name is Gesya Gelfman. Please come in."

"Am I the first to arrive?" he asked, checking her over with his eyes.

"Yes, but I'm sure the others will be here shortly," she replied, glancing back at him.

She took his hat and coat and led him into the dining room.

Within a few minutes, more soft knocking was heard. Gesya answered once again.

This time, three men appeared.

One was Andrei Zhelyabov, a member of the *Narodnaya Volya's* Executive Committee. He was quite an unusual looking man. He was over six feet tall with a long pointed nose and an enormous black mustache, which seemed to sweep into a full growth of hair on his chin and lower cheeks.

The second man was Nikolai Sablin, who had joined the group at the same time Gesya had, and they had already been involved in several sexual encounters.

The third man was introduced as Nikolai Rysakov.

"Please follow me, gentlemen. We're about to start the meeting."

Sophia greeted the three men and asked each to have a seat.

"May I have your attention?" she asked as she stood in front of the group. "I'd like you to meet Nikolai Sablin and Nikolai Rysakov. They have recently joined Narodnaya Volya, and, of course, you know Andrei Zhelyabov."

Stepan immediately got up and offered them a handshake.

"It's a pleasure to meet you," answered Nikolai Sablin, a short but dignified well-dressed young man.

"I too," replied Nikolai Rysakov.

After everyone settled in, Andrei Zhelyabov stood at the head of the table.

"Good evening," he said, his eyes exploring each person. "I'm happy to see you're responding to each other favorably. We all have to work as a group in order to fulfill our hopes of bringing about a revolutionary change in our country."

Andrei closed his eyes slightly and then opened them wide.

"This evening, I want to introduce you to a newly formed cell under the leadership of Nikolai Rysakov. We have put together a plan to be executed on the 17th of February, which will finally rid the country of a cruel and oppressive ruler.

"I called this meeting because most of you are aware of the recently failed attempt on the Tsar's life. Well my friends, we will not stop until we have succeeded in accomplishing our objective. We must remove the Tsar and all the evil associated with his rule, and we will not rest until we put into place a new social order. We want change and dammit, we'll get change."

Immediately, everyone rose to their feet.

"Please sit down," Andrei said, gently stroking the hair on his chin. "We'll have plenty of time after I finish for your reactions but for now, please bear with me.

"We have a perfect window of opportunity next month to carry out our objective. At this time, I would like to turn the meeting over to Stepan."

"Stepan stood from his chair with his hands crossed.

"Let me start by giving you a bit of my background," he began. "My father was a peasant who struggled all of his life. With help from a friend, I learned carpentry and have worked in several factories throughout St. Petersburg.

"I recently was employed at the Winter Palace, and they allow me to sleep in the basement. I see a perfect opportunity for me to set off a bomb. All I need is for someone experienced to make the explosive device and show me how to set the timer, and I will do the rest."

Nikolai Rysakov raised his hand. Stepan acknowledged him.

"Now I understand why I've been asked here today. I've studied engineering at the Institute of Mining in St. Petersburg, and I know everything there is to know about explosives. I'll show you how to do it. We'll have a few meetings, and you'll be able to set off a bomb with your eyes shut by the time I get finished with you."

Stepan's enthusiasm lit up his face.

"Great," he said. "That's exactly what I want to hear. A meeting will be set for next week, and we'll put this new plan in motion."

Stepan again addressed the group.

"On February 17, the Tsar will be entertaining guests for dinner. Early that morning, I'll place the bomb into my toolbox and smuggle it into the Palace. I'll put it in the ceiling directly under the area where the Tsar will be dining and set it to go off one-half hour after the Tsar is expected to arrive.

"Next, I'll need someone with a horse and carriage waiting at an agreed location to pick me up after I have armed the bomb.

Nikolai Sablin's hand immediately shot up.

"I will be happy to provide your escape," he said eagerly.

"Good. I knew I could count on you," Stepan replied. "So far, it looks as though most of the details have been worked out. And lastly, I will need a ticket to Moscow and one from Moscow to Odessa. Do I hear any volunteers?"

Sophia raised her hand and, with her heart hammering deeply within her chest, spoke forcefully and repeatedly, "I will do it. I will do it."

A few moments later, Gesya stood in front of the group. She could feel sweat beading on her forehead and felt her heart in her mouth while she spoke.

"Sophia should not get both tickets," she said, stumbling over every other word. "She should only get a ticket from St. Petersburg to Moscow. I'm certain she will raise suspicion if she purchases both tickets. Let me go to Moscow and purchase the ticket to Odessa."

Andrei joined Stepan at the head of the table and spoke.

"Everyone must carry out their task. I have every confidence in you. I think we should have a vote to decide if Gesya is ready to do her part in furthering the cause. Let's have a show of hands to give Gesya the opportunity to prove herself."

Gesya darted a glance across the room and saw that all the members had raised their hands in agreement. How excited she was. For the first time she felt she was truly part of something.

Andrei looked around the room.

"Is there anything else anyone wishes to discuss?" he asked, pleased that the meeting had gone so well.

A hush came over the group.

"Judging from your silence," he said, just before he sat down, "I think we have covered everything. I expect all of you to coordinate with Stepan, and remember, I must be kept informed at all times. This meeting stands adjourned. Now for the refreshments."

Gesya brought out several trays filled with sliced onions, sliced gherkin, fresh kielbasa, potato salad, and black bread. Small glasses filled with vodka were placed on trays, accompanied by tall glasses and a bowl of jam. Long-handled metal spoons were provided to scoop up the jam and to break the shock of the hot tea being poured into the glasses.

Andrei rose from his seat again and tapped on his glass with his spoon.

"Before we partake in this wonderful feast, please join me in a toast."

He raised his glass up high.

"To success and long live *Narodnaya Volya*."

The rest of the group stood and held their glasses up high.

"To success and long live *Narodnaya Volya*," they replied in unison.

Then they took a healthy swallow of vodka.

The hour was approaching eleven and except for Andrei Zhelyabov and Nikolai Sablin, the rest excused themselves and left.

Because of their involvement in the "Trial of the 193," Andrei and Sophia had become very good friends. In fact, he considered her his closest friend. But recently, although he liked the warm and friendly dealings they had had, he wanted more than a platonic relationship.

Later that evening, he spoke his feelings.

Sophia had always admired him and enjoyed the connection they had but this particular night, he began making sexual advances toward her. She could not resist his attention so, in order to have more privacy, he convinced her to invite him into her bedroom.

While they lay in bed, he began to kiss and fondle her. She closed her eyes and made her lips move perfectly against his and deepened the kiss by grabbing the back of his neck to bring him closer. The lovemaking went on for quite a while until neither could hold back and within moments, sensual gratification had taken place.

Andrei had stirred up feelings in her that she did not think she had for him. Although she had encounters with other men, it was merely to satisfy her sexual needs, but Andrei had awakened in her not only a physical need, but an emotional one as well.

Then he said something that surprised her.

"I've been thinking about you and have wanted to get close to you ever since you joined the organization. I see in you a woman who is strong and unafraid, and I can see us becoming a great team."

Somehow, during the conversation, they began discussing the concept of free love, which was becoming very popular among revolutionary groups.

"What are your thoughts on free love?" he asked, gazing lovingly into her eyes.

"The idea of having sexual relations according to one's choice," she replied, "and without being restricted by marriage or other long-term commitments, sounds like a very progressive idea and..."

"But for me," Andrei interrupted, "if I loved a woman, I would not want her to be with anyone else."

Sophia soon realized Andrei felt although free love was acceptable for others, it was not acceptable for him and marriage was an important part of a serious relationship. Neither one said another word on the subject.

Meanwhile, Gesya and Nikolai had gotten involved that evening. From the beginning, she had been brainwashed to his way of thinking regarding free love.

At first, he used systematic and often forcible pressure to make her conform until she finally gave in and became totally subservient to him.

After several meetings, the final plans for February 17 had been completed, and all they had to do was wait for that fateful day.

According to the customary practices associated with *Narodnaya Volya* and similar groups, before a new assassination attempt was to be carried out, those involved would have to pick up and move to another location.

"Are the two of you prepared to leave?" Andrei asked, as he and Nikolai entered the women's apartment.

"Yes, we're all packed and ready to go," answered Sophia, grabbing her suitcase.

Gesya and Nikolai had settled into a two-bedroom apartment on Telezhnaya Street located in a heavily populated working-class neighborhood.

The apartment was small except for a large dining room. Built into the center of the left wall was a brick, wood-burning fireplace, surrounded by a wooden mantle. The insert where the fire burned was constructed of cast iron, and one could hear the wood crackling as a high fire roared in the grate.

Directly above a rectangular wooden table hung a red, glass lantern chandelier in the shape of a bell jar with a four-arm external candleholder, and as the lit candles glowed from the fixture, it cast a shadow on the high yellow ceiling.

Andrei and Sophia moved into a one-bedroom apartment located in a remote area of town and as far away from Gesya and Nikolai as possible to avoid being linked to them.

Living together was unconventional at the time, and since Andrei believed in the sacrament of holy matrimony, he was persistent in asking Sophia to marry him.

Late one evening, she surprised him and accepted his proposal, and a week later, they were married, with Gesya and Nikolai in attendance.

On the day after the assassination attempt, Andrei wondered, while he sat at the kitchen table eating his breakfast, if they were successful.

Sophia had gone out to get a newspaper.

The door opened, and when she entered the room, the look on her face immediately conveyed to him the plan had failed. She threw the newspaper on the table and took a seat. Andrei picked it up and observed in large print in the center of the front page:

"ATTEMPT ON TSAR'S LIFE FAILS"

Andrei began to read:

*Yesterday, on the 17th of February, an attempt was made on the life of our beloved Tsar Alexander II. An explosion was set to go off in the dining room, while the Tsar was entertaining his guest, Prince Alexander of Battenberg. Because the Prince had arrived an hour late, the dinner was delayed, and the dining room was void of the royal family and his guest. The persons responsible for this cowardly act are being sought by the police and will be apprehended.*

Sophia said nothing for several moments, and then, with her voice cracking with every word, spoke.

"Again we have failed."

Andrei threw the newspaper down on the table and took hold of Sophia's hand.

"Don't worry," he replied, trying not to show his disappointment. "The odds are very much in our favor. Despite our unsuccessful attempts, I'm certain we're getting closer to putting an end to the Tsar's rule.

"We have good men who are well educated in the field of science and engineering, and they are highly proficient in their knowledge of explosive materials. I'm sure it's only a matter of time before we succeed."

"You're right, Andrei," Sophia replied, placing her hand on top of his. "At least, the good news is, it looks as though Stepan has gotten away."

"Let's hope so, Sophia. We have you, Nikolai Sablin, and Gesya to thank for what we hope is his successful getaway."

◄O►

Faivush had finished his formal education and had acquired a position in Kiev as a teacher in a non-Jewish school. Because the government in Kiev placed restrictions on organized Jewish life, Jewish education was difficult to find. The last Jewish school was shut down in 1878, and most Jewish families living in Kiev had no choice but to give their children a secular education.

He continued attending meetings of his socialist group, putting together various written works and secretly distributing them among the students at the university.

Not hearing from his sister since her arrest in October of 1877, he was beside himself with worry, but he figured if she did not die in prison, she was still active in revolutionary groups. Perhaps she felt it would be too risky to get in touch with him, and the best thing she could do was to disappear from his life.

◄O►

The apartment on Telezhnaya Street was dimly lit as Nikolai Sablin and Gesya Gelfman prepared to hold a meeting of the *fighting squad*, which was the code name for the cell that was specifically formed to carry out the next attempt on the Tsar's life. The meeting was to be held at six o'clock in the evening, and the participants were instructed to arrive two at a time, at fifteen-minute intervals.

Andrei Zhelyabov and Sophia were the first to arrive. Andrei had spent many months intent on developing another plan to assassinate the Tsar, and at last he had come up with an idea he thought was flawless.

"We've waited patiently for this day to arrive," he said, as he took his heavy overcoat off and handed it to Gesya.

"Yes," answered Nikolai. "Gesya and I can't wait for the meeting to begin."

When each gave the other a warm embrace, they could sense excitement in the air.

"Where are the others?" Nikolai asked, pacing up and down the room."

"Calm down, Nikolai," Andrei replied, raising his voice slightly. "We have to take our time. Remember, we can't afford to make any more mistakes."

Within fifteen minutes of Andrei and Sophia's arrival, there came several knocks at the door.

Timofey Mikhailov and Ignacy Hryniewiecki, new members of the group, made their entrance.

Timofey was an uneducated son of a poor farmer. He was employed as a hired hand and steam boiler operator in several plants in St. Petersburg, and it was in one of these plants he became interested in revolutionary politics, joining the *Narodnaya Volya.*

The other man, Ignacy Hryniewiecki, was born into an impoverished Polish family and at the age of twenty, moved to St. Petersburg to pursue mathematics at the Polytechnic.

During this time, while studying the history and language of the Russian people, he was persuaded to attend meetings of the *Narodnaya Volya.* He came to know Andrei Zhelyabov and Sophia Perovskaya when their services were enlisted by *Narodnaya Volya* to secretly spread revolutionary propaganda among the students at the university.

The next to arrive was Nikolai Rysakov who had recently become a member of the *fighting squad.*

The last to make his entrance was Ivan Emelyanov, a cabinetmaker by vocation and also a new member of the group.

Everyone was seated, and all eyes were on Andrei, as he calmly stood to address the gathering.

"Good evening members of the *fighting squad,*" he said, giving each a smile. "I believe all of you have an idea why you are here today." And with his fist lightly touching the table, he cried, "This time we will not fail. All of you are here because you have joined in our latest plot to assassinate the Tsar. I have drawn up a plan on how we can rid our country of this evil ruler once and for all.

"Sophia," he said, handing her a stack of papers, "please pass out a copy of my proposal. Study it very carefully, my friends, for you must put it to memory."

He paused for a moment and took a sip of water.

"Each one of you has a specific job to do. Failure to follow through with your assignment will cause the plan to fail and under no circumstances do we want that to happen."

Those in attendance fixed their eyes unwaveringly on Andrei, while he continued speaking.

"The assassination will take place on Sunday, the thirteenth of March at approximately eleven-thirty in the morning. Remember, we will have less than two weeks to prepare for the most important day of our lives.

"I have engaged Nikolai Kibalchich, an explosives expert, who has built many bombs for us before, to put together four bombs to be ready the day before the assassination.

"After the bombs are assembled, he will meet with the bomb throwers and show them how to detonate them. I have assigned four of you to be the designated bomb throwers. Please stand up when I call your name.

"We wish all of you good luck," Andrei said. "Remember these men. Their names will go down in history. You may sit down, gentlemen. Please allow me to continue.

"On the morning of the assassination, I'll be standing nearby to make sure everything goes according to schedule. It is well known that the Tsar goes to the Mikhailovsky Manege every Sunday for the military roll call. He travels in a closed carriage, usually accompanied by six Cossacks, while the Tsar's guards and the chief of police follow closely behind.

"The route taken is always from the Catherine Canal and over the Pevchesky Bridge, and we know exactly when the carriage is scheduled to arrive.

"Sophia will stand at a specified location near the canal, alongside the bystanders and will raise a red scarf the moment the carriage is about to pass through.

"Nikolai Rysakov will be near the canal, carrying a bomb concealed in a small package wrapped in a white silk cloth. When he sees Sophia lift her scarf, he'll know the carriage will soon be approaching and will throw the bomb under the carriage and seek his escape."

Nikolai Sablin quickly raised his hand.

"And what happens if somehow the plan fails?"

Andrei cleared his throat and cried, "It cannot fail. That's why we have four bomb throwers.

"Ignacy Hryniewiecki will be nearby, ready to throw the second bomb, and if that fails, we have two other bomb throwers, Ivan Emelyanov and Timofey Mikhaylov. They will be standing by to throw their bombs when the Tsar's carriage attempts to return to the Palace. That's why I say this latest plan will be successful. There's no way the Tsar can survive."

He placed his hands behind his back and made a circle around the room, facing the group once again.

"Is there anyone here who sees any flaws in this plan. If so, speak up now."

The room went silent. The silence lasted for several seconds.

Nikolai Sablin rose slowly to his feet.

"It's a great plan," he said as he stood in support. Following his lead, the rest of the *fighting squad* stood.

All agreed this latest scheme was indeed infallible. And to have three men as backup in case the first bomb failed to do the job was ingenious.

"Good," Andrei said as a smile crossed his face. "Your support indicates you have accepted my proposal. I could not ask any more of you."

Andrei, very pleased, motioned for Gesya to collect all papers and notes to be thrown into the fireplace and to begin serving the refreshments.

Although Gesya had been accepted by the group and was considered part of the *fighting squad*, she could not overcome the fact she was still being treated as a servant. However, she was happy they had taken her into their confidence and would be used as a backup for Sophia.

A few days before the planned assassination, the Okhrana, the secret police, arrested Andrei Zhelyabov on suspicion of plotting to assassinate the Tsar. On the day the assassination was to be carried out, in spite of Zhelyabov's absence, the group decided to go ahead and execute the plan without him.

On Sunday, the 13th of March 1881, the procession of Tsar Alexander II went according to schedule. As soon as the Tsar's carriage neared the Catherine Canal, Sophia raised her scarf to alert Nikolai Rysakov. He aimed for the carriage but the bomb exploded in front of the Cossacks, killing some of them.

The Tsar, being concerned for his men, stepped out of the carriage. This was a perfect opportunity for Ignacy Hryniewiecki to toss his bomb. The Tsar lay quiet in a puddle of blood and within hours, he was dead.

Nikolai Rysakov, the first bomb thrower, was arrested immediately after the assassination, and in order to save his life, he informed on his fellow conspirators.

They were quickly apprehended except for Ignacy Hryniewiecki, the second bomb thrower, who was mortally wounded from the force of the explosion; Nikolai Sablin, who took his life before the police had a chance to arrest him; and Ivan Emelyanov, who disappeared and was never seen nor heard of again.

Although Alexander II was attempting to reform Russian society along moderately liberal lines, he was proceeding too slowly. Prior to his assassination, he had drawn up plans for an elected parliament that was to be available to the Russian people.

If he had lived, Russia might have evolved into a government dominated by an elected legislative body. Upon his death, he was succeeded by his son, Alexander III, who was a more repressive monarch than his father had ever been.

After Alexander III's coronation, the first thing he did was to compromise the plans his father had made for the advancement of the Russian people.

Secondly, he directed the Okhrana to take into custody all those who were suspected of being in opposition to his rule.

Thirdly, because of Alexander II's murder, pogroms were set into motion throughout the Russian Empire.

And finally, the assassination of the Tsar stirred up the anarchists to commit brutalities in order to topple the government.

"Don't close the shop yet!" Mrs. Bleekman shouted as she came running in, looking as though she were about to explode. "You won't believe what I've just read."

"Calm down," Uncle Morris replied, waving a paper fan in front of her, thinking she was going to faint at any moment.

"Stop that," she said, pushing the fan away from her face. "The Tsar has been assassinated. It happened Sunday. Here it is in the Kovne newspaper."

"May I see the paper, Mrs. Bleekman?" Uncle Morris asked.

He took the paper from her hands, sat down and began to read.

*A member of the revolutionary group called the Narodnaya Volya assassinated the Tsar in the streets of St. Petersburg. It occurred while the Tsar was on his way to the Mikhailovsky Manege for the military roll call. The Tsar's grandson, Nicholas, age twelve, witnessed his grandfather's death.*

Uncle Morris thought for a moment and then put down the paper.

"I'm not surprised it happened," he said. "After a few attempts on the Tsar's life, the subversives have finally accomplished their goal. My only fear is the killing of the Tsar will have grave repercussions for the Jews of Russia.

He glanced down at the floor and then looked up at Mrs. Bleekman.

"Maybe those two young men from the shtetl who just left for America did the right thing. Perhaps it's time for Lena, Sarah Taube, and I to go too."

Thirteen-year-old Sarah Taube sat on the bench near the window and listened while her uncle expressed his fears.

# Chapter 5 – Dimitri Bogdonovich

## March 1881 - Kiev, Ukraine, Russian Empire

Anatoly cried, "Let me in, Faivush," as he pounded the front door.

"What's wrong?" Faivush asked, thinking something serious had happened to his friend.

"Have you seen the newspaper this morning?" Anatoly asked, holding the paper close to Faivush's face.

"No, Anatoly. I usually get the paper on my way to work. What's gotten you so upset?"

"They've arrested another one of the assassins and published their name."

Anatoly hesitated but felt compelled to ask.

"Your last name is Gelfman, isn't it?"

"Yes, you know it is," Faivush replied.

"Please tell me you don't have a sister named Gesya?"

Beads of sweat broke out on Faivush's forehead. Why was Anatoly asking me about Gesya, he thought, and what kind of trouble had she gotten herself into this time?

He grabbed the newspaper out of Anatoly's hand and scanned the front page. In large letters it stated that Gesya Gelfman, a member of the *Narodnaya Volya*, was arrested as a co-conspirator in Tsar Alexander II's assassination.

Faivush fell silent. It was as if a dagger had plunged into his heart. He wondered how his sister could have allowed herself to be involved in such a thing, and he realized there was no way he could deny being related to her.

"Yes, I do have a sister named Gesya," he answered, "but I haven't heard from her for more than four years. I can't believe she's been implicated in the Tsar's assassination."

"Tell me what happened when you last saw her?" Anatoly asked.

After regaining his composure, Faivush took a seat, wiped his brow with the sleeve of his shirt and began to relate the sad story of his sister's life and how they had reconnected when he first moved to Kiev.

"We saw each other often for dinner, but she never let on she had gotten herself involved with a group of revolutionists. I later learned she was arrested and sent to prison for two years."

Anatoly sat down beside Faivush. "What was the name of the group she belonged to?" he asked.

"I never found out. In any case, I haven't heard a word from her since."

"You mean you never tried to find her?"

"No. I wanted to but a friend suggested I stay away. He said I could have been accused of being mixed up with the group she was involved with."

"I hadn't thought of that. Your friend probably gave you good advice."

"Yes, I'm sure he did but all these years I felt guilty. I should have tried to find her after she was released from prison.

"My sister was naïve and easily influenced by others. I think she wanted to fit in and be part of something. I really don't think she knew much about revolutionaries, and I truly believe she was totally misled."

"How can you say that?" Anatoly asked. "She may have been naïve at first but I certainly think, after belonging to the *Narodnaya Volya*, she was systematically indoctrinated to their beliefs. Take you, for instance. When you first came to Professor Vladimerskii's meeting, you didn't know much about social justice, did you?"

"No, I didn't," Faivush replied.

"But as you continued attending his discussion groups, you soon learned about the policies and practices based on socialism. I believe your sister knew exactly what was going on."

Faivush thought for a moment.

"It's well known that the *Narodnaya Volya* is a left-wing terrorist organization," he said. "How could she have chosen to join such a group?"

"Who knows why people do what they do," Anatoly replied. "Anyway, there's nothing you can do for your sister now. Remember, you don't want to arouse any suspicions about your activities and of those who are near to you."

Anatoly moved his chair close to Faivush and looked him in the eye.

"I would suggest, though, that you change your name and move out of Kiev immediately. You certainly don't want to be connected to your sister, especially now. I'm sorry to say, my friend, but you must distance yourself from her. I know it's cruel, and I'm sure you love your sister dearly, but you have to think of your hopes and dreams for our country."

Faivush knew his friend had given him good advice but still it was a hard decision for him to make.

After careful consideration, he said to Anatoly, "You're right, of course. The future belongs to us and much to my dismay, there's nothing I can do for my sister."

"I'm glad you see it that way but what about your name?"

Faivush thought about the question and then his eyes lit up.

"I've got it," he said, striking the table with the palm of his hand. "The last year of school, I befriended an exceptionally bright student. He repeatedly got the highest grades in all of his tests. I felt I was in competition with him, but he somehow always managed to reign supreme."

Faivush had Anatoly sitting on the edge of his chair.

"Go on," he said. "Get to the point."

"Unfortunately, soon after graduation, I learned my friend had passed away. I can take his name and still be able to claim I graduated from the Saint Vladimir University in Kiev."

"So what will you call yourself?" Anatoly said impatiently.

"Dimitri Bogdonovich," Faivush blurted. "That's what I'll call myself. Dimitri Bogdonovich."

Faivush knew he had to leave Kiev in a hurry, as he felt it was only a matter of time before the secret police would catch up with him.

Anatoly thought for a moment before he spoke.

"I think the best place for you is St. Petersburg. It's a big city and there you can find another job, perhaps in teaching and since you'll be changing your name, no one will ever connect you to your sister."

A smile came to Faivush's face. "You've read my mind. That's exactly the city I was thinking of."

After a long silence, Faivush rose from his seat and put his hand on Anatoly's shoulder.

"What I really want to do is write for an underground newspaper connected with one of the revolutionary groups just as you're doing."

"There are plenty revolutionary groups scattered throughout St. Petersburg," Anatoly replied, "and these days most of them have an underground press." He reached in his pocket and pulled out a pen and paper and hastily jotted down a few words.

"Here, Faivush. I mean Dimitri. I've written down the name of someone I know in St. Petersburg. He's a good man who will help you find what you're looking for."

Faivush slipped the paper into his pocket and thanked him.

"You've been a good friend," he said. "I'll never forget you. I know it's too dangerous for us to correspond. Perhaps someday we'll meet again."

The two men shook hands, embraced, and said their goodbyes. And within an hour, Dimitri was on a train heading for a new city, a new identity, and a new life.

Dimitri had settled into a one-bedroom apartment in the center of town and after a few interviews, he was accepted as a secondary school teacher at the K. May Gymnasium and Natural Science College, a top accredited private school in St. Petersburg.

Several weeks later, he visited Anatoly's contact and, after much discussion, was directed to a socialist group that not only had an underground press but also met most of his requirements.

Soon, after he joined the group, he began writing revolutionary articles, which were published in many underground revolutionist and socialist-leaning newspapers.

On Thursday, the 20th of April 1881, the trial for the remaining conspirators accused of Tsar Alexander II's assassination was held. No one denied the allegations made against them, with each making a short statement.

Nikolai Kibalchich, the bomb maker, stood before the court and appeared to be calm. Instead of making an argument for his life, he went on about how explosives were made. The court was fascinated and listened attentively to his long description and when he was finished, he took his seat.

Sophia Perovskaya rose slowly from her place and, with a serious look on her face, stated to the court only her name and age. She appeared unemotional, said nothing in her defense, and promptly sat down.

Andrei Zhelyabov was next to appear. He turned to the judge and expressed only that he strongly believed in what he was doing and had no regrets and if given the chance again, he would repeat his actions.

Now it was Gesya Gelfman's turn. She go up from his chair and began by describing how she left her family as a young girl to keep from entering into an arranged marriage. After leaving home at sixteen, she was involved with revolutionaries and shortly afterward, became sympathetic to their cause.

"Have you nothing more to say?" asked a member of the court.

"No, I do not," she answered as her voice trembled.

"Then you may sit down."

Timofey Mikhailov was up on his feet even before his name was called. He told the court he had joined the group mainly because they spoke up for the working class. He said nothing more and took his seat.

Lastly, Nikolai Rysakov stood and made himself known. He gave no logical argument in his defense and stated he never took part in any of the group's prior rebellious undertakings. He excused himself and sat down.

After the court heard the statements given by each of the accused, it was determined they were all guilty as charged and the sentence was death by hanging.

Gesya Gelfman looked at the judges and slowly raised her hand.

"Yes, do you wish to make a statement?" a judge asked, motioning for her to rise.

"Yes, if I may," she answered in a low voice.

"Then speak up. What do you have to say that will make a difference in the court of law?"

Gesya turned to face the judge.

"I would like to inform the court I am three months pregnant and beg that my sentence be postponed until I have my child. Please have mercy," she cried.

The judges were taken by surprise. They clustered together and had a quick consultation. After a few moments, a judge announced that the court had decided to stay her execution until a determination could be made.

"You will be sent to a penal institution where you will be incarcerated until your child is born," he said. He continued with the ruling, stating the remaining assassins were to be taken to Semenovsky Square and sentenced to be hanged the following morning.

The next day, while Dimitri was on his way to work, he purchased a newspaper. On the front page in large letters, the headline read:

ASSASSINS TO BE HANGED

Although he had expected the worst, he still could not believe his sister was being given the same harsh sentence as the others. He continued to read.

*All the assassins of Tsar Alexander II were found guilty and sentenced to death by hanging. The execution is to be held today. After her sentencing, Gesya Gelfman stated she was three months pregnant.*

Dimitri stopped reading. Again, he read that portion of the article. He was shocked at the news. He had to pull himself together before he could go on.

*The judge ordered her execution to be delayed until forty days after the birth of her child as the execution of a pregnant woman is prohibited. It is thought the fetus is completely without fault of the sins of the mother. For the next six months of her pregnancy she will be confined to the Peter and Paul Fortress prison in St. Petersburg.*

Dimitri felt relieved. At least his sister's execution was postponed, and she would not be executed along with the others today.

As the morning mist shrouded the skyline of the city, the convicted assassins, with the exception of Gesya Gelfman, were awakened at precisely six o'clock.

As soon as they dressed, they were asked to put a long black garment over their clothing and after they were fed, signs displaying the word *regicide* were hung around their necks.

With their ankles and wrists chained, the convicted prisoners were led into the courtyard and put into a large open cart to begin their trip to Semenovsky Square, where the executioner was awaiting them.

Approximately eighty thousand people gathered to watch the hanging. Some in the crowd, in sympathy with the *Narodnaya Volya,* kept their mouths shut, while others, as soon as they saw *regicide* signs around the prisoners' necks, shouted, with hatred in their voices, *"Killers of the Tsar! Killers of the Tsar!"*

The next twenty minutes were devoted to reading the sentences of each of the prisoners, followed by the signing of the official records.

Prior to placing large black hoods over their heads, the conspirators said an emotional farewell to each other, but Nikolai Rysakov was ignored by everyone.

Before the group climbed the steps of the gallows, Andrei Zhelyabov hobbled over to Sophia, gave her a kiss and whispered in her ear, "We've accomplished our objective. The Tsar is dead."

There was a particular order in which the convicted were to be hanged. The one thought to be the guiltiest was to witness the executions of the others and once they were all pronounced dead, he would be the last to dangle from the rope.

Nicholai Kibalchich, the least guilty, was first in line. Death was kind to him as his neck snapped quickly.

Second, was Timofey Mikhailov. The first and second attempts proved unsuccessful as the rope broke both times. The third attempt worked but only after the rope was made stronger.

Next came Sophia Perovskaya. She died instantly.

Fourth, was Andrei Zhelyabov. He was not as lucky as Sophia. His body twisted and turned for several minutes until the Angel of Death claimed him.

Finally, it was Nikolai Rysakov's turn. Up until the very end, he thought his sentence would be commuted. Since he cooperated with the government by turning in his fellow conspirators, he felt he would have a good chance to go free. However, he was thought to be the guiltiest, mainly because he threw the first bomb.

After realizing he would not be let off, a wave of panic came over him. As they put his head in the noose, he continued to struggle until the trap door opened, and there he swayed until his body went limp.

Silence came over the spectators. The event was over, and there was nothing more to see, so they quietly left the square.

The bodies were removed, put into gray wooden coffins, placed onto wagons, and laid to rest at an undisclosed graveyard.

Immediately after the trial, Gesya Gelfman was sent to the Peter and Paul Fortress. There, she was to spend the remainder of her pregnancy. Living conditions in the prison could not have been more austere.

While confined, she never received any medical care for her pregnancy. Because she was named as being among those conspirators who plotted the assassination of the Tsar, she was treated more severely than the others.

Life in prison was beyond belief, and she was beginning to have doubts if she would ever live to see the birth of her child.

The news of the State's unfair treatment of a pregnant woman and especially the sentence of execution for a woman, spread throughout Western Europe and in the foreign press as well. Women's suffrage groups put together campaigns opposing Gesya's imprisonment and to challenge her eventual hanging.

Due to worldwide publicity, the Russian government decided to postpone her execution indefinitely and move her from the Peter and Paul Fortress prison into a labor camp in Siberia.

Dimitri continued to search the newspapers for information. Finally, in the local newspaper, he spotted a brief sentence regarding his sister's fate.

It said Gesya Gelfman, one of the convicted assassins of Tsar

Alexander II, was moved today to an undisclosed Siberian prison camp where she will spend the remainder of her pregnancy. The article did not say more.

He was glad to learn her place of confinement was changed to a more humane institution. Perhaps she would survive after the birth of her child and remain there for the rest of her life. But then, he thought, living out the rest of her life in prison could be a sentence even worse than death.

Again, he wondered how she could have gotten herself into this mess. As his friend Anatoly had said, "She probably knew exactly what was going on. It was for a good cause and to her it was worth the risk."

◄O►

On the morning of Yom Kippur, the holiest of holidays for the Jews, Gesya went into labor. Because her case attracted such a display of public opinion, it was suggested by officials of the Okhrana that she be attended by a physician who dealt with obstetrics and if he needed assistance, the prison doctor would be available.

"Her cervix has widened sufficiently," the attending physician said as he prepared for the delivery. "She's ready to give birth."

When the baby's head came through the birth canal, the prison doctor took notice of a tear at the opening of the vagina and suggested it be sewn up to avoid a possible infection.

The attending physician looked down at his patient and said, "We have no need for that," and began cleaning his surgical tools. "And besides," he snorted, "she is a Jewess, isn't she? A convicted killer of the Tsar. She will soon get what's due her."

Gesya gave birth to a seven pound, six ounce baby girl. Several days later, she began experiencing bouts of high fever and irrational fits of behavior. Because her wound was never stitched, the laceration never healed.

Sometime in mid-November, she developed peritonitis, usually caused by a bacterial infection and by January the following year, her condition became acute. At no time was any attention given to her ill health.

Throughout her long period of untreated illness, Gesya managed to nurse her daughter. The child filled her heart with intense feelings of love. It was something she had never experienced with anyone before, other than her brother, and certainly not with the father of her newly born infant.

On the morning of the 25th of February 1882, Gesya's daughter was taken from her. It was the last time she would ever see her.

The same day her daughter was removed from prison, Gesya developed a severe infection and high fever. Six days later, isolated and alone, Gesya was dead.

According to the medical records, she died from an infection, but those who knew her said, "She died from a broken heart."

A few days later, Dimitri learned his sister had met her death in prison and was to be buried at an undisclosed location. There was no mention of what happened to her child and feelings of guilt began eating away at him. How alone and helpless she must have felt. As her brother, he had a moral obligation to stand by her no matter what, but he failed to do so, and for that he would never forgive himself.

Because of Gesya's tragic demise, Dimitri became even more infuriated with the Tsarist regime. At one time he thought a slow, non-aggressive move to socialism was the only way to bring about a better life for the Russian people.

His ideas rapidly changed when he realized in order to transform the injustice brought about by the Imperial rule, he would have to choose an organization that was more militant. Peaceful change would take too long and violence would be the only way to accomplish a quick takeover and practically overnight, he was transformed into a revolutionary, militant extremist.

During the next few months, a series of pogroms occurred. The government investigated the causes, and it was determined it was due to the exploitation of the gentiles by the Jews and the liberal policies of Alexander II. Temporary laws against the Jews known as May Laws were proposed and enacted on the 3rd of May 1882 by Tsar Alexander III.

Jews were forbidden to live outside certain towns and boroughs, they were prohibited from obtaining mortgages or becoming lessees of real estate outside such towns and boroughs, and they were prevented from conducting business on Sundays and on the main Christian holy days.

These actions were relevant only to the governments within the Pale of Jewish Settlement—the western area of the Russian Empire in which the Jews were allowed to live.

After fourteen months, Dimitri joined the Emancipation of Labour Group, known for being the first Russian Marxist group. Through the underground papers, many in the organization, including

Dimitri, did a great deal to translate Marxist writings into Russian.

The group's founder, Georgi Plekhanov, prepared two drafts that would later become the foundation of the Russian Social-Democratic Party, and Dimitri helped publish and distribute these papers among the various revolutionary groups throughout the country.

Dimitri acclimated to his new mission in life, fueled by hatred of the Tsarist regime and plagued by his guilt of not reaching out to his sister, while the Jews in the Pale of Settlement acclimated to the May Laws, fueled by their desire to adhere to their customs and traditions, plagued by anti-Semitism.

# Chapter 6 – Partners

## March 1884 – Shidleve, Kovne Guberniya, Russian empire

Shidleve, approximately 100 miles Northwest of Vilne, was a small town populated by a few hundred families. It had a main street with a marketplace and shops. As was true in other small shtetls, the houses in the business sections were of two stories, with storefronts on the lower level and living quarters above.

Charles Grazutis lived in Shidleve for many years with his mother, Chaya, father, Avigdor, and sisters Jenny, Bessie, and Freida. When his parents passed away, his aunt and uncle assumed the responsibilities of taking care of his sisters.

Charles was able to rent a small room from the local tailor, Benjamin Schneider, who gave him an apprenticeship in his establishment. He was an elderly man who had recently lost his wife and had one son named Byrum, whom he had taken into the business. Mr. Schneider was a very kind and generous man and considered Charles almost like a son.

Charles learned the skills of tailoring in a short time. Mr. Schneider did not believe in sewing machines so everything was made by hand, requiring many days to make a suit or a dress. Mr. Schneider had an excellent reputation and had orders from towns as far away as Shirvint and Vilkomir.

"Charles, open the door. I must tell you the news," a voice called.

The pounding at the door startled Charles, who was wrapped in a black and white prayer shawl and deeply engrossed in his morning prayers. Recognizing that the excited caller was his friend and co-worker Chaim Gluckman, he put a marker between the pages of the prayer book and placed it softly on the table.

"What's all the commotion about, Chaim?" he asked as he

stumbled to open the door. "You've interrupted my prayers. It better be important or you'll be in big trouble with the Almighty," he said with a smirk.

Chaim, a short, heavy-set young man with a hint of mischief in his eyes, asked, "Remember Jacob Ratner, the tailor from Shirvint?"

"I think so," answered Charles. "Didn't he buy a Singer sewing machine a few months ago?"

"Yes, that's the one. Well, he's leaving for America, and he's selling his Singer. Now is our chance to buy it and open our own tailor shop, and the best part is I think we can get it for a very good price."

Chaim stood with his blue eyes looking directly at Charles, anxiously waiting for his reaction.

"This is good news," Charles said. "It's an opportunity for us."

He placed his large, firm hands on Chaim's shoulders, and said in a quiet voice, "You have done well, my friend. You have done well."

Chaim Gluckman and Charles had read articles in local newspapers describing how the sewing machine had revolutionized tailoring in large cities and factories were being opened where mass quantities of clothing could be produced in a short time. They had dreams of some day opening their own factory but for now, they were only interested in getting Jacob Ratner's sewing machine.

The next morning, after their prayers, they hitched up the horse and wagon outside Mr. Schneider's shop. Luckily, they had several deliveries to make in Shirvint that day so it would be easy to make the extra stop.

The road to Shirvint was rugged. It had rained so the earth was muddy. Charles had to remove mud from the wagon wheels on several occasions. Finally, as the noonday sun began to break through the dark gray clouds, they arrived at their destination.

When the horse came to an abrupt halt in front of a small wood-framed house, Jacob Ratner, a short, round-bellied man with red curly hair, came running out.

"Welcome, my friends. I see you are anxious to purchase my machine." He pointed his finger toward the front door and motioned for them to go in. There on the floor stood that strange looking creation.

"It's a Singer," he said, being careful not to sound too excited as he knew they were about to negotiate a price.

Walking around the machine with his hands clenched behind his back, Charles asked, "How much do you want for it?"

Mr. Ratner looked out the window and then at Charles.

"I'll make a good price for you," he replied.

After Jacob Ratner told Charles and Chaim the price, Charles slapped the table and doubled over with laughter.

"If we had that much money," he said with his hands on his hips, "we would buy the entire Singer sewing machine factory. Anyway, Mr. Schneider will fire us as soon as he learns we have brought back this complicated contraption. You know, Chaim, how he says the sewing machine is the curse of the devil. Every stitch is the same and no human being can make a stitch like that."

Charles looked around and noticed Mr. Ratner had gotten rid of most of his possessions and only a small suitcase stood by the door.

"Well, I guess we'll have to return home empty-handed. Maybe we'll come back in a few weeks with more money."

He and Chaim slowly walked toward the front door.

"Wait," Jacob Ratner called out, as beads of sweat ran down his brow. "Perhaps we can come to an agreement. Since I'll be sailing in a few days, I'll make a sacrifice."

He then offered Charles a substantially lower amount.

Without hesitating, Charles held out his hand.

"Let's shake on it," he said.

Charles reached into his pocket, handed over the money, and he and Chaim bid Mr. Ratner goodbye, wishing him *a gute parnosseh* in America—a good livelihood in America.

Charles and Chaim, happy they had gotten a great bargain, lifted the sewing machine onto the wagon and began their journey home.

For the next few months, Charles and Chaim spent a good deal of time planning the opening of their shop.

As time went on, Charles began to have reservations about actually making that final commitment. With the May Laws enacted two years earlier, he feared, at any moment, even more restrictions could be placed on the Jews.

"Did he want to live in a land that was so anti-Semitic," he asked himself? He did not. There was something better out there, and he was determined to find out what it was.

How ashamed he felt having to tell Chaim, after all these months, he had changed his mind, but it was something he could not put off any longer.

One Sunday evening, while taking a leisurely walk, Charles spotted Chaim sitting alone under an old birch tree.

"Chaim, I need to discuss a matter with you that's been worrying me for some time."

"Yes. I've noticed something has been weighing heavily on you," Chaim replied, as he raised himself from the ground and wiped away the dirt from behind his trousers.

Charles led Chaim to a nearby bench.

"You know me well," he said. "I'm sorry, but I've decided to leave for America. I cannot live here any longer, not knowing what I could be missing elsewhere in the world."

"I certainly can understand why you wish to leave Lithuania," Chaim said, "but America, that is a puzzle to me and besides, I've heard it's not all that wonderful there. I guess you'll have to see for yourself. This I know about you. So go with my blessing."

Charles took Chaim's hand and shook it.

"Thanks for understanding," he said. "You've been a good friend to me."

"I feel the same about you," Chaim replied, and it was obvious that the friendship these two men shared was deeply felt.

Aunt Lena and Uncle Morris had been up for several hours, preparing the breads, pastries, and rolls for their customers.

This was not an ordinary day. They, along with Sarah Taube, were closing the bakery early and traveling to Shidleve to see Charles Grazutis off to America. Sarah Taube had not seen Charles for several years, not since the family went to Shidleve for his mother's funeral.

Whenever Sarah Taube thought of Charles, a warm feeling would come over her. She often remembered the night of her mother's funeral when he first visited her and Aaron. How gentle he was, and she never forgot it was then when he first called her Sarala.

Sarah Taube rose early that morning and spent some considerable time thinking about what she was going to wear. She wanted Charles to notice her. She quickly slipped on the beautiful, light green dress her aunt had had the local seamstress make for her for Rosh Hashanah. She fastened the five pearly, white buttons and carefully tied the big, white sash behind her back.

As she gazed into the mirror, turning around several times to make sure there were no threads hanging or buttons unfastened, her mind began to think thoughts of a young girl who was quickly becoming a woman. She was sixteen years old and already being considered for marriage by the town matchmaker.

Who will I marry, she wondered, as she opened a glass jar full of rose water and combed it through her long, brown hair. With a single motion, she pulled her hair tightly into a bun, neatly centering it on the back of her head, securing it with two straight pins.

How wonderful it was that Charles was going to America, she

thought. She wondered whether Aaron would ever send for her. It was still her dream to join him, but she was beginning to have her doubts as to whether he would ever follow through with his promise.

"Are you ready," a voice sang from behind the door. "We have lots to do before our trip."

Sarah Taube was so preoccupied with her thoughts that she did not hear Aunt Lena's call.

"Sarah Taube, are you ready?" her aunt asked again. "We need you to help display the baked goods. Put on an apron and hurry and eat. It's getting late, and the customers will be here soon."

"I'm ready," Sarah Taube replied, throwing open the door.

This morning the entire world looked beautiful to her. She was going to Shidleve to see Charles again.

"There," Charles said, giving the suitcase one last look. "I think I've packed everything. All I have to do now is fill this knapsack with provisions to last me for at least two weeks."

His friend, Chaim looked on with an expression of sadness on his face.

"I still don't understand why you want to go to America," he said.

Charles lifted his suitcase from the wooden bench and placed it firmly on the floor.

"I have an aunt and cousins living in Pittsburgh," he replied. "They have written many times inviting me to visit. I want to see for myself what it's like. Are the streets really paved with gold? Will I be able to make a living? Don't worry, though. If I see it's not for me, I'll come back and never think of America again."

It was early in October and the sun was beginning to set, casting its shadows on the rooftops of the small wood-framed houses.

Charles heard the clatter of hoofs outside.

"Welcome," he said as he opened the door and greeted Sarah Taube and her aunt and uncle. "Please come in and make yourselves at home. What is that delightful fragrance I smell, Sarala?" he asked, following her into the living room.

Sarah Taube was embarrassed.

"It's water scented with rose petals," Aunt Lena replied. "After she washes her hair, she combs it through to give it a sweet smell. They sell it at the General Store. She's never without it."

"Aunt Lena, please," Sarah Taube whispered.

Charles, realizing Sarah Taube felt uncomfortable, immediately changed the subject.

"Let me look at you, my Sarala," he said, stepping aside to observe her more closely. "This can't be my Sarala? You've grown into a beautiful young woman."

Sarah Taube blushed at the compliment and looked away.

Before long, the room filled with friends and relatives who had come to wish Charles good luck and a safe journey.

Aunt Lena reached into a straw basket and presented him with three salamis and a challah.

"Something to eat on the trip," she said as they exchanged smiles.

"Thank you for your thoughtfulness," he replied and placed the items into his knapsack.

"I have something for you too," Sarah Taube announced, giving Charles a shy smile. "It's a sweet cake made from a recipe my mother gave me when I was a child."

"If you made it, my Sarala, I know it will be the best I've ever tasted."

Each time Charles called her his Sarala, her heart would beat faster. Sadness came over her. Charles was leaving, and she probably would never see him again.

"Will you be visiting Aaron?" Aunt Lena asked. "I'm sure he would love to see you."

"Yes. He'll be picking me up as soon as the authorities clear me. He knows when my ship will be arriving and has invited me to spend the day before I leave to visit my relatives."

"Please give him our love," Aunt Lena said.

"I will," Charles replied, looking in Sarah Taube's direction.

The rest of the evening was spent eating, drinking and talking about America. Most agreed it was a wonderful land, full of personal and religious freedom and lots of good food and good jobs for all who wanted to work.

"My goodness, it's getting late," Uncle Morris said, glancing at his watch. "We must be going. We have a long trip ahead of us."

Charles motioned for Sarah Taube to come closer.

"Be sure to take good care of yourself," he whispered, as he leaned over and placed his strong, warm hands on her shoulders.

Sarah Taube's eyes filled with tears.

Charles gently wiped them from her face.

"There's no need to cry, my Sarala. I promise I will write as soon as I get settled."

"Please, I'll be expecting your letter," she replied.

Charles watched from the door as they quietly left.

After Uncle Morris helped Aunt Lena and Sarah Taube into the wagon, he pulled himself up, took hold of the reins and led the horse onto the road.

Sarah Taube gave Charles one last look, and as she waved goodbye, she thought about how Aaron had promised he would send for her and hadn't kept his promise. Charles promised to write. Will he keep his promise?

# Chapter 7 – Charles in America

## October 1884 - New York City, USA

Aaron looked quickly at the clock on the kitchen wall. Time for his departure was drawing near and he had to hurry.

The October days were becoming quite brisk, so he put on his heavy, wool jacket and wrapped a dark brown scarf around his neck before he flew down the stairs of his third floor apartment.

Thankfully, he had enough time to hop onto a horse-drawn streetcar that had pulled over. He was heading for Castle Garden where he would meet Charles who was scheduled to arrive at three in the afternoon.

Within an hour, the trolley stopped in front of the immigration station. Aaron jumped off and entered the main building where an official pointed him toward a room at the end of the hall.

Many of the arrivals had been processed and were eagerly awaiting the appearance of a familiar face to take them away from the chaos and lead them toward a new and better life. It reminded him of when he first came to America as a greenhorn, but now he was on the other end, ready to welcome a new immigrant as he had been welcomed years ago.

Aaron scanned the crowd. Then he heard a voice yelling, "Aaron, Aaron, it's me!"

He turned around and saw a tall, dark-haired man carrying a black valise and a knapsack draped over his shoulder.

"Charles! Charles! I can't believe it's you!" he shouted. "How did you ever recognize me?"

"It was easy," Charles replied, holding up a small photograph. "Your sister gave me this before I left. She thought it would help pick you out in a crowd and it worked. I would never have recognized you, otherwise. You're not that skinny little boy I remember. When was it—seven years ago?"

"Yes, Charles. I was fourteen years old when I left Shavlan. So you think I've changed that much?"

"Certainly. Look at you. You've grown into a handsome young man."

Aaron was over six feet tall with sandy brown hair and green eyes, and the resemblance to his sister was uncanny. He had a pleasant disposition and Charles recognized these fine qualities.

"Come, let's catch the next streetcar," Aaron said, taking hold of Charles' suitcase. "You must be tired and hungry. My place is less than an hour from here."

As the trolley came to the Lower East Side, Charles was amazed to see so many businesses along the thoroughfare.

"That's where I work," Aaron said, pointing to a bakery halfway down the street. "I work there every day, except Sunday. Sunday is my day off."

Charles immediately picked up on Aaron's comment.

"You mean you work on Saturday? On the Sabbath?"

"It's America. If you want to work on Saturday, it's okay, and if you want to take off on Saturday, that's okay too."

Jews who don't observe the Sabbath, Charles thought. Already he was having doubts about the country.

After traveling for a while, the streetcar came to a stop in front of a row of five-story tenements.

"This is where I live." Aaron said, grabbing Charles' suitcase. "Let's get off."

Aaron led Charles toward a tall, brick building and pulled out a key. "Fortunately for you, my apartment is only on the third floor."

They proceeded to walk up three flights of stairs with Charles breathing heavily with every step.

When they got to the third floor, Aaron motioned for Charles to follow him down a long hallway, stopping in front of a brown, wooden door.

"Come in. Take off your coat and make yourself comfortable," Aaron said as he placed Charles's suitcase on the floor. "I'll get dinner started. I'm sure you must be starving for a home cooked meal."

"May I offer you a cigarette?" Aaron asked and pulled out a shiny brass case.

Charles hesitated. He had smoked cigars before but never cigarettes.

"Go on, try it," Aaron urged. "Everyone in America smokes. It's considered quite fashionable."

Charles reached into the case, took out a cigarette, placed it in his mouth and lit it.

"How do you like it?" Aaron asked.

"I like it very much," Charles replied as he puffed away."

"I knew you would. But be careful. It can become quite addictive. Anyway, this is my apartment. I know it's small, but I have everything I need and at least it's my very own place. The only thing I share is the bathroom down the hall. The rent is reasonable, and I make a fairly good wage, so I'm able to afford it, thank G-d."

Charles looked around, noticing the apartment was adequate for Aaron's needs.

The living room held a sofa and two chairs, and off to the side was a small kitchen table, two benches, an icebox, and a stove. In the adjoining room stood a single bed and a nightstand.

"Tell me the news from home," Aaron asked, as he began preparing the evening meal. "I've lost track of time here in America. It's been over a month since I've heard from my sister. Did you see her before you left?"

"Yes I did. Your sister still has hopes of coming to America. She mentioned you were saving up for her passage, but she wondered what was taking so long. I didn't realize you've been here for over seven years, so I'm curious myself to know why you haven't sent for her."

Aaron pulled up a chair and sat down.

"At first, I felt guilty leaving my sister with Aunt Lena and Uncle Morris, but I realized she was better off living with them than here with me. Who would have taken care of her while I worked? What would have become of her? So I put the idea in the back of my mind and decided not to pursue the matter any further. Someday, I'll send for her. I want you to know I have not forgotten my promise, but its best to leave things this way for now."

Charles saw that Aaron was sincere, but Sarah Taube would be disappointed if she knew how he felt.

"There, it's ready," Aaron announced, inviting Charles to sit at the table. "I hope you enjoy what I've put together and, by the way, you don't have to worry because everything is strictly kosher."

Charles felt relieved. At least he was observing one of the laws of the Torah, he thought, but he most definitely was not keeping the laws of *Shabbat*.

"Aaron, I didn't know what a good cook you were," Charles remarked, pleasantly surprised at the wonderful spread.

"When you live alone, you quickly develop a knack for cooking," Aaron said proudly. "We bachelors have no choice in the matter.

Right, Charles?"

On the table was a basket filled with soft rolls, a plate of boiled brisket with roasted potatoes, a bowl of green peas, and a dish of lettuce, tomatoes, and cucumbers. For dessert, there was a glass container filled with stewed fruit, followed by a pot of hot coffee.

Aaron presented his newly arrived guest with a wonderful feast, and before they began to eat, he and Charles recited the prayer for the beginning of the evening meal.

Aaron and Charles had a delightful conversation while eating. Aaron was eager to hear about the old country, and Charles was equally eager to hear about America.

"What do you intend to do while you're here?" Aaron asked, offering to place another spoonful of fruit into Charles' dish.

"That's easy," Charles replied, covering the bowl with his hands. "No thank you. I'm afraid I can't eat another bite. But to answer your question, I plan to visit my aunt in Pittsburgh for a few days and once I return, I'll be looking for a job as an apprentice in a clothing factory. When I've become proficient at my job, I plan to open my own tailor shop."

"Here in America you'll have many opportunities," Aaron said as he began collecting the dishes. "If you're willing to spend the time, there's always someone who is willing to show you the ropes. Of course, as long as you put in the hours and work hard, the rewards will surely follow.

"By the way, when you return from your visit, you're more than welcome to stay with me until you find a job, and when that happens, you'll be able to get a place of your own as I've done."

"Thank you," Charles replied, helping Aaron clear the table, "and I will definitely take you up on your offer."

"Now let me prepare a bed for you. I'm sure you must be exhausted after your long ocean voyage."

Before they retired, Aaron pointed out to Charles where he could catch the local trolley.

"There you will take the ferry to New Jersey," he explained, "which will take you to the railroad terminal to pick up the train to Pittsburgh."

The following morning, Aaron prepared breakfast and by eight o'clock, they were both on their way—one going to Pittsburgh to visit family—the other going by trolley to report for work.

By the late nineteenth century, almost eighty-five percent of the New York garment industry was located below 14th Street. Many Eastern European Jewish immigrants found jobs in the garment industry and tailoring was one of the few careers available to them.

Once returning from visiting his relatives, a reputable clothing manufacturer in New York City hired Charles as an operator. Not too long after that, he was fortunate to have been accepted as a boarder in a boarding house run by a respectable middle-aged landlady.

◄O►

A heavy December snow had fallen overnight, and the streets were carpeted with soft white powder. Aunt Lena and Uncle Morris stayed in bed longer as the snow practically crippled the community. Generally, the women remained at home unless it was necessary for them to go out.

"Let's make fewer baked goods today," Aunt Lena said and began preparing the rolls, cakes and pastries.

"I agree," Uncle Morris replied, staring out the window at the large snowflakes covering the oak trees outside the bakery.

"Does it look as though the sun will come out?" Aunt Lena asked.

"No, but it's early. Perhaps the sun will emerge later in the morning. If so, the snow will melt, and we may get customers after all."

Sarah Taube came down the stairs.

"Take your time eating your breakfast," Aunt Lena said. "We're only going to make a few items in case anyone shows up."

It was now ten o'clock. The baked goods were put on racks to cool, and there was nothing more to do except to wait and see if the weather improves.

Aunt Lena heard a thump coming from outside. To her surprise, it was the mail carrier, Mr. Steadman.

"Hurry and let me in!" he shouted, standing outside shivering.

Uncle Morris led him into the kitchen and helped him off with his boots, while Aunt Lena offered him a glass of hot tea.

"Come, sit by the stove," she said. "You need to warm up. What brings you out in this kind of weather?"

"I have to deliver the mail, don't I? I especially have to deliver this letter to Sarah Taube. It's from America, and I know how she looks forward getting letters from there."

"Mr. Steadman has a letter from America, Sarah Taube," her aunt called. "Come into the kitchen."

As soon as Sarah Taube heard the words "letter from America," she threw down the mop she was using to clean up the snow Mr. Steadman had left on the floor and came running in.

"I believe you have a letter from New York," Mr. Steadman said and handed her a wet envelope.

Sarah Taube's face crinkled in disgust.

"It's soggy, Aunt Lena."

"Come, give it to me, my child."

Aunt Lena took the letter out of the envelope, placed it on a plate, put it in the oven and after a brief wait, she retrieved a completely dry letter.

"It's a trick I learned from Mrs. Levitan at the General Store. I observed how she dried an order of writing paper, which had been sitting under a leaky roof in her storage shed."

Sarah Taube wrapped her arms around her aunt and gave her a hug. "You're so clever," she said, "but now I must go upstairs to read my letter. It's from Charles, you know."

Aunt Lena and Uncle Morris watched as Sarah Taube held the letter tightly against her chest. As she climbed the stairs to her bedroom, she called out, "I'm so happy he has written. I was beginning to think he had forgotten me."

*24 November 1884*
*My dear Sarala,*

*I have some good news. I have found a job as an operator working in a large clothing factory. My hours are from 7:30 a.m. until 5:30 p.m. with Saturdays and Sundays off. Thank G-d I do not have to work on the Sabbath.*

*The second part of my good news is I have found a nice Jewish woman who rents out rooms. I pay her monthly and home-cooked kosher means are included.*

*New York is not a very pretty place. There is no countryside, no grass or trees. There are only tall, cold-looking buildings. Many people here are hustlers. They look for ways to make a living, and they don't care who they walk over to do it.*

*I spend so much of my time wondering if I made the right decision to come here. But I know I must give it more time. Hopefully, I will grow to like it.*

*Aaron is doing well. He speaks English fluently and was recently made a manager at the bakery. He loves it here and is completely Americanized, not like me.*

*I will end my letter by saying please write.*

*Take care and regards to your family,*
*Charles*

Life in Shavlan had become very lonely for Sarah Taube. Of course, Aunt Lena and Uncle Morris were very kind and often expressed how much they loved her but something was missing from her life.

As Aunt Lena and Uncle Morris had predicted, the sun came out, the snow began to melt and by early afternoon the streets were passable.

A dozen customers came in and by late afternoon, the entire stock was gone.

After the dinner dishes had been cleared, Sarah Taube went to her bedroom, sat down in her favorite chair and began her reply to Charles.

◄O►

Late one January evening, after returning to his apartment from a long day at work, Charles was excited to find a letter waiting for him. It was from his Sarala. She wrote of how happy she was learning he had found a nice place to live and he had found a good job. She told him nothing of importance or interesting ever happens in Shavlan and life goes on just about the same day after day.

After wishing him good luck in his job, she ended her letter, *"Your Sarala."*

◄O►

A month had passed and Sarah Taube was happy to have received another letter from Charles. As usual, she went up to her room to immerse herself in its contents. The correspondence between them continued with each letter strengthening the bond between them, extending across two continents.

Time flew and it was the 8th of September 1885, the day before Rosh Hashanah. Sarah Taube, Aunt Lena, and Uncle Morris had finished baking the rounded loaves of challah and honey cakes.

"I love this holiday, and I love baking honey cakes," Aunt Lena said. "It's a way to express our wishes for a sweet new year. I've made these honey cakes with a recipe handed down by your great-grandmother, Lena, whom I'm named after. You too will pass them on to your children and your children's children."

Sarah Taube wondered if she would ever have a family. At the rate she was going, she could not imagine herself married, let alone having children. As she completed her thought, Mrs. Bleekman came into the shop.

"Aunt Lena poked her head out from behind the counter.

"Good morning, Mrs. Bleekman. How may I help you?"

"It's awfully hot in here," Mrs. Bleekman replied, fanning herself with her pocketbook. She began perspiring heavily. "I must take off my coat. I feel faint."

"It's the hot oven," Aunt Lena replied. "In a few minutes we'll be taking out the honey cakes, and then the shop will cool down as soon as the fire is smothered."

Mrs. Bleekman was taken to a nearby bench and given a glass of water.

"Here, this will make you feel better," Aunt Lena said, holding the glass close to Mrs. Bleekman's lips. "You could be having a hot flash. I get them myself occasionally."

"Hot flash!" Mrs. Bleekman screeched. "I'm much too young to be getting a hot flash."

Mrs. Bleekman spotted Sarah Taube behind the display case.

"How are you, my dear?" she asked, giving her a long stare.

"I'm fine," Sarah Taube replied. "Excuse me. I have to attend to the honey cakes in the oven."

Sarah Taube always felt uncomfortable whenever Mrs. Bleekman came into the shop. She could not tolerate her stares and would, on occasion, look fixedly at her until she would be forced to look away.

Mrs. Bleekman earned her living by setting up *shidduchs*—an arranged marriage between two willing people of the opposite sex. It was the way she went about it that disturbed Sarah Taube. The word discreet was definitely not in Mrs. Bleekman's vocabulary.

"Are you feeling better?" Aunt Lena asked, gently feeling the woman's forehead to make sure she did not have a fever.

"Yes, thank you," replied Mrs. Bleekman, standing up and reaching for her coat. "I don't know what came over me. My goodness, I've forgotten why I came here in the first place. Yes, now I remember. Give me two of those round challahs—the ones with the raisins."

Aunt Lena wrapped up the challahs and thanked her for the purchase, wishing her a very happy and healthy Rosh Hashanah.

"The same to you and your family," Mrs. Bleekman replied, placing her parcels into a small wooden basket. "We have to get together soon," she said, giving Aunt Lena a quick wink.

Aunt Lena, of course, knew exactly what was meant by that wink.

Mrs. Bleekman had recently contacted her with regard to a possible introduction between Sarah Taube and the shoemaker's son.

Aunt Lena felt that Sarah Taube was not even close to thinking about marriage, but it was only a matter of time before the topic would to be brought up.

By now, the bakery was full of customers, eager to pick up their honey cakes and challahs. The holiday was fast approaching, and the ladies were in a hurry to return to their homes to prepare for the joyous celebration.

Before noon, the shelves of baked goods were stripped clean, the shop closed, and Sarah Taube and her family began preparing their own house for the festive occasion.

◄O►

Charles wondered where the time had gone. He had lived in New York City for almost two years and other than seeing Aaron on occasion, his work had consumed the better part of his life.

The room he rented from his landlady, Mrs. Gittleman was adequate for his needs. After her husband died, she converted her three-story home into a boarding house so she could support herself. She had six male roomers occupying the second and third floors and maintained the first floor as her own living quarters, serving meals in her kitchen.

This evening, when Charles returned from work, Mrs. Gittleman alerted him that he had received a letter.

"It's from your family in Lithuania," she said as she did each time he received a letter from Sarah Taube. He quickly took the letter off of the hallway table, thanked her, and climbed the stairs to his room.

Charles always looked forward to reading mail from his Sarala. It calmed him after he had spent a long, tiring day glued to the sewing machine.

Through her letters, he could temporarily escape his feelings of emptiness and loneliness. He had developed a fondness for her, and the friendship they shared had become important to him.

Sarah Taube and Charles continued to correspond on a regular basis. Charles would write about his life in America, and she would write about the boring life she led in Shavlan.

◄O►

Late one afternoon, as Aunt Lena was about to close the bakery, Mrs. Bleekman came in, looking quite excited. She and Aunt Lena immediately headed for the back room.

"Sarah Taube," Aunt Lena called, "please clean up and lock the front door. Mrs. Bleekman is staying for dinner."

Sarah Taube was suspicious. There were rumors that Mrs. Bleekman was concerned about her position as village matchmaker.

Since many young men were leaving for America, the townspeople were worried that there would not be enough eligible men to go around for the young women who were approaching the age for marriage. Mrs. Bleekman was working overtime to fill the demands made by families with marriageable young girls.

Sarah Taube knew the time would come when Aunt Lena and Uncle Morris would want to arrange for her to meet a suitable young man. After all, she was eighteen years old and well over the age to marry. She could not help but wonder whom Mrs. Bleekman had chosen for her.

"It must be the shoemaker's son, Hershel," she whispered to herself. She noticed he was coming into the shop to make purchases for his mother, and he would stare at her with his bulging, black eyes when he thought she wasn't looking. G-d in heaven, please don't let it be him, she thought.

At the table that evening, Uncle Morris sat quietly eating. He did not want to be a party to any discussions involving Sarah Taube and the obvious matchmaking schemes, which were going on between Aunt Lena and Mrs. Bleekman.

"How is business?" Mrs. Bleekman asked as Aunt Lena handed her a platter of baked chicken and crisp roasted potatoes.

"Business is fine," Uncle Morris replied, stuffing a fork full of chicken into his mouth.

"The evenings are getting warm now that summer is approaching," Aunt Lena said, passing a basket of freshly baked rolls to Mrs. Bleekman.

Sarah Taube could feel the tension building, and she wondered when Mrs. Bleekman was going to bring up the main topic of conversation.

Back and forth went the chatter and finally, after talking about trivial matters, the main subject materialized.

Mrs. Bleekman reached for her napkin to wipe her lips.

"Did you know, Sarah Taube, that Hershel Zimmer, the shoemaker's son, will be finishing his apprenticeship soon? He's such a nice boy. Have you seen him lately?"

Sarah Taube knew immediately this was not the first time the shoemaker's son's name had come up. Obviously, talks had been going on for a while, and they were now making an effort to introduce her to the idea of meeting this young man.

"Pass the rolls, please," Sarah Taube asked nonchalantly.

Mrs. Bleekman handed the plate of rolls to Sarah Taube, looking at her for an answer.

"Well, have you seen him?" she again asked, raising her voice slightly.

Sarah Taube placed a roll on her plate.

"Yes, I've seen him in the shop a few times last week," she replied.

What she really wanted to say was she would prefer that Mrs. Bleekman stop meddling in her affairs and when the time came for her to get married, she would pick someone of her own choosing. But she refrained from speaking her mind, mostly because she knew her aunt would not approve of her being rude to one of her customers.

Nothing else was said regarding Hershel Zimmer. The conversation continued to be more about the weather, business and other simple topics. Sarah Taube was relieved knowing Mrs. Bleekman's visit would end shortly, soon after dessert was served.

A feeling of panic came over Sarah Taube that night when she thought about the discussions that went on during dinner. She knew it would not be long before Mrs. Bleekman would again try to put together a match between her and the shoemaker's son or anyone else for that matter.

What was she to do? She must write Charles and tell him of her suspicions. She pulled out a sheet of writing paper from her box of stationery and began jotting down her thoughts.

*12 May 1886*
*Dear Charles,*

*I hope this letter finds you in good health. I am now eighteen years old, and I believe Aunt Lena has been discussing with Mrs. Bleekman, the matchmaker, the possibility of putting together a shidduch with me and some eligible young man here in Shavlan or perhaps in a nearby town.*

*There's another strange thing I've noticed. Every now and then young men come into the bakery. They tell me they're running an errand for their mother and need help selecting baked goods.*

*I have seen these men walking to the synagogue for their Torah studies, and I'm suspicious that I am about to be matched with one of them. I have no intention of marrying anyone, especially someone I do not know or even like.*

*I care for you very much and greatly respect your opinion, so I'm asking your advice in this matter. Please, if you know how to get me out of this situation, I would appreciate it. Give my best to my brother, and I hope to hear from you soon.*
*Your Sarala*

Charles was distressed to learn his Sarala could soon be married. He needed to write immediately and declare his intentions and if she felt the same, at least she would wait until he had made some decisions about what he was going to do with the rest of his life.

He closed his eyes, clearly composing the letter in his mind, before he took to the pen.

A letter arrived from Charles this afternoon.

*29 June 1886*
*My dear Sarala,*

*I am saddened to learn of your family's intention to marry you off. From the very first time we met, I felt a great deal of affection for you, and I believe my affection has grown into something more serious.*

*The idea of you being married to someone else has aroused strong emotions in me, and I could not bear your being with anyone else.*

*I have some serious thinking to do about my future but whatever decision I make, it will include you, my Sarala.*

Sarah Taube's heart began to flutter as she held the letter close to her chest. At last, he was saying the words she waited to hear and, in his own way, he had declared his love for her.

She felt a stir of happiness within the depths of her soul.

After taking a deep breath, she continued to read.

*I will stay here a while longer but by the new year, I plan to come home, and we can discuss further my intentions. Meanwhile, do not make any rash decisions until I return.*

*Write soon, my Sarala.*

*All my affection,*
*Charles*

Sarah Taube reread the letter several times before she placed it in a box marked, "Letters from Charles".

Charles had made it clear to her that he cared for her and nothing could ever tear her away from him. Even if she had to wait years for his return, she would do so.

After all, he was her *besherter*—her soul mate.

After attending the Sabbath services at a nearby synagogue, Charles was about to take his leave when an attractive young woman tapped him on the shoulder.

"Hello," she said in a heavy Yiddish accent, looking as though she had met him before.

"Hello," he replied, taking a quick look. "Do I know you?" he asked politely.

"Yes. I believe we've met before," she said, stepping in front of him so he couldn't pass.

In an attempt not to appear rude, he asked how she knew him.

"You work at Mendelsohn's Clothing Factory, don't you?"

"Yes I do," he replied in a slow, hesitant way. "How do you know this?"

"I work there, too. Don't you remember the other day when you held the door open for me? It was early in the morning, and I had packages in my arms."

After thinking about it, Charles remembered the incident but, at the time, he hadn't paid much attention to it.

Before he knew it, they were walking in the same direction, heading back to his boarding house.

"My name is Yetta Solomon," she said, "and what may I ask is your name?"

"Charles Grazutis," he replied, feeling a bit more at ease with her.

They continued to walk for several more blocks with Yetta making frivolous conversation. Charles listened and was becoming more annoyed with each passing moment. He did not want to waste any time with this woman and wanted to get home as fast as possible. Perhaps there was a letter waiting for him from his Sarala.

"Well, this is where I live," Charles said, stopping in front of steps leading up to the boarding house. "It was nice talking to you."

Yetta, realizing she lived a block away said, "I live not too far from here, and yes, I enjoyed very much talking to you. May I call you Charles?"

Charles stared at her strangely but did not answer. He merely excused himself and proceeded to walk up the eight steps leading to the front door.

"Goodbye," Yetta said, looking up at him from the bottom of the steps, "and when you see me at work on Monday, say hello."

Yetta had emigrated with her brother, Harry almost five years ago. She was from a small town in Russia called Turov and like all immigrants in America, she and her brother were looking to make a better life for themselves. They were devoted to each other until last year when he unexpectedly got married and that was when their relationship began to fall apart.

Yetta felt Sybil, her new sister-in-law, was jealous of the connection she had with Harry and was determined to break them up. Sybil told vicious lies about Yetta to Harry.

Harry tried to reason with his wife but she wouldn't listen and so he continued to see Yetta secretly. Finally, he could not handle the situation any longer and ended all contact with his sister.

Like most young, single immigrant women, her only hope for surviving and raising her standard of living was to catch herself a man, and she had set her sights on Charles.

The weekend passed and it was Monday morning.

When Charles entered his place of employment, he heard a voice call, "Stop, Charles. Wait for me."

It was Yetta. He had almost forgotten about her but hearing her voice in her distinctive accent made him recall their meeting the previous Saturday.

"Let's have lunch," she said. "I'll call for you at noon."

Charles was not used to anyone taking such an interest in him, especially a single female who was expressing herself openly and unashamedly. She was definitely not a well-mannered or ladylike young woman and was certainly the complete opposite of his Sarala.

Sure enough, as soon as the noon hour appeared, there was Yetta, standing beside his sewing machine.

"I know of a great lunch counter a few blocks away," she said. "They sell the best kosher hot dogs."

"My landlady always packs me a lunch," Charles replied, "but I'll join you in a cup of coffee."

"Very well," she answered, linking her arm into his.

As they walked down the street, her body rubbed against his, and Charles sensed that she wanted more than a casual relationship.

Charles, being a very prim young man, was horrified at his body's reaction to this woman and felt he had to distance himself from her.

This woman was so controlling that Charles felt as though she were leading him around by the nose. He was already thinking about what to say so she would leave him alone and latch on to some other poor soul.

"I would like to know how long you've been working at Mendelsohn's?" she asked.

Charles gave her a strange look.

"It's been more than two years," he replied. "Why do you ask?"

"Well, I was wondering why you haven't been given a promotion by now. I've heard there's an opening for a foreman."

As soon as Charles heard this, he was agitated and thought he, at least, should have been considered for the position. After all, he had been at the job for more than two years and was well qualified. Seeing how angry Charles was, Yetta suggested once he returned from lunch, he should speak to the boss.

"May I have a word with you?" Charles asked as he opened the door to the manager's office.

"Come in, come in," his boss said. "What can I do for you?"

Charles spoke about the opening for foreman and wondered why he wasn't considered.

The boss came around the corner of his desk and invited Charles to take a seat.

"You've been here for over two years, and I'm well aware you are one of my best workers but because your work is so good, I really didn't want to take you away from it.

"After all, if I made you foreman, who would do the work to make the fine clothing this factory produces? So, my friend, I've given the position to someone else whose work was not as good as yours. This will allow you to continue doing the work in grinding out the best quality of products."

Charles sat there with his mouth open. He had worked so hard only to be told his work was too good for him to be considered for a supervisory position.

At quitting time, Yetta stopped by to inquire how his meeting had gone. Charles did not want to discuss the matter with her. She was a stranger and, besides, she was now really getting on his nerves. He did not want a woman prying into his business. All he wanted was to be left alone.

When Charles came home from work that evening, a pleasant surprise was waiting for him. It was a letter from his Sarala.

Charles climbed the steps to his second floor room, pulled up a chair by the window and read through the letter before placing it in an envelope.

A smile came to his face. This was exactly what he needed to calm him down and take his mind off of what had transpired that afternoon.

---

There was hardly a trace of snow on the ground as Sarah Taube threw open the shutters of her small, narrow room. The morning sun shone brightly and a refreshing smell permeated the air. Spring would be here soon and she could hardly wait.

Purim, the celebration of the deliverance of the Jewish people from persecution in the ancient Persian Empire, was tomorrow.

Sarah Taube hurried to get dressed, as she had to help Aunt Lena and Uncle Morris prepare the special holiday pastry, hamantashen.

She heard bustling about, so she grabbed her apron and ran down the narrow, wooden stairway leading to the kitchen.

As Uncle Morris was loading the peat into the oven to keep the fire going, Aunt Lena had already prepared the dough and was cutting out the triangles for the pastry.

"Oh, you're up," Aunt Lena said. "Reach in the pantry and fetch the prune and poppy seed fillings. The triangles are ready to be filled and folded."

Aunt Lena had already made the breads, cakes, and cookies while Sarah Taube slept.

From time to time, she would allow her niece to sleep longer, especially if the shop was busy the day before. She would say with a chuckle, "Sarah Taube, you're a growing girl and need your beauty sleep." This would be her way of letting her niece know she could sleep late the following morning.

Twenty minutes had passed, and Sarah Taube knew by the smell that the hamantashen were ready.

"They're done," she said, taking one hamantashen off of the hot baking sheet and setting it aside for herself.

By now many customers had gathered, patiently waiting for the bakery to open. They had already shopped for the items they needed to make the festive foods for Purim and because they wanted the breads and pastries to be fresh, Aunt Lena's bakery was usually the first stop they would make the morning of the eve of a holiday.

"Is everything out?" Aunt Lena asked, glancing at the display case.

"Yes, everything is out," Sarah Taube replied.

One by one, the women entered the shop.

Mrs. Shimmel was the first in line. She was a tall, beautiful brown-eyed young woman with a face that could charm any young man. She had recently wed Isaac Shimmel, the blacksmith.

Prior to getting married, Isaac had been known as the town bachelor and had not been the least bit interested in getting married. Mrs. Bleekman finally worked her magic and was able to arrange a meeting between the two of them and after a few months, a match was made. It was another one of Mrs. Bleekman's success stories.

Mrs. Shimmel loved to entertain and was one of Aunt Lena's best customers and whenever she came into the shop, she was given special attention.

"Good morning, Mrs. Shimmel," Sarah Taube said, appearing

from the side of the counter, "and how may I help you today?"

Mrs. Shimmel was busy deciding what she wanted and did not answer for a while. Finally she looked at Sarah Taube and said, "I would like eight hamantashen, four with prune and four with poppy seed."

Sarah Taube very carefully placed her purchase in a bag, wishing her *a guten yontif*—a good holiday.

Before the morning was over, all the baked goods, except for the ones set aside for the proprietors, were gone.

Just before Uncle Morris latched the front door, Mr. Stedman came in with a large burlap bag hanging over his shoulder.

"I have a letter for you," he said, giving Sarah Taube a chuckle. "Maybe it's a letter from New York," he added, pretending he hadn't looked at the return address.

"Thank you," she said politely and took the letter from his hands. He turned around, threw the mailbag back over his shoulder and left the premises.

At last, the exhausted trio could retire to their quarters.

With letter in hand, Sarah Taube plopped herself down on her bed and began to read.

*"I miss you very much,"* he wrote.

Again he mentioned returning to Lithuania. Sarah Taube felt both happy and sad at the same time.

She was happy because she would see him again but, on the other hand, she could not understand why he did not like America. The idea of emigrating there was the only thing that made any sense to her. He continued to convey his feelings, ending his letter, *"Affectingly, Charles."*

Sarah Taube smiled as she put the letter back in the envelope and placed it in her special box marked, "Letters from Charles", along with all the other letters she had received from him over the years.

Correspondence between them continued with letters coming on a regular basis, but it was already three months into the new year and still no Charles. Was he ever going to come back? She was beginning to have doubts.

Charles was pleased with his recent change in employment. He was doing good work and was happy in his new job. Mr. Hamburg, his employer, had recently called him into his office.

"I'm impressed with the excellent work you're doing," he said as he walked to the front of his desk. "If you keep this up, I'm afraid I'll have to give you more responsibilities, and you know what that means, don't you?"

Charles did not know what to say.

After waiting a few moments, Mr. Hamburg said loudly, "It means a step up the ladder, my boy and an increase in salary. Perhaps even a job as foreman."

Charles was elated to finally hear he was appreciated.

"Thank you, Mr. Hamburg for those kind words. I've learned a great deal working in the garment industry, and if I'm to be considered for a supervisory position, I will do my best."

"Keep up the good work," Mr. Hamburg said, shaking him firmly by the hand.

Charles could not have been happier. He received recognition from his boss and felt it was only a matter of time before he would be given the opportunity to supervise and direct others.

"Hold the door for me. I'll be there in a minute," a voice called one morning as Charles was about to enter his place of work. He recognized the voice immediately. With an accent like that, it could only be Yetta Solomon from his old workplace.

Running down the street was this voluptuous woman, waving her hand as her long, black skirt swung about her legs. "I thought it was you," she said almost out of breath.

"What are you doing here, Yetta?" Charles asked, not expecting to see her.

"Surprise. I work here too. I don't want you to think I've been following you, but when I found out you left Mendelsohn's to come and work for Hamburg and Sons, I thought to myself, I really miss that nice gentleman. I bet he's getting paid a lot more than what he got at Mendelsohn's. Was I right?"

Charles hesitated for a moment. "Yes," he felt compelled to say. "I did get a slight increase."

Charles had been very careful to avoid Yetta's clutches and when he left his last job, he was certain he had accomplished his goal. But here she was, as usual, snooping around in an attempt to find out all she could about his private business.

Every time he would look up from his sewing machine, go to lunch, or get ready to leave for the day, there she was. What could he do? Because they worked in such close proximity and she was a female, he had to be well mannered and a perfect gentleman toward her at all times.

Months had passed, and it was almost the middle of December. Charles kept wondering if America was really where he wanted to settle. Even though America was still not a country he was fond of, he liked his job and thought he soon would be considered for a promotion.

The company was growing and more people were being hired. Because the place was getting overcrowded, Charles heard that Mr. Hamburg was seriously thinking about opening another factory, and he hoped he would be in the running to head it up.

He tried to keep away from Yetta but everywhere he went there she was, eager to start a conversation. Even the men at the workplace were beginning to make off-color remarks.

Late one afternoon, Charles was called into Mr. Hamburg's office.

"Do you know Yetta Solomon?" he asked. The grin, when it finally came, spread slowly across his face.

"Yes, I do," answered Charles, wondering why her name was brought up.

"She's quite an attractive young lady, isn't she?" Mr. Hamburg said with a snicker. "I've noticed the two of you see quite a lot of each other."

Immediately, Charles knew what Mr. Hamburg was getting at. Charles may have been what they called a "greenhorn," but he had been in America long enough to recognize an employer who was looking to take advantage of, or make unfair demands on, one of his female employees. And in this case, it was Yetta he was after.

A feeling of revulsion came over him, and the sight of this man he had respected now filled him with disgust.

"Are you having an affair with her?" Mr. Hamburg asked.

"No, we're friends," Charles replied, shocked at this man's bluntness.

"Well, it would be nice if you were to stop seeing her. I find her very appealing, and I would like to get to know her better, if you know what I mean.

"With you out of the picture, I think I would stand a good chance with her. So what do you say? By the way, an opening for foreman will be coming up. I'm thinking very seriously of considering you for the job."

Charles wondered whether Mr. Hamburg was offering him a bribe. It certainly sounded like a bribe.

Even though Charles had no romantic interest in Yetta and gave her no reason to believe he did, the thought of Mr. Hamburg, a married man, being so blatant about going after her in such a shameful manner was beyond belief.

It was at that point when Charles came to a few decisions about what he wanted to do with his life and staying in America was not one of them. Mr. Hamburg's lechery resolved all of his conflicts.

"You know, Mr. Hamburg," Charles said, showing displeasure in his voice, "you totally disappointed me today. Even if you were to offer me a partnership, I would turn my back on you.

"You have a lot of nerve bringing me to your office and telling me what you have in mind with regard to one of your employees. I would have expected you, as the owner of this establishment, to conform to accepted standards of Jewish morality and respectability. Where is your sense of decency?"

Mr. Hamburg sat in shock. To hear one of his employees address him in such a manner was appalling to him.

"You can do whatever you want in your factory," Charles continued, "but to ask me to stop seeing one of your female employees so you can take advantage of her makes me sick."

Mr. Hamburg's face turned red as he stood from behind his desk and huffed out his irritation.

"You can forget about being promoted to foreman of this factory," he said, pointing his finger toward the door. "You're fired. Pack up your belongings, stop by the accounting office to get your pay, and leave these premises immediately."

"With pleasure!" Charles shouted as he stomped out of the room, slamming the door behind him.

When Charles walked out of the building that afternoon, he ended his work at Hamburg and Sons and also ended his stay in America.

He realized he had wasted years of his life and achieved nothing. He came to America to find himself but instead, there was nothing in America for him to find. Perhaps, he thought, his experience was meant to teach him that his place and future was in his shtetl in Lithuania.

# Chapter 8 – Charles Returns

## February 1888 – Shavlan, Kovne Guberniya, Russian Empire

A soft voice spoke, "Hello, Sarala."

Sarah Taube's heart skipped a beat and she began to shake. She had just opened the bakery and her back was toward the front door and was busy arranging the trays of pastries neatly on the shelf.

It had to be Charles, she thought. Who else would call her, Sarala? She turned around.

"It's you," she said, bursting with happiness at seeing him.

"Yes, Sarala. I could not stay away from you any longer."

Sarah Taube's heart was pounding as Charles came closer to her. He smiled, reached for her hand and led her toward a warm fire blazing in the wood-burning stove.

"I missed you so much," he said.

Sarah Taube could not keep her emotions hidden and now that they were face to face, she finally told him how she felt.

"I missed you too," she replied as her green eyes glistened with joy.

Charles, still holding her hand, said, "Sarala, do you think you could be happy with someone like me?"

Sarah Taube did not have to think twice.

"Yes," she answered. "All these years, I've thought of no one but you."

"That's exactly what I wanted to hear," he said as he gently let go of her hand. "I need to speak with your aunt and uncle."

Sarah Taube ran up the stairs to inform her family.

"Welcome back," Aunt Lena said, inviting Charles to take a seat.

Charles, in his nervousness, puffed on a cigarette.

"Tell me," Aunt Lena asked, politely handing him a small dish to flick his cigarette ashes into, "what brings you here this morning?"

"As you know," Charles began, taking another draw before he spoke, "I've spent more than three and a half years in America but, almost from the beginning, I could not get accustomed to the American way of life."

Uncle Morris turned his chair toward Charles.

"So tell me, why then did you stay so long when you knew you weren't happy?"

Charles, not wanting to tell him why he really left, replied, "Why? I stayed mainly to get the experience I needed to open my own tailor shop. When I realized I couldn't tolerate living there any longer, I knew it was time to leave.

"I missed my shtetl and the people I left behind, which brings me to the reason I'm here today. I want to live in Shidleve, open a tailor shop, get married, and settle down."

Charles took his time lighting another cigarette, then inhaled deeply.

"The two of you," he began, as he placed the cigarette on the small dish Aunt Lena has provided him, "cannot have failed to notice I've been corresponding with Sarah Taube over these past years."

"Yes. We are aware of that," Uncle Morris replied, giving Aunt Lena a quick look.

"Well, I began to think of your niece often and soon realized I had very deep feelings for her, so I'm asking for her hand in marriage. I will try to give her a good life and be a good husband to her."

Aunt Lena and Uncle Morris looked at each other, and the expressions on their faces clearly displayed their approval. He was a mature young man, and they truly believed he would make Sarah Taube happy. But without hearing from their niece's lips that she wanted to be wedded to him, they could not yet give their blessings.

"Sarah Taube," Aunt Lena called from the second floor. "Are there any customers in the shop?"

"No, Aunt Lena."

"Then come up. Your uncle and I wish to speak to you."

"Come, sit," Aunt Lena said. "Charles has told us he cares for you and has asked for your hand in marriage. What are your feelings, my child?"

The look on Sarah Taube's face spoke her feelings. She wrapped her arms around her aunt and looked at Charles.

"Yes," she answered. "I very much want to marry him."

"Then it's settled," Uncle Morris said as he stood from his chair. "We give our blessings and wish you much happiness."

At dinner that evening, Charles made it known that he wanted to continue living in Shidleve and open a tailor shop with his friend, Chaim.

"Doesn't Shidleve already have a tailor shop?" Aunt Lena asked.

"Yes," Charles said. "There is one."

"Do you think there will be enough business for two tailor shops in one small shtetl?" Uncle Morris asked.

Charles looked at Sarah Taube and then at Uncle Morris.

"I'm not sure," he replied, realizing he had not thought through his business plans.

Aunt Lena glanced at Sarah Taube, Uncle Morris and Charles and smiled. "Why don't you open a shop here? We haven't had a tailor for over a year. The last one left for America, and I'm sure he's not coming back."

"You're probably right," Charles said, again looking in Sarah Taube's direction. "What do you think, Sarala? Would you want to stay here in Shavlan after we marry?"

Sarah Taube thought her place was with her husband and was willing to live wherever he preferred. But now that she had the opportunity to voice her opinion, she rose from her chair and with a smile on her face said, "I think opening a tailor shop here sounds like a good idea."

Sarah Taube surprised herself. This was the first time she displayed such a forceful personality to her future husband, and she wondered whether this assertive behavior would grow stronger in the days and years to come.

"Good," Charles said, not thinking that Chaim was anticipating being partners with him in a shop in Shidleve. "Since we're all in agreement, I'll set up my business here in Shavlan."

After much discussion at dinner, it was decided the wedding would take place in May. Charles left shortly after dessert, eager to return home to notify his family of the good news.

When Sarah Taube finished helping her aunt with the dishes, she went to her room, pulled out a pen and sheet of paper and began by telling Aaron of her engagement and up and coming marriage. Her thoughts were coming so fast that her pen could barely keep up. She was a young woman whose dreams of marriage and family were about to become a reality.

*"It would make me the happiest girl in the world,"* she wrote, *"if you would escort me down the aisle..."*

"Get up my beautiful one," Aunt Lena said, shaking her niece gently by the shoulders. "You have to open the shop with your uncle this morning. I must speak to Rabbi Broide to make arrangements for the wedding."

The rabbi of Shavlan was Zev Wolf Broide. He was a short man in his middle twenties with dark hair, prematurely graying at the temples and was married and had two young sons.

As is often true in the rabbinical community, his marriage had been arranged. Years ago, a rabbi from a nearby town was in search of a husband for his young daughter, Rachel, so the matchmaker from that town made arrangements for Rabbi Broide to meet with his prospective bride.

They had a great deal in common, especially since Rachel's father was a rabbi, and they could converse on many subjects about Jewish customs and other related matters.

After courting for several months, they married. Rabbi Broide returned to Shavlan with his new bride where he taught the Torah to the young boys in the congregation. Within the year, however, the congregation's rabbi died, and Rabbi Broide took over his position.

"Good day to you," Lena said to the *rebbetsen*—rabbi's wife. "I must speak to the rabbi. I have some wonderful news."

"What could be so wonderful that you have come so early?" the *rebbetsen* asked, as she welcomed Lena into her home and offered her a seat.

Lena folded her hands and sat up in her chair. "My niece is getting married, and we plan to have the wedding in May. I need to ask the rabbi if he still has openings for that month."

"Say no more," the *rebbetsen* replied and quickly walked over to the rabbi's study.

"Come out," she said. "I have some good news. Lena's niece has received an offer of marriage, and she's hoping you will have time in May to perform the ceremony."

"Mazel Tov!" he shouted as he came running out of his study with his appointment book and began flipping through the pages. "Ah," he said, "I see I have penciled in the shoemaker's son's wedding the first Tuesday in May."

"The shoemaker's son is getting married?" Aunt Lena questioned, raising her eyebrows. "I see Mrs. Bleekman did not waste any time."

"No, she didn't," was the rabbi's reply. "Anyway, she found him a lovely young woman, and his parents seem to be happy with the *shidduch*—an arranged marriage. Now let's get back to finding you a date. What about the 22nd of May? It's a Tuesday. There seems to be an opening."

Lena was pleased to hear he still had a Tuesday available. Tuesday was considered the luckiest day in the week for weddings, according to Jewish folklore, so she gave her consent.

"Well, it's done," Aunt Lena said to Sarah Taube as she entered the bakery late that morning. By now, the place was filled with customers and within minutes, everyone knew about her niece's forthcoming marriage.

The women shouted, "Mazel Tov! We wish the future *khosn*—the groom, and *kah'leh*—the bride, much love and happiness."

Lena was happy to see so many customers in her shop, and she knew those who were present would spread the word of her niece's engagement far more quickly than she could.

◄O►

When Charles returned to his home in Shidleve, he shared the news with his relatives, and they could not have been happier. He had found someone he loved and who loved him in return.

It occurred to him, however, with this marriage, he would be taking on a great deal of responsibility. No more running around from place to place, trying to find himself. He would have to tame his wanderlust, settle down and provide for his bride, his Sarala. Perhaps he thought that this was what he was searching for, and fate would have it that he had found it so close to home.

Many of Charles' relatives lived in various shtetls throughout Western Lithuania, but he had not kept in touch with most of them so his family was small.

His late father, Avigdor, had two married brothers living in Shidleve. After Charles's father and mother passed away, his father's younger brother Lazer and his wife Hannah took in his sisters, Bessie, Jenny, and Freida. His father's older brother Myer and his wife Sadie had no children and had been thinking about emigrating to America.

Charles had to make arrangements for his move to Shavlan and, most importantly, he had to tell Chaim about his change in plans, and he hoped that Chaim would not be angry and would understand.

When Charles left for America, Chaim remained in Shidleve and continued to work for Mr. Schneider. The Singer sewing machine he and Charles had purchased sat on the floor of the shop for several months, but soon Mr. Schneider realized it may be a good idea for him to begin experimenting with it.

He allowed Chaim to make clothing using the Singer, and when Mr. Schneider saw that production increased and he was getting many more orders, even from other towns, he realized the Singer was a good thing.

In the past, it took a week to produce a man's suit, but now it only took a few days to cut, sew, and fit the customer. Mr. Schneider was finally convinced the sewing machine was not the curse of the devil but an invention of a genius. At first, Chaim loaned the machine to his employer but within a few months, Mr. Schneider had acquired one of his own.

Chaim smiled when he saw Charles at work this morning.

"I have some good news," Charles announced, grabbing Chaim around his shoulders with both hands.

"What news?" Chaim asked curiously.

"I'm getting married, and I bet you can't guess with whom?"

"Let me see," Chaim replied, placing he hand on his chin. "Could it possibly be Sarah Taube?"

"How did you know?" Charles asked, baffled by Chaim's reply.

"How did I know? She's all you've been writing about in your letters. Of course, I began to suspect you were taken with her, and when you wrote me you were coming home, I was certain it was to ask for her hand in marriage."

"Chaim," Charles said, smiling from ear to ear, "I can't hide anything from my best friend, can I?"

"No," grinned the delighted man. "I guess I know you much too well. Anyway, congratulations and what may I ask are your plans?"

"I must be frank with you my friend," Charles replied, as Chaim guided him toward a wooden bench off to the side of the room. "As much as I would like to stay in Shidleve and open a shop with you, I'm afraid my plans have changed. I'll be moving to Shavlan and opening a shop there."

When Chaim heard Charles' reply, he sat down next to him.

"I fully understand," he said. "You have to do what's best for you and your bride."

Chaim did not let on his true feelings. He was deeply hurt and disappointed in hearing that Charles' plans to open a shop did not include him. When first he learned Charles would be returning from America, he had hoped that they would still be partners. He said to himself, "Partners we'll never be but our friendship will go on forever."

Charles was pleased that Chaim took the news so well and added he would be honored if he would act as his best man.

Without even thinking twice, Chaim replied, "It would give me great pleasure to stand up for you," and the two men embraced warmly.

Early the next morning, Aunt Lena was on her way to see Mrs.

Jacobs, the town caterer. Mrs. Jacobs' house was conveniently located a short distance from the town's synagogue and as Lena knocked on the door, the aroma of warm bread permeated the air, reaching her from an open window.

"Who's there?" Mrs. Jacobs asked.

"It's me, Lena from the bakery."

"*Oy vey*. You caught me at a very busy time. I'm making ready for the shoemaker's son's engagement party next Tuesday and my hands are full of flour. Come in and make yourself at home. I'll be with you shortly."

Mrs. Jacobs, a tall, dignified looking woman, was not especially attractive but her personality was quite charming. She was good at what she did and she knew it.

"Please forgive me for taking so long," she said, wiping her hands with a dishtowel. "By the way, I've already heard the news. Mazel Tov."

When Lena told her customers of her niece's impending marriage, she suspected that her customers would spread the word around town quickly, but they had done so even more quickly than she had anticipated.

"So tell me, what brings you here?" Mrs. Jacobs asked, taking a seat next to Lena.

Lena crossed her legs and leaned forward. "I've come to engage your services. As you already know, my niece is to be married, and her uncle and I plan to throw her an engagement party."

"And where and when do you plan to have this party?"

"I plan to have it in my home on Sunday, the 15th of April, at one o'clock in the afternoon, and I was hoping you would be free to provide food for my guests. Please be so kind as to check your schedule."

Mrs. Jacobs opened her journal and began turning the pages.

"Ah, you're in luck, my dear," she said, placing her hand on the page. "That date is still open. Do you wish to reserve it?"

"Yes, I do," Lena replied as she grinned her approval. "Also, I have written down a few dishes I think will be suitable."

"Your choices are good," Mrs. Jacobs said, glancing over the selections.

"Oh, there's one more thing," Lena added. "I would like the food to be brought to my house and personally served by you. It will allow me to be free to spend time with my guests and, of course, I'll pay you extra."

"Certainly," Mrs. Jacobs replied, making a note in her book.

Mrs. Jacobs paused before asking the next question.

"And what about the wedding plans?"

*"Oy.* I can't believe it. I've left out the most important date. I hope you still have the 22nd of May open."

Mrs. Jacobs once more referred to her journal.

"You're in luck again. That date is still available. Do you wish to reserve it?"

"Yes," Lena replied as she sank into her chair and let out a sigh. "I'll think about the menu for the wedding later and bring it to you in a few days."

After dinner that evening, Lena composed an invitation and with Sarah Taube's approval, sent her notes to Mr. Miller, the local scribe.

*In honor of their betrothed, Sarah Taube Fineberg and Charles Grazutis, the family of Sarah Taube invites you to join us at our home to celebrate their engagement. The luncheon will be held Sunday, 15 April 1888, at 1:00 p.m. Until then we remain, Aunt Lena and Uncle Morris.*

A week later, a positive response was received from Charles' family. Aunt Lena quickly notified Mrs. Jacobs, telling her thirteen people will be expected for lunch, including Uncle Morris, Sarah Taube and herself.

Time flew quickly and the day of the happy occasion had finally arrived. Sarah Taube, before slipping into her dress, combed rose water through her long brown hair and, with a single motion, pulled her hair tightly into a bun, neatly centering it on the back of her head, securing it with two straight pins.

As she looked into the mirror and saw her reflection, she thought it was not too long ago when she stood before that very same mirror and wondered if she would ever become a bride. But now she no longer wondered because she was marrying the one man in her life who was dearest to her heart.

Within minutes they heard knocking at the door.

"Come in," Aunt Lena said as she and Uncle Morris greeted their guests. "Let's go upstairs and make ourselves comfortable."

"My wife, Hannah and I are very pleased to be here," Uncle Lazer said. "May we congratulate you and your wife on your niece's engagement."

Standing beside them were Uncle Meyer and his wife, Sadie.

"We were very glad to hear the news, and we wish for the happy couple a lifetime of love and happiness."

Next, Charles' sisters Bessie, Freida, and Jenny greeted Aunt Lena and Uncle Morris.

"And who is this gentleman," Aunt Lena asked, noticing that Jenny was holding on tightly to a young man standing beside her.

A blush spread across Jenny's face. "Please meet Nathan, my fiancé," she replied. "We've recently become engaged."

Lastly, Chaim greeted his host and hostess.

"So happy to make your acquaintance," he said, offering a handshake to Uncle Morris.

When Sarah Taube and Charles made their entrance, the entire family stood up and shouted, "Mazel Tov!"

After a moment or two, Uncle Meyer and Aunt Sadie stepped forward. Uncle Meyer and his wife were people with strong emotions, but they were inclined to conceal them from the eyes of others. They did not embrace Sarah Taube but instead, presented her with a small box tied with a decorative ribbon.

"What a lovely surprise," Sarah Taube said, giving them a warm embrace. She sat down on the sofa and very carefully unwrapped the gift. Inside was a small silver cup.

"It's the *Kiddush* cup Charles's dearly departed father used to recite the blessing on the Sabbath," Uncle Meyer said. "Since your Aunt Sadie and I will be leaving for America, we thought you would like to have it as a keepsake."

Charles was taken by surprise when hearing his uncle's comment about leaving for America.

"Why are you leaving so soon," he asked?

"It was time for us to leave, and..."

Aunt Sadie quickly interrupted.

"I have a married sister living in a place called Galveston, Texas and for years she's been asking us to come. I'm sure your uncle and I will adjust quite nicely. After all, it is America." Then everyone called out, *"Zolst leben un zein gezun*t." You should live and be well.

Conversation flowed freely and after Mrs. Jacobs passed around the appetizers and served the fruit punch, she signaled for Aunt Lena to invite her guests into the dining room. Lunch was ready to be served.

The discussion about the upcoming wedding was the main topic of conversation. The guests were enjoying themselves, and it seemed as though the two families were quite compatible.

The spring breeze made a soft whistling sound as it rustled through the trees. Night would soon fall, and it was time for the guests to return home.

"If I can help in any way with the wedding plans," Charles asked, gently taking Sarah Taube's hand, "please let me know."

The following afternoon, after the bakery had closed, Aunt Lena put together the wedding invitation and offered it to her niece.

Even in a small shtetl, special attention was always given to personally invite not only the immediate relatives and friends but also the entire Jewish community.

The invitation read:

*Praised is love; blessed be this union. May the Bride and Bridegroom rejoice together!*

*We wish your presence at the wedding of our dear niece, Sarah Taube Fineberg, to Mr. Charles Grazutis on Tuesday, the 22nd of May 1888, at 7 p.m.*

*Khosn Kah'leh Mazel Tov. Zay azog gut aktsye arayn undzer glik—Bride and Groom Mazel Tov! Please share in our happiness.*

Sarah Taube only had to read the invitation once before she gave her approval. "It's perfect," she said, giving her aunt a tender kiss on the cheek.

Aunt Lena smiled. "I'll drop it off at Mr. Miller's house but before I go, I have a few surprises for you. Come. Let's go into my bedroom."

Aunt Lena reached into her wooden chest where she stored her treasures and gently pulled out a carefully wrapped parcel.

After unwrapping it, she took Sarah Taube in her arms. "I've been saving this for you for many years. This was your mother's wedding dress and veil. Before she fell ill, she asked me to keep it for you to be worn on your wedding day."

It was as if a bolt of lightning had struck Sarah Taube's heart. Seeing her mother's wedding dress and veil stirred up emotions in her, which had remained dormant for many years.

She lay sobbing on the bed while Aunt Lena stroked her hair, the way she did when she was a child.

"Stop your tears. This is not the time for tears. Your mother always dreamed of you marrying one day."

Sarah Taube looked at her aunt and wiped her face with the back of her sleeve.

"You're right," she said and with great care, picked up the dress and held it against her body.

It was a simple, white ankle-length dress with pearly buttons spread around the bodice and an attached belt that tied in the back.

"Try it on," Aunt Lena spoke. "Let's see how it fits."

As Sarah Taube slipped into the dress and placed the veil on her head, her aunt's eyes began to swell.

"How much like your mother you look, my sweet child."

"Now look whose crying," Sarah Taube observed. "Remember, you said no tears."

Sarah Taube was about to leave the room.

"Stop," Aunt Lena called. "Don't leave yet. There's more."

Again, she reached into the wooden chest and pulled out three brass candlesticks wrapped in an old worn cloth.

As soon as Sarah Taube saw them, she knew exactly who they belonged to. "Those are the candlesticks *Mammeh* used to light the Sabbath candles at sundown every Friday. I wondered what had become of them."

Sarah Taube took the candlesticks and held them close.

"There's one more thing," her aunt said and again reached into the chest and pulled out a reddish-brown handmade copper pot. The pot puzzled Sarah Taube.

"There's a good reason why you don't have any memory of this pot," her aunt replied, holding the pot up in the air. "Your great-grandmother made gefilta fish in this very same pot for the Passover holidays."

Sarah Taube sat in deep thought and then let out a smile.

"Thank you, Aunt Lena. I know exactly what I'm going to do with it."

"And what might that be, my child?"

"I'm going to make gefilta fish for Passover in this pot just as my great-grandmother once did."

Within a few days, the invitations were completed and distributed to the immediate family and guests and, as per tradition, to the Jewish community.

Arrangements were made for the tablecloths to be rented from the local gentiles, and the chairs, tables, benches, kitchenware, and plates would be borrowed from the Jewish locals.

Mrs. Jacobs would provide the candlesticks, utensils, glasses, and decanters, and the wine would be made by the local wine makers and delivered the day of the wedding.

Late one afternoon, as the bakery was closing, the town yenta, Mrs. Schemer came running into the shop.

"*Oy*, I'm so glad I made it in time," she said, glancing at the display case. "I see you've sold out of your apple cake. Now what will I serve to my guests for dessert this evening?"

"Don't fret, my dear," Aunt Lena replied. "Try one of my cinnamon and sugar coffee cakes."

"Well," Mrs. Schemer said, "if I must, but I did have my heart set on your apple cake. By the way, did you hear the news?"

"What news?" Aunt Lena asked, looking up from the counter.

Mrs. Schemer leaned toward Aunt Lena and whispered, "Don't say you heard it from me, but the shoemaker's son, Hershel has run away. And what's even worse is he has run away with a *shiksha*—a non-Jewish female.

"Before he left," she began, "he told his father he did not want to stay here and marry, and he had been carrying on with an older woman for some time.

"He said he hated being a shoemaker, and he and his *shiksha* were going to run off, get married, and go to America. What do you think of that?" she asked with her hands on her hips.

Aunt Lena's eyes opened wide with shock, thinking she nearly agreed to a *shidduch* between her niece and this miserable young man.

"What can I say," she replied. "I feel sorry for Hershel's father and especially for the bride-to-be, but she's certainly lucky Hershel decided to run away with his *shiksha* now instead of after they were married."

Mrs. Schemer expected Aunt Lena to mention that her niece was at one time being considered as a match for Hershel, but Aunt Lena was too smart to give in to this habitual gossipmonger so she refrained from further comment. She wrapped up the coffee cake, handed it to her, and wished her a good evening.

After careful thought, Aunt Lena decided when she saw Mrs. Bleekman, she would not say a word about the incident. It would be considered a black mark against her reputation.

Mrs. Schemer would soon see to it that the entire shtetl would hear about it and, unfortunately, nothing could be done to shut her mouth. The only good thing to come of this was that her niece did not fall prey to Hershel's deceitfulness.

As Sarah Taube was about to open the bakery the next morning, the door flew open.

"A letter for you," Mr. Stedman announced.

A smile came to Sarah Taube's face. "It's from my brother," she said and sat down near the window and began to read.

A scream rang out from Sarah Taube's voice.

"Yes, Aaron is coming!" she shouted to her family.

While they ate their dinner that evening, they heard knocking at the front door.

"It's Aaron. I know it's Aaron," Sarah Taube said, pushing herself away from the table.

There he was, her brother, standing outside with his arms outstretched.

It was not unusual for letters to arrive after the individuals themselves had already appeared, especially when the letters came from overseas.

Aaron was a grown man now and not the teenaged boy Sarah Taube had remembered. She threw her arms around his neck and welcomed him.

"Let me look at you," he said, holding her in his arms. "What a beautiful young woman you've become."

Sarah Taube took his suitcase and led him into the kitchen.

"Welcome home," Aunt Lena and Uncle Morris said with tears in their eyes.

"I'm happy to be here," Aaron replied, looking around. "I see nothing has changed."

"You're right," Uncle Morris answered. "Nothing much ever changes in Shavlan."

"This is the way it's always been," Sarah Taube cried out, "and it will always be this way."

Aunt Lena looked at the three of them. "Enough talk. Aaron must be tired from his trip, and I'm sure he's hungry."

They sat around the table, eating, talking, and laughing as if all the years of separation had never taken place. Sarah Taube was happy. The wedding was one day away, and all the important people in her life were here.

The sun was beautiful as its morning rays appeared through Sarah Taube's curtains and seemed to reach out to find her face.

The birds were singing sweet-sounding tunes while they flew from tree to tree, and she could smell the violet blossoms from the lilac bushes outside, sending their sweet aroma into her room.

It was the fourth Tuesday in May, the day of Sarah Taube and Charles' wedding.

Aunt Lena heard Sarah Taube moving about in her room.

"Are you up, my child?" she asked, knocking softly on her door.

"Yes," Sarah Taube replied. "Please come in."

"I've brought your breakfast," she said, placing the tray on Sarah Taube's lap. "Don't worry about anything. Try to relax. I'll be back at five to help you dress."

Sarah Taube took Aunt Lena's advice. After a warm bath, she washed her hair and tried to stay calm.

Precisely at five, Aunt Lena called from outside Sarah Taube's room.

"Time to make yourself ready for the most important day of your life, my child. May I come in?"

"Yes," Sarah Taube answered. "I'm so excited. I can hardly stand still."

Aunt Lena lifted Sarah Taube's hair and gently slipped her sister's wedding dress over her niece's shoulders and placed the veil on top of her head. Her eyes began to water and she said smiling, "You look beautiful, my child. Your mother would be so proud of you today. Now we must hurry. Rabbi Broide is waiting."

Aaron and Aunt Lena appeared linked in Sarah Taube's arms, while the rabbi, preceded by a three-piece band playing *klezmer*, chanted from his prayer book.

A wedding in Shavlan was a *simcha*—a Jewish celebration. What a beautiful sight it was to observe relatives, friends and the entire Jewish community heading up the hill toward the old wooden synagogue.

This was a very special synagogue. It was built in the mid-seventeenth century and although the outside structure was plain, once you stepped inside, it was as though you had gone back through a portal in time.

The entire *bimah*—the podium, was carved of wood and stood in the middle of a large room. It was considered by many to be a beautiful work of art, and Jews from surrounding areas would come to worship in this remarkable house of G-d. The shtetl of Shavlan was very lucky to have such a wonderful place where the Jewish community could meet for religious worship and happy occasions.

Before the ceremony, Rabbi Broide invited the bride, the groom, the wedding party, family members and closest friends into a small private room to perform two short rituals.

The first was the signing of the *ketubah*, the binding marriage contract, which had to be read, signed by the bridal couple, and witnessed by two guests who could not be blood-related family members to the bride or groom.

The second was called the *badekenish*, a ritual where the groom covers the bride's face with her veil. It was a custom derived from the biblical account of Jacob's first marriage when he was deceived to marry the heavily veiled Leah instead of Rachel, his intended bride.

After these rituals were completed, it was time to enter the synagogue where the ceremony was to begin.

On the *bimah* stood four local Jewish elders selected by Aunt Lena to hold up the poles attached to the large hand-embroidered chuppah.

Rabbi Broide stood under the chuppah behind a circular table, which held a Bible and a silver goblet filled with wine. As soon as he picked up the Bible, the room went quiet, signaling for the wedding procession to begin.

Slowly, Aunt Lena, Uncle Morris and Aaron walked Sarah Taube down the aisle and as they approached the *bimah*, they each gave her a kiss. Then Aaron gave his sister to Charles, and they both stood under the canopy.

Rabbi Broide looked around the sanctuary and smiled before he spoke.

"Family and friends of the Bride and Groom: Welcome to the wedding of Sarah Taube Fineberg and Charles Grazutis on this lovely spring evening. Your attendance reminds them of how fortunate they are to have such wonderful people in their lives..."

Sarah Taube heard every word the rabbi was saying but it seemed like a dream. She felt herself going through the motions of the ceremony—circling the groom seven times—hearing Charles pledge he would be faithful to her by repeating the Hebrew vow after the rabbi, with the giving of the rings—seeing Charles lift her veil—drinking the wine, and lastly, the breaking of the glass in memory of the destruction of the Temple in Jerusalem.

As soon as Sarah Taube heard the rabbi say: "Mazel Tov. You may kiss the bride," it was then she realized the ceremony had ended, and she was now Mrs. Charles Grazutis.

Charles took his bride's arm, and they both walked up the aisle and out the front door. It was a short distance to Mrs. Jacob's reception hall and all followed the couple, dancing and singing happily to the *klezmer* music played by the musicians.

The bride and groom sat in the middle of a long, rectangular table surrounded by those they loved. The band had established themselves along the left side of the hall, leaving space for dancing in the center of the room. There was a small table located to the right of the entrance where guests placed their gifts and outside the building, additional tables were set up for the overflow of people.

Traditionally, the celebration would begin with the gifts ceremony. Most of the guests' gifts were not monetary but the immediate family always gave money.

One by one, the family members stood, each stating their name, what side of the family they were on, and how much money they were giving to the bride and groom.

Next, Chaim stood and lifted his glass toward the couple.

"To Charles and Sarah Taube," he said as he voice rang out among the guests. "May all your dreams come true, and may you always remain as happy as you are today.

"Since I will be leaving in a few weeks to take a job in Johannesburg, South Africa and because you will be opening your tailor shop shortly, my gift to you is the Singer sewing machine we both acquired years ago. I won't be needing it since there will be plenty of sewing machines where I'm going."

Charles rose from his chair and looked at Chaim.

"I knew you wanted to leave Lithuania, but I didn't think it would be so soon. Thank you for this wonderful gift, and I wish you much success and good fortune."

You could hear a pin drop as the two men embraced.

Then a guest stepped forward and called out, "Now let the celebration begin."

Uncle Morris made the blessings over the challah and wine, followed by the klezmer band playing wedding music in front of the newly wed couple. Mrs. Jacobs began serving dinner. Music was played throughout the evening for all to enjoy.

Those who could not fit in the wedding hall were enjoying the festivities from outside and availing themselves of the additional tables filled with food and drink.

Time seemed to pass quickly and the hour was nearing midnight.

Soon after the dessert was served, the guests offered their congratulations and politely set out for home.

Aaron was the last to leave. He took Charles' hand and gently kissed his sister.

"Goodbye," he said. "Sorry I have to leave so soon, but I'm opening a new bakery and I'm anxious to get back."

Charles put his hand on Aaron's shoulder. "Good luck," he said. "Your sister and I wish for you to meet a good woman and settle down."

Aaron looked deeply into Sarah Taube's eyes and replied, "If only I could find a woman as sweet as my sister."

Aunt Lena and Uncle Morris led the newly married couple outside where a driver was waiting. Charles shook Uncle Morris warmly by the hand and kissed Aunt Lena. "Thank you both for everything," he said as a teardrop formed at the corner of his eye.

"It was our pleasure," Uncle Morris replied, glancing in Sarah Taube's direction.

After the couple climbed into the carriage, the driver took them on a slow, romantic drive along the outskirts of town before dropping them off in front of their new home.

When they entered the front door, Charles took Sarah Taube by the hand and led her into the bedroom. At long last, they were alone.

"I love you very much," he said, sitting her down on the bed.

He saw a smile on Sarah Taube's lips and she whispered in his ear, "I love you too."

Charles lit the candles beside the table and gave her a loving touch. "May our lives be filled with happiness and everlasting love," he said and as her thick brown hair flamed against the light, he saw a flicker of a smile pass across her face. The curtains were drawn and within a short time the flames of the candles began to burn fiercely.

When sleep finally came to the couple, each dreamed their own dream. Sarah Taube dreamed of a family and to be with Charles, while Charles dreamed to be with his Sarala and to be a success.

# Chapter 9 – Shtetl Life

## May 1888 – Shavlan, Kovne Guberniya, Russian Empire

The rays of the morning sun came through the shutters, brightening the entire room. At first, Sarah Taube did not know where she was but soon realized this was the first day of her married life as the wife of the man lying next to her, the man she loved.

Charles awoke.

"I love you very much, my Sarala," he said.

"And I love you," she answered back.

She let her eyes linger on him suggestively.

The curtains were drawn and once again they were in each other's arms.

After getting dressed, Sarah Taube and Charles shared their first breakfast together.

"May our lives be filled with much happiness," Charles said to his bride.

"And may we always be as happy as we are at this moment," Sarah Taube replied, thinking how happy she was looking forward to her life in the shtetl and dismissing, for a time, her dream of going to America.

Charles had rented a small storefront house located on the main street near the General Store and close to Aunt Lena and Uncle Morris' bakery.

It was a typical storefront house. There was a kitchen next to the shop with a wood-burning stove and three more rooms in the back. The house also had an attic which could be used for storage and additional rooms, if necessary.

"Come outside," Charles said. "I want to show you the grounds."

When Sarah Taube walked to the front of the house, she saw three lilac bushes up against the right side of the wall. They were already in bloom with purple, heart-shaped blossoms, gracefully cascading from their stems. Lilacs were one of Sarah Taube's favorite flowers. Her mother also loved them, and she remembered her saying lilacs were a symbol of love.

"Sarala, come and see the other side," Charles said excitedly. "The property is not very large but large enough to have a small garden."

When Sarah Taube came around the corner of the house, she noticed three large apple trees in front of a fence.

"We have apple trees on our land!" she cried. "Look, they already have blossoms."

"I'm so pleased you're happy," Charles replied, "but if you like what you've seen so far, wait until I show you one more thing."

He led her to the front of a small shed.

Sarah Taube hesitated for a moment, not knowing what to expect but curiosity got the best of her and as she opened the door, there stood something that totally shocked her.

Charles pointed to the surprise with a broad smile.

"I thought you would want one of your own."

"It's a cow!" she shouted. Thank you so much. This house is the best wedding gift you could ever have given me."

"I'm glad, my Sarala," he said as he folded her in his arms and kissed her, "but now that you've seen the outside, let's go inside and look at my shop."

The room was large enough for Charles to have his sewing machine, tables for cutting and sewing, and an area where fabrics could be stored.

"It's perfect," he said. "I can't wait to open for business."

After a few moments of not speaking, he looked at Sarah Taube and asked, "Sarala, what do you think we should call the shop?"

Sarah Taube put her hand on her chin and her eyes gleamed.

"I've got it," she said innocently. "Why don't we call it Charles' Tailor Shop? After all, it is a tailor shop and you are a tailor, aren't you?"

Charles nodded his head in agreement.

"Now that's a wonderful name," he said, grinning like a Cheshire cat. "How did you ever come up with a name like that?"

Sarah Taube turned her head toward Charles and responded to his grin with a smile, realizing he was poking fun at her.

Charles remembered seeing a square piece of wood leaning up against the house. This would make a good sign for my shop, he thought.

Later that day, he chiseled the name into the wood and carefully hung it from two long, sturdy pieces of timber, which he set upright in the ground, directly to the left of the front door.

When Charles was in America, he wanted to become a successful businessman but he failed. And where he was now in life was a far cry from what he wanted for himself. After some reflection, he looked up at the sign and thought, even though I did not succeed, I will begin a new life with my Sarala.

He stood in front of the sign with his hands behind his back.

"How does it look, Sarala," he asked, feeling deep pleasure as a result of his accomplishment.

Sarah Taube nodded, giving him her approval.

He looked at the sign once again and thought, "The only thing missing is my sewing machine, but Chaim will be delivering it in a few days, and then I'll be ready for my first customer."

Word of mouth that the shop was about to open had already traveled throughout the shtetl. With the money Charles saved in America and the cash gifts he and Sarah Taube received from relatives, it would be enough to sustain them until his business took off.

Sarah Taube was happy to be near the General Store. The owners, the Levitans, had lived in Shavlan for years, and their daughter, Shaina was almost the same age as she.

When Shaina was a little girl, her mother would send her to Aunt Lena's bakery to purchase bread for the Sabbath and pastries for the holidays. She always asked for Sarah Taube's assistance and from then on they became good friends.

Not too long after Shaina married Saul Schuman, her parents retired and turned the General Store over to her and her husband. Shaina's husband was a very learned man and besides running the business with his wife, he also held several religious positions.

A few days later, as promised, Chaim dropped off the sewing machine. Sarah Taube made tea and served her famous *kichlach*—a Jewish sweet cracker. He and Charles reminisced about the time they spent working as apprentices for Mr. Schneider and especially how they purchased that magical sewing machine.

"I've been wondering," Charles asked as he dunked a piece of *kichel* into his hot tea, "why did you decide to leave Lithuania so soon?"

Chaim pushed his chair away from the table and crossed his legs.

"I thought now would be a good time" he replied, "and besides ever since the May Laws were put into effect six years ago, Jewish businesses have suffered. I didn't want to get caught up in it if I were to open my own business."

Charles looked across at Chaim. "It hasn't affected me yet, but it's too early to tell since I'm just starting out. Anyway, good luck in South Africa and be sure to write."

"Wait just a minute," Chaim replied. "You're not getting rid of me that fast. I won't be leaving until the middle of June."

Sarah Taube placed another *kichel* on Chaim's plate. "Come for dinner next Thursday," she said. "We want to spend time with you before you leave."

The following week, late in the afternoon, just as Charles was about to close the shop, he heard someone pounding on the door and shouting at the top of his voice, "Let me in! I need to talk to you! I haven't much time!"

To Charles' surprise it was Chaim.

"I'm coming," Charles called out, wondering what all the excitement was about.

"I came to say goodbye and to ask a favor," Chaim said, almost completely out of breath.

"Of course, anything, but I though you weren't leaving until the middle of June?"

"There's been a change in my plans," Chaim replied nervously and began wiping the sweat from his brow. "I have to leave Lithuania now. I fear for my life."

"Fear for your life!" Charles shouted.

Charles led Chaim into the kitchen where Sarah Taube was preparing dinner. He sat him down, drew up a chair, listening carefully to the circumstances that brought him to their doorstep so unexpectedly.

"I planned on leaving in a few weeks, but my life has changed drastically in the last few days."

"What do you mean?" Charles asked.

"You remember Gideon Ehrlich?"

"I believe so. Wasn't he one of your childhood friends?"

"Yes, he's the one. I hadn't seen him for a while, and a few days ago I ran into him in Kovne, while I was picking up my travel documents. We began talking, and he invited me to meet him at a nearby meeting hall. He said I would be very interested in listening to the speaker.

"I didn't think much of it and he seemed friendly enough, so after I took care of my personal business, I went to the address he had given me. And this is when my troubles began.

"After listening for a short time to the speaker, it became clear to me he was the head of some secret group of revolutionists whose aim was to overthrow the Tsar. Can you imagine that? What had my so-called friend gotten me into?

"I knew I had to get out of there fast, so I looked for the nearest exit. As soon as I got up, the doors flew open and a group of armed soldiers came marching in, aiming their pistols toward the crowd."

Chaim stopped for a moment to collect his thoughts.

"Go on," Charles urged, anxious to hear the rest.

Sarah Taube handed Chaim a glass of tea and after taking a few sips, he continued.

"I saw men and women running in every direction. Guns went off, and people began to drop to the floor. Thank G-d, I managed to escape out of a second floor window, jumping onto a large tree and climbing to the ground. My horse and wagon were waiting a few blocks away and as I ran, I could feel my heart pounding. That's the reason, my friend, why I must leave as soon as possible."

"Don't be so hasty," Charles advised. "Perhaps nothing will come of it."

"I can't take that chance. I don't know if Gideon was captured or killed. If he's still alive and being held by the authorities, they could get names from him, and I'm worried he may tell them I was among those attending that night."

Chaim looked down at the floor and back at Charles.

"I did a very foolish thing in trusting this old acquaintance of mine, and it may be a matter of life or death if I stay."

"Since you put it that way," Charles answered, "I agree. You must get out of the country quickly."

Sarah Taube sat, not saying a word. How was it possible she thought that during a public meeting the police could enter the premises and arrest or even kill you? She could not imagine such things could happen.

She was a naïve, young woman going about her business, and the politics of the country did not interest her. Putting food on the table and living from day to day in a fairly peaceful shtetl was all she needed in life.

Charles stood and placed his hand on Chaim's shoulder.

"Is there anything I can do?" he asked.

"As a matter of fact, there is. I've made arrangements to be secretly smuggled out of the country tonight, and I must ask a favor of you."

"Anything, Chaim," Charles replied, eager to offer a helping hand.

"I'd like you to notify Mr. Schneider that I won't be able to finish my jobs, and after I'm well out of the country, you can tell him the circumstances which led to my leaving. Finally, please give my family my goodbyes, and tell them I'll be contacting them as soon as I arrive in Johannesburg."

"Don't worry," Charles said. "Concentrate on getting away safely and write me as soon as you get to South Africa."

Sarah Taube picked up from the table one of the apple cakes she had baked for the morning deliveries and wrapped it with a protective cover to keep it fresh.

"Please accept this," she said, handing him the package. "It's something to remember us by and to fill your stomach during your long journey. May G-d bless you and keep you safe."

"Thank you," Chaim replied, choking back tears.

Charles walked over to a small cabinet and reached into the drawer.

"I want you to accept this small gift," he said and slipped into Chaim's hand a leather pouch filled with Russian rubles.

"G-d bless you," Chaim said. "The two of you have been good friends."

Not wanting Charles and Sarah Taube to see tears flowing down his face, he said his goodbyes and disappeared into the night. Charles and Sarah Taube looked at each other and wondered if they would ever see him again.

Charles's work had met with a great deal of approval among the villagers and even though he was in business for only a short time, he already had several customers scheduled for fittings.

Sarah Taube also kept busy working in Aunt Lena's bakery and to earn extra money, she baked pastries and breads to sell at the market.

One morning, as Charles was about to open his shop, a horse-drawn carriage pulled up. To his surprise, it was Mr. Sadunas. He recognized the man as being one of Count Simonis' servants.

Because of his bravery in battle, Count Simonis' ancestor, Andrius Semeta was granted a large piece of land located in the northwestern region of Lithuania known as Siaulenai—Shavlan. Through the generations, the land, which was part of an estate and Manor House, was handed down to Semeta descendants and was eventually inherited by the count's father, Vytautas Simonis. Those who inherited land through their ancestors were considered a ruling class and members of the nobility.

"Hello, Mr. Sadunas. May I help you?" Charles asked, greeting him at the front door.

"Yes, may I come in? Count Simonis has sent me. He is in dire need of a tailor and needs some adjustments to his tuxedo."

Charles thought this was a strange request because the Simonis family usually did business with the tailors in Kovne and, as a rule, not with Jewish tailors. In any case, Charles was not going to question why he was chosen and agreed to go.

"Sarala, my first appointment is with Mr. Adler. He's going to a wedding next month and needs to be fitted for a suit. If he should come early, tell him to wait and I'll be back soon."

Charles gathered his black leather bag filled with scissors, needles and threads and with Mr. Sadunas' help, lifted the sewing machine into the carriage.

The Manor House was less than two miles away and once they got close, Mr. Sandunas led the horse through the gates and up a long driveway lined with tall oaks, standing like soldiers guarding their fortress.

Charles had counted five gardeners before he even set eyes on the house. After arriving, they entered a large double door which led to the foyer.

"Follow me," Mr. Sadunas said and escorted Charles into a room off of the main entrance. "Wait here. I'll get the count."

Count Simonis had been married for over two years and had a one-year-old son named Vytas.

When the count's father died a few years ago, he inherited his title and the entire estate, consisting of thousands of acres. There were several mills, farmland, and many orchards, which were maintained by local townspeople.

After a short wait, the count appeared fully dressed, wearing a black coat, waistcoat and trousers.

"So glad you could come. I've heard you are quite an accomplished tailor, and I need you to fix this tear in the sleeve of my coat. I'm having an important business meeting this evening, and it's formal attire."

"Could you please take off your coat," Charles asked, "so I may examine it?"

He studied the torn sleeve carefully before he spoke.

"Yes, I can fix it," he said. "It's only a slight tear. If you'll have Mr. Sadunas help me bring in my sewing machine, I'll get started."

Charles immediately went to work and in a short time, the tear was mended.

"Please try it on to make sure it's to your liking," Charles said and helped him on with the coat.

"You've done an excellent job," the count replied, viewing himself in a mirror. "Perhaps you can stop by in a few weeks. I would like you to make a suit for me. How much do I owe you?"

Charles was happy his work was held in such high regard. He related the cost and politely bid the count goodbye.

When Charles came home, Sarah Taube was awaiting his arrival. She was apprehensive at first, wondering if Charles was able to repair the tuxedo to the count's satisfaction, but when Charles came in wearing a smile, she knew everything was fine.

"Tell me what went on between you and the count," she asked, offering him a glass of water, "and what did the Manor House look like?"

"I'll tell you all about it at dinner Sarala but first I must tend to my customers."

He had been gone not quite three hours, and already there were several people waiting and by the end of the day, he had enough jobs to keep him busy for many weeks.

At dinner that evening, Sarah Taube once again asked to hear about Charles' experiences at the Manor House.

"Tell me about the count and what the Manor House looks like?" she asked with slight impatience in her voice.

A smile crossed Charles' face.

"All right, my Sarala. I know you're very curious to hear about my experiences this morning."

Sarah Taube placed her fork down on her plate, folded her napkin and patiently waited for Charles to begin.

"When I first entered the foyer, I saw a curved staircase leading up to the second floor and from what I could see, it was the most elegant house I have ever seen and perhaps will ever see in my lifetime."

"I wish I could have been there," Sarah Taube sighed. "Tell me more."

"I will try, my Sarala but first, let me gather my thoughts. Oh, yes. The furnishings were quite elaborate. But remember, I did not go into all the rooms.

"I do recall in the foyer there were two settees with upholstery of beautiful silk jacquard. I have only seen silk jacquard once when I worked in the factory in New York."

"What else did you see?" Sarah Taube asked, hanging onto his every word.

"The only other room I entered was the room next to the foyer. I think it must have been what they call the drawing room. Exquisite brocade draperies hung on every window, and there were fine paintings everywhere. It was in this room that I waited for the count.

Charles paused for a moment to clear his throat.

"Go on," Sarah Taube urged.

"Calm down, Sarala. There's really nothing more to tell. After all, he employed me as his tailor, not his personal confidant."

Sarah Taube went quiet and her expression changed to one of

sadness.

"No, Charles. You most definitely are not his personal confidant. We are shtetl Jews from Shavlan trying to eke out a living."

"Now Sarala, cheer up. It's not so bad and anyway, he did ask if I would consider doing more tailoring for him. Think of it as a good opportunity to increase my business."

There was a long silence.

"You're right, Charles. I should be thankful for what we have."

Months had passed since Charles and Sarah Taube were married, and she began to think about a family. After all, she and Charles had discussed the matter and they both wanted children.

Before the end of the year, she found herself pregnant but unfortunately, after a few weeks, she miscarried. Aunt Lena tried to console her, telling her that it was nature's way of getting rid of a badly formed child or perhaps one who would be born sickly. She encouraged her to be patient, and they would be blessed in G-d's own time.

Over the next few years, Charles' tailor shop prospered, developing a loyal following among the townspeople, but Sarah Taube felt her life was not complete.

As she awoke this morning, she found herself engulfed in sadness. After going through several more miscarriages, she was convinced she would never carry a child to term.

The following afternoon, she made an appointment with Rabbi Broide.

"Come in," he said, motioning for her to take a seat. "Please tell me why you're here today."

Sarah Taube folded her hands and placed them on her lap.

"I've already had three miscarriages, and I feel as though Charles and I might never have a child."

The rabbi rose from behind his desk and walked slowly over to her.

"I know about your miscarriages and I've been saying prayers. Do not worry. Within the year, G-d willing, you will conceive. Now go and prepare for this new life which will soon be entering your body."

Sarah Taube's cheeks became flushed with excitement. If the rabbi says I will have a child, she thought, then I'll go home and prepare for the new arrival. She thanked the rabbi and left to tell Charles of his prophecy.

As soon as she entered the house, Charles saw a change in her.

"The rabbi said I will have a child," she said with joy in her heart.

Charles was pleased.

"See, my Sarala, if we are patient, good things will happen."

It had been one year since Sarah Taube's visit with the rabbi. Recently, she had missed her menstrual period and noticed her breasts had become tender.

After a visit with Mrs. Rubin, the midwife, her suspicions were confirmed. She was pregnant. She did not want to show too much excitement but thought it was time for her to share the news with her husband. That evening she prepared his favorite meal.

"What is this delightful aroma I smell?" he asked, entering the kitchen.

"It's stuffed cabbage. Your favorite," she replied, as she untied her apron and placed it on the chair.

Charles began with the blessing, "Blessed are You, Lord our G-d, King of the Universe..."

As soon as Sarah Taube heard him say, "amen," she began serving the piping hot dish.

A smile came to Charles' face.

"Sarala, do you have something you wish to tell me?"

"How did you know?" she asked.

"In the past, whenever you've made my favorite dish, it's always been because you've had good news. So what is it this time, my Sarala?"

Sarah Taube could not hold back her excitement.

"I'm with child, my husband. I'm with child."

Charles stood and placed his arms around her.

"You've made me very happy today," he said. "See. The rabbi's prophecy has come true. It was from Rabbi Broide's lips to G-d's ears."

Nine months passed quickly and early one morning, as Sarah Taube rose from her chair, a gush of water splashed onto the floor. Her water had broken. Mrs. Rubin had told her this would be one of the first signs her body was preparing for labor.

The townspeople were very lucky to have Mrs. Rubin. Since there was only one doctor in the area who lived in the next town, it was a blessing that she was available to deliver the babies of Shavlan.

"Charles, run and fetch Mrs. Rubin," Sarah Taube called out. "Tell her my water has broken, and I'm going into labor."

Charles' brows lifted in surprise. Trying desperately not to panic, he placed the "Closed" sign on the front door of the shop and carefully helped Sarah Taube to a cot in the kitchen. Then he ran to Mrs. Rubin's house to give her the news.

"I'm not surprised," she said, taking her glasses off and placing them in her dress pocket. "I suspected she was getting close to term."

Without delay, she grabbed her satchel and hurried out the door.

"I'll need your assistance, Mr. Grazutis," she said once she entered the house.

"Tell me what I need to do," he replied, wiping his forehead with the sleeve of his shirt.

"Good." She placed her bag on the floor, adjusted her spectacles delicately on the bridge of her thin nose, and rolled up her sleeves.

"First, you need to heat a pot of water, and I'll need some blankets and sheets. Before you do anything, wash your hands in soapy, hot water."

After several hours, Mrs. Rubin asked Charles to wait in the next room. "I'll be able to handle the rest myself," she said.

Mrs. Rubin was quite good at what she did, having delivered many babies over the years. The doctor was only called on if there was a serious problem. And in most cases, when this occurred, he would not arrive in time to save the mother or the child.

Charles paced back and forth nervously and after a few more hours, he heard a clap and the sound of a baby crying.

"It's a girl!" Mrs. Rubin shouted from the kitchen. "You have a beautiful, healthy baby girl."

When Charles came into the room, he saw his Sarala holding their daughter in her arms. He had tears in his eyes.

Sarah Taube smiled.

"I want to call her Ruchel after my mother," she said and on the 14th of August 1895, Charles and Sarah Taube welcomed their first child into their home.

After a few months, Sarah Taube found herself pregnant again.

Nine months passed quickly.

"I don't want you to exert yourself," Mrs. Rubin said, knowing Sarah Taube was due at any moment. "Try to stay home and rest. Your aunt can do without you. If you like, I'll stop by and tell her you won't be coming to work this morning."

"Don't be silly," Sarah Taube replied. "I want to go. Besides, she's depending on me to bring over the breads and pastries I've baked this morning."

"I'll tell you once and only once," Mrs. Rubin said firmly, "judging from my examination, you could go into labor at any moment."

After stating her concerns, without another word, she marched out the door.

Charles was not at home. He had used his last few yards of gabardine and was in need of more fabric. He heard that Mr.

Schneider had purchased a large order, so he went to Shidleve to replenish his stock.

Sarah Taube gathered up her baked goods, placed them in a wicker basket, collected little Ruchel and left, heading up the street toward her aunt's shop.

"You shouldn't have come this morning," Aunt Lena scolded, grabbing the wicker basket from her niece's hands. "I would have sent Uncle Morris to fetch the baked goods. Go home and rest and leave Ruchel here."

After thinking it over, Sarah Taube said, "You know, Aunt Lena, you and Mrs. Rubin might be right. I am feeling tired. I probably should be home resting."

As Sarah Taube was about to leave, she felt a tightening in her abdomen and pain in her lower back. These were signs she was all too familiar with. She reached for a chair and shouted, "Tell Uncle Morris to get Mrs. Rubin quickly! I think I'm going into labor!"

Uncle Morris ran on his old bony legs as fast as he could to tell Mrs. Rubin what had happened. Without delay, they returned to the bakery, and Mrs. Rubin prepared for the delivery of Sarah Taube's second child.

Aunt Lena and Uncle Morris paced nervously up and down the hallway.

Within a few minutes after the clock struck twelve, the sound of a baby crying rang throughout the house.

"It's a health baby boy," Mrs. Rubin sang out, holding the newborn in her arms. And on the 2nd of June 1896, a second child was welcomed into the Grazutis family.

Sarah Taube looked up at her Aunt and Uncle.

"I'm going to name him, Yankel after my father. May he rest in peace."

Three years passed, and Sarah Taube found herself pregnant again. And on the 31st of May 1899, she delivered a healthy baby girl whom she named Gitka after Charles' late mother.

To help Sarah Taube out with the children, Charles would take Ruchel along on various jobs, both in Shavlan and other nearby shtetls. When the count called on Charles to make him a suit, he always brought Ruchel along.

Whenever Charles showed the count the latest styles and materials, Ruchel would always play with Vytas, the count's young son. And when it was time for them to leave, as Charles led the horse down the long driveway toward the gates, Ruchel would look back at the Manor House, seeing Vytas staring out the window at their disappearing wagon.

While Jews from the Pale of Settlement continued to emigrate from Shavlan to a life in America, peasants in Russia were leaving the farms in the countryside to work in the new factories in the cities.

Tsarist Russia was on the front wave of its industrial revolution, and it was changing the fabric of society but because of the corruption of the state, life for those at the bottom of the ladder did not improve and actually became more difficult.

# Chapter 10 – The Bolsheviks

## June 1903 – St. Petersburg, Russian Empire

It had been four years since Dimitri decided to join the Russian Socialist Democratic Labour Party (RSDLP), which combined all the revolutionary organizations into one united group and primarily supported the beliefs of Karl Marx. They recruited help from the radical intellectuals and the urban working class and publicly approved a complete social, economic, and political revolution.

Vladimir Lenin, a member of the RSDLP, believed in a more militant policy than many in the organization. In June of 1903, during the party meeting in Brussels, Belgium, a point occurred where Lenin was able to rally a short-lived majority, naming his group Bolsheviks, meaning "majority" in Russian.

This action caused the RSDLP to break into two groups with opposing views on how to implement Marx's philosophy, the Bolsheviks led by Lenin and a pacifist group called the Mensheviks, meaning "minority" in Russian.

The Mensheviks thought Russian socialism should develop slowly and without bloodshed. They believed that a democratic republic should replace the Tsar's government peacefully, whereby the socialists would work together with the liberal bourgeois parties.

The Bolsheviks, on the other hand, wanted to form a group of professional revolutionists, under strong party control, to lead the working class in an effort to seize power by force.

From this time on, this division caused conflict. Subsequently, the Bolsheviks became a separate political party completely unconnected to the RSDLP.

Dimitri admired Lenin for many years. He read a good deal of articles by him and completely agreed with his beliefs that by using

Marxist theories, one could totally carry out a political revolution.

He had learned Lenin's father worked as a director of educational institutions and, in recognition for his outstanding work, was promoted into the Russian aristocracy, so Lenin himself was from a bourgeois background. One of the main factors that pushed Lenin to support revolution was his brother's execution by the Tsarist Government for an assassination attempt on the Tsar.

Dimitri could relate to Lenin's feelings because he too had begun to feel more radical toward the Tsarist Government when his sister was treated so poorly while imprisoned and especially because it resulted in her untimely death.

After his sister, Gesya died, Dimitri adjusted to living his life alone. He was absorbed in his new identify and his new mission in life. All the thoughts of that young Jewish boy entering the university were lost in the deep recesses of his memory.

One balmy Saturday afternoon, while Dimitri was taking a leisurely walk in the park, he saw a well-dressed young man running toward him.

"Faivush! Faivush! Stop! It's Isak from Mozir!" he shouted. "Don't you remember me?"

Dimitri walked faster, pretending not to hear him.

The man continued to run after him.

"Stop!" the young man shouted again.

Almost completely out of breath, he finally caught up with Dimitri.

"Don't you remember me, Faivush?" he repeated once again. "You saved my life when I was a child."

Dimitri shrugged his shoulders.

"I'm sorry," he replied. "You've made a terrible mistake. My name is Dimitri Bogdonovich. I don't know this person you're referring to. Please let me pass."

Without saying another word, Dimitri left Isak standing there with a pitiful expression on his face. Isak looked as though his best friend had abandoned him. And indeed, he had.

Dimitri continued to walk without ever looking back. Of course, he knew this kind young man was his friend Isak and although he wanted to reach out to him, he realized it would not be possible to ever rekindle their friendship. Dimitri's life had changed so drastically from that of that little boy his friend knew, and he was glad Isaac had remembered him with the love they had shared when they were young boys.

The following day, Dimitri decided he was going to join the Bolshevik Party and would attend his first meeting in less than an hour. It was to be held at a secret location in an area of town where he had never been.

He was in the prime of life and still full of hope and promise. He felt optimistic about the future of Russia and believed very soon Lenin would be successful in putting Marxist principles into practice. There was no doubt in his mind that it was only a matter of time before the Bolsheviks would gain control and overthrow the Tsar, making way for Lenin to become head of state.

As the konka, a horse drawn tram, made its last stop near an area far from the center of town, Dimitri rushed to get off. Because he was unfamiliar with this part of St. Petersburg, he cautiously walked along the road. After entering a side street, he stopped at the last house on the block.

Dimitri walked up the steps to the front door and banged firmly with the heavy brass knocker and as he waited for the door to open, he could hear footsteps.

When the door opened, standing before him, clothed in a plain brown, long-sleeved dress, appeared the most bewitching young woman he had ever seen and even her drab clothing could not hide her loveliness. She was of average height and had beautiful, black hair and a well-endowed body. She introduced herself as Aleksandra Petrova. Dimitri was immediately smitten.

Aleksandra was born into a typical bourgeois family. She studied at the St. Petersburg Women's Courses, one of the few educational institutions available to females. After finishing her studies in 1890, she was actively drawn into revolutionary work and before long, she became a professional revolutionist with the *Narodnaya Volya.* Many professional revolutionists were devoted Marxists who spent the major part of their time organizing the party so they could lead workers in a revolution.

Later, she joined the Bolshevik faction of the RSDLP and worked in an illegal printing house helping to smuggle party literature between various revolutionary groups. She was active in distributing propaganda and provoking public agitation for social reform, especially among women.

Her admiration for Lenin grew rapidly as she became more familiar with his political beliefs. She read he wanted to abolish discrimination against all Russian women and believed women should be given more opportunities to take part in the social revolution stating that without them, a dramatic change could not take place.

"Come in," she said in a pleasant voice. "You must be here for the meeting. May I have your name?"

Dimitri did not answer. He was struck by her beauty and could think of nothing else.

"May I have your name?" she asked again, but this time she raised her voice and stretched out her arms to welcome him.

"I'm sorry. I'm Dimitri Bogdonovich," he said as he engulfed her small hands into his.

"Please follow me," she said and led him into a room where a group of men were sitting in straight-backed chairs around a long wooden table. A few looked familiar from previous RSDLP meetings. Within minutes, the voices quieted down and at the head of the table stood Aleksandra.

"Good morning," she said in a voice that commanded attention. "My name is Aleksandra Petrova, and I'm the Secretary of the Bolshevik's newly formed St. Petersburg Committee."

She did not waste time and began discussing her ideas for furthering the revolutionary cause.

She spoke of how they should become more involved in writing and publishing articles and how these articles could be distributed among various groups throughout the area. She made suggestions of how they could be used as party agitators to arouse and excite the working class and hopefully bring them around to their way of thinking.

After she finished talking, many in attendance contributed their ideas where they could be useful participants in fighting for social justice. Since Dimitri had already taken part in writing and publishing articles, it was decided he would continue to work in that capacity.

Aleksandra was pleased the way the meeting turned out and, as it drew to a close, made everyone aware they would not be assembling at that location again. Each of these secret gatherings were to be held only one time at any given address for fear of being found out by the authorities.

"I was very impressed with your meeting," Dimitri said, moving slowing in Aleksandra's direction. "You did a great job in getting your ideas across, and I believe it went well."

After staring at him for a few moments, she replied, "Thank you for those kind words, Mr. Bogdonovich."

"Please call me Dimitri."

"Yes, Dimitri. I'm glad you found the meeting enlightening. That was my intention, and I believe I got my points across. Now, however, there's a lot of work to be done, and I'm very eager to get started."

As the conversation continued, Dimitri became even more

infatuated with her.

"Will you consider joining me for a late lunch?" he asked while his eyes explored her body. "It would give me great pleasure to exchange ideas with you while enjoying some good food."

Aleksandra thought for a moment before answering.

"Yes," she replied. "That would be nice."

As soon as they stepped outside and headed into the bright summer afternoon, the thoughts of the day became less important.

A feast of beautiful red and yellow blossoms flanked the small garden surrounding the brick pathway, which led to a konka parked a few blocks away. Without a word passing between them, Dimitri took Aleksandra by the hand and they ran to catch the car.

"Where are we going?" Aleksandra asked, almost completely out of breath.

"The Summer Garden. Have you been there during this time of year?"

"No. I've been there during the fall but never in the summer."

"Well, my dear, you're in for a delightful surprise. There's a lovely little teahouse in the pavilion."

After the konka crossed the Nevsky Prospekt, heading up toward Sadovaya Ulitsa, Dimitri caught sight of St. Michael's Castle.

"This is our stop," he said when the konka came to a halt. They got off, and they began walking slowly up the hill toward one of the entrances behind the Castle across the Swan Canal.

"What's your favorite part of the garden?" he asked.

"I'm fond of the beautiful marble sculptures but my favorite is of Cupid and Psyche. I love the way it extends out into the Swan Moat, depicting the precise time when Psyche falls in love with Cupid while she leans over his sleeping body, holding a lamp to his face."

It was interesting to Dimitri that she chose Cupid and Psyche. It indicated to him, despite her disciplined behavior, deep down she was a woman who could express emotion.

"Do you come here often?" she asked.

"No, not too often," Dimitri replied, still holding her hand, "and occasionally, especially in the spring and summer, I like to wander through the park."

As they headed toward the pavilion, they walked through some of the most breathtaking ornamental grounds.

"Look," Aleksandra pointed out. "There's the statue of the great Russian fabulist, Ilya Krylov in front of the teahouse. I don't remember ever seeing this one."

"Come, Aleksandra. You'll have plenty of time after we eat to enjoy the rest of the park."

On entering the establishment, the hostess escorted them to a table tucked away in a quiet corner.

"Have you eaten here before?" Aleksandra asked.

"Yes, I've eaten here several times. But of course, I've eaten here always by myself but today is different. I have a beautiful, young lady accompanying me."

Dimitri reached over and placed his hand on hers. Aleksandra did not pull away. The food was ordered and as they ate, the conversation continued. They talked about their likes and dislikes, interesting places they had traveled and, in general, anything that did not disclose their previous activities with the RSDLP.

After they finished their main course, the waiter brought over a dessert tray filled with pastries and a large samovar brewed with the house's traditional smoky flavored tea known as Russian Caravan.

Dimitri leaned over toward Aleksandra and held her hand.

"This is a very special tea," he said. "Do you know the history behind it?"

"No," replied Aleksandra, feeling the warmth of his hand on hers.

"The tea got its name because it was originally imported from China by way of camel caravans, which took many months to arrive at their final destination. Because of the caravans' campfires along the way, the teas took on a distinct smoky flavor and this became a common feature of tea throughout Russia."

Aleksandra looked at Dimitri and smiled.

"That's very interesting," she said. "I've learned something new today."

Being together brought them contentment they had never known before, and little did they know their first meeting would have turned into such a pleasurable afternoon.

"Where has the time gone?" Dimitri asked, glancing at his watch.

"It's gone by much too fast," she replied.

"We still have time to enjoy the rest of the park," Dimitri said, taking hold of her hand once again.

After looking at a few more sights, it was close to five o'clock and the place was about to close. Dimitri asked where Aleksandra lived and much to his surprise, her apartment was very close to his.

When they reached their stop, they got off the konka and walked for several blocks until they came to Aleksandra's building.

"This is it," she said. "I'm on the second floor, Apartment 201A."

Dimitri looked at Aleksandra with longing eyes, and it was obvious he did not want the evening to end. He yearned for more of Aleksandra, and she had a strong desire for more of Dimitri.

Reaching into her handbag, she pulled out a silver plated key.

"I'll get it," Dimitri said, taking the key from her hand.

He slowly opened the door but before he could set foot inside, a harsh squeal startled him and a silver-blue ball of fur leaped out.

"Oh," Aleksandra said, "please don't be alarmed. I want you to meet Matreshka, my little Russian doll."

She picked up Matreshka, a beautiful, green-eyed female Russian Blue with large pointed ears and introduced her to Dimitri.

"What a relief," Dimitri said, wiping his brow with the back of his hand. "It sounded like a baby crying."

"I know," Aleksandra replied, cuddling her cat in her arms. "It's not the first time I've been told that. I've had her for over two years now. She keeps me company when I'm here alone."

Dimitri was about to stroke Matreshka's soft, silver-blue fur when she opened her mouth and let out a sharp hissing sound.

Dimitri pulled away.

"It usually takes her some time to get used to strangers. Although she's very intelligent and can be very playful, most Russian Blues tend to be hostile around people they've just met."

Aleksandra placed her adored house companion on the floor.

"Would you like to come in for a while," she asked. "My roommate is spending the night at her boyfriend's place and won't be home until late tomorrow morning."

"Yes, I would love to," Dimitri replied. "We've had a very busy day. I want to sit and rest for a while."

"Would you like something to drink? Some vodka, perhaps?"

"No, not yet. If I had vodka now it would put me to sleep and then what would you do? You would have to put me up for the night, and I'm sure you wouldn't want that?"

Aleksandra and Dimitri exchanged glances, suggesting neither one would mind if they were to spend the night together.

The hour was late and Aleksandra hadn't realized it was close to dinnertime.

"Would you like to stay for supper? I don't have much here but I'm sure I can prepare something."

Dimitri was experiencing a strong desire for something but it wasn't food he was longing for.

"I'm not hungry," he answered. "Maybe later."

Almost instantly, their eyes met.

"Do you mind," she asked, "if I change into something more comfortable. I've been in these clothes all day and I need to loosen up. I'll won't be long," she promised.

A few minutes later, Aleksandra reappeared wearing a white negligee.

"Now that's better," she said as she sat down on the sofa, moving her warm body next to his.

Dimitri never felt closer to her than at that moment. She reached over and pulled his face toward hers. Then she raised her hand and, using up and down strokes, began to rub the nape of his neck.

"Does that feel good?" she asked teasingly.

"Yes, don't stop," he replied and began caressing her breasts.

Before long, she was kissing him with intense emotion, and it didn't take long before their strong sexual feelings took over. Dimitri continued to explore her body and could feel her heart throbbing from beneath her flimsy nightgown.

"Quick," she whispered in his ear. "Let's go into my bedroom."

"We'll never make it in time," Dimitri murmured softly.

"We can make it. Hurry."

Dimitri lifted Aleksandra with his strong arms and carried her into the next room. He placed her on the bed and continued to explore her soft, velvety body and she continued to caress his. And within minutes, they both worked themselves into an all-consuming passion. Neither one could hold back. The most intense and exciting moment of the night had occurred and to both, a climax had been reached.

Dimitri rose from the bed and stretched his muscles.

"All of a sudden I'm hungry," he said.

"Me too," Aleksandra replied. "Sex always makes me hungry."

They both got dressed and went into the kitchen.

Aleksandra was silent for a few moments. "I hope you don't think I go to bed with every man I meet for the first time," she felt compelled to say. "I must tell you I believe wholeheartedly in free love, and both men and women have the right to sexual pleasure without it being the business of the State or anyone else."

Dimitri was taken back at Aleksandra' statement so early in their relationship. "Go on," he urged, wanting to hear more.

"I feel it's important to establish a close connection with someone before jumping into lovemaking. I felt differently with you though and went against my principles for the first time."

"Aleksandra, you're a grown woman with strong emotions. You have to follow your heart and stay with what makes you happy. Sometimes standing on principle is not always the best way to run your life."

Aleksandra was pleased with Dimitri's reply, and it was yet another reason why she felt close to him.

She looked into her cupboard and sighed. "All I have is black bread and jam, and I can make some tea. How does that sound?"

While they sat in Aleksandra's kitchen, enjoying their late night meal, they both realized there was great potential between the two of them for a long and lasting relationship.

During the next month, Dimitri and Aleksandra spent many happy hours together.

One day, Aleksandra learned that her roommate, Svetlana was getting married and would soon be moving out. Aleksandra did not like living alone and wanted to discuss her options with Dimitri.

The following Sunday, Dimitri invited Aleksandra to one of his favorite restaurants, The Palkin, one of the oldest restaurants in St. Petersburg. After they finished their meal, Dimitri could not wait any longer.

"Now tell me, Aleksandra. What is this important matter you wish to speak to me about?"

The restaurant was crowded and although they had a private table in a quiet corner, she felt she needed to lower her voice so those nearby could not hear what she was about to say.

She took one last sip of tea, cleared her throat and pulled her chair close to his.

"Dimitri, you remember when I mentioned to you that my roommate would be moving out soon and you know how I don't like living alone."

"Yes," he said, wondering what she was leading up to.

"Well, since I have a two-bedroom apartment in an excellent location, I thought it would be nice if you moved in with me. That way, I would not be lonely, and we could see each other all the time. What do you think?"

"What do I think?" Dimitri replied loudly.

"Shh! Not so loud," Aleksandra whispered.

Dimitri looked around.

"No one is paying attention to us," he said, lowering his voice. "Anyway, it's a good idea, and we would share in the rent and everything else."

A pinkish blush spread across Aleksandra's face.

"Then it's decided?" she asked. "You agree to move in?"

"Of course I agree," Dimitri whispered in her ear.

After living together for only a month, both Aleksandra and Dimitri had become quite used to each other. It was as if they had never been apart. They both liked the same things and life could not have been better.

One evening, while Dimitri was on his way home from work, he stopped to buy a newspaper.

"Aleksandra, did you hear the news?" he asked, entering the

apartment.

"No. What news?" she replied, taking his hat and coat.

"It's in all the papers. Yesterday, a group of Japanese destroyers launched a surprise attack on our eastern fleet anchored in Port Arthur, Manchuria without even declaring war. It was a naval base leased to us by China."

"I remember reading something about it," Aleksandra said. "The Tsar's Minister of Interior was pushing the Tsar to expand the Empire and plans were being made to take over Constantinople, Manchuria and Korea. Of course, Japan would not stand for this kind of aggression. No wonder they attacked."

Dimitri thought for a moment before he spoke.

"I think the Tsar was hoping for a conflict with Japan, and it looks as though he's going to get his wish. By doing this, he thinks he can rally the people around him and awaken a feeling of patriotism among his subjects. I believe his plan will have the opposite effect. The people don't want war. They want social justice."

Aleksandra raised her voice slightly.

"They most certainly do," she replied, "and you and I will see to it that these changes will come about very soon."

Although Matreshka was having a hard time adjusting to Dimitri, after a while she settled down and began tolerating his presence but deep down she still viewed him as an intruder, hissing at him whenever Aleksandra was not around.

Every evening, after Aleksandra and Dimitri would kiss goodnight, the cat would jump on the bed and snuggle up between them. Aleksandra would wrap her arms around Matreshka and fall asleep.

This did not sit well with Dimitri. He wanted all of Aleksandra's affections and did not want to share any of it with a Russian Blue. Aleksandra was oblivious to all that went on, and she thought the two roommates she loved dearly were living together in love and harmony.

Dimitri would go to work during the week, while Aleksandra devoted most all her time organizing and arranging union strikes and bringing women together for meetings to educate them regarding their human rights. Even though a great deal of Aleksandra and Dimitri's time was taken up with subversive activities, they still had time to fit one another into their busy lives.

# Chapter 11 – A Trip to Moscow

## June 1904 – St. Petersburg, Russian Empire

Dimitri asked one morning, as he was finishing his breakfast, "How would you like to take a vacation to Moscow?"

"Moscow! What could we possibly do in Moscow?" Aleksandra asked. She knew Dimitri well enough to know he had planned something spectacular, and she was merely teasing him.

"All right. I cannot keep it from you any longer," he said, while he poured himself another cup of coffee, stirring in a meager spoonful of sugar. "I've gotten tickets to the Bolshoi Theater to hear Feodor Chaliapin. He'll be performing in the opera, *"The Maid of Pskov"* as Ivan the Terrible.

He paused for a moment and asked, "You do like opera, don't you?"

Aleksandra rose slowly from her chair and put her arms around Dimitri.

"I love opera," she replied, giving him a kiss on the cheek.

"Then you're in for a treat, my darling. I thought we could take a train next Tuesday afternoon, check into the Hotel National, do some sightseeing Wednesday, and go to the theater Thursday evening to see Chaliapin's performance. How does that sound?"

Aleksandra looked at Dimitri and smiled.

"It sounds perfect. We both have to get away, and this trip is exactly what we need."

Dimitri pushed his chair away from the table and stood up. "I can't wait to check into the National? It was built last year and is considered one of the most beautiful hotels in the world. I've read somewhere it's the only hotel in the city with elevators."

"Was it hard getting reservations?" Aleksandra asked. "How in the world did you manage it?"

Dimitri smiled. "It was easy. When I heard the hotel only took guests who were highly recommended, I asked Mr. Krakau, the Director of my school, to put in a good word. He visited the hotel a few months ago and said he would be happy to do me a favor.

"He did mention when he first arrived there, he couldn't help but notice the majority of the hotel's clientele were made up of businessmen, aristocrats and members of the Tsarist administration. So I'm warning you, we will be mingling with these Capitalists. Do you think you still want to go?"

Aleksandra raised her shoulders slightly.

"If it's only for a few days, I think I'll be able to manage it," she said as her lips curled into a beautiful smile.

The day of their trip could not come fast enough and before long, Dimitri and Aleksandra were on a train heading for Moscow.

When they walked through the revolving door of the hotel, Dimitri registered like any businessman would do. He and Aleksandra went up the elevator as any bourgeois couple would do and tipped the bellhop like any aristocrat or Tsarist administrator would do.

Nothing they did or how they acted made them any different from the bourgeoisie with perceived materialistic values and conventional attitudes.

Dimitri and Aleksandra could not see the hypocrisy of their actions. Weren't they acting exactly like the people from the society they wanted to destroy?

They thought they were far superior to the other guests because they were looking out for the workers and peasants and this made them different, which made them even more entitled to these luxuries.

The following morning, Aleksandra was the first to awaken. Not remembering to shut the drapes the night before, she witnessed the sun's first appearance, rising from behind one of the buildings.

"Hurry, Dimitri," she said, gently shaking him. "Open your eyes. You have to see this magnificent sunrise."

Dimitri opened his eyes and wished he had kept them closed. The light coming into the room was so bright that he had difficulty focusing.

"There, I'm fine now," he said, looking out the window. "You're right, Aleksandra. It most definitely is magnificent."

After breakfast, Aleksandra and Dimitri left the hotel.

The day was beautiful. The temperature was warm, and a gentle wind could be felt working its way through the statuesque trees lined up along the main thoroughfare.

Aleksandra and Dimitri walked, hand in hand, along the boulevard, pretending they had lived in Moscow for most of their lives. They were here to have a wonderful, romantic holiday and were bent on leaving their political lives behind.

After an hour, just as they approached a narrow side street off of Teatralnaya Square, Dimitri spotted a small café.

"We should stop and have lunch," he said. "I'm getting hungry."

"That's a good idea," Aleksandra replied, "and since it's such a lovely day, let's sit at one of the tables outside."

When Dimitri studied the list of dishes available, he noticed there was not much in the way of complete meals. Instead, the menu contained several soups, salads, teas, and desserts. However, he did see a soup that immediately caught his eye.

"Look. They have *okroshka*. The last time I had it was when my mother made it when I was a child. I'm going to order it. It will bring back pleasant memories."

"*Okroshka*. Isn't that a cold soup made with vegetables, boiled potatoes, eggs and cooked meat?"

"Yes, it sounds as though you've had it before."

"Had it before. I practically ate nothing but *okroshka* when I was a child. You have to remember, I came from a lower middle-class family and there were five of us children. My mother had to make the food go a long way, so soup was one of the frequent dishes in our household."

"Does that mean you're sick of *okroshka*?" Dimitri asked.

"It's been a while since I've eaten it but if you're having it, so will I."

Moments later, the waiter brought out two bowls of *okroshka* and a small dish of *smetana*—sour cream. As they sat, eating their soup, Aleksandra was reminded of her early childhood, but she never spoke about it to Dimitri, and he never pressed her for information.

Dimitri was about to order dessert, when he felt a sudden drop in temperature and noticed the sun had disappeared behind a dark cloud.

"We better leave," he said. "It looks as though a storm is coming."

He paid the bill, took hold of Aleksandra's arm, and they both ran back to the hotel.

Ominous dark clouds appeared as their hotel came into view. Within minutes, there was an outburst of lightning and thunder, followed by strong winds and a torrential downpour. By the time they reached the hotel, they were drenched.

"Take off your clothes," Dimitri said and began wrapping a

blanket around her. "You don't want to catch a cold."

"You do the same," she replied, wiping his forehead with a towel.

Aleksandra and Dimitri stood in front of a large window, and they could see in the distance a vortex of violently rotating winds. It seemed to have the appearance of a funnel-shaped cloud.

"It looks like a tornado," Dimitri called out.

"A tornado," Aleksandra cried. "Russia doesn't have tornados."

"Well, it looks like a tornado to me, but the good news is it's heading away from us. Let's stay in our room for the rest of the evening."

"I agree," Aleksandra said, pulling the window drapes shut. "We don't want to be awakened by the sun creeping into our room like it did this morning."

"Sun," Dimitri called out. "From the looks of it, I don't think we'll be seeing the sun any time soon."

After taking warm baths and having their dinner sent up to their room, they both retired early. Tomorrow was the 30th of June and their first opportunity to experience an opera at the Bolshoi Theater.

Shortly after ten the next morning, Dimitri awakened. Aleksandra was still asleep. Quietly, he got out of bed and peeked through the curtains. The rain had stopped, but the sky was still darkened with clouds.

After a while, Aleksandra began to move.

"Are you awake, my darling," Dimitri asked, placing his hand softly on her cheek.

Aleksandra opened her eyes, wrapped her arms around him, and gave him a kiss.

I'm awake now," she smirked.

"Let's get dressed and have breakfast," he said. "Afterward, we can go to the third floor. I hear there's a reading room with a large library where the latest magazines and newspapers are delivered. I would like to catch up on the news."

Aleksandra laughed.

"I thought you didn't want to know about the news while we're on holiday."

"Well," he replied making a joke, "I want to be sure the Tsarist government hasn't engaged in conflicts with any other countries since we left St. Petersburg."

There was an air of excitement when Dimitri and Aleksandra entered the library later that morning.

"What's all the commotion about?" Dimitri asked an elderly gentleman who was hobbling around on his cane.

"You mean you didn't hear?"

"Hear what?"

The old man handed him the newspaper.

"Read it for yourself," he said and quickly left the room.

On the front page in large letters appeared the words:

TORNADO HITS MOSCOW SUBURBS

"I was right," Dimitri said. "It was a tornado." He stared at the headline and thought to himself, this was an omen of doom. Just as the tornado caused damage to Moscow, the coming revolution will wreck havoc on the Tsarist regime, allowing a worker's paradise to rise from the ruins.

"You were right," Aleksandra replied. "We witnessed it happening before our very eyes."

Dimitri put down the paper and looked at Aleksandra.

"We were fortunate that the storm headed in another direction. If it hadn't, we probably would have been killed soon after the tornado had taken shape and struck ground."

When they returned to their room, Dimitri smiled and slowly took off his jacket and his shirt. Aleksandra returned his smile and removed her dress, allowing it to fall to the floor. Once they were both unclothed, they fell onto the bed. Dimitri stroked her long black hair while Aleksandra kissed him tenderly.

After they had made love, Aleksandra fell back on the pillow and said, "Now I know why I love you so much. Don't ever change, my darling." Dimitri held her in his arms until they both fell asleep.

"Wake up," Aleksandra said, shaking Dimitri lightly. "We have almost slept the evening away. It's almost four o'clock, and we have to get dressed for dinner." She placed her silky hand on his forehead and began rubbing it gently. He still did not wake up, so she let him sleep and began to dress.

Twenty minutes later, she shook Dimitri again. He still did not wake up. Aleksandra began prancing around the room, hoping this would awaken him.

Suddenly, he sat up in bed, giving her a strange look. It seemed as though the echoes and scents he was experiencing had awakened in him some long lost memory.

"Dimitri, Dimitri. Why are you looking at me so strangely?"

"I'm all right," he replied. "It must have been something you did that made me react so."

He thought for a while and then it came to him. Aleksandra had finished washing her hair and was combing rose water through its long black strands. Of course, he had witnessed her doing this many times. Somehow, the vision of her doing it at that moment and the scent of the rose water, brought back memories of his beloved sister, Gesya and how she used to wash her hair and use the rose water in a similar fashion.

Aleksandra felt she had done something to upset him and thought it was best not to bring it up.

"Get dressed," she said. "We need to hurry. Didn't you say our restaurant reservation was for five o'clock?"

"Yes, my darling," he replied, eagerly jumping out of bed.

The restaurant was located on the second floor and was decorated in Louis XV furnishings. It had an elaborate fireplace embellished with white marble and a metal lattice, and the ceilings were adorned with beautiful paintings.

Aleksandra could not help but stare.

"May I have your name, sir?" the maître d' asked, greeting them at the entrance.

"Dimitri Bogdonovich. If you would be so kind, I would prefer a table away from the crowd."

"Yes, sir. Please follow me."

After they had studied the menu, the maître d' approached them.

"May I make a suggestion?" he offered.

"But of course you may," Dimitri replied. "What do you recommend this evening?"

"May I suggest you start with our most delicious pate with truffles, followed by a hot bowl of broth. Next, I recommend a small, delicate green salad and for your entrée, you must try our Gatchina trout served with boiled potatoes and baked mushrooms."

"How does that sound, my darling?" Dimitri asked.

"It sounds perfect," she answered.

At that moment, their eyes met and words could not describe what they were feeling for each other.

When Dimitri looked around, he noticed a dignified older man sitting alone, and the waiters were very attentive to him. While the food was being served, he politely asked for the gentleman's name.

"He's the famous composer, Nikolai Rimsky-Korsakov," the waiter replied. "We're honored to have him dining with us this evening."

After they finished their main course, Dimitri looked at the clock hanging on the wall.

"Goodness, it's a little after seven. I'm afraid we'll have to skip dessert. The opera starts at eight o'clock sharp. We'll have to grab a cab, though. I hear there's still debris on the ground from the storm."

"The Bolshoi Theater and hurry," Dimitri said, as he and Aleksandra climbed into a carriage outside the hotel.

The theater was filled with members of Russia's wealthiest social classes, but this did not bother Aleksandra or Dimitri. They felt ballet and opera were totally acceptable for them to enjoy and appreciate. In other words, it was perfectly fine for them to surround themselves with these evil people as long as it satisfied their needs. Such actions by others in the party, however, were strictly frowned on.

"Listen to this, Dimitri," Aleksandra said, browsing through the program. "It says Feodor Chaliapin appeared here in October, 1901 when he first premiered as Ivan the Terrible in the *"The Maid of Pskov."* I'm not familiar with the opera, but it was written by Nikolai Rimsky-Korsakov, the very same gentleman we saw this evening."

"That's probably why we saw him," Dimitri said. "I'm certain he's sitting somewhere in the audience."

When Aleksandra looked around, she spotted the gray-haired composer sitting in a box seat very close to the stage.

She continued to skim through the program, trying to read as much as she could before the performance.

"It says here, Chaliapin was mainly self-taught, and his career began in St. Petersburg at the Imperial Opera."

"St. Petersburg. What year was it?"

Aleksandra was about to answer when the lights flickered and after a few stragglers made their entrance, the theatre darkened and the orchestra began playing the overture.

When the overture ended, the red velvet curtain rose. Act One, Scene One was about to begin. From then on, the audience's attention was held captive until the final act and scene had concluded.

The performers were given a standing ovation and expressions of approval continued for several moments.

After the second curtain call, Feodor Chaliapin came out and motioned for everyone to quiet down.

"Thank you for your kind response," he began. "Please allow me to introduce the magnificent composer of the opera you have seen here this evening. Let us give a welcoming hand to Nikolai Rimsky-Korsakov."

Chaliapin looked up into the balcony and began to clap, and then the entire audience stood and joined him in a round of applause.

Nikolai Rimsky-Korsakov rose from his seat and stretched out his arms to welcome the attention.

It was an endearing moment, and one that will always be

remembered by those in attendance that beautiful summer evening.

One morning, six months later, while Dimitri was reading the newspaper, he learned that on the 3rd of January, a strike had occurred at the Putilov Irons Works Factory in protest to the firing of four workers. The strikers demanded that the workers be rehired, but the management rejected their demands.

Dimitri and Aleksandra discussed the possible ramifications of the incident.

"Perhaps this will present itself as an opportunity to overthrow the Tsarist Government and put a socialist government in power," Dimitri said, as he folded the paper and placed it on the table.

Aleksandra reached for the coffee pot and poured Dimitri a cup of coffee. "Perhaps it will," she replied. "Perhaps it will."

Sunday, the 22nd of January 1905 was a date in Dimitri's life that would never be forgotten.

He and Aleksandra had finished an early breakfast as a cold mist began to settle into the wintry landscape. Aleksandra gathered up the binder she had packed the night before, full of subversive pamphlets.

Within a few hours, there was to be a peaceful demonstration at the Winter Palace, led by a popular Russian priest, to present a petition to Tsar Nicholas II, asking for certain reforms and improvements for the working class.

It was arranged that Aleksandra and several cohorts deliver the pamphlets to a group of students who would be waiting nearby to distribute them in an attempt to influence and arouse the demonstrators.

Dimitri decided not to attend because he was in the middle of finishing an article, which was due to be published in one of the popular underground newspapers.

"Be careful, Aleksandra," Dimitri warned and helped her on with her coat.

"I wish you were coming with me," she said and placed her arms around his neck.

"Remember," Dimitri said, "be sure to come straight home after you've given out the material."

He held her close, they kissed, and she disappeared into the chilly wintry morning.

When Aleksandra approached the Winter Palace, she could see what looked to her to be an innocent march made up of unarmed workers and their families.

Meanwhile, Dimitri began having second thoughts about letting Aleksandra attend the protest without him, so he quickly put on his coat and hurried out the door.

When he came within site of the demonstrators, a strange and frightening feeling came over him. He saw soldiers of the Tsar's Imperial Guard take aim and fire a few shots over the heads of the crowd. The soldiers then fired their rifles directly into the masses. People were dropping everywhere. Innocent men, women and children were being slaughtered. It was a cold-blooded massacre.

Aleksandra was standing nearby and witnessed most of the scene through a mist of tears. Dimitri's eyes searched until he caught sight of her. Frantically, he ran in her direction.

"Aleksandra! Aleksandra!" he shouted. "Hurry! Run! Don't look back!"

Aleksandra, hearing Dimitri's voice, turned around and began running toward him.

"Dimitri! Dimitri!" she cried as tears continued to roll down her cheeks.

After the Tsar's troops fired their last shots, a lone soldier was able to fire off one hard, rising bullet into the crowd.

Aleksandra ran into Dimitri's arms.

"You're safe, my darling," he said. "I've got you."

Aleksandra lay quiet. The soldier's stray bullet had made its last journey into the dear life of Dimitri's beloved.

She looked up at him and said with her last breath, "I love you, my darling. Don't ever forget me."

Dimitri held her close and as her body lay motionless, he felt all the love inside him drained forever from his heart.

When the Tsar's soldiers ceased their firing, more than one thousand men, women and children had been injured or killed. What was supposed to be an innocent demonstration by the people turned out to be a bloody massacre—an incident that would go down in Russian history.

Instead of silencing the crowd, the actions taken by the Tsar's Guard energized the masses more and united the peasants, workers, and middle-class intellectuals to rise up against the tyranny of the monarchy, thus was born the Revolution of 1905.

Even though the workers and peasants wanted economic freedom and the well-to-do middle-class sought drastic political change, together a united front was formed against the Tsar.

It was more than a month since Aleksandra's murder on that cold January morning. Dimitri had gotten rid of everything that reminded him of her, except for her dearly loved Matreshka.

Matreshka was well aware that something very precious in her life had been taken, and each night she would let out a howling cry before she would curl up on the floor near the side of the bed where Aleksandra once slept.

Although Dimitri took good care of Matreshka, mainly because Aleksandra would have wanted him to, he never felt close to her. In fact, there were times when he wished her dead. The pain of seeing Matreshka without his Aleksandra was almost too much for him to bear. However, he felt obligated to take care of the cat in reverence to Aleksandra's memory.

One rainy evening, as Dimitri was getting ready for bed, he noticed Matreshka sleeping in exactly the spot Aleksandra once occupied. This was quite unusual, because she never slept there after Aleksandra's death.

When Dimitri reached to pull the covers over his body, Matreshka opened her eyes, crawled up next to him, and let out a loud, doleful cry. It sounded to him like a prolonged wailing noise such as that made by a strong wind. Then Matreshka tumbled off the bed and lay motionless on the floor.

"Matreshka! Matreshka!" Dimitri shouted but there was no answer. Matreshka was again a happy, contented Russian Blue who had joined Aleksandra and now Dimitri was truly alone.

As the year progressed, there was more agitation among the people. The Bolshevik Party saw an opportunity to incite the workers even further. This was their chance to promote their communistic theories among the masses.

The university students gave out more pamphlets and flyers and more speeches were made to large crowds. Dimitri and fellow members jumped at the opportunity to express their discourse to large audiences and this time the disgruntled crowds listened.

Students, factory workers, revolutionaries, doctors, and teachers took to the streets demanding change. Strikes were taking place throughout the country, crippling the entire Russian economy and to add more misery, Russia had lost the Russo-Japanese War.

In October, out of desperation, the Tsar issued the October Manifesto, allowing the formation of the workers' parliament, freedom of the press, the right to assembly, and the right to vote. The workers' uprising, however, failed to remove the Tsar, and he later abandoned many of the promises he had made.

The following January, Lenin was elected to the executive committee of the Russian Socialist Democratic Labour Party. Dimitri listened, while Lenin spoke to the Bolshevik Party members. After hearing his address, Dimitri was immediately inspired since they both were of the same thinking, and he wished one day he would meet this man he so admired.

Dimitri helped publish many of Lenin's writings and speeches, which were distributed among the working class. He went to secret meetings held in factories throughout the Russian Empire, spreading Lenin's ideologies wherever possible and before long, Dimitri's reputation had become well known.

One evening, Dimitri came face to face with Lenin at one of his rallies to raise money for the party. In the past, Dimitri had seen him from a distance but now he was standing so close, he could reach out and touch him.

"Good evening," Lenin said, reaching for Dimitri's hand.

"It's a pleasure to meet you," Dimitri replied, shaking Lenin's hand vigorously.

"I've heard good things about you," Lenin said.

Gazing directly into the eyes of this giant of a man," Dimitri replied, "You inspire me."

"Keep up the good work," Lenin called out as he rushed to another speaking engagement.

Lenin spent a good deal of time finding ways of raising money for the party. Through his lectures, he was able to secure large pledges from several Moscow millionaires, which contributed to the management of the organization.

Dimitri continued writing articles and making speeches at various factories and other places, spreading the Party's ideologies, along with the writings of Lenin. He was eager to carry out the dreams of this man he so admired to make a better world for the good of the common people.

As an obedient member of the Party, Dimitri used his work like a drug to mask the emptiness he felt in his heart for the loss of his Aleksandra. Never again would he find another woman like her, he thought.

Jews in the Pale of Settlement continued to toil under the oppression of the May Laws, struggling to eke out a living, while being subjected to increasing anti-Semitism.

Some gave up and emigrated, while those who remained prayed in their synagogues for change, still maintaining their customs and traditions.

As the rest of the world moved forward into the twentieth century, Russia seemed to stand still. The tidal wave of increased commerce in the western world bypassed Russia, leaving it behind.

When will the inevitable change come, Russians wondered?

# Chapter 12 – The Wandering Jew

## February 1905 – Shavlan, Kovne Guberniya, Russian Empire

In the early hours of the morning, on the 2nd of February, Sarah Taube gave birth to a beautiful baby girl, whom she named Chaya after Charles' grandmother, of blessed memory.

"Hello. May I come in?" Shaina asked, tapping softly on the front door.

"Of course," Sarah Taube replied. "I've just finished giving Chaya her bath. I'll be there shortly."

A while later, Sarah Taube entered the room, holding her five-day-old daughter tightly against her chest.

"Another beautiful child," Shaina said, "and how are you feeling?"

"I'm feeling fine," Sarah Taube replied, gently placing Chaya down in the crib. "With each pregnancy, the deliveries seem to be easier. Here, let me get you a glass of hot tea. I was about to make one for myself."

"Do you plan to have any more children?" Shaina asked.

It's not up to me," Sarah Taube replied. "It's up to *der oybershter in himl*." The highest one in heaven.

"I feel the same way. You know how much Saul and I wanted another child. After my son was born, I thought I could never conceive again, and last month when I delivered my Rifka, I was the happiest woman on earth."

"And how is your business," Sarah Taube asked, handing Shaina a plate full of freshly baked *kichlach*.

"Things are good, but I find I rarely have time for myself. Saul is under a great deal of pressure running public institutions, so he doesn't have much time to help me in the store. I worry that he has taken on more than he can handle."

"You should talk to him," Sarah Taube replied. "Maybe there's someone who would be willing to take over some of his duties?"

"You're right," Shaina said, breaking off a small piece of *kichel* and placing it in her mouth. "I'll have a talk with Saul soon."

A few months later, when Shaina was about to close the store, her husband felt pain in his chest and dropped to the floor. By the time she got to him, he was dead, apparently of a heart attack.

Shaina felt guilty. If only she had spoken to him earlier to try to convince him to ease up on his workload, he might still be alive.

Shortly after his death, Shaina fell into depression. Her two sisters were frantic with worry. Not knowing what to do, they contacted Sarah Taube and asked if she could come for a visit.

"Hello, is anyone home?" Sarah Taube called. No one answered. She gently pushed the front door open and when she entered the living room, she found Shaina lying on a sofa, staring up at the ceiling.

"Shaina, speak to me. Are you all right?"

When Shaina heard Sarah Taube's voice, she began to move.

"It's you. I'm so glad you've come."

"What's been troubling you?" Sarah Taube asked, surprised to see her in such a state.

Shaina sat up and began to cry.

Sarah Taube reached into her pocketbook and handed her a handkerchief.

"Here, dry your eyes and then we'll talk."

Shaina wiped her tears and blew her nose.

"Remember the last time we met, I discussed with you how Saul was working so hard, and you suggested I speak to him about getting help?"

"Yes, I remember."

"I have only myself to blame for his death. I never got the chance to speak with him and now he's dead."

"You mustn't blame yourself for Saul's death. It was his time. It was *bashert*." Written in the book of life.

Sarah Taube reached for Shaina's hand.

"You're a strong and capable woman, and you have two children to raise. For their sake, you have to pull yourself together."

Shaina stood up and straightened her shoulders.

"Thank you for coming," she said. "You've given me some good advice. You're a dear friend."

All Shaina needed was a visit from Sarah Taube to make her realize she had to accept her husband's death and whether she blamed herself or not did not matter.

She continued to operate her store and built it up to be one of the most successful businesses in town. Her two sisters, who were unmarried, moved in with her and helped run the business and take care of the children.

After two years, once again Sarah Taube found herself pregnant, and on a sunny spring morning on the 19th of April 1907, another child came into the lives of the Grazutis family. A beautiful baby boy was born, and he was named Avram after Charles' late father.

Six months later on a Thursday morning, while Sarah Taube was preparing to go to market and Charles was preparing to open for business, Aunt Lena and Uncle Morris came into the shop.

Sarah Taube was concerned because they were not in the habit of visiting on a day the bakery was open.

"We need to speak to you and Charles," Aunt Lena said.

Sarah Taube and Charles dropped whatever they were doing and sat down.

After hesitating for a moment, Aunt Lena spoke.

"Your Uncle Morris and I, after long consideration, have decided to sell the shop and leave for America."

Sarah Taube couldn't help herself. Her jaw dropped to the floor as her eyebrows shot toward the ceiling.

"Isn't this sudden?" she asked.

"No, my dear. We've been thinking about it for a while now. Your uncle has cousins living in a town called Baltimore, and they have invited us to stay with them. They own a grocery store and have offered Uncle Morris a job."

"I can't believe what I'm hearing," Sarah Taube said as her voice quivered with emotion. "It never occurred to me that the two of you were unhappy."

This news left Charles speechless. He sat there, not saying a word.

"It's not that we're unhappy," Aunt Lena replied, "but your uncle and I have been troubled about the country and the changes that have been made over the years. These changes have not been good for our business, so we believe now would be a good time to make the move."

There was nothing more to say. Sarah Taube knew in her heart their decision was the right one. Day by day, the government was increasingly cracking down on the Jews throughout the country, and she wondered when Charles would realize his shop would soon be affected.

She hugged her aunt and uncle and wished them good luck and a safe journey and yearned for the day when she and her family would also be relocating to the one place she dreamed of for most of her life.

Aunt Lena and Uncle Morris would be selling the bakery and moving within the next few months. It was a very sad day in Sarah Taube's life. Once more, she was losing family members and again she was being left behind.

For many months, Charles' sister Bessie had made it known that she was not happy living in Shidleve. She was a young woman of marriageable age but no eligible young men in town interested her and if she remained in Shidleve, she would probably die an old maid.

She had always been interested in moving to England so when Charles realized how unhappy she was, he bought her a ticket to London. The following month, she left Shavlan to begin her journey.

Shortly after arriving in England, she wrote Charles a letter, telling him she had met a nice young man on board the ship and a few days before landing, they were married. Her husband's name was Bernard Myers. He was a cabinetmaker and had a good job waiting for him. They had settled in the East End of the city, and they were very happy.

Approximately three weeks after Bessie left for London, Charles' sister Freida and Uncle Lazer and Aunt Hannah informed him they were also leaving for America.

Aunt Hannah had several cousins who had emigrated from Lithuania to a small town called Ellwood City, near Pittsburgh, Pennsylvania, so they decided to relocate there as well and take Freida with them. Since Charles felt there would be no future in his sister's staying behind, he agreed.

With more family members leaving, a feeling of melancholy came over Sarah Taube. Again, she felt isolated and abandoned by those she loved. She knew Charles had not changed his mind about America and she, much to her displeasure, had no choice but to respect his wishes. After all, he was the man of the house, and he always knew best, she thought.

One evening, after she put the children to bed, she decided to have a talk with Charles.

Charles pulled out a cigarette and as they sat at the kitchen table, she poured him a glass of tea.

"I've observed lately that you have not been yourself," Charles said while he puffed away. "Have I done something, Sarala to make you unhappy?"

"Charles, I wish to speak about something that's been worrying me for some time. Our family has gotten smaller since most of our relatives have left, and soon the children will forget about ever knowing their *eygeneh*"—relatives.

Sarah Taube sat there waiting for his reply.

He took a sip of tea and said nothing.

This angered her.

"What I'm trying to tell you is I don't think I can live out the rest of my life in this place. I want to go to America. I have a feeling things here will soon get bad. It's already difficult for us and with more and more of our people leaving, it will get even worse."

Charles remained silent for some time. Finally he rose to his feet and said, "Sarala, I'm trying to understand your feelings. I realize conditions here have changed. But you know I was not happy living in America, and I've told you many times I will never go back."

Sarah Taube tried once more to convince this man that to emigrate would be the most sensible thing for their family but as much as she tried, she saw it was futile for her to continue. Being a proper Jewish wife and mother, she felt she had to obey her husband. She immersed herself in caring for her children and tried to stifle her desire to take them and leave for America.

One month later, after an uneventful summer, a stranger came to the front door. He was dressed in a worn tuxedo with a fluffy, red handkerchief tucked in the pocket of his jacket.

"Hello," he said in a friendly voice. "My name is Makso Rubinstein, and I'm a photographer from Shavl. I will be scheduling family photographs here in Shavlan. Would you be interested?"

"How soon can you get started?" Charles asked.

Mr. Rubinstein took out his pocket watch attached to a long chain hanging from the inside of his coat pocket and said, "I can schedule you in an hour."

Sarah Taube quickly dressed the children in the clothing they wore only on special occasions. Unfortunately, Yankel was attending *kheyder*, a Jewish school, studying for his bar mitzvah.

An hour passed and the photographer returned with his camera in hand and all the photographic equipment needed to take the portrait.

Mr. Rubinstein posed the family in front of a pleasant backdrop and told them to be perfectly still. "Ready?" he said. "One, two, three!" The flash powder went off and the photograph was taken.

"I require a deposit," he told Charles, "and I'll be back in two weeks with the finished portrait."

Two weeks later, as promised, Mr. Rubinstein returned with the photograph and the family was quite pleased with the results. Sarah Taube put it in a metal frame and placed it inside her kitchen cupboard.

After six months, conditions for the Jews in the Pale of Settlement had become much worse since the anti-Semitic "May Laws" were enacted in 1882. It was becoming more difficult to take part in long-established occupations such as manufacturing, and what was most alarming was they were now being excluded from government service.

In the spring of 1910, Charles' brother-in-law, Nathan was leaving for America where a job was waiting for him in Baltimore. Aunt Lena and Uncle Morris, who had recently settled there, invited him to stay with them until he found a job.

It was decided, it would be best for his wife, Jenny and their two children to stay behind until he could send for them and before he left, he asked Charles to look after them.

Three months went by and Jenny had not heard from her husband. Charles was not happy about it, thinking Nathan had abandoned his sister and her family. It was also becoming a burden for him to care and support them.

Charles waited patiently for Nathan to take responsibility, but he did not. At least he should be sending his wife money, he thought. The more he thought about it, the angrier he got, so he decided to send a letter to Aunt Lena, explaining the situation.

After a month, Aunt Lena wrote.

*Dear Charles and Sarah Taube,*

*I'm not surprised to hear Nathan has not been a good husband to our Jenny. He's been seen carrying on with women in the area. The men come here to find better jobs with the expectation of sending for their families once they have saved enough money for their passage. However, as time goes by, many forget what brought them here in the first place.*

*The Jewish organization in Baltimore developed a way to solve some of these problems. Landslayt, our fellow countrymen, who are affiliated with various shtetls, contribute to a fund. When money is collected, they buy passage for the wife and family. Once the family arrives, the husband reverts back to being the devoted man he was before leaving the old country. Otherwise, he is made to feel ashamed by his peers. I think this is what we should do for our Jenny.*

*In the meantime, the landslayt will see that Nathan gets in touch with her, sends her money, and apologizes for not writing. Usually these men come around to being good husbands after the landslayt give them a talking to.*

*I hope the family is well. Uncle Morris and I are very happy. We love it here, and I only wish you and your family could join us. Kiss the children for us.*

*With Love,*

*Aunt Lena and Uncle Morris.*

As Aunt Lena stated, within a few weeks, Nathan sent Jenny an apologetic letter but still no money. The *landslayt* were disappointed in him and managed to collect enough money for his family's passage and within a few months, Jenny and her family were on their way to America.

Yet again, more family members were leaving to make a better life for themselves in America.

Conditions were not getting better for the Jews of Lithuania, and many were leaving their shtetls to settle in other countries. By now, even Charles was feeling the effects of this mass emigration.

Most of his customers were religious men whose custom was to wear black suits to synagogue. With the men leaving, the call for new suits diminished greatly.

This had an effect on Charles's tailoring business, creating less calls for new suits and also less repairs on old garments. Sarah Taube knew it would only be a matter of time before Charles would be thinking about joining Chaim. They had continued their friendship by mail, and she was afraid Charles would set his wanderlust eyes on South Africa.

One evening, after the children had gone to sleep, Sarah Taube and Charles sat at the kitchen table, discussing what they would do if they could no longer earn a living in Shavlan.

Charles poured himself a cup of coffee and lit a cigarette.

"Where would we go and what would happen to us?" Sarah Taube asked.

"I would have to look for another opportunity some place else," Charles replied calmly, flicking some ash from his cigarette onto a plate.

Once again, Sarah Taube saw an opportunity to discuss her feelings. "Won't you reconsider our leaving for America?"

Charles stubbed out his cigarette, leaped to his feet, and left the room without saying a word. He was painfully aware if he had stayed one minute longer, they would have harsh words to say to each other.

Sarah Taube couldn't sleep that night. Many thoughts were racing through her mind, and for a moment, just a moment, she again contemplated taking the children and leaving. But where would she go?

It had been more than three years since Sarah Taube had given birth to little Avram and again she found herself in the family way. She was in her ninth month and ready to deliver. This would be the sixth child born to her and Charles.

After going through a very easy labor, on the 3rd of January 1911, she brought into the world a healthy baby boy.

"His name will be Masha, after your grandfather. May he rest in peace," she said as Charles looked on with approval.

The following year in early June, Sarah Taube found herself in the family way once more and about to give birth. She was busy in the garden, planting late spring seedlings. Although it was getting harder to carry out her day-to-day activities, this did not keep her from performing them.

Ruchel, who was now seventeen years old, had taken on many responsibilities, both in watching her brothers and sisters and in managing the household. She was conscientious and made sure her mother was not subjected to excessive demands in her present condition.

The sky had filled with large dark clouds, and Ruchel suspected a storm was heading their way. She called to her mother, "*Mammeh*, a storm is coming. Hurry and come into the house."

Sarah Taube, with the help of her daughter, collected the garden tools and hurried into the house.

All at once, Sarah Taube felt a pain that was much too familiar.

"Go and get Mrs. Rubin!" she yelled, "and tell her my time is near."

Ruchel ran to the midwife's house, but she was not at home and by now the storm had gotten stronger. What was Ruchel to do? Her father had gone to a nearby town to make a delivery and would not be home until dark. Her mother was alone, and she knew she had to get back, so she headed home in the midst of the downpour.

Ruchel, completely out of breath and drenched from head to toe, ran into the house.

"Where is Mrs. Rubin?" her mother asked, by now in considerable pain.

"*Mammeh*, she wasn't there. What are we to do?"

"Don't worry, *myne kind*, but I'm afraid you'll have to help. First, go and change your wet clothes."

Ruchel obeyed her mother's instructions and within minutes returned.

"Tell me what to do, *Mammeh*?" she asked.

"Quickly, prepare some hot water and heat the scissors over the fire. Then get some binding tape and place it on the table beside me, along with two sheets and some towels. I will time my contractions. Be ready to hand me whatever I ask for."

Ruchel patiently waited by her mother's side.

"It's time," Sarah Taube called out, trying to stay as calm as possible for her daughter's sake. "First, prepare the sheets and place them under my body. Then go and get the pot of hot water but be careful not to burn yourself."

The contractions were now coming very fast and after a short time, the cervix had widened enough for Ruchel to see the baby's head. Sarah Taube pushed gently and within minutes, the complete expulsion of the baby took place.

As Ruchel held open her arms to catch her newborn sibling, she called out, "It's a girl, *Mammeh*."

Sarah Taube cleaned the child and took the sterile binding tape from Ruchel's hand and very carefully clamped and cut the umbilical cord. Then she cleaned the baby and wrapped her in a warm blanket.

"I've named her Fraida after your father's great-grandmother. May she rest in peace."

Ruchel, throughout her life, would never forget the day she helped bring her sister Fraida into the world.

Eight months passed and the clash of opposing views between Sarah Taube and Charles had not changed. This morning, while Charles was in the kitchen having breakfast, she could tell from his demeanor that something was bothering him.

Ruchel had taken on the responsibility of making sure Yankel and Gitka were out of the house in plenty of time so as not to be late for school, while Chaya was in charge of taking care of her younger siblings.

Sarah Taube waited patiently for the morning routine to end. Once the children were off to school and the younger ones were playing outside, she closed the door and made her way to the kitchen.

"It there something troubling you?" she asked as she sat down beside him and poured herself a glass of tea.

Charles reached for a brown envelope and held it up.

"Sarala, I've received a letter from Chaim. I'm sure you have sensed I have not been happy. In the past, even though we did not have a great deal of freedom, we were, for the most part, able to go about our business and practice our religion. Now, conditions are not as good, and I truly believe it's time for me to leave."

Sarah Taube seemed reluctant to discuss the matter. She listened anyway, while Charles continued to present and explain his reasoning for making his decision.

"Over the years, I've been pressured to join various political groups but I refused, and it was only last month I was asked to join the Russian Social Democratic Labour Party and I again refused. By not joining these groups, I've been looked upon by many as being against Jewish socialist movements. And now the government has placed restrictions on us who engage in traditional occupations like shopkeeping. This directly affects us, Sarala. Soon, we will not be able to earn a living in this country. Then what will we do?"

"So what have you decided?" Sarah Taube asked impatiently.

"I'm getting to that."

"Chaim has written many letters asking me to visit and has even offered me a job. He says in South Africa there is religious freedom, no obvious anti-Semitism, and more opportunities than in most other places."

Charles paused. "I've decided to take him up on his offer."

This came as no surprise. Sarah Taube had suspected he wanted to leave for quite some time, and he was waiting for the right opportunity to tell her.

"I agree it's becoming much harder for us to make a living," she said, trying to control her anger. "But Africa! You know it has never been my desire to move there. Going to America has always been my dream.

"You are a kind man and have been a good husband and father, but you're not considering my feelings. When I speak your ears are open, but when I finish speaking, you act as though you have not heard a word I've said."

Charles looked at her, showing not even the slightest spark of interest in what she was saying.

Sarah Taube sank into her chair and sighed hopelessly.

"Then go, my husband!" she shouted. "The children and I will be fine."

A gigantic smile spread across Charles' face, and his eyes lit up like the evening sky after a shooting star had entered the earth's atmosphere. It was as though she had set him free.

Charles rose from his chair and took Sarah Taube by the hand.

"You won't be sorry, my Sarala. Try to look at it as an opportunity that might change our whole life."

Sarah Taube attempted to smile, but it was as if the effort would wound her.

"I plan to settle my affairs and leave in two months. Also, during my absence, I've decided to hire Mr. Koppel, a tailor I know from Shidleve, to run the business. If my plans work out the way I expect them to, I'll sell the shop and send for you and the children."

Would he travel aimlessly from place to place like a wanderer, Sarah Taube thought, or would he, at last, find what he was looking for. In a few months, she would have her answer.

Two months later, all the preparations had been made. Charles' passport was renewed, his papers were in order, and he was eager to begin his trip. He planned to visit his sister Bessie in England and continue on to Johannesburg.

"How will I know where you are in case I have to get in touch with you?" Sarah Taube asked, as she placed the last article of clothing into his old battered suitcase.

"There's nothing for you to worry about, my Sarala," he assured her.

"Here, I've made a copy of my itinerary so you'll have an idea where I am."

Sarah Taube's head began to spin.

"Such a complicated trip," she said, expressing total confusion.

"It's not that complicated, and it's not as if I've never been out of the country."

Charles's face grew serious.

"Sarala, I leave everything in your hands. Conditions can change almost over night so always take notice of your surroundings. Pogroms can happen at any time, as you well know, so don't go out at night, lock your doors, and make sure the children are inside before dark."

The door flew open and Yankel entered, completely out of breath.

"I thought I had missed you, *Tateh*. I ran as fast as I could from Rabbi Broide's study. Have a good trip, and I hope some day to be able to travel to far away places like you."

Charles grabbed his son around his shoulders and looked in his eyes.

"Maybe some day you will, *myne zun*—my son. For now, the most important thing is for you to keep up with your studies."

Promptly, there was a knock at the door. The driver had arrived to take Charles to the train station in Shavl.

"Now children, take good care of yourselves and listen to your mother." He encircled them with his arms and gave each a kiss and with a tear in his eye, he turned to Sarah Taube and said, "Tell them about me, Sarala so they don't forget me."

He kissed her on the lips, placed his suitcase into the wagon, and lifted himself onto the seat.

Sarah Taube removed the handkerchief from her pocket and wiped her eyes. Again, a feeling of abandonment took hold of her, while she watched Charles disappear down the road, wondering whether or when she would ever see him again.

As Charles caught sight of his family one last time, he could feel his heart beating and his cheeks were flushed with excitement, thinking about the new adventure he was about to embark upon.

# Chapter 13 – London

## March 1913 - East End, London, England

By the middle of the 19th century, many Eastern European Jews had emigrated to America, Palestine and South Africa to escape deteriorating conditions in their respective countries, and many were from small settlements outside large cities and towns. Some ran away to England and settled in the East End of London, preferring to live near people of the same faith.

As more immigrants arrived and settled in the East End, overpopulation became a primary concern. Overcrowding led to unsanitary conditions, which affected the hygiene and health of the inhabitants.

In 1885, Lord Nathaniel de Rothschild, a well-known Jewish philanthropist and others, decided to put together a Company and build flats that would provide for large families. These buildings were known as tenements and mostly everyone could afford the reasonable rents.

At long last, Charles, after an exhausting trip, had arrived. Typically, the weather was cold, wet and unpleasant. He grabbed a taxi and directed the driver, a round faced, middle-aged man, to take him to the East End.

"Blimey! Where abouts in da East End are yew going?" the driver asked.

"Take me to the Rothschild Dwellings at Flower and Dean Streets," Charles said, holding on tightly to his suitcase.

"Wight away," the man replied.

The cab driver, after twenty minutes, stopped in front of a tall, brown building, which looked more like an old deteriorated warehouse.

"Dis is it, gov'nuh," he said as he stopped close to the curb and called out his fare.

Charles handed him the money, grabbed his suitcase and exited the cab, hesitating for a moment before entering the building.

It was an unpleasant-looking building and his sister lived on the sixth floor. Up each flight he climbed, huffing and puffing, stopping to catch his breath before he could tackle the next flight. And by the time he reached the sixth floor, he was exhibiting extreme physical fatigue.

After pausing for a few moments in order to restore his normal breathing pattern, he knocked on the front door of his sister's flat.

"Who are you?" a small oval-faced boy with curly hair asked."

"I'm your uncle," Charles said, gently patting him on the head. "What's your name, young man?"

"My name is Leonard," he replied, looking up at Charles with his big brown eyes.

Charles could hear his sister calling in the background.

"Who's at the door, Leonard?"

"You can come in now," the child said.

"Charles, I didn't think you would be here so soon," his sister said as she came running out to greet him. "This is my son, Leonard. You remember, I wrote you about him."

Charles stretched out his arms, and he and his sister embraced.

"How have you been?" he asked as she led him into the living room.

"I've been fine," she answered, pointing to a chair for him to sit in. "Bernard has a good job, and we hope to move to a better part of town but this is all we can afford now. So tell me, where are you headed after your visit?"

"I'm going to Johannesburg, South Africa. You remember my friend Chaim?"

"Yes, I believe so. Wasn't he your best man at your wedding?"

"Yes. That's the one. He offered me a job working in his tailor shop. I'm thinking if I like it, I'll send for Sarah Taube and the children."

"Why would you want to move to that godforsaken place?" his sister asked, shrugging her shoulders, clearly unable to believe he would consider such a thing. "If I could do it all over again, I would have gone straight to America like Jenny and Freida did."

Charles grew angry. He leaned forward in his chair and looked Bessie straight in the eyes.

"Bessie, let's not talk about my personal life. You don't know anything about it. Are you happy?" he asked, quickly changing the subject.

"Yes, I am, but I can guess why you're asking. It's because of the way I met Bernard, isn't it?"

"Yes it is. I was shocked to learn you had married a perfect stranger."

"I'll tell you the story," she said and pulled her chair close to him. "Bernard and I were two lonely people onboard a ship heading for a country we knew nothing about. We found each other. He's a good man and I've grown to love him."

Bessie sounded content with her life and that was all Charles wanted to know.

"You wrote that Bernard is a cabinetmaker. Has he found a job in his line of work?"

"Yes. Once he demonstrated his skills, one of the best furniture makers in London snatched him up. I hope he decides to stay here in England," she added, looking as though she were about to cry.

Charles was taken by surprise. "Why would he want to leave? He has an excellent vocation, and I'm sure he'll always be able to find work."

"I'll let Bernard explain it to you when he comes home."

"And when might that be," Charles asked, glancing at his watch.

"He usually gets home around six. Little Leonard will let both of us know when he arrives. You'll understand what I mean soon enough."

Within the hour, the clock on the mantle began producing a series of ringing sounds until the hour of six was struck.

"It's six o'clock! My Daddy's home!" Leonard shouted, prancing up and down the room.

As soon as Bernard came in, Leonard jumped into his arms.

"Daddy, did you bring me anything?" he asked, hugging and kissing his father.

"Here, son. Put your hand in my pocket and see for yourself."

Leonard reached into his father's pocket and pulled out a red toy train.

"Thank you, Daddy," he said, disappearing into his room.

"And who may I ask is this?" Bernard asked, glancing in Charles' direction.

"Don't you remember," Bessie replied. "I told you my brother was coming from Lithuania to pay me a visit."

"Ah, yes. So this is your brother Charles. So glad to finally meet you."

"Likewise, I'm sure," Charles answered, holding out his hand for a handshake.

While Bessie was in the kitchen preparing dinner, Charles and

Bernard sat down for a friendly chat.

"Your sister mentioned that you may be thinking of leaving. From what I understand, you have a good job working for a good company so why would you want to relocate elsewhere?"

"Because of Palestine," Bernard called out. "That's why I want to leave."

Charles knew exactly what Bernard was referring to as soon as he heard the word, Palestine.

"You're a Zionist," he said. "Now I understand why you want to go to Palestine."

"That's exactly right. We Jews need a homeland. The countries we live in don't want us. The only solution to the persecution our people have endured throughout our history is to establish a homeland in Palestine. And according to the bible, it was always our land.

"When Bessie and I first moved here, I read about a man called Chaim Weitzman. Have you heard of him?"

"Yes. I remember reading an article about him."

"Well, Chaim Weitzman, who was from a small village near Pinsk, was a very educated man who studied chemistry in Germany and Switzerland. He lectured at the University of Manchester and settled here soon afterward.

"Early on in his career, he became a dominant figure in the Zionist movement. I went to some of his lectures and agreed with his beliefs that if we Jews move to Palestine now and take part in its development, we will have our own Jewish State.

"Enough about anti-Semitism!" Bernard yelled. "At least in Palestine I will feel like it's truly my home."

"What about Bessie?" Charles asked, glancing toward the kitchen. "What does she think about this?"

"I've discussed it with her, but she doesn't feel as strongly as I do. Naturally, she worries about Leonard. Palestine may not be the place to bring up a child. I'm not moving yet. I'm thinking about it. What are your feelings about Zionism?"

Charles did not speak for a moment in order to give a greater force to his answer.

"When the *Mashiach*—Messiah comes, then we will have our State of Israel. According to Traditional and Orthodox Jewish teachings, the Messiah will be the chosen one who will descend from his father through the Davidic line of King David. Then and only then will he send for us and bring us back to the Land of Israel."

Charles saw that Bernard did not like his reply but continued anyway.

"It is believed by many, including me, that the Messiah and only the Messiah can lead us into the Promised Land."

Bernard and Charles realized they had different opinions, and it would be a waste of time to continue, so the topic was dropped.

After a while, Bernard brought up another subject.

"I understand you've been to America, but it did not work out for you and you returned to Lithuania. If you're looking for the perfect place to settle down, you'll never find what you're looking for because perfection doesn't exist."

Bernard was now treading in very dangerous territory. Charles was obviously offended by his remarks and thought who was he to tell him about the ways of the world and what he wanted out of life?

"You don't even know me," Charles said, angrily, rising from his chair. "How can you assume to know what's in my mind and..."

Bernard, becoming aware of what he had said, interrupted.

"I'm sorry. I should not have spoken to you that way. Please accept my apology. I was only relating what your sister had told me."

In the kitchen, Bessie could not help but overhear her husband and her brother going at it as if it were a verbal sparring match.

"Dinner is ready," she said, calmly entering the room. "Enough talk. Let's enjoy our few days together."

Charles and Bernard, realizing Bessie had overheard them arguing, looked at each other and being the well-brought up gentlemen that they were, shook hands, both expressing their regrets for not being able to accept the other's point of view.

After only knowing Bernard for a few hours and despite their disagreements, he came across as being a very pleasant and good-natured young man. And it was obvious to Charles that he loved his son and seemed to be a loving and devoted husband to his sister.

Charles spent the next two days enjoying the time spent with Bessie and her family. He explored London to see if he would be interested in resettling there if things did not work out in South Africa and before long, it was time to continue his journey.

He caught a train from London and made his way to Southampton in time to board the Union-Castle Mail Steamship Company Limited's regular Thursday's four o'clock sailing to Cape Town.

Charles was excited to be traveling to a new country and looking forward to new adventures, completely putting out of his mind that he had left his wife and children alone in a country full of violence and hatred.

# Chapter 14 – South Africa

## April 1913 – Cape Town, South Africa

The rays of the sun spread its warmth on Charles's face as he headed toward the train. It was very crowded, and he was forced to move hurriedly through the car in search of an empty compartment. When he approached the end of the aisle, he spotted one and quickly placed his body on the seat next to the window.

Within a few moments, an attractive middle-aged woman with flaming red hair and dressed in a green, one-piece outfit entered the compartment.

"Are you holding this seat for anyone?" she asked in a pleasant voice, pointing to the seat directly across from him.

"No, it's vacant," Charles replied, not even looking up to see who was speaking. He reached into his knapsack and pulled out a newspaper and began to read.

"Then you won't mind if I join you?" she asked, dragging her suitcase behind her.

"Not at all," he answered and continued reading.

She attempted to lift her large, brown valise up into the overhead storage area but was having little success in doing so. She was breathing heavily and seemed not to have enough strength to lift it up and out of the way. Being the gentleman he was, Charles put down his newspaper and volunteered his services.

"Thank you. It's quite uncommon to find such a chivalrous young man in this part of the country," she said, while she maneuvered her body comfortably into the seat. "Let me introduce myself. My name is Madeleine Solvey. I live in Johannesburg and where are you headed, if I may ask?"

"Actually," Charles replied, "I'm heading for the same place."

She gave him a warm smile. "Now that's a coincidence, isn't it? Will you be living there permanently?"

Charles finally looked up at her and said, "Yes, I plan to."

"Well, I certainly hope you enjoy Johannesburg. The place can get pretty raunchy at times. Will your wife be joining you?"

By now, Charles had become clearly annoyed with this woman. He was a man of few words and resented the fact that this stranger was asking him all these personal questions. He was about to cut her off when, as the train was pulling out of the station, a round-faced, bald-headed gentleman came rushing in and collapsed into the seat next to Charles.

"I thought I was going to miss the train," he said, almost out of breath. "Looks like I made it just in the nick of time and..."

"My name is Madeleine Solvey," the female traveler said, breaking into the conversation before the stranger had a chance to continue speaking. "This is... Sorry, what is your name?" she asked, pointing in Charles' direction.

He folded his newspaper and placed it on his lap. "My name is Charles Grazutis."

"I'm David Schoenberg," said the stranger. "Glad to meet you, Miss Solvey."

"I beg your pardon. It's Mrs. Solvey. I'm a widow. Have been for nearly twenty three years."

David turned to Charles. "Glad to see you again," and the two men shook hands.

"Do you two know each other?" Mrs. Solvey asked, checking for a wedding ring on David's finger.

"Yes. We met briefly on board the ship coming here."

"Why are you late?" Charles asked. "You almost missed the train."

"I was out of cigarettes, and I thought I could find a shop nearby where I could pick up a pack. When I realized it was taking too long and I might miss the train, I gave up and hurried to get here."

"Would you like one of mine?" Charles asked, as he reached into his coat pocket.

"Don't mind if I do."

Charles pulled out another cigarette for himself and searched for matches. Mrs. Solvey quickly dug into her handbag, pulled out a booklet of matches and proceeded to light both of the gentlemen's cigarettes.

"Thank you," Charles and David said and began puffing away.

"So tell me, Mr. Schoenberg," Mrs. Solvey asked, leaning forward in her seat, "what brings you to South Africa?"

"Work. That's what brings me to South Africa. I've been out of work for quite some time and when my friend, Josef wrote me a letter offering me a job, I decided it was time to leave Lithuania and try my luck elsewhere."

"What does this Josef do? Is he a salesman?" she asked.

"A salesman? Of course not. You must be joking. He's a millionaire. He and his father own a big department store in Johannesburg. It's called Labinovitch and Son. I'm sure you've heard of it."

"Heard of it. Of course I've heard of it. It's the biggest department store in town. They are one of the richest families, and you can be sure they would never think of living in Johannesburg. No, it's too slummy for them. They live in Braamfontein and, I might add, in a very ritzy area."

"Good for them," David replied. "They've worked very hard all these years. Why shouldn't they profit from the fruits of their labor?"

"Tell me, David," Charles asked in an attempt to change the subject, "where will you be living when you get to Johannesburg?"

"I don't know yet. I'll have to look around once I get there."

Mrs. Solvey's eyes lit up.

"I have a room you could rent, and my place is right in the heart of Johannesburg. Would you be interested?"

"Interested. I most certainly would be interested, Mrs. Solvey."

"You may call me Madeleine," she said, laughing lightly.

"Of course, and you can call me David. By the way, Madeleine, I'm very curious to know how long you've lived in Johannesburg?"

"It's a very long story. If you have the time, I certainly don't mind telling you."

Both David and Charles seemed eager to learn more about her so they settled in, and Madeleine began to recount past events leading up to her present life, as the train headed north through the South African countryside.

"I came here with my husband Andrew in 1890," she began. "Before then, we lived in London, England.

"We were newly married," she said and began twisting her wedding ring around her finger. Andrew was ten years older than I and had done some extensive traveling before we met. He had heard that Johannesburg was in need of skilled workers with engineering knowledge to manage a new process. So naturally, he thought this would be a great opportunity for him, especially since he had the qualifications and experience.

"For me though, coming here was most distressing. I had never been out of London so moving to a strange land with strange customs completely overwhelmed me. However, I loved my husband and would have gone anywhere with him."

Madeleine stopped talking for a moment, looked at the two gentlemen and asked, "If I'm boring you, I can stop."

"No, not at all," they said eagerly. "Please go on."

"Johannesburg was a wild frontier back then. The city was undeveloped, and small roughly built shacks and mud huts extended across the land as far as the eye could see. In 1886, shortly after gold was discovered, a large number of people emigrated to Johannesburg from all over the world, and they came with many of the skills they had learned in the countries they lived in."

"Many of the immigrants were Jews from Lithuania," Charles added.

"Not only Lithuania but also from England as well," Madeleine replied.

"It wasn't long after gold was discovered when Johannesburg became the biggest community in South Africa. In a short time, the gold mines were taken over by large mining companies, and they acquired a great deal of wealth. Anyway, to make a long story short, my husband was able to buy stock. Everyone was buying stock and..."

David interrupted. "I remember reading about it. It was a big story in those days. So what happened?"

Madeleine paused for a moment, stared out the window and then continued.

"Things were going well for us, but my husband had a strong feeling something bad was about to happen. In 1895, he sold our stock and with the money, we bought a small hotel in a nice section of town.

"It was lucky we got rid of our stock when we did because within a few months, the bottom fell out of the market. It seems someone had dropped a large number of shares onto the London stock exchange, causing hysteria among the shareholders.

"Stock prices began to drop, forcing the monetary unit of South Africa into a financial downswing. Fortunately, my husband and I came out smelling like a rose. At least we had a way to make a living but most people lost everything."

"It was a wise decision you and your husband made in purchasing the hotel," David remarked.

"Yes, and my Hotel Victoria still remains one of the most popular hotels in the area, and I still operate it the same way Andrew and I did years ago, with a few minor changes, of course."

"You mentioned you were a widow," David said. "What happened to your husband?"

"What happened to my husband? A tragedy happened to my husband. Living conditions were still pretty primitive then and, although new towns were built to accommodate the arrival of large numbers of foreigners, there were still many areas that were full of unsanitary conditions, causing frequent occurrences of infectious diseases. And some fatal, I'm afraid."

Madeleine voice started to crack and she stopped talking.

"Go on," David urged, not realizing that she was under a great deal of stress finishing the story.

"Please forgive me," she said. "It brought back unpleasant memories. My husband was one such person who was caught up in an unwelcome situation. One evening, he came down with a fever and infection of his lungs, and although he fought very hard, the angel of death came and took him from me. It was then when my world collapsed."

Charles and David were speechless. After this long dissertation about her early life in Johannesburg, it was a total shock to hear the outcome of how her husband had met his death.

"I'm sorry Madeleine," David said, reaching for her hand. "Sounds like you've had a difficult life but you survived. I'm curious though. Why are you still living here when you lost your husband years ago?"

"I had no family back in England, and I had grown accustomed to a certain lifestyle. The town was growing by leaps and bounds, and I wanted to be part of it. So here I am twenty-three years later."

Throughout the evening, the three of them continued to engage in conversation. Early the next morning, the conductor announced that the train would be arriving in Johannesburg in twenty minutes.

Madeleine looked at the men and smiled. "Goodness, we're almost there. I thoroughly enjoyed this trip and could not have asked for better traveling companions."

"Likewise, I'm sure," David replied.

"Yes, I enjoyed it too," Charles said, "and by the way, David, as soon as you get settled, stop by and see me. It's called Chaim's Tailor Shop."

"And you do the same," David replied and scribbled down the address of his place of work.

When the train pulled into the station, Charles felt obliged to take down Madeleine's valise, and she, of course, thanked him.

He grabbed his suitcase, left the compartment and handed his ticket to the collector.

"Charles! Charles!" someone yelled, waving his hands up and down.

There in plain sight was Chaim, standing on the platform.

"I can't believe its really you," he said, grabbing Charles by the shoulders.

"Great seeing you, Chaim. It's been a tiresome journey, and I'm happy to finally be here."

Chaim led Charles down a narrow street, heading toward a red electric tram that had stopped in the center of the road.

"Come, let's get on. It will drop us off near my shop."

While the tram moved through the streets, Charles turned his head back and forth. There were people everywhere and pubs on practically every corner. When he would fix his eyes on one attraction, the tram was already passing and going on to another.

"Aren't you impressed with what you're seeing?" Chaim asked.

"I am. I didn't think the city was so well developed, and it looks as if it's still growing."

"It's been growing like this for years. With the discovery of gold and everyone flocking here to try their luck in mining, Johannesburg needed people with skills like tailors, blacksmiths, carpenters, and bakers."

"You mean like us?" Charles asked.

"Yes, my friend. They were looking for people like us from small shtetls, and that's why there's a large Jewish population here."

"Get ready to get off. My stop is coming up."

Chaim's tailor shop was right at the corner of Commissioner Street and Market Square. Market Square was a mixture of deafening sounds and smells. The street consisted of a conglomeration of shops, selling everything from rolls and pastries to pots and pans.

"This is it," Chaim said, standing in front of a two-story building. "Come in. Let me show you around."

When Charles entered the shop, he saw a large poster hanging in the center of a wall.

*Chaim Gluckman, Proprietor*
*Complete line of the newest materials for suits and overcoats*
*You name it and we can make it*
*Ready to wear clothing available*
*Reasonable prices and satisfaction guaranteed*

Charles was impressed.

The store consisted of three large rooms. The front room was a waiting room, the second room displayed the merchandise, and the third room was the actual workshop. Chaim had two employees who did the measurements, cutting and sewing, while he ran the business and did the selling.

"If you notice, Charles, I carry ready-to-wear clothing. The businessmen still come in for three-piece suits made to order, but now I also accommodate the working-class community.

Chaim put his hands on his hips. "Well, what do you think of my little operation?"

"I think you've done well for yourself, but do you think you have room for me?"

"Room for you. "I would not have offered you a job if I thought I could not take advantage of your talent. Believe me, I have more work than I can handle.

"My customers keep coming back, and I'm happy to say I also have a good walk-in trade. Here, no one gets turned away. I guess that's why I have such a good reputation. I even have customers coming from as far as Cape Town. Now do you see why I need you?"

Charles nodded his head. "Yes, I do. I'm ready to start right away but first, I'd like to settle into the room you've found for me."

"That's no problem. It's not too far from here. I'll take you there now."

Three months had passed, and Charles easily adjusted into his new routine. It was like old times when he and Chaim worked for Mr. Schneider, except Chaim was now Charles' employer.

Late one morning, while Chaim was finishing a custom-made suit, three men entered the premises. Two of them were dark-skinned Indians, one dressed in a business suit and black tie, while the other was dressed rather strangely, wearing a white Indian dhoti and shawl. The third man was white, dressed in an expensive European suit.

Chaim recognized the strangely dressed man and alerted Charles that he was a man called Gandhi—the one who had recently made headlines in the local newspaper because he was the leader of the workers' strike in Natal.

"You're right," Charles said, remembering he had seen Gandhi's picture and read that very same article.

Charles walked over to the men. "Gentlemen, may I help you?"

"Yes you may," said the European. "My name is Hermann Kallenbach. We were attending a rally a few blocks away, and the crowd got quite aggressive. Unfortunately, during the struggle, the pocket on my jacket ripped. I noticed your shop and was wondering if you could repair the tear while I wait?"

"Please take off your jacket," Charles asked and examined the pocket closely. "Yes, I'm quite sure I can repair it. And within a short time, the coat pocket was mended. "Please try it on."

Mr. Kallenbach looked carefully at the pocket. "You're done an excellent job. How much do I owe you?"

"There's no charge," Charles replied, shaking his head. "It didn't take me long, and if ever you need my services, I would be most happy to accommodate you."

By this time, the Indian wearing the dhoti slowly walked over.

"Where are you from?" he asked.

"I'm from Lithuania."

"Are you here alone?"

"Yes, I am. I've read about you in the newspaper so I recognized you. You are called Gandhi, yes?"

Gandhi nodded. "You speak English but it is not the King's English. Where did you learn it?"

"In America."

"Why did you not stay in America?"

"Because the Jews in America were not religious enough for me."

"Oh, so you are a religious man?"

"I try to be."

"And why did you leave Lithuania?"

Charles did not think he was going to have such a serious talk with this man and before he knew it, he was in deep conversation with him.

"Being a religious Jew in Lithuania is more difficult than being an Indian in South Africa. In Lithuania, we frequently have pogroms where the Russian soldiers and even the local Gentiles come into our shtetls and indiscriminately kill every Jew they can find. Men, women, children, it does not matter. It's a manifestation of anti-Semitism and is condoned by the government and military authorities."

Gandhi listened closely as Charles continued.

"After a while, things go back to normal as if nothing had happened. You talk about your people not having all rights of citizenship here. Well, my people have been denied their rights for not one or two centuries but for two thousand years. We Jews are invited to live in many different countries but are never given the freedoms and opportunities the rest of the citizens have."

Gandhi lowered his head in deep thought, and after a few moments, began speaking to Charles as though he were lecturing a student.

"There is only one road for the Jews. They must abstain from abuse, while safeguarding their self-respect. If I were a Lithuanian Jew, I would dare the Lithuanians to open fire at me or hold me prisoner, instead of surrendering to their prejudiced behavior. And if all the Jews carried out this elective hardship, it would bring them limitless internal power and pleasure."

Charles was stunned by Gandhi's remarks. No one spoke. And within a short time, Gandhi and his entourage left the shop.

Chaim, hearing the conversation, walked over to Charles and put his hand on his shoulder.

"Gandhi's pacifist methods may work against the British because the British are an educated and decent people, but it won't work if we Jews used the same methods because the Lithuanians are an uneducated and prejudiced people."

"Yes, and thank goodness we and others like us disagree with this man's philosophy," Charles replied.

Late that afternoon, while Charles and Chaim were preparing to close the shop, a man came in, carrying a jacket draped around his arms.

"Is it too late for you to repair a loose button on my jacket?" he asked.

Charles took the coat from the man's hands and looked at it. "Yes, I can fix it while you wait," he replied.

"You're Charles Grazutis, aren't you?"

"Yes, I am. How do you know me?"

"Don't you remember? I met you on the ship, and then we rode on the train from Cape Town to Johannesburg. I'm David Schoenberg."

Charles thought for a moment and then it came to him.

"Ah, yes. I thought your face looked familiar. As I recall, you were going to work for your friend who owned a department store here in Johannesburg. Did that turn out well for you?"

"I'm very happy. I couldn't have asked for a better job, and after only a few months, I'm managing a large section of the store and making lots of money."

Charles handed him the mended jacket.

"Where are you living now?" he asked.

"Well, Charles, do I have a story to tell. Do you have the time? I noticed when I first came in, you were about to close the shop.

Charles did not want to appear rude.

"Chaim," he called, "you can leave. I'll close the shop as soon as my friend is ready to go."

"Now that we're alone, David, tell me what happened?"

"You recall the woman we met on the train, Madelaine Solvey? Remember, she offered me a room in her hotel."

"Yes, I remember. Go on."

"When we got off the train, we took a tram over to her place. There was a restaurant and a pub within walking distance, which I thought was odd, since she said her hotel was in a nice section of town. She led me up the stairs and into a room and told me to make myself comfortable, and later we could discuss the rent. She said dinner would be served at seven and to meet her in the dining room.

"A few hours after my nap, I went downstairs and into the dining room where Madelaine was waiting, along with six of the most beautiful women I've ever seen.

"They were dressed in stunning gowns and long diamond earrings dangled from their ears. The conversations were relaxed and most enjoyable and after we finished our dinner, the ladies excused themselves."

Charles looked annoyed.

"How much longer does this story go on?" he asked.

"I'm getting to it," David replied and took a long breath. "After dinner, I thanked Madelaine for her hospitality and went back to my room to settled in for the night. It must have been ten o'clock when I heard the door open and felt a warm body slip into bed.

"What is your pleasure?" the voice asked.

"I immediately turned on the light and, to my surprise, lying there completely naked was one of the women from dinner.

"I'm sorry," she said. "I must have made a mistake and gone into the wrong room. She quickly gathered up her flimsy negligee and left. It was then I realized that Madelaine was running a house of ill repute, and this strange woman was a lady of the evening."

David's eyes opened wide. "What do you think about that?"

Charles stood there with his mouth hanging downward limply. "I'm totally shocked. But as Madelaine explained, she had to survive when her husband died, and it was the only way she knew how. So then what did you do?"

"Of course, I finished out the night, and the next morning I packed, left some money on the dresser, and vacated the premises. Anyway, I reported for work that morning, and my boss found me a very nice room in a boarding house very close to my place of work. I'm sorry my tale took so long, but now you see why I couldn't leave anything out."

"I certainly do, and I'm glad you were able to find yourself a suitable place to live."

"Look at the time," David said, glancing at the clock hanging on the wall. "It's getting late. I better be heading home. It was nice talking to you. Don't be a stranger. Come see me at the department store. Remember, it's called Labinovitch and Son. I'm in the furniture department, second floor."

After Charles closed the shop, he went home, ate his dinner and sat down to write Sarah Taube a letter. Sleep did not come easy to him. He missed the sound of his Sarala's voice and the warmth of her body lying next to him.

# Chapter 15 – Workers Unite

## June 1913 – Johannesburg, South Africa

Two men entered Chaim's Tailor Shop carrying signs, "Join the Workers Union" and "Workers Unite Now."

Chaim, who was completely against unions, recently read that this particular group had organized trade unions in their countries of origin, and now that they had moved to South Africa, they had undertaken the task of organizing unions here.

My employees do not need to join a union, Chaim thought to himself. I pay them fair wages, give them benefits and periodic raises, and offer them excellent working conditions, always complying with the labor laws of the country. So what could a union do for them that I am not already doing?

Chaim stood quietly, pretending he was an employee, allowing the uninvited men to sound off their ideas. Not getting any favorable responses, they became agitated. They raised their voices in anger threatening if the employees did not join, things could get unpleasant.

"Wait a minute!" Charles shouted. "Are you threatening us?"

"No, of course not," one of the men replied. "We're having a friendly conversation. That's all."

"I think it's time for the two of you to leave," Charles said, pointing his finger toward the door. "We've heard all that needs to be heard. Take your signs and do us a favor, don't come around anymore."

The two men, without saying another word, grabbed their signs, slung them over their shoulders, and walked out. Nothing more was said about the incident until later that day. The other two employees had already left for the day and only Chaim and Charles remained to tally up the receipts, close the shop, and retire for the evening.

"Why do you allow these men to come into the shop?" Charles asked.

"I let them come and talk," replied Chaim. "After listening to them, my people know they are treated well, and there is no need for them to join a union. Thank you for speaking out against those leftist radicals. They led you to believe they were good people but, after a while, they could not hide the fact that they were nothing but hooligans."

"I'm glad they finally got the message," Charles said. "Hopefully, we have seen the last of them."

"I hope so," answered Chaim, glancing at his watch. "It's time to close up. We've had a busy day."

Chaim went out the front door and over to a side entrance, which led to his apartment on the second floor, while Charles, who had moved into a second floor, one-bedroom apartment a few blocks away, began walking home.

When Charles came close to his apartment, two men wearing dark overalls jotted out from the corner. He noticed their faces were covered with black cloth that fitted tightly over their noses and mouths, and he could see only their peering eyes staring at him. One of the men grabbed him by his arms, while the other began punching him.

"Take that," he said and continued to hit him. "This will teach you to keep your mouth shut when we do our best to help the workers."

"That's enough," said the other man. "You can let him go. Remember, we only want to scare him, not kill him."

Then the two ran, leaving Charles lying in the middle of the street writhing in pain. Realizing he needed immediate attention, he dragged himself back to the side entrance leading up to Chaim's apartment and, with great difficulty, began banging on the door.

"Who's there?" Chaim asked, stretching his head out the second floor window.

"Help, it's me!" Charles screamed. "I've been attacked!"

"My G-d! I'm coming right down!"

Chaim desperately tried to support the weight of his friend's body, while he helped him up the stairs.

"What happened?" he asked."

"I was assaulted by two men, and I'm certain they were the men who spoke at the shop today."

Seeing how much in pain Charles was, he replied, "We can talk about this later. I'm going to call for an ambulance and take you to the hospital."

Charles was promptly ushered into the emergency room, while Chaim waited in the hallway.

After an hour, the door opened and the doctor, a tall, lean man with half-moon spectacles on the end of his nose, came out.

"Are you his friend?"

"Yes. Is he all right?"

"Luckily, he only has a few bruises around his ribs and there appears to be nothing broken. I've given him some medication to be dispensed as per my instructions but for now, he needs bed rest until his body heals. As soon as I fill out a police report, he'll be discharged. In any case, he's going to need someone to go home with him and make sure he follows my orders."

Chaim patiently waited until Charles came out.

"I'm fine," Charles said, bent over with pain.

Chaim got a taxi and, instead of taking Charles home, instructed the driver to return to his apartment.

"I want you to stay with me until you're feeling better."

"You don't have to do that," Charles replied, stumbling as he walked.

"As I said, you'll be staying with me until you're well enough to take care of yourself."

Charles was too exhausted to argue.

That evening, Chaim moved Charles into a small guest room and made sure his every need was attended to.

"Thank you for all you're doing for me," Charles said and began to drift off.

Chaim pulled down the shades and drew the curtains.

"Get a good night's rest, my friend," he whispered.

The next morning, Charles heard someone at the door.

"Are you awake? It's me, Chaim."

"Come in," Charles replied, trying desperately to sit up in bed.

Much to Charles's surprise, standing before him was a short, rather attractive brown-haired woman.

Chaim introduced her.

"I want you to meet Sadie Behman. She'll be taking care of you while you're recuperating. She will bring you your meals and make sure you have everything you need. I'll be going downstairs now to open the shop."

Charles was not pleased with what Chaim had done. He did not need anyone to assist him, especially some strange woman.

"Pleased to meet you," Mrs. Behman said, as she fluffed up his pillow and placed it firmly behind his back. "I've brought your breakfast. Is there anything else I can do for you before I leave?"

"Look here, Mrs... What did Chaim say your name was?"

Sadie looked at him with her big blue eyes. "It's Mrs. Behman but you may call me Sadie."

"Look here, Sadie. I'm all right. Leave me alone. I'm quite capable of taking care of myself."

"Hush," she said, bringing her finger to her lips. "Chaim is in charge, while you're in his care. He made it perfectly clear. He said you will probably try to discourage me from helping you, but I am to go ahead and do whatever I think necessary to bring you back to health."

Before Charles could say another word, Sadie left.

After eating, he felt tired and fell asleep, and within minutes, he was dreaming of his Sarala. There she was at the kitchen table, pouring him a glass of hot tea and serving her freshly baked *kichlach*.

"Did they come out good," she asked while sitting in the chair next to him.

"Yes, my Sarala. This batch is the best batch you've ever made."

Sarah Taube smiled, leaned over and wrapped her arms around his shoulders.

At that moment, Sadie arrived.

She called from behind the door. "May I come in? I've brought your lunch."

Sadie's voice startled Charles, and he felt someone shaking him with such force that he opened his eyes and sat up in bed yelling, "Sarala, don't leave me!"

"Charles, calm down," Sadie spoke softly. "You must have had a nightmare. You were screaming some woman's name."

Charles looked up at Sadie and said angrily, "My dear lady, it was not a nightmare. I dreamt I was with my dear wife. Why did you have to wake me?"

"I'm sorry. You were tossing and turning in bed. I honestly thought you were having a nightmare."

Because Sadie heard Charles call out, "Sarala, don't leave me," she assumed his wife had left him, and the reason he left Lithuania was to start a new life in South Africa.

"Please forgive me, Charles said when he realized he was speaking harshly to this woman who was being kind to him. I didn't mean to snap at you."

"Of course," she replied, gently placing the tray of food on his lap. "I understand."

For the next several days, Sadie never failed to show up with meals, and after the fourth day, Charles was feeling much better. He was gaining strength and well on his way to recovery.

"So tell me," Charles asked, curious to learn more about his caregiver, "how did a nice woman like you wind up in South Africa?"

Sadie cleared the lunch dishes and placed them in the sink before she spoke.

"I guess Chaim didn't tell you I'm a widow and have been for many years."

"No, he never mentioned it," Charles replied, surprised she was living in the country alone.

"Originally, my husband, Solomon and I lived in a small village near Minsk in Russia. We had known each other ever since we were children. Our families were very friendly, and it was planned that Solomon and I would one day marry.

"In 1890, when I was twenty and Solomon was twenty-two, we were wed. I will never forget how handsome my Solomon looked that day with his beautiful green eyes and wavy black hair."

"Are you all right, Charles?" Sadie asked. "Shall I go on?"

"By all means, do," Charles replied, curious to know as much about Sadie as possible.

"Solomon worked for his Uncle Assa who owned a small tavern, but when his uncle died and left the business to him, it was then he decided to leave Russia. He had dreams of becoming wealthy, so he made the decision to try his luck in South Africa. He sold the tavern, and we came here and settled in Cape Town."

"When was that, Sadie?"

"The year was 1897," she said, briefly pausing for a sip of water. "It was two years before the outbreak of the Boer War."

"You mean you and your husband were here during the war?"

"Yes, we were."

"May I ask what your husband did in Cape Town before the war?"

"That's another story," she replied and took a deep breath.

"I'm listening," Charles said. "Please go on."

"When we first arrived, we got a nice apartment not too far from the business district, and after a few weeks, we joined a nearby synagogue. The congregants made us feel welcome and before long, we had made a few good friends.

"One Saturday morning, after religious services, Solomon was introduced to a very nice gentleman named Hyman Markovitz who happened to be the president of the synagogue. They engaged in conversation, and when Mr. Markovitz heard that Solomon was looking for a job, he offered him a position in his business.

"What kind of business did he have?" Charles asked, moving his chair close to Sadie.

Sadie reached for the teapot and poured Charles and a glass of tea.

"We didn't know at the time, but Mr. Markovitz was an extremely wealthy man and owned a very large furniture factory. Solomon worked in the factory as a manager in the distribution center. Things were looking up for us and within a short time, we had established ourselves as upstanding citizens of the community."

"It sounds as though you and your husband were very happy."

"We were, but unfortunately it did not last long. When the Boer War broke out in 1899, everything changed in our lives."

Solomon volunteered his services as an ambulance driver, transporting wounded soldiers to the hospital.

Sadie continued to relate the life she lived with her husband until Solomon's untimely death.

At this point in her story, she dissolved into tears. She quickly wiped them away and, after taking a brief pause, regained her composure and continued.

"There's a little wooden bench right next to my husband's grave and when I visit, I sit on the bench, close my eyes, and meditate."

Charles reached over and gently placed his hand on hers.

"I bet you have some interesting stories to tell."

"I do. There's one more incident I think you will enjoy hearing. Are you up to it?"

Charles leaned back in his chair. "Yes, please go on."

Sadie cleared her throat before she continued.

"During the war, I worked in a hospital, and one afternoon in February 1901, I was called into the Director's office. He said he was on his way to an important meeting, and a very special gentleman named Winston Churchill would be arriving within the hour to visit an injured military friend. He asked if I would look after him?

"I told him I would be happy to. I had read about Winston Churchill in the newspaper. He was the one whose story had made all the newspapers around the world. Sometime in November of 1899, while Churchill was in Natal reporting on the Boer War for the London Morning Post, he joined an armored train as part of a scouting expedition. The train was heading North where Boer patrols had been detected.

"The train was ambushed by Boers north of Frere in Natal and all on board were taken prisoner. Since Churchill was on the train and appeared to be much too active during the conflict, one of the Boer generals made the decision to take him to Pretoria and imprison him, along with the others. But they could not keep Churchill confined to a cell for long. He managed to make a break for it and hid away on a coal train, moving east in the direction of Mozambique. Eventually, he escaped through the Boer lines and was reunited with the British Army."

"Shall I stop," Sadie asked, not wanting to tire Charles out.

"No. I'm fine. Please continue."

"While waiting for Churchill's arrival, one of the hospital attendants brought a rather pleasant-looking, blond-haired young man into my office. He introduced himself as Winston Churchill. He said he was on his way back to England and wanted to see how his friend George Malone was doing.

"As soon as he and I walked into George Malone's room, he let out a smile. "It's wonderful to see you, Winston," he said. "You're quite the hero, old chap. Quite the hero."

"What a great story, Sadie."

"I have some more interesting stories Sadie said, "but I'll save them for another time. I should leave you alone to rest."

"I have one more question for you and then I'll stop. I'm eager to know how you made a life for yourself after your husband's death?"

"With what I've learned in helping the doctors and nurses during the war, I left Cape Town and became a practical nurse at one of the hospitals here in Johannesburg. During my free time, I volunteer my services to people in the community who need my help recuperating from illnesses or injuries."

"You mean like me?"

"Yes, like you."

Charles reached over and gently put his hand on hers.

"I admire you very much. You have strength and compassion. How come an attractive woman like you never remarried?"

Sadie crossed her arms lightly over her chest, tilted one hip and gave him a raised eyebrow. "The truth is, "I gave my heart away a long time ago and never got it back." She paused. "That is until now."

Charles gave Sadie a smile. "I can't believe I'm telling you this, but ever since I left Lithuania, I've been lonely and longing for the touch of a woman."

He got up, put his arm around her and whispered in her ear, "Thank you for taking care of me."

She whispered back in his ear, "The pleasure was all mine."

Before Sadie left for home that afternoon, she refilled his cup with tea, and as her body brushed against his, he thought if he ever did allow himself to be with another woman, it would be with Sadie.

# Chapter 16 – The Count's Son

## July 1913 – Shavlan, Kovne Guberniya, Russian Empire

Ruchel, Sarah Taube's first born, had grown into a beautiful young woman, highly sought after by the few remaining single Jewish men in the community. But she was ahead of her time in her thinking and could never accept the shtetl's backward views toward women.

One warm, summer afternoon, while Ruchel was on her way home from visiting a friend, she noticed the count's son, Vytas riding on his white stallion a short distance away. She had not seen him for a while and had wondered what had become of him. On several occasions, he had noticed her around town and remembered when they played together as children when she accompanied her father to the Manor House.

Vytas was quite a handsome young man. He was tall, blond, and slender, with a sharply sculptured face, and the resemblance to his father was striking.

"Hello, Ruchel," he said in a soft melodic voice.

She returned the greeting.

"Hello, Vytas. What are you doing so close to town?"

"I ride my horse here often, hoping to run into you," he replied politely.

Ruchel glanced up at him and blushed. How dignified he looked sitting in the saddle, and she too remembered so fondly playing with him as a child.

"I've been away attending school in Germany, and I'm home for the summer," he said, thinking to himself what a lovely young woman she's become.

"That must be why I haven't seen you in a while," she replied, giving him a flirtatious smile.

"Would you like to go for a ride near my father's orchard?" he asked.

Ruchel knew her mother would not approve but being nearly eighteen, headstrong and impetuous, she accepted.

He got down from his horse and gently lifted her up onto the saddle. Then he mounted the stallion and rode away, heading out of town toward the fruit orchards near the Manor House, with Ruchel holding on tightly around his waist.

When they approached the orchards, Vytas pulled on the reigns, and the stallion came to a stop. He slowly dismounted and reached for Ruchel. She lowered her arms onto his strong shoulders as he lifted her and, with a gentle motion, placed her firmly on the ground.

There was no communication between them while they strolled hand in hand along the pasture covered with broad leaves and purplish, flowering spikes. They were well aware that each was enchanted with the other.

There were hundreds of apple trees in the orchard and as they came closer, Vytas leaned over and gave Ruchel a gentle kiss on the lips. Ruchel was taken by surprise. She did not expect him to exhibit such a bold display of affection. In fact, this was the first kiss she had ever received from a young man, let alone a *shaygets*—non-Jewish boy. What would her mother think of her spending the day with this outsider? She felt ashamed.

"We better get back to town. My mother will be wondering where I am."

"If that is what you want my lovely princess, your wish is my command."

"Lovely princess," he called her. How romantic he was, and, at that moment, she truly felt like a princess. It seemed to her like a page out of a fairy tale.

He took her once more into his arms and after carefully lifting her back onto the saddle, he remounted and gracefully rode away, heading back to town.

"May I see you again?" he asked.

Ruchel did not answer.

How could she possibly meet him again? She would be going against everything her mother believed in. "Jews must marry Jews," she remembered her saying, but being with Vytas was exciting. They would only see each other for a short time, until summer was over. She would be very secretive and that way her mother would never find out.

Vytas stared into her eyes and a smile crossed his face.

"May I see you again?" he asked once more.

"Yes, I would like that very much," she replied. At last, some excitement in her life she thought, and to her it was worth the risk of not telling her mother. She thanked him for the ride and walked through town, heading toward home.

In the weeks that followed, she and Vytas met often by a shallow brook near a wooded area outside of town.

One day, as Sarah Taube was leaving for market, Mrs. Bleekman approached her. It seems she had seen Ruchel in the distance, riding out of town with a young man on a white horse. According to her, he did not look as though he belonged in the shtetl. In fact, he did not look like any of the Jewish young men in the village.

After thinking about it, she realized he reminded her of the count and how he looked many years ago when he went riding around town on his white stallion.

Mrs. Bleekman was a very smart woman and one could be sure nothing could get passed her. She knew immediately it must have been the count's son who was entertaining Ruchel in such an outlandish manner.

Of course, she refrained from telling Sarah Taube who she thought this young man was because she did not want to upset her any more than necessary.

Sarah Taube thanked Mrs. Bleekman and said she would handle the matter when she returned from the market that evening.

Later that day, Sarah Taube waited for Ruchel to return from visiting a friend.

"Ruchel," she called. "Come into the kitchen and have a seat. Is there anything you need to tell me?"

Ruchel knew, by the sound of her mother's voice, that someone had spotted her with Vytas, and she would now have to tell her mother the truth.

There was a long pause and then she spoke.

"Yes, *Mammeh*," she said, showing signs of regret. "It's about the count's son."

Sarah Taube put a lid on the pot of stew cooking on the stovetop and pulled up a chair.

Ruchel sat at the kitchen table and told her mother everything that had happened.

Sarah Taube was disappointed to hear that her daughter had been seeing a gentile and, what made it even worse, it was with the count's son. Most Jewish mothers would have lost their composure but not Sarah Taube. She was completely in control and expressed her displeasure.

"I forbid you to see him," she said, as she sat back in her chair and folded her arms. "It can only lead to unhappiness for the two of you."

"But *Mammeh*, it was entirely innocent."

"Let me finish. We do not mix with these people. This is how the world works, *myne tay'er tochter*—my dear daughter. You are a bright and beautiful young woman and have your entire future ahead of you. Don't mess it up by seeing this man so I'll tell you again, you must stop seeing him."

Ruchel cried hysterically. She sniffed and wiped her lower lashes with the back of each hand.

"Forgive me," she cried. "It was a little excitement in my life. I'm lonely and unhappy, *Mammeh*. I don't want to wind up matched with some rabbinical scholar who will sit all day and study the Torah, while I slave to provide him with the kind of life he's used to. I have to get out of this place. Please let me go to America."

Sarah Taube placed her hands around her daughter's sweet face.

"You know I love you very much. I understand what you're going through as I was young once myself. I will write your father and explain the situation to him. In the meantime, you must promise you will stop seeing this man. It is shameful and unacceptable."

From the tone of her mother's voice, Ruchel knew she had no choice but to put an end to her friendship with Vytas, and she clearly did not want her mother humiliated in front of the entire Jewish community.

The following afternoon, Ruchel greeted Vytas at their usual meeting place. She noticed he had a sorrowful expression on his face and just as she was about to explain what had happened with her mother, he interrupted.

"I must tell you something," he said, taking hold of her hand. "One of our servants spotted us together. My father was very upset when hearing the news. He reminded me that someday I will inherit his estate and will have to choose a wife with similar background. He's sending me to school in Switzerland next month, hoping I can forget you." He looked deeply into Ruchel's eyes and said, "I'm sorry, my sweet princess."

While Ruchel listened, she could not bring herself to tell him the same thing had occurred with her family.

"I probably will be leaving for America in a few months," she said. "I truly believe we were thrown together by fate. I also believe our lives have been predetermined, and it was inevitable our relationship would end. But I will never regret nor forget the wonderful times we shared together."

"Nor will I," Vytas replied. He pulled her close, wrapped his arms around her waist, and kissed her gently on the lips.

"Memories of you will always remain in my heart," he said and kissed her again.

"And you will always remain in my heart," Ruchel replied as a teardrop left her cheek.

Ruchel, for the remainder of her life, would treasure the relationship she had had that summer with Vytas, her handsome young nobleman.

Four months had passed since Charles had left for South Africa. Mr. Koppel, by now, had established himself as a competent tailor. Fortunately, he owned a horse and wagon, which made it easy for him to travel back and forth to town.

Charles had made an arrangement with him whereby a percentage of the profits would be given to Sarah Taube to help manage the household. He would open the shop on Monday and Thursday of each week to look after the customers, while Sarah Taube would continue to sell her baked goods in town and operate her stall at the market each Thursday to earn extra money.

It was a typical morning for the Grazutis family. Ruchel had taken her sister, Gitka to school, Yankel had gone to his Torah studies, Chaya was taking care of the younger children in the back yard, and Sarah Taube had finished preparing the evening meal. She had made a chicken stew and left it on the stove to simmer until she returned from the market that afternoon.

"Chaya, come into the kitchen," She called. "I've heard that some of the villagers have been going into our houses and stealing food. You'll have to watch very carefully to make sure my stew is not stolen or else we'll have nothing to eat for dinner."

Several hours had passed. Avram was playing, "Jump the Step," a game where each child would jump off the step onto the ground, landing on one foot. Masha and Fraida were patiently waiting their turns.

When Chaya spotted a strange man entering their house, she remembered her mother's warning and ran into the kitchen. By the time she got there, the man had run away. Nothing was touched and the stew was still on the stove simmering, just the way her mother had left it.

Upon returning, she found Avram lying on his back. She ran over and began shaking him but he did not move.

"*Avramicha, Avramicha*," she called. He lay there with his eyes closed, not making a sound. Chaya was frightened and did not know what to do.

Fortunately, Ruchel, Yankel and Gitka had come home for lunch in time to witness little Avram lying there. Ruchel immediately ran to Mrs. Rubin's house to tell her what had happened.

When Mrs. Rubin saw Avram lying on the ground not moving, she suspected he had hit his head when he fell, and when she picked him up, she saw that her suspicion was correct. Directly behind his skull was a large rock. She quickly lifted Avram in her arms and carried him into the house.

"Ruchel, run to the market and get your mother!" she yelled.

"*Mammeh, Mammeh*," Ruchel cried when she caught sight of her mother. "Come home! Avram is hurt!"

"Open your eyes, my son," Sarah Taube cried. "Wake up. Wake up."

Chaya began to cry as she expressed to her mother what had happened.

"Don't blame yourself, *myne kind*," Sarah Taube said, gently touching her daughter's face. "You're not responsible for what has happened."

Mrs. Rubin applied hot compresses to Avram's forehead and rubbed him down with alcohol, hoping this would revive him but his condition did not change.

Sarah Taube quickly called for Mr. Koppel, who was waiting on customers.

"I need your help," she said.

"What has happened?" he asked.

"You must go to Shidleve and fetch the doctor. Avram is hurt."

Mr. Koppel dismissed his customers, hitched the horse to the wagon and rode away.

While everyone awaited the arrival of the doctor, they all prayed. Mrs. Rubin had seen cases like this in the past, and she was convinced Avram had suffered some sort of brain injury.

"The next few hours will be critical and if he does not wake up, I'm afraid the outcome will not be good," she said.

Everyone hovered around Avram's bedside, praying he would return to them healthy and happy, just as he was earlier that morning.

"*Avramicha, Avramicha*," Sarah Taube cried. "I should never have left you. Dear G-d, why are you punishing me?"

Within a few minutes, they heard a gurgling sound coming from his throat, and his eyes opened for a brief moment and then closed. His breathing stopped, and the angel of death had claimed another life.

"I blame myself for this," Sarah Taube spoke as tears flowed down her face. *"Gott hov mir schtrofn."* G-d has punished me.

As for Chaya, this tragedy would never leave her thoughts. All through her life, she would remember that horrible summer morning and blame herself for what had happened to *Avramicha*, her precious little brother.

Avram had been gone for less than a month when Sarah Taube received a letter from Charles. "Should she write and tell him about Avram?" she asked herself but after much thought, she decided against it. He would blame himself for what had happened, and she did not want to place that kind of guilt on him. She did, however, write about the relationship Ruchel had had with the count's son.

Charles was upset when he read her letter and was thankful his daughter had put an end to it. It was then he realized he would have to think seriously about sending her to live with his sister Freida in America.

Ruchel, who recently turned eighteen, still had high hopes of going to America. Her aunt had written her many times asking her to come. She would always say there was plenty of room and most importantly, Ruchel would have many opportunities to meet eligible young men.

One evening, while Sarah Taube was looking out the window waiting for Ruchel to come home, she noticed several young *shkotzim*, non-Jewish boys, lingering near the General Store. She watched as Ruchel approached them.

Quickly, they leaped out and surrounded her, not letting her pass. Ruchel was not prepared for this and began screaming. Sarah Taube grabbed a broom, flung open the door and began running toward them. About that time, a group of townsmen were walking by. When the boys saw them, they ran away. Because Ruchel was beautiful, the young, gentile males were always giving her the eye.

After this incident, Sarah Taube made up her mind. Ruchel had to leave Lithuania as soon as possible. She immediately wrote to Charles, telling him what had happened and just before she ended her letter, she stopped short and thought about her words before she continued.

*"I'm sending Ruchel to America to live with your sister with or without your permission,"* she wrote.

---

Charles cursed to himself when he thought about the anxiety his Sarala was going through, and he'd done nothing to help. He wired her the passage money and wrote: *"See to it that Ruchel gets to America safely."*

At the synagogue last Saturday, Sarah Taube learned of a family in Shavlan named Davidson who were planning to leave for America within the next few months. Mr. Davidson had traveled there a few years earlier and had recently returned to bring his wife and two daughters back with him to settle in New York.

Sarah Taube arranged to have them over for dinner this Sunday at seven o'clock to discuss the possibility of taking her daughter along with them.

Ruchel suggested that Gitka, Chaya, Fraida and Masha be sent to Shaina's house for the evening. A serious conversation could then be had without interruption. Yankel was not coming home that evening. The rabbi had invited him for dinner and to stay over.

When the Davidsons arrived at seven, both Sarah Taube and Ruchel greeted them with welcoming smiles.

"It's a pleasure to meet you," Mr. Davidson said, introducing his wife, Eva and daughters, Sophie and Deborah.

Mrs. Davidson immediately reached into her bag and presented Sarah Taube with a beautifully wrapped *babka*—a twisted cake with a brown sugar-cinnamon filling. "I hope you enjoy it," she said. "It's from a Russian recipe handed down from my grandmother, Sarah Feigel."

Sarah Taube thanked her, took the cake from her hands and led the family through the shop and into the kitchen.

While dinner was being served, all engaged in a casual exchange of words. Then the main topic of conversation came up—the trip.

Sarah Taube suggested if the Davidsons chaperone Ruchel to America, Ruchel could assist in the children's care.

Mrs. Davidson glanced at the children and then at Ruchel.

"Would this be all right with you, Ruchel?" she asked. "I hope you're aware the children can be quite a handful."

Ruchel winked at the children and smiled. "They seem like very sweet girls to me."

The girls looked at Ruchel and giggled.

"Then it's settled," Mr. Davidson said. "I'll go to Kovne and book from the Ticket Agency a "package" deal, which includes rail travel from Lithuania to Bremen, Germany or Hamburg, depending on the port the shipping company uses. Will Ruchel be going on to another state or is she taking up residence in New York?"

"No. Ruchel will be going to Ellwood City, a town near Pittsburgh, Pennsylvania, to live with my husband's family," Sarah Taube replied.

"In that case, with her package, I'll include train fare from the U.S. port to a train station near Pittsburgh."

"By the way," Sarah Taube asked, "what kinds of accommodations are available on the ship? I've heard many of the newer ships have replaced some of the steerage accommodations with four and six-berth, third class cabins. And they serve meals, even kosher ones, in dining rooms with long tables. I don't want my Ruchel traveling in steerage."

"I know about the newer ships and will try to sign on to one," Mr. Davidson replied. "I'll need a small deposit," and related the amount to her.

Sarah Taube went into the next room and brought out the required amount. "I'll pay you the difference when I see you next."

After dinner, Sarah Taube served the *babka*.

"It's delicious," she said. "It tastes as good as my Aunt Lena's."

I'll take that as a compliment," Mrs. Davidson replied, "and thank you for inviting us. It was a pleasure meeting you and Ruchel."

Within a week, Mr. Davidson returned.

"I have all the documents," he said, reaching into his folder, "and I was fortunate to get reservations on the *George Washington*. You'll be happy to know that the ship was built in 1909, and it's one of the newer ones we spoke about. I've booked a four-berth, third class cabin for me and my family, and I was able to get a room nearby for Ruchel with the same accommodations. And to let you know, she will be sharing the cabin with three other women.

"The ship will be leaving Bremen, Germany on the 17th of September, so we have to leave Lithuania on the 12th in order to get to Germany in time for the sailing."

"I'm happy to hear the cabins will be close to each other," Sarah Taube said. "Knowing this makes me feel more at ease in letting my Ruchel go."

"You need not worry," Mr. Davidson replied. "You can be certain I will look out for my family as well as your lovely daughter.

"By the way, the cost of the trip was quite reasonable. The complete package for Ruchel came to a total of seventy U.S. dollars. In addition, she will need fifty dollars to show the immigration authorities she is not indigent and will not become a ward of the state."

"I was expecting a much higher fee for the trip," Sarah Taube said and handed him the additional money.

"Please have Ruchel ready before noon on the 12th. I've arranged for a driver to take us to Shavl, and there we will take the train to Kovne."

At last, Ruchel was leaving for America.

"Thank you, *Mammeh,*" she said as she hugged her tightly.

Then Ruchel began to cry.

"*Mammeh,* I don't want to leave all of you behind. What if I never see you again?"

"You're talking foolish," Sarah Taube said, wrapping her arms around her daughter. "You have to go for this may be your only chance. I expect to hear good things from you and remember, you mustn't be afraid to dream a little bigger, my child."

There was no time to waste. Sarah Taube immediately sent Aaron a wire, giving him Ruchel's date of departure and the ship's expected time of arrival. She also sent Freida a wire, giving her all the details.

Sarah Taube was happy knowing her daughter was fulfilling her dream of going to America. She did not lose hope that one day she would fulfill her dream of going there too.

In all the letters Charles had sent, he never mentioned how he was getting along, except he was continuing to work for Chaim and was doing well.

Sarah Taube selfishly hoped he would not be successful in South Africa and, even though he had misgivings about America, she wished he would finally come to his senses and realize it would be the best place for their family.

# Chapter 17 – Ruchel's Trip

## 12 September 1913 – Shavlan, Kovne Guberniya, Russian Empire

Ruchel was wide-awake long before the sun rose this morning. She had just finished packing. Sarah Taube handed her an envelope containing her passport, tickets, spending money, fifty U.S. dollars and all the other papers needed for the trip. She also placed some non-perishable food into her suitcase, which she figured would last for several days until she arrived in Germany.

Ruchel looked out the window and saw, approaching from the road, a horse-drawn wagon.

"The Davidsons are here, *Mammeh*," she called.

Yankel came running across the street from the rabbi's house.

"I thought I had missed you," he said and handed her a small wooden box.

She pulled out a beautiful heart shaped, gold locket hanging from a chain. "I love it," she said, holding it up to her chest. "Thank you, Yankel. I'll treasure it always."

Slowly, the family escorted Ruchel to the wagon.

"Be good and listen to *Mammeh*," Ruchel said as she kissed her siblings goodbye.

Now, the saddest moment was about to take place. It was time to say goodbye to the one woman she had known and loved all of her life.

"*Mammeh*, my dearest *Mammeh*," she said with tears in her eyes, "I will miss you."

Sarah Taube gently folded Ruchel in her arms and gave her a kiss. *"Zay gezunt, myne tay'er tochter."* Be well my dear daughter.

"Don't worry, Mrs. Grazutis," Mr. Davidson said, helping Ruchel into the wagon. "I promise I'll take good care of her."

When the driver led the horses down the road, Ruchel saw her family fading in the distance. She looked away and then glanced back but by then, they had already disappeared from view. A strange feeling came over her. Will she ever see her family again?

Even though the road to Shavl was not far, it was a most unpleasant ride. The terrain was uneven, and there were many sudden jolts along the way. After traveling for some time, the driver dropped them off at the railroad depot, unloaded their belongings and wished them a safe trip.

There were many people patiently waiting by the tracks, some carrying personal items like pillows, blankets, and small pots. They too were emigrating from Lithuania with intentions never to return.

Within a short time, the train came and in less than two hours, they had arrived in Kovne, where they boarded another train, traveling west to Germany.

After being on the train for two days, the Davidsons and Ruchel had finally arrived at their destination. Mr. Davidson quickly led them toward the ship's personnel who were holding up signs showing they represented the North German Lloyd Shipping Line. They announced that anyone booked on the *George Washington*, sailing on the 17th of September, follow them onto a bus.

"We're taking you to one of our private hotels," the shipping line representative announced.

It was the practice of the shipping lines, who were taking immigrants to America, to provide their steerage and third class passengers, coming from countries in central and eastern Europe, food and housing until their respective ships sailed.

After the bus reached its destination, everyone was asked to get off and enter the building with the red sign saying, "North German Lloyd Shipping Company."

"In this hotel," the representative continued, "you will be fed and housed until your ship has docked and is ready to take on passengers for the return trip to New York. If everything goes smoothly, you'll be ready to sail on the 17th. Good luck and Bon Voyage."

"Next in line," a young man called out.

The Davidsons and Ruchel stepped forward.

"May I see your documentation?" he asked.

One by one, he went through their papers. After approving their paperwork, he handed them tags containing their names and numbers.

"Please pin the tags onto your clothing," he said, "and follow the officer to Room 1, where you will be disinfected and vaccinated."

This procedure was done to rid both the passengers and their luggage of bacteria and insects before they were allowed to mingle with those who had already been processed.

Once the Davidsons and Ruchel were finished being processed, they were told to go to Room 5.

An officer greeted them when they entered.

"You are being placed in quarantine and free to enter the main floor of the hotel, but you are not to leave the building until you are ready to board the ship. Please wait here for further instructions."

After thirty minutes, a well-dressed middle-aged woman came into the room. Her name was Mrs. Becker, and she was a representative of the shipping line.

"I will be your main contact while you're in this facility," she said, "and once you have settled into your rooms, I will take you on a tour to familiarize yourselves with the layout of the building. Please do not take off your nametags because they will be used as identification.

"You may be wondering why you were instructed not to leave the building. Since you've been disinfected and vaccinated, we want to make sure you do not catch any communicable diseases before you board your ship.

"Tomorrow, you'll go through a long process, so I suggest you retire early. I will call on you at nine o'clock in the morning. By the way, your ship is expected to arrive this Wednesday."

After taking them up a flight of stairs to their temporary living quarters, she told them they could go downstairs to the dining room and partake of the buffet. She added that breakfast, lunch and dinner would be served each day they were there.

Ruchel barely had time to put down her suitcase when Mr. Davidson knocked at the door.

"Mrs. Davidson, the children and I are hungry," he said. "Let's go down to the dining hall. And remember, be sure to come to our cabin at nine o'clock in the morning."

When Ruchel returned to her room that evening, she was surprised to see a young woman sitting on the edge of the bed. "You must be my roommate," she said and proceeded to introduce herself.

"My name is Raisa Brodsky," the young lady replied. "I'm from Stolin, Russia. I've been traveling for many days in order to get here in time for the sailing on the 17th."

"I'm glad to meet you," Ruchel said and sat down beside her. "I'm scheduled to take that very same ship. Are you traveling alone?"

"Yes. I'll be meeting my fiancé, Alfred when I arrive in America. We're to be married in New York where he lives. Where are you from?"

"I come from Shavlan in Lithuania. It's a very small town. I'm sure you've never heard of it."

"No, the name does not sound familiar."

The two women liked one another right away and after chatting for a while, they washed their faces, brushed their teeth and retired for the evening.

When Ruchel joined the Davidsons in their room the following morning, she found Mr. Davidson sitting on a chair with his legs crossed, reading the local newspaper.

Nine o'clock sharp, a knock was heard at the door. Mrs. Becker had come to take them to their medical exams. She led them down a flight of stairs and into a large room. By this time, there were many people waiting in line.

"Stay here and be ready to answer when your name is called," she said and wished them good luck.

Running her finger down a long list of names, a nurse announced, "Ruchel Grazutis, please step forward." She pulled a curtain around the examining area to create some privacy and gave Ruchel a white-checkered gown to change into.

A doctor, a short man with a shiny baldhead, wearing rimless spectacles, entered the cubicle. He did not introduce himself.

"I'm going to read off a list of ailments," he said rather abruptly. "You will answer yes or no. Have you ever been diagnosed with trachoma, tuberculosis, scarlet fever, diphtheria, heart disease, blood disorders, or any other life threatening diseases?"

Ruchel was so taken aback by his list of ailments that she didn't answer immediately.

"No," she finally replied.

"Good. It sounds as though you are quite a healthy young lady. Now I'm going to listen to your vitals."

He opened the front of her gown, allowing it to drop to the floor.

Ruchel felt awkward standing there naked and exposed.

He took her pulse, temperature, respiration rate, and blood pressure.

"So far, everything looks good," he said with a sneer. "You may put the gown back on."

What followed next was what Mr. Davidson described as the worst part of the examination.

"I'm now going to examine your eyes for trachoma. Is there any history of trachoma in your family?"

"No," Ruchel answered.

"You, of course, know this is a highly contagious disease and if found, it means immediate rejection," he smirked. "You will have to return to your country. Russia, isn't that where you're from?"

"Yes," Ruchel replied.

He told her the test was going to be uncomfortable and proceeded to roll back her eyelids, using a buttonhook, to check for the eye disease in question. Mr. Davidson was right. It was the most painful examination she had ever experienced.

"Everything looks good," he said. "You are a lucky girl."

After standing there for a moment, he took off his glasses, placed them inside the pocket of his white coat and left the cubicle.

Ruchel, from the very beginning, did not like this man's attitude. She felt he was lacking in compassion. Even though his job was monotonous, she would have expected him, as a physician, to conduct himself in a more sympathetic way and was pleased her unpleasant experience had finally come to an end.

When she returned to the waiting room, she found that the Davidsons had already finished their examinations.

"How did everything go?" Mr. Davidson asked.

"I did fine," Ruchel replied, not wanting to go into her unpleasant experience. "What about you and your family?"

Mr. Davidson smiled. "We all passed. Let's go and get some lunch. It's time to relax and enjoy the rest of our afternoon."

After lunch, Ruchel decided to go back to her room. The morning's experience had totally exhausted her, and she needed to unwind. When she returned to her cabin, she saw Raisa lying on the bed, curled up beneath the covers.

"Raisa," Ruchel whispered when she came closer. "Are you all right?"

Raisa did not answer. After a few moments, she pulled the covers away and began to cry.

"Something terrible has happened. I was coughing during the medical exam, and they told me they suspected I might have tuberculosis. I may have to go back to Russia. Shortly, I have another appointment to be retested. What will I do if the new test shows up positive? Alfred will be waiting for my call. I feel as though it's the end of my life."

At first, Ruchel did not know what to say. The way Raisa was speaking about the end of her life was upsetting to hear.

Ruchel took Raisa by the hand.

"I'm sure everything will be fine. You need to hear the results of the second test. Doctors make mistakes too."

Raisa wiped the tears from her eyes, got up, straightened her dress and combed her hair. "Wish me luck," she said and quietly left the room.

While Ruchel lay resting in bed, her eyes began to droop, and she dozed off.

"Wake up," a voice spoke softly. "I have wonderful news. I passed."

"Did I hear right?" Ruchel said, opening her eyes slowly. "Did you say you passed the test?"

"Yes. The second examination showed no signs of tuberculosis. I had just recovered from a cold last week, and when the doctor examined my chest, he heard some wheezing. After listening a few times, he concluded that the sound he heard was from the aftermath of my cold. He said I was free to go."

Ruchel put her arms around Raisa.

"I'm so happy for you. See, I told you everything would be fine."

Raisa leaned over and gave Ruchel a kiss.

"Thank you. If it weren't for you, I could never have found the courage to be retested."

It was almost five o'clock in the evening and time to meet the Davidsons for dinner.

"Come join us," Ruchel said, pulling Raisa up from the bed.

'I'll eat later," she replied, not wanting to impose.

"I would never forgive myself if you didn't come. The Davidsons are good people and would love to meet you."

Ruchel lightly knocked on the Davidsons' door.

"Come in," he said as he rose from his chair. "We were going to call for you, and who is this lovely young lady?"

"This is Raisa, my roommate. I hope you don't mind but I've invited her to join us for dinner."

Mr. Davidson took one look at Raisa. "Mind. How could I possibly mind? Now I'll be sitting with five lovely young ladies instead of four."

Deborah placed her hand over her mouth and giggled.

"By the way," Mr. Davidson added, "this afternoon, I saw Mrs. Becker in the hallway, and she informed me our ship had arrived on schedule. After breakfast tomorrow, we'll be transported to the terminal where the ship is docked. We need to pack our suitcases tonight, leaving out the clothes we'll need in the morning.

"One more thing before we eat. We'll need to answer a series of questions before we board the ship tomorrow so remember if you take your time when answering, you'll have no difficulties getting through it. Now let's go to dinner. I'm starving."

The dining hall was set up cafeteria style. There were five long tables in the center of a large rectangular room with three counters surrounding the perimeter.

One counter contained trays of cold dishes, salads, meat platters, herring, black bread and dairy products, while the second counter held all the hot dishes including soups. The last section displayed the desserts, which included streusel topped coffee cakes, pies, cookies, and containers of coffee, tea and milk.

After looking around, Ruchel spotted six empty seats.

"Let's eat," Mr. Davidson said, pointing to his stomach. "I'm getting hungrier by the minute."

"I can't wait to get to America, *Tateh*," Deborah whispered in her father's ear.

"Yes," her father replied. "Neither can your sister, your mother, nor I."

The next morning, Ruchel and Raisa had gotten up early to prepare for their departure. A few minutes before seven, they met the Davidsons' in the main lobby where Mrs. Becker was already greeting the other passengers.

"May I have your attention," she said as she stood in front of the crowd. "The buses are ready to take you to the terminal where you will go through the final procedure. Once you've passed, you'll be allowed to board the ship."

"Everybody out!" the driver announced, stopping in front of a large, flat-roofed building. There were four long tables inside with one official manning each table.

"Next in line," the examiner announced.

"That's us," Mr. Davidson said to his family.

After a while, the Davidsons returned.

"It went smoothly," he said with a grin. "It's your turn Ruchel. Don't be scared. Listen to the questions carefully before you answer."

"Next in line," the examiner announced.

Ruchel stepped forward.

On his desk was a large log called the Manifest, listing the names of the passengers sailing for the United States on the *George Washington*.

The Manifest was always filled out by the shipping company prior to sailing, on forms provided by the U.S. Immigration Service.

Every port of entry in the United States needed these documents, listing the names of all steerage and third-class passengers, in order to process them through the Immigration System.

"Good morning, young lady," the officer said. "May I see your passport, travel packet, medical examination certificate, vaccination certificate, and disinfection certificate and any other papers you may have as identification?"

"Yes, sir," was Ruchel's reply as her hands shook slightly.

After carefully going through each document, the examiner said, "I see everything is in order. I will now ask you a series of twenty-nine questions and record your answers in the ship's Manifest. You are to be truthful and answer to the best of your ability. Do you understand?"

"Yes sir, I do."

The examiner asked for her name, age, marital status, occupation, nationality and so on, until he finished asking the last question. He then scribbled some words on the Manifest and spoke again.

"I would like to inform you on behalf of the North German Lloyd Shipping Company that you have successfully answered all the questions. Congratulations and welcome aboard. Before you board the ship, you will be disinfected one last time. Please go to the sign that says: Entrance to Ship, Disinfection Ahead."

"Where is Raisa?" Ruchel asked, after joining Mr. Davidson and his family.

Mr. Davidson first looked at his family and then at Ruchel.

"Raisa has already been approved, but she had some personal matters to attend to before she went to her cabin."

After the final disinfection, they boarded the ship, which was to be their home for the next two weeks. A diagram of the ship's layout and a brief description of its amenities were presented to the passengers when they came aboard.

The ship had eight decks.

The first-class passenger section included thirty-one cabins, luxuriously designed.

The second-class cabins were decorated in a pleasant manner.

The third-class cabins were decorated in a suitable design for their class. The beds had iron frames and were arranged in two tiers. There was a mattress on each bed, along with a white sheet and a wool blanket enclosed with a bright floral cover. The sheets were always cleaned at the beginning of the voyage and were not cleaned again during the trip. The cabins were supplied with a small washbasin, towels, drinking cups, and a pitcher that was filled by a steward each day with fresh water. In addition, small tin cans were provided in case of seasickness.

The third-class dining room was called the dining salon where meals were served daily. The room held close to three hundred people at one sitting. The tables were covered with blue tablecloths and matching napkins, and the dishes were of heavy ceramic. The food was included in the price of the ticket. A steamship company with ships carrying 1,500 to 2,000 immigrants in third-class could make a profit of well over 50,000 U.S. Dollars on a single one-way voyage.

The stewards carried out their responsibilities with a good deal of attention to the passengers. They cleaned the floor in the dining salon after each meal and washed the decks and passageways between the cabins daily, but the floors in the cabins were washed and swept only as needed.

The Davidsons and Ruchel were directed down several stairs, which led into one of the enclosed lower decks where the sign in the hallway read: Third-Class Cabins 1-10 Straight Ahead.

After Ruchel unpacked, she felt tired, placed her head on the pillow and fell asleep.

There was light knocking at the cabin door. Ruchel did not answer. The rapping grew louder and it finally awakened her.

"Who's there?" she asked as she sat up in bed and rubbed her eyes.

"It's one of your roommates. Is it all right to come in?"

Ruchel straightened the covers and fluffed the pillow.

"Yes, please come in."

There, to her surprise, stood Raisa. The two of them burst out laughing.

"I never expected to see you as my roommate," Ruchel said, smiling from ear to ear.

"Neither did I," answered Raisa. "I guess it must have been *bashert* that we should be sharing the same cabin."

"You're right," replied Ruchel as she rose from her bed. "I could not have asked for a better roommate."

"Are you ready?" Mr. Davidson called from outside. "We want to go to lunch. Have you already met your roommate?"

When Mr. Davidson came into the cabin, he and Raisa broke out in laughter.

Seeing them grinning, Ruchel knew they had played a trick on her.

"I confess," Mr. Davidson said with a chuckle. "When we found out Raisa's cabin number was the same as yours, we decided to withhold the information from you. It was an unexpected surprise, wasn't it?"

Ruchel looked at Mr. Davidson. "Yes, it most certainly was and a much welcomed surprise at that."

They noticed a sign in big letters just before they entered the dining salon: KOSHER FOOD.

Mr. Davidson smiled. "I'm happy to see it. When I signed up for this ship, they said there would be an area where we could get kosher food approved and supervised by a *mashgiach*—an overseer of kosher food. I was told this was an additional feature the newer ships adopted as an incentive to entice Jewish travelers."

Ruchel and Raisa took a tray and began moving down the line. There were platters full of rye bread, jams, hard-boiled eggs, vegetables, salads, baked sauerkraut with apples, boiled fish and herring.

Next on display were desserts including coffee cakes, apple strudels, and German chocolate cakes, followed by large jugs of milk and urns full of black coffee.

"The food is quite good," Mrs. Davidson said as she spread jam on her bread. "Even the girls are enjoying the German dishes."

"Naturally, everything is good," Mr. Davidson replied. "They have to keep us happy in third-class. They make all their money from the third-class passengers and, of course, steerage.

"If we're satisfied with our accommodations, we'll recommend them to others and that's exactly what the steamship company wants. It's a business and the more people who book with this company, the quicker they fill up their ships and the more money they make.

"After we finish dessert," Mr. Davidson said, looking at his watch, "may I suggest we return to our cabins and get some rest. The ship will be sailing at six o'clock this evening and if we want to see her cast off, we should meet outside my cabin at five-thirty."

When Ruchel and Raisa returned to their cabin, they saw two young ladies huddled together on one of the lower berths.

Both women stood up.

"Hello," one of them said, offering her hand in friendship. "You must be the ladies were sharing this cabin with. My name is Feige Rowin and I'm from Kolna, Russia."

She, like Raisa, was engaged and explained she was to meet her fiancé, Jordan, at the "Kissing Post," as soon as she passed her final examination at Ellis Island.

The Kissing Post was an area on the first floor at Ellis Island and led from the Great Hall to the Social Services Area. It was a designated place to meet new arrivals and was named the kissing post because it was where new immigrants met their relatives with kisses and tears of happiness.

"My name is Becky Biegun," the other woman said, "and I'm from Slobar, Lithuania. I'm traveling with my brother, Gershom but unfortunately he's staying in steerage."

Ruchel noticed that Becky appeared to be unhappy about something.

"Is anything wrong?" she asked.

Becky sat down on the bed. "Yes, there is. Don't get me wrong. I'm very happy to be going to America but I feel sorry for my brother. Steerage is horrible.

"My parents arranged for us to live with our relatives in New York, but they only had enough money for one of us to travel in third-class. My brother volunteered to go steerage in order for me to have better accommodations.

"Now that I've seen steerage, I can honestly tell you it's terrible. He's staying in one of the large compartments where bunks are stacked up by three's along two sides of the room. The men sleep on the left side while the women sleep on the right. They're given a tin cup and plate, and their food is handed out on wooden counters."

Ruchel was puzzled and thought for a moment. "So where do these people eat?"

Becky raised her shoulders slightly.

"From what I could tell, most were eating in their berths or sitting on the floor. I'm sorry my brother has to go through this. I wanted to change places with him but he wouldn't hear of it."

The girls had no idea that steerage was so bad. They had heard stories about it and knew it was the cheapest way to get to America and agreed that before the voyage ended, they would see for themselves how horrendous the conditions were.

"Goodness, it must be close to five-thirty," Ruchel said. "We need to go. We have to pick up the Davidsons."

Within minutes, the Captain sounded a low-pitched foghorn.

The weather was quite brisk and as the ship headed toward the open sea, the women felt its gentle rocking, commenting that the air was fresh and crisp and quite invigorating.

"Let's go inside," Mrs. Davidson said, feeling as though her legs were about to give out. "It's getting chilly, and I'm beginning to feel a little woozy. I hope I'm not getting seasick so soon."

Mr. Davidson took hold of his wife's hand.

"You'll feel much better after you've eaten and speaking of eating, I do believe it's time for dinner."

Mr. Davidson always knows when it's time to eat, Ruchel thought. He never misses a meal.

Once back in their cabin, Ruchel and Raisa washed their hands and faces, drying them with one of the towels hanging on a rod and prepared for dinner.

Feige and Becky were tired, so they decided to skip dinner and catch up on some much needed sleep. After saying goodnight, Ruchel and Raisa took their purses and headed out the door.

It was dark in the hallway and while they continued walking, a man leaped out and grabbed hold of Ruchel's pocketbook. Raisa began to pound at him with her fist. Ruchel regained control of her purse and began to strike him repeatedly.

When they saw a steward at the end of the corridor, they screamed to get his attention. The attacker broke loose and by the time the steward got to them, he had escaped, heading down the stairway.

"Are the two of you all right?" he asked.

"We're fine," Ruchel answered, her voice cracking as she spoke.

"Can you make a positive identification?"

"It was too dark," Raisa replied.

The steward led them to a lighted corner of the hallway.

"You'll need to fill out a report so there will be a record of the assault. This kind of thing happens quite often during these sailings, and you should be careful not to move about the ship alone, particularly at night. It's better to travel in twos or threes. Even better, it's safer to be escorted by a male."

Most women would have lost their composure after such an experience but not Ruchel and Raisa.

"Thank you for your help," Ruchel said. "We'll be sure to pass on your suggestions."

When they met with the Davidsons, Ruchel related the incident to them. Mr. Davidson was absolutely livid on hearing the news.

He took Ruchel to one side. "I feel totally responsible for what has happened. I promised your mother I would keep you safe. I'm afraid I've failed to keep my promise."

Ruchel tried to console him.

"Don't blame yourself. You can't be with me all the time."

"Yes, but I can make sure your in your room safely each night."

After dinner that evening, Mr. Davidson and his family walked Ruchel and Raisa back to their cabin, making sure they locked the door behind them.

# Chapter 18 – Crossing the Atlantic

## 18 September 1913 – North Sea

Ruchel heard Raisa and Feige moving about.

"Are you girls going to breakfast?" she whispered. Becky was still asleep.

"Yes," answered Raisa. "Can you peak into the hallway to catch the steward's attention. We need fresh towels and water."

Ruchel opened the door slightly and looked out.

"May I come in?" the steward asked. "I'll be refreshing the water and towels every day, usually around this time in the morning."

With all the commotion, Becky had awakened. Four young women sharing a small cabin was a situation that would challenge anyone's good intentions, but they realized they were lucky to be in a private room. There were those who were less fortunate on the ship.

Before leaving for breakfast, Ruchel related to Becky and Feige the unpleasant encounter she and Raisa had had last night.

Becky turned around and placed her hand on Ruchel's shoulder.

"My G-d. Are you and Raisa all right?" she asked.

"We're both fine." Ruchel replied. "I think the attacker may have been hurt. We punched him so hard that he may have gone to the clinic to tend to his injuries. Anyway, may I suggest if you girls have any valuables, you wrap them in a handkerchief, tie it in a knot and pin it onto your undergarment."

The girls looked at each other and laughed.

"We know about that trick," they said.

They had learned about this Eastern European practice early on from their mothers and grandmothers. In the old country, this was the usual way for women to conceal their money and jewelry.

"Please remember," Ruchel added, "you have to be on guard at all times. And when you move about, try to go with at least one other person for your own protection. Are we all ready for breakfast?"

"Yes. We're starving," said Raisa and Feige.

"I'm going to wait and visit my brother," Becky replied.

While the girls made their way down the dimly lit hallway, they kept a firm grip on their purses, especially after the experience two of them had had the night before.

After breakfast, Ruchel, Raisa and Feige decided it would be a good time to explore the ship.

It was a warm September morning and the sea was without wind. Not surprisingly, the deck was crowded with others seeking to escape their tight quarters. There were people from Slovakia, Poland, Lithuania, Russia, White Russia and Germany and some were dressed in their traditional ethnic garments, displaying their own distinctive character. Many looked as though they had spent their last dime in order to make that final leap, hoping to seek a better life.

The smell of the fresh ocean air was invigorating. The girls continued to stroll up and down the teak wood deck and, after a while, found a row of empty chairs, quickly plopping themselves down.

"I can't wait to see my fiancé," Raisa said. "I miss him so much."

"How did you meet him?" Feige asked.

"We've been friends since we were children. A few years ago our friendship became serious and we got engaged. It was then Alfred decided to come to America."

"What does he do in America?" Ruchel inquired.

"He gives instruction in Hebrew in one of the leading rabbinical colleges in New York, but his dream is to study law. In fact, when he's able to master English, he intends to work his way through the educational system and go to university."

All of a sudden Raisa stood from her chair and her eyes filled with tears.

"Let it all out," Feige said. "Soon, the two of you will be reunited, and you will have forgotten all the lonely months you spent away from him."

Raisa wiped her eyes and gave Feige a smile. "You're right. Soon we'll see each other again."

The ship started to move faster as a gentle breeze began to stir. The girls were so involved in conversation, that they had not taken notice of the hour and didn't hear the striking of the ship's bell. Ruchel figured it must be eleven o'clock and suggested they return to their cabin to freshen up before lunch.

When they came close to the cabin, Ruchel saw Mr. Davidson

waiting nearby and from the expression on his face, he looked upset about something.

"Ruchel, I'm glad you're back," he said, motioning for her to open the cabin door. "Mrs. Davidson is feeling poorly, and I'm afraid being confined in such tight quarters with the children has become a strain on her. Can you take them for a while? She needs to be by herself, and the girls need some social interaction to keep them busy."

"Of course, Mr. Davidson. I can take the girls for a stroll around the deck and afterwards we'll have lunch."

"Thank you, Ruchel," and motioned for her to sit down.

"When I left for America a few years ago," he explained, "Mrs. Davidson could not deal with the girls. She stayed with my parents in Shavlan and as much as they tried to help her, it was never enough. I truly believe she was close to having a breakdown. I'm sorry to have to tell you about these problems."

"No, I'm glad you did. Now that I know, I'll make it my business to help out more."

On the fourth day, the ship made its final stop at Cherbourg, France to pick up passengers traveling to New York. The sea had become rougher but nothing to be alarmed about. The weather remained calm and the ship was making way nicely.

Ruchel, during the next few days, attended to the needs of the Davidson children from the moment they got up until their bedtime.

This afternoon Mr. Davidson called her aside.

"I'll be taking the girls at six o'clock. Both Mrs. Davidson and I would like you to take a break. I hear there's going to be music in the salon this evening. Please go with your friends and enjoy yourself."

"Are you sure, Mr. Davidson? Won't that be too much for Mrs. Davidson?"

"No. In fact, Mrs. Davidson was the one who suggested it and besides, I'll be around to help."

After spending the entire day taking care of the children, Ruchel was looking forward to the entertainment after dinner.

"Good night my sweet girls," she said as she dropped them off in front of their cabin.

"Have fun, Aunt Ruchel," they replied. They had recently begun calling Ruchel, aunt, and it did her heart good hearing them call her by that name.

After they finished their meal that evening, Ruchel and her roommates could hear music, and one could sense an air of excitement spreading throughout the third-class corridors. There were large crowds everywhere, blocking the halls and stairways, trying to get closer to the entertainment.

When they entered the hall, they noticed a young man standing on a platform holding an accordion. He was a man of short stature with hair brown in color and uncombed.

"His name is David Kosner," Becky said, glancing in his direction. "He comes from Slovakia. My brother told me about him. He met him while walking through the main deck the other day. You'll never guess how he managed to get on this ship without paying?"

The girls looked at each other and raised their shoulders slightly.

"How would we know?" Raisa replied. "Hurry and tell us."

"Well," Becky began, "my brother told me while David was in line to purchase his ticket, one of the steamship officials heard him playing. He told David that if he wanted to entertain the first and second-class passengers, the fee for his passage in third-class would be waived."

"Then why is he here and not still playing for first and second-class passengers?" Ruchel asked.

"He plays for them while they're at dinner. Later, they're entertained by a four-piece string quartet. You know how these people love to waltz.

"Once David has finished his performance, he's allowed to leave and the rest of the evening is his own. He enjoys being with people of his own kind. He said to my brother, 'Those rich passengers traveling in first and second-class accommodations are stuck-up. Just because they have succeeded in becoming wealthy, they turn up their noses at us.'"

At that moment, Becky's brother, Gershom came into the room.

"I'm glad you brought your friends to listen to David play," he said. "He's quite talented, you know."

Becky, realizing her friends had not yet met her brother, introduced them.

After a while, David stood in front of the crowd and asked for their attention.

"Hello!" he shouted in order to be heard. "My name is David Kosner, and I come from a city in Slovakia called Bratislava! I wish to play for you several melodies, some of which you will be most familiar with!"

As soon as he began playing, a loud cheer came from the audience. After many days at sea, everyone was starved for any kind of diversion. They started to clap their hands to the rhythm of the music. Many grabbed partners and began dancing. The event caused quite a stir, and it was a night thoroughly enjoyed by all.

Just as David was leaving, Gershom got his attention.

"Come and join us," he called. "I want you to meet my sister and her friends."

When David looked at Feige, he was immediately taken with her, and as she held out her hand to welcome him, he tactlessly held on. He had a blatantly flirtatious manner she found revolting, and it was obvious she had no interest in him.

The more she ignored him, the worse it got until she could not tolerate his forwardness any longer. She politely excused herself and went back to her cabin.

According to the captain's daily message, the ship was on course as she sailed the North Atlantic, heading for the United States. She had picked up speed to approximately 18 knots and the sea was comparatively calm.

Ruchel was busy most of the time looking after Sophie and Deborah, helping out as much as possible. Mrs. Davidson was regaining much of her strength and was taking part in more of the children's activities, which allowed Ruchel more time to enjoy the ship and be with her friends.

She had not yet gone down to explore the steerage section, "the hole," as it was called. Today, she had free time after lunch, while the children were taking their naps, to actually see this horrid place where it was said, "people were packed together like cattle."

Becky brought some rolls, cheese, and fruit from the dining room to give to her brother because, according to him, the meals were getting worse.

"Are you ready?" she asked, placing the food in a small bag.

Ruchel looked at her as a crinkle formed on her forehead.

"I'm as ready as I'll ever be," she replied.

Becky led the way down the stairs until they came to the steerage section.

People were packed together like sardines, and they could smell a heavy odor of rancid food and unwashed bodies. Because there were many people crammed into such small quarters with inadequate facilities for maintaining personal hygiene, it was hard for anyone to keep clean.

Ruchel could see passengers eating meals from tin mess kits and as they were eating, they were sitting on their bunks or on the floor. It was exactly as Becky described but seeing it in person made it more believable.

"I see Gershom," Becky said, waving her arm to get his attention. "Quick, let's hurry. He's putting on his shoes. He must be leaving.

"Gershom, wait!" she shouted. "I've brought you food!"

Gershom, hearing his sister's voice, jumped down from his bunk.

"I was getting ready to go on deck to get some fresh air," he said, looking a little peaked.

Becky held up her bag. "What about the food?" she asked.

Gershom frowned. "I prefer eating it on deck."

Ruchel could tell that Becky was beside herself with worry, and it was not good for her brother to see her this way. As long as his sister was in a good place, it was all Gershom was concerned about. He was big and strong and even though he was confined in such tight quarters, it was only for a short time. Dreaming about America was all he needed to keep him going.

When they walked out on deck, they immediately noticed the general mood of the passengers had changed. Some were playing shuffleboard, some were playing cards, children were throwing balls and women were knitting. It was a way for them to pass the time since there was not much to do except eat, sleep and try to keep active.

While Gershom sat on a deck chair eating, Ruchel and Becky each pulled up a chair next to him and the three engaged in conversation. The sky was clear, and the ocean sparkled in the sun and after a while, the chatter stopped. The sea was tranquil, and they had fallen asleep to the gentle rocking of the ship.

It was early the next morning and well into the second week of the journey. A covering of gray clouds marked the sky. The ship began to roll from side to side and with each movement, the sea became more aggressive.

Ruchel and her roommates were awakened by the whistling of the wind. Everyone had to hold on to the railings of their bunks to keep from falling out. It was apparent, after many days of calm weather, a storm was brewing.

"Girls," Mr. Davidson said softly from outside the door, "let's go have breakfast."

Ruchel was not at all surprised at hearing Mr. Davidson's plea for food.

"Are you sure you want to eat?" she asked. "The ship is swaying back and forth."

"That's what I mean," he replied, raising his voice slightly. "We have to move fast before the storm gets worse. Hurry and meet me at my cabin."

Ruchel and her roommates were curious about the storm and wanted to see the effects the strong winds were having on the ship. Although almost impossible, they managed to get dressed and head down the hallway toward Mr. Davidson's cabin.

Ruchel began knocking. The door flew open and Mr. Davidson rushed into the hallway, followed by his family.

"Let's get to the dining salon as fast as we can," he said. "Everyone, hold on to me."

It was a struggle but they finally made it.

"Where is everyone?" the children asked, looking around at the empty seats.

"They're probably seasick and are throwing up in their cabins," Raisa said, holding her nose with her finger.

Dishes were flying through the air, glasses were breaking as they hit the cabinet doors, and tablecloths and napkins were being tossed about everywhere.

"Quick! Let's grab some food before the entire salon disappears!" Mr. Davidson shouted.

Everyone grabbed as much food as they could and headed down the stairway, twisting and turning to avoid obstructions in their path. Finally, they made their way back and, with food in hand, disappeared into their cabins.

The storm strengthened as the hours passed. Now even Ruchel and her roommates were feeling the effects of the turbulent wind and raging sea.

"I knew we shouldn't have eaten," Ruchel said, holding her stomach.

Within a short time, their heads began to ache, and they became dizzy and sleepy. It was clear they, like all the others, were experiencing the symptoms of motion sickness and were going to be ill very soon.

"I feel like throwing up," Ruchel said as her face turned a horrid green.

Raisa, Feige and Becky joined in. They were as sick as Ruchel.

Within a few minutes, they each grabbed a pail and headed out the door and up the stairs toward the open deck.

When they reached the top, to their disappointment, the doors to the outside deck were roped off and no one was allowed to exit. This was standard procedure to prevent passengers from being washed overboard during turbulent seas.

By this time, Ruchel and her roommates knew they had no choice. Their bodies were telling them they were about to throw up and within minutes, they vomited into the metal pails.

"I feel much better," Ruchel said, wiping her perspiring brow with the sleeve of her dress.

"We feel better too," Ruchel's roommates said, happy the ordeal was over.

When they headed down the stairs, they could hear mothers' voices attempting to calm their frightened children. The smell of vomit, along with the body odor of unclean passengers, had spread throughout the third-class and steerage sections and the stench was overpowering.

It was nearly five o'clock in the evening when the worst of the storm had passed. The sea had settled down with only slight waves appearing while the ship continued its journey.

Ruchel wondered how the Davidsons had faired during the morning's excitement. It was time for dinner and as she expected, Mr. Davidson would probably want to have a good meal.

"We've been napping ever since we got back," Mr. Davidson said with a yawn as he opened the door. "When we returned to our room this morning and ate our breakfast, we came down with a case of nausea. I'm afraid the rocking of the ship had gotten to us and..."

Mrs. Davidson quickly cut in. "I remembered when I had experienced a spell of nausea last year and heard the best treatment for it was to lie on your left side with your eyes closed. So we got into our beds and in a short time the nausea was gone and because the rocking of the ship was so soothing, it put us to sleep."

"You were very fortunate," Ruchel replied. "Practically the entire third class and steerage passengers had gotten sick, including us."

"Well, now that everything is ship-shape, so to speak," Mr. Davidson said, giving Ruchel a quick wink of the eye, "are we ready for dinner? I'm starving.

"It's not bad," Mr. Davidson said, observing that the dining room was completely back to normal. The floors were swept of all debris, tables and chairs were turned right side up, and all the food that had been tossed around during breakfast was picked up and discarded.

"At least, it's in much better shape than we left it this morning," Mr. Davidson said, grabbing a tray off the shelf. "Let's see what they have to eat."

"There he goes again," Ruchel whispered to herself. "He's thinking about food so things must be getting better."

On the counter stood a medium-sized vat containing hot chicken soup, an urn filled with hot tea, saltine crackers, cheese, and a container filled with jam. The server mentioned that these items were good to eat when recuperating from a bout of seasickness and were recommended by the ship's doctor.

After finishing their dinner, Mr. Davidson and his family escorted Ruchel and her roommates back to their cabin.

The next day, it was announced by the captain that the ship was making good time, despite the storm they had had the day before. And the best news was in less than forty-eight hours the ship would be arriving in the Harbor of New York City. By now, most of the people were restless and after almost eleven days at sea, anxieties were building up among the passengers.

Early on Saturday morning and to everyone's delight, an announcement was made by the captain that a get-together for third class and steerage passengers was planned to celebrate their last Saturday on board the ship.

After the evening meal, Ruchel and her roommates went to the ship's third class entertainment salon to take part in the happy event. Tables and chairs were set up, and there were four musicians standing on a wooden platform near the center of the room.

Ruchel thought it was strange seeing David standing beside the musicians, looking as though he were part of the group.

Mr. and Mrs. Davidson and their daughters arrived and sat down at a nearby table.

"What's David doing up there?" Feige asked.

"I've heard from several people," Mr. Davidson said, "that these men are from the Ukraine and are called *Der Fraylekh Muzikers*—The Happy Musicians.

"They recently signed a contract with the William Morris Agency in New York. But unfortunately, their accordionist was rejected during his medical examination in Bremen and had to return home.

"Since they were already committed and a great deal of money was involved, the group continued with their original plan, hoping they could pick up an accordion player in America."

"So why is David among them?" Feige asked again.

"I was getting to that," Mr. Davidson replied. "It seems when David was entertaining several nights ago, one of their members happened to hear him play, and he was asked to perform for the group. They couldn't believe their ears. He was one of the most talented accordionists they had ever heard and he was offered a job."

It was a surprise to everyone, hearing the news about David. Feige was especially surprised since she thought he was wasting his time hoping to become an entertainer. Even though she thought his behavior was unprofessional and, as a result, he would be unlikely to succeed, it was obvious his talent far outweighed his shortcomings.

The bandleader began to play a short tune on his clarinet.

"May I please have your attention?" he said. "My name is Ben Kogan, and I would like to introduce you to the rest of the members of *Der Fraylekh Musicians*."

As their names were called, the crowd stood, giving each a round of applause.

"Now for your pleasure," he said, "we will perform several well known tunes."

The most beautiful sounds came out of the instruments, and everyone began clapping their hands and swaying their bodies to the rhythm of the music. After finishing, the bandleader made an announcement.

"If there are any requests, please stand up."

Ruchel slowly stood from her seat.

Hesitating for a moment before speaking, she asked, "Do you know *Der Heyser Bulgar*?"

The players huddled together. "Yes, we do," one of the members replied.

It was Ruchel's favorite tune. She had heard it played many times at various occasions in Shavlan.

After the band finished, a gentleman sitting in the back of the room stood.

"Can you play a *horah*?"

"Of course we can," replied the bandleader.

While the musicians played, men, women and children gathered in a big circle, holding each other's hands, dancing counterclockwise in a particular sequence of three steps forward and one step back.

The circle grew larger as more people broke into the line. Even Sophie and Deborah joined in the fun.

It seemed as though the dance would never end. When the music finally stopped, most of the children fell to the floor, while the adults plopped into the nearest chairs.

After the band had completed their performance, they thanked the crowd for being so gracious and in appreciation, the passengers rose to their feet, giving the musicians one last round of applause.

Immediately following, it was announced that refreshments were being served.

Gershom stood and waved for Ben, David, and the rest of the musicians to join him.

"You boys are pretty good," Mr. Davidson said.

"Thank you," Ben replied. "You obviously know good music when you hear it."

"That's a bit strong," Mr. Davidson chuckled. "I'm not an expert by any means, but I do know your kind of music is very popular in America. Most of the immigrants who have settled in the Lower East Side of Manhattan would probably pay good money to hear you play."

Feige saw David staring at her. She tried to circulate around the room but his eyes followed her everywhere. He finally cornered her near the exit.

"How are you, Feige?" he asked. "Did you enjoy the music?"

Not wanting to make a scene, Feige answered him.

"I enjoyed the band very much and wish all of you good luck. Perhaps one day my fiancé and I will be able to see you in concert."

She purposely made it known she was engaged, hoping this would discourage him from any further flirtations and to her amazement, her strategy worked. The look on David's face was priceless. This was the last thing he expected to hear.

"Congratulations," he said and quickly walked away.

After an exchange of pleasantries, the evening ended, and the steamship company's aim of providing an unforgettable celebration was achieved.

The following morning, Ruchel was the first to open her eyes.

"Girls, get up," she said softly. "We have a lot to do today. Remember, tomorrow we arrive in New York."

When Becky and Feige heard Ruchel mention New York, they jumped out of bed and began dressing. Raisa wanted to sleep a while longer, so she agreed to meet them later.

By this time, the dining salon was filled to capacity and, of course, the Davidsons were already sitting at a table.

"Come over here," Mr. Davidson called, pointing to their table. "We have plenty of room."

"Hurry, Aunt Ruchel. Sit next to us."

"Sit down and eat a nourishing meal," Mrs. Davidson said. "Please keep in mind, young ladies, we all want to be as healthy as possible for our examination tomorrow when we enter Ellis Island."

Raisa had not shown up for breakfast and the girls wondered what had happened to her.

After eating, Ruchel, Feige and Becky headed back to their cabin to pack and read the material the captain had prepared regarding their disembarkation. They found Raisa sitting on the edge of her bed.

"Where were you," Ruchel asked, observing a sad expression on Raisa's face.

"I'm sick, really sick," she moaned, her voice trembling. "When I got up this morning, I began coughing, and it went on for quite a while. As I wiped my mouth, I noticed blood on my handkerchief, so I decided to go to the nurse's station. When I got near the door, I hesitated to go in. It would not be good for them to see me this way I thought, so I came back. Tomorrow, when I get to Ellis Island, I'll have to go through the medical examination again. What if I don't pass?"

Ruchel sat down beside her. "Stay calm. Perhaps you caught a cold like you did before."

"Raisa did not answer and pulled the covers over her body.

Her roommates did not know what to say and felt bad for her.

They continued to pack and, after a while, laid themselves down on their beds and fell asleep.

It was almost five o'clock before Ruchel awoke and realized they had slept through lunch.

"Get up, girls," she said, rushing around the room. "We need to meet the Davidsons for dinner."

"You go ahead," Raisa replied. "I don't feel well."

"You have to eat something," Ruchel said. After several attempts, she finally persuaded her to get dressed and to make an appearance.

"Come, let's enjoy ourselves," Mr. Davidson said, stretching out his arms in welcome. "This is our last dinner together before we leave the ship."

Ruchel noticed that Raisa was still in low spirits and, although she was not coughing, something did not look right with her.

"Try some hot broth," she suggested.

"Thank you," Raisa replied and began to eat slowly.

After a while, Mr. Davidson pushed himself away from the table and stood.

"It's been a pleasure knowing such lovely young ladies," he said, smiling at each one of them. "May your lives be filled with happiness and prosperity, and perhaps one day we shall meet again."

Raisa reached into her pocketbook, took out a pen and a slip of paper and jotted down her fiancé's address and telephone number. "Here," she said to Ruchel, with an expression of sadness on her face. "Keep it in a safe place."

# Chapter 19 – Ellis Island

## 29 September 1913 – New York Harbor, New York, USA

Ruchel could hear the blasting of the ship's horn. She and her roommates had awakened early and were already dressed and awaiting instructions as to when they could vacate the vessel. They heard noise coming from the upper deck. When Ruchel took a peak outside, she saw people running toward the stairs.

"What's all the commotion about?" she asked.

"I heard that the ship will be passing the Statue of Liberty soon," a young girl replied, "and everyone is rushing on deck to see her."

Ruchel and her roommates set out for the deck to join the Davidsons who were among those eagerly waiting for the Lady to appear. In less than twenty minutes, a colossal, neoclassical sculpture came in view and captured the attention of the entire crowd. People got down on their hands and knees to pray to this icon of freedom.

"Thank God! Thank God!" they cried.

"There she is," an old woman said as tears flowed down her wrinkled face.

Ruchel grabbed Sophie and Deborah and placed them in front of her so they could get a better look.

The ship went up the Hudson River and docked, and the first and second-class passengers were allowed to disembark. It was not required for them to go through the inspection process at Ellis Island since it was thought because their tickets were higher priced, they would not be a financial burden on the government.

At last, it was the steerage and third-class passengers' turn to leave the ship. After returning to their cabins to get their belongings, Ruchel, her roommates, and the Davidsons headed for the departure area.

Tags were pinned on the passengers' clothing, stating their name and Manifest number, and they were given documents required for clearance. Everyone patiently waited until they were led onto a ferryboat.

As the boat moved steadily toward the dock at Ellis Island, a large building appeared. All on board disembarked and were led up a flight of stairs to the second-floor registry room in the Great Hall where medical personnel, looking for communicable diseases and physical impairments, evaluated them.

After the Davidsons and Ruchel were checked and approved, they moved to the next phase of the examination, the one feared by all the immigrants, the test for trachoma. Even though this probe was done in Bremen, one final examination at Ellis Island was compulsory.

When it came time for Raisa's physical evaluation, it was noted she was coughing and spitting up blood. The doctor placed the letter "P," which stood for possible lung disorder, in blue chalk on the front of her coat. She was then removed from the line and taken to a nearby area where a more extensive examination could be performed.

Mr. Davidson was not concerned about the trachoma test and felt it was merely a formality, since they had all passed when it was done in Bremen, but still it needed to be performed. The last phase of the examination was about to begin, the asking of the "twenty-nine" questions.

There were long tables divided into sections and behind each section sat an inspector and an interpreter who were fluent in several languages. Most of the questions were the same ones asked before such as name, date of birth, country of origin and so on. There were also several trick questions like, "Has someone in America promised you a job?" If you answered yes, you would be at risk for deportation because the immigration law prohibited the employment of anyone who could possibly fill the position of an American citizen.

When the Davidsons' turn came, Ruchel could hear one of the inspectors asking Deborah to walk over to her father. This was asked of small children to make sure they were not crippled. Sophie was asked her name to make sure she could hear and talk.

Since Mr. Davidson had been through this process before, he was well aware of the questions the inspectors would ask. Prior to the trip, he had reviewed the queries with his family and Ruchel so they would be prepared to give the correct answers.

After the last question, Ruchel could see the inspector marking each of the Davidsons' tags with a stamp of approval. Big smiles appeared on their faces. All was well with the world. They were approved to enter the country.

Now it was Ruchel's turn. Sitting beside the examining officer was a woman who appeared to be in her thirties.

"My name is Mrs. Rosen," she said. "I'm with the Hebrew Immigrant Aid Society. The officer will ask you questions and if you do not understand, I will interpret for you and will relate your answers to him."

The officer began by asking Ruchel the same questions asked of her before boarding the *George Washington*. As she answered, he checked the Manifest to make sure her responses were the same as the ones given before. He was well trained in human behavior and could tell if someone was lying. After Ruchel had answered the final question, the officer put down his pen.

"Everything seems to be in order," he said. "You are free to go."

Mrs. Rosen pinned onto Ruchel's coat a tag, noting her uncle was to meet her at the Temporary Detention Center, and she had a railroad ticket to continue on to Pittsburgh. She explained that this detention center was a place reserved for immigrants meeting relatives or needed to resolve minor problems.

"Good luck," she said, "and welcome to America."

By the time Ruchel was able to see the last of her friends being processed, she noticed Raisa being escorted down a hallway.

"They tell me I am to be deported!" she cried. "I will never forget you! May your life be filled with joy and happiness! *"Ad'yeh, myne tay'er fraynd."* Goodbye my dear friend.

Ruchel lifted her hand to her mouth and threw a kiss and within seconds, she saw Raisa, the girl she had grown to love while on board the ship, disappear through the doors of the Great Hall.

"Come, follow me," Mr. Davidson said. "I'll take you to the Temporary Detention Center to meet your uncle. He took hold of Ruchel's hand, and they all walked into a large room.

A brown-haired, dignified-looking man tapped Ruchel on the shoulder and asked her name.

"My name is Ruchel," she said, recognizing him from a recent photograph her mother had given her.

"I'm your Uncle Aaron," he said and stretched out his arms to welcome her.

"Yes," I know," Ruchel replied. "I'm so happy to meet you."

Mrs. Davidson and the children surrounded Ruchel.

"Goodbye," Mrs. Davidson said. "I wish you much happiness."

The children put their arms around Ruchel and each gave her a kiss. Lastly, Mr. Davidson stepped forward and took Ruchel's hand. "Have a wonderful life and may all your dreams come true."

"Come children," Mrs. Davidson said. "We have to hurry. We have to get on the ferry before it fills up."

Rochel watched from the hall as the Davidsons disappeared.

"Tell me, Ruchel," Uncle Aaron asked, "I understand you have a train ticket for Pittsburgh and will be living with your father's family in Ellwood City."

"Yes," Ruchel replied and pulled out the ticket and handed it to him.

"I was thinking, would you like to spend time with your Aunt Clara, Cousin Tessie, and me? Perhaps you can take an early train in the morning."

"Yes," Ruchel replied. "I would like that very much."

"Wonderful," Aaron said, taking hold of Ruchel's suitcase. "But first, before we go to the train station to change your ticket, I'll call my family and tell them to meet us at Ratner's and you'll be staying over. You'll like Ratner's. It's a nice kosher dairy restaurant."

It was almost five o'clock in the evening and as the ferry glided over the Hudson River, Ruchel leaned over the railing and looked toward the Manhattan skyline, wondering what her life was going to be like in her adopted country.

Once the ferry docked, they took a short ride by trolley to Penn Station. There, Uncle Aaron was able to book a ticket to Pittsburgh, leaving the following morning at seven o'clock.

After sending a wire to Ruchel's family in Ellwood City, telling them of the change in plans, they were on their way to Ratner's on the Lower East Side of New York.

"Welcome," Mr. Ratner said. "How many will be joining you for dinner?"

"There will be four in our party," Uncle Aaron replied. "My wife and daughter will be arriving shortly."

"And who is this lovely young lady?" Mr. Ratner asked.

"This is my niece, Ruchel. She arrived from Lithuania today. This will be her first experience eating in an American restaurant so please give her the red carpet treatment."

"What a very pretty young lady," he said. "Is she married? I know of a nice Jewish boy who is looking for such a beautiful girl."

"She has plenty of time to think about men," Aaron said, giving him a polite chuckle.

"What do you mean, plenty of time?" Mr. Ratner replied, raising his eyebrows. "The boys will soon be swarming around her like honey bees gathering nectar. I guarantee it.

"Follow me," and escorted them to an area away from the swinging doors of the kitchen.

"This table is reserved for my very special customers," he said. "I'll keep a lookout for your family."

To Ruchel, the size of the restaurant was enormous. There were so many tables and people eating and laughing as if they did not have a care in the world. It was different from Shavlan where most people were struggling to earn a living and to put food on the table. No wonder America is called the *land of milk and honey*, Ruchel thought.

"Here they are," Mr. Ratner announced, as he led Aaron's wife, Clara and his daughter, Tessie to the table.

Tessie was taller than her mother and well developed for a girl of thirteen. Her eyes were dark brown and her black hair fell to her shoulders in a mass of tangled curls. She was a friendly and outgoing young woman who was not afraid to speak her mind, one of many distinguishing characteristics of young women born in America at the turn of the century.

After hearing about the relatives from Lithuania, Clara and Tessie were excited to finally be meeting one of them. Ruchel got up and gave them each a warm embrace.

"She's lovely, Aaron," Clara said. "Your sister was right. She certainly would be the most beautiful girl in the room. We'll have to introduce her to a nice young man."

"Mother, she's been here less than a day and already you're thinking about finding her a husband. I'm sure she's perfectly capable of finding a man. Remember, she's in America now."

"It's all right, Tessie. I'm sure your mother meant well."

Aaron quickly changed the subject and called for the waiter to bring the menu.

After everyone made their selections, Aunt Clara turned to Ruchel.

"How is your mother getting along now that your father is in South Africa?"

"She's doing well," Ruchel replied, appreciative of her aunt's inquiry. "She takes good care of the children and continues to sell her baked goods at the market."

Aaron kept quiet and from his facial expression, one could read his thoughts. He felt Charles should never have left his sister and the children alone in that godforsaken place. He should have brought the family to America years ago.

While enjoying their meal, they were distracted by a commotion coming from the front door. Mr. Ratner passed their table, escorting a gentleman accompanied by an entourage of attendants. Aaron immediately recognized the gentleman. "It's Al Jolson."

Aunt Clara and Tessie stood up to catch a glimpse.

Aaron explained to Ruchel that Al Jolson was an up-and-coming

Jewish entertainer who had become very popular in the last few years, appearing in musical comedies at the Winter Garden Theater.

"You'll be happy to know he was born in Lithuania in a town called Srednik in Kovne Guberniya," Aaron said. "I had heard after his performances, he often comes to this restaurant to enjoy a good Jewish meal."

A short time later, much to their surprise, Mr. Ratner brought Al Jolson over to meet them.

"Good evening," Al Jolson said, looking in Ruchel's direction. "It's a pleasure to meet you and your wonderful family. Ratner has told me you're from my country. What do you think of America so far, my dear?"

"I've only been here less than a day," Ruchel replied, "and from what I've experienced, I'm sure I will love living here."

"Well, young lady, I've been admiring you from the very first moment I walked passed your table. You're quite a beautiful young woman. Would you be interested in getting into the entertainment field?"

Ruchel was extremely flattered and the flirtatious side of her was quickly awakened. "I'm not quite sure, Mr. Jolson. What do you have in mind?"

"Show business! That's what I'm suggesting for you and with your looks, you could go far. And if you have any talent, that's even better.

"In case you're interested, the owners of the Winter Garden are always on the lookout for attractive newcomers. Give me the word, and I could get you an interview for one of the openings in the chorus line."

Ruchel continued to converse with him regarding the possibilities available to her in the entertainment world, but the conversation was getting well over her head, and she knew she could not keep up the pretense much longer. What was this chorus line he was referring to? This did not sound kosher to her.

Meanwhile, Ruchel's uncle was growing impatient and was about to speak.

Ruchel quickly stepped in. "Thank you for your interest in me. I'm afraid I have other plans, and they do not include show business."

"Well, I tried," Jolson said, and handed her a copy of his playbill. She kindly asked for his autograph and he obliged.

"If you ever change your mind, my dear, please look me up."

Without further ado, Jolson said his goodbyes and returned to his table.

"A lot of firsts have happened to you today," Uncle Aaron said. "You've had your first American meal in an American restaurant, and now you've met your very first American performer."

"Yes, Uncle Aaron. I've already experienced much during my brief time here."

When Aaron and the family began to exit the restaurant, Mr. Ratner greeted them again, wishing them a good evening.

"Lots of luck and happiness to you," he said, helping Ruchel on with her coat. "If you're ever in the neighborhood, stop by for a bite to eat."

While they strolled amid a beautiful September evening, a pleasant, warm breeze could be felt as it gently ruffled the awnings on top of the storefronts that lined the streets of the Lower East Side.

"My house is not far from here," Aaron said and when they approached his street, Ruchel noticed a long row of buildings.

"These buildings are what we New Yorkers call Brownstones," Uncle Aaron explained. "They got their name mainly because of the reddish-brown sandstone covering the structures. Come, here we are. This is my house. Let's go in and get settled and then we can talk some more."

Ruchel was impressed as she climbed the twelve wide steps leading to the double doors of the building and thought Uncle Aaron must be rich to be able to afford such a beautiful home.

"Take off your coat and make yourself comfortable," he said and accompanied her into a large parlor off the main entrance.

"I'll go in the kitchen to make a pot of tea and prepare dessert," Aunt Clara said. "Tessie has gone to her room and will be down shortly."

"Tell me, Ruchel, what do you think of our America?" Uncle Aaron asked.

"It's beyond my wildest dream, and I have my parents to thank for making this all come true. I could not have lived in Shavlan for one more day. I hated it so."

"You mean you were that unhappy?"

"Yes, I was. I'm sure you remember what Shavlan was like when you left to come here as a young boy. Nothing has changed and, in fact, it has gotten worse. I only wish *Mammeh* could convince *Tateh* to leave South Africa and bring the family here."

Uncle Aaron pulled up a chair and, in a soft voice, began to relate his thoughts.

"When your father first came here many years ago, he tried to get used to the American way of life. But after a few years, he decided this was not the place for him. I feel bad about not keeping my promise to your mother. I should have sent for her a long time ago. Look what has happened. Everyone has gone, even Aunt Lena and Uncle Morris. And to make things worse, your father has left her alone in a country that could turn from bad to worse."

"What about me," Ruchel replied, very upset at what her uncle had said. "I was selfish in wanting to come here. I did not think of *Mammeh* either."

"That is different, my dear. Your mother always dreamed of a better future for you and had written me many times, telling me she wanted to get you out of Shavlan."

Uncle Aaron was about to continue the conversation when Aunt Clara opened the door and announced tea and dessert were being served.

"What's for dessert?" Tessie asked as she came prancing down the stairs.

"It's something special," her mother replied. "When your father called to say Ruchel would be spending the night, I thought she would enjoy tasting a traditional American dessert, so I thought of getting an apple pie. When I got to our bakery, they had sold the last one, so I had to get a Boston cream pie instead. I have since learned Boston cream pie also originated in the United States or I should say Boston. You should know, Ruchel, it's really a cake and not a pie."

Tessie began to laugh hysterically.

And because Tessie laughed, Ruchel laughed, although she wasn't sure why.

"Mother, it's still called Boston cream pie. You shouldn't confuse Ruchel or else she'll be calling it Boston cream cake."

Now even Uncle Aaron laughed.

Ruchel took one bite. "It's delicious, Aunt Clara. This is another first for me. Now I have tasted my first American dessert."

Uncle Aaron glanced at the clock, pushed himself away from the table, and took Ruchel's hand.

"We should go to sleep," he said. "Remember, we have to get up early in order for me to drop you off at the train station."

Aunt Clara and Tessie stood from their chairs and wrapped their arms around Ruchel.

"We loved having you," Aunt Clara said. "If you're ever in New York, please come for a visit."

Uncle Aaron carried Ruchel's suitcase up the stairs and showed her to the guest room. "Get a good night's rest," he said. "I'll wake you at five."

The following morning, after breakfast, a taxi drove Ruchel and Aaron to Penn Station in time for Ruchel to catch the early morning train to Pittsburgh.

"Have a pleasant trip and give my regards to the family," were Aaron's last words before the train pulled away.

Charles quickly adapted to his new life in South Africa. Chaim treated him well, and while he had hoped to uncover some business opportunities, none presented themselves.

He was unhappy that Ruchel had to be sent to America and was saddened by the fact that he was losing control over the geographic dispersion of his family. This was a constant worry to him and kept him up many nights, thinking about what he could have done to change it.

Sadly, because he was a private person, he could not share his thoughts with Chaim, his closest friend or Sadie, who had become his social companion.

# Chapter 20 – Gitka

## November 1913 – Shavlan, Kovne Guberniya, Russian Empire

Late one afternoon, Sarah Taube came into the shop carrying a letter in her hand.

"We have a letter from Ruchel," she said.

Yankel was studying with the rabbi and would be late coming home for dinner.

"*Mammeh,*" Fraida said, clapping her hands, "we can't wait to hear about Ruchel's trip."

Masha, on the other hand, seemed uninterested and walked out of the room. Sarah Taube was not at all surprised by his reaction. With each passing day, he was becoming more obstinate and unmanageable. He was an inconsiderate and self-centered little boy who, even at his young age, thought only of his own needs.

The fall sky was beginning to darken. Sarah Taube grabbed three candles and placed them in her mother's three brass candlesticks and opened the letter.

Ruchel wrote about her sea voyage, her visit with Uncle Aaron, and her new home in Elwood City. Sarah Taube's heart was warmed knowing Ruchel was happy in America and wished for Charles to come back so they could go there too.

Three months later on a cold, rainy morning, Gitka had taken ill. It was determined she had contracted diphtheria, a bacterial disease of the respiratory tract, which had been spreading among the children in town.

Since it was a highly contagious disease, usually acquired by direct physical contact, the other children were temporarily sent to live in Shidleve with one of Mr. Koppel's relatives.

Five days had passed since Gitka had come down with the illness, and by now, she had gotten worse. Gitka's breathing and swallowing became more strained. Mucous oozed out of her mouth and she could barely speak.

As she lay in bed, shivering and gasping for breath, Sarah Taube drew the covers closer to her body and placed warm compresses on her throat.

Mrs. Rubin arrived each morning to care for Gitka and today, as soon as she set eyes on her, she knew the chances of her recovery looked bleak.

Sarah Taube held her daughter's hand and stroked her forehead, but the expression on Mrs. Rubin's face told her everything she needed to know.

Sarah Taube cried, *"Helfn myne kind."* Help my child.

Gitka looked up and with her last ounce of strength, squeezed her mother's hand and then her brown eyes closed. Gitka was gone and Sarah Taube was again helpless to save a child.

Late that evening, when Mr. Koppel brought the children home, sadly, Sarah Taube had to tell them about their sister's death.

"Why did Gitka die, *Mammeh*?" Chaya asked as tears rolled down her cheeks.

"We don't know why these things happen, *myne kind*, but we must not question *der oybershter in himl,*" Sarah Taube replied, stroking her daughter's sad face.

"It's time to say your goodbyes," she said, motioning for the children to come closer. "We have to prepare for the funeral tomorrow."

Yankel could not believe Gitka was gone. They had had a special relationship and no matter what transpired, they always looked out for each other.

He kneeled beside her bed and cried.

"I will miss you, dear sister and all the ways you showed me how you cared. The memory of you will stay in my heart forever."

The following morning the burial took place sharply at ten o'clock.

While the immediate family gathered around the sacred area, Rabbi Broide recited the appropriate prayers. Then the body, wrapped in a white shroud, was lowered into the freshly dug grave and in less than twenty-four hours, Gitka had been laid to rest next to her dearly departed brother Avram.

Sarah Taube had to remain strong, especially for the children and not show her emotions. When she was alone, however, she would break down and cry, "G-d, why have you forsaken me?"

One late afternoon, Shaina came to visit.

"We do not know why these things happen," she said in an attempt to console her friend. "You have four others who depend on you and for their sake, you have to show strength in the face of adversity.

"Remember when my husband died? I will never forget when you comforted me. You made me realize, even with all the trouble in my life, I had to go on for the sake of my family, and my advice to you is to do the same."

Sarah Taube, with tears in her eyes, reached for her friend.

"I feel better now that we've talked," she said. "My children mean the world to me and they must come first."

She wiped the tears from her face and expressed her gratitude for Shaina's compassion. There was nothing that could ever break the bond these two women shared.

Sarah Taube had never written Charles about Avram's death and was well aware the longer she waited, the more difficult it would become. How could she write him about Gitka?

She decided it would be best to wait until he came home. By telling him now, it could throw him into a fit of depression.

She felt the same concerning Ruchel. Why spoil her happiness when she was adjusting to her new life. So for that reason, she decided to answer Ruchel's last letter without mentioning the tragedy that had befallen her sister.

One Sunday afternoon in June of 1914, Charles sat down to take stock of his life and what he had accomplished during the past year. He came to work for Chaim, and he was still working for Chaim. Regrettably, there had been no business opportunities which presented themselves to him that he could take advantage of.

Was the year lost, he thought? No. He learned a lot about himself and came to realize he wanted to live in a city and not a small shtetl like Shavlan. Keidan in Lithuania was the place he had in mind. There he could be a success, and he was sure his Sarala would like it too.

He heard a knock at the door.

"Who is it?"

"It's Sadie. I was visiting a friend nearby and thought we could have dinner together."

"I'm coming right out." He quickly reached for his sweater, leaving his thoughts behind.

# Chapter 21 – War

## July 1914 – Shavlan, Kovne Guberniya, Russian Empire

One summer afternoon, just before Sarah Taube was about to close her stall in the market, Mrs. Bleekman came by to purchase a loaf of bread.

"It's terrible about the assassination last week," she said.

"What assassination?" Sarah Taube asked.

"You mean you haven't heard?"

"No, I'm afraid not. Tell me what happened."

"A Bosnian Serb assassinated Archduke Ferdinand of Austria and his wife, while they were in Sarajevo. I read it in the Kovne Yiddish newspaper yesterday, but it shouldn't be of concern to us. Anyway, I thought I would mention it."

"You're right. It should not be of concern to us, but whenever things like this happen, it's never good for the Jews."

Several weeks later, Sarah Taube read in the newspaper that Austria-Hungary blamed the Serbian Government for the attack on the archduke. Austria-Hungary issued an ultimatum to the Serbian Government containing an extensive list of demands, which would effectively revoke Serbia's independence.

The demands were rejected, causing Austria-Hungary to cut off diplomatic relations, and on the 28th of July, they declared war on Serbia.

The article continued to state that because of this, a chain reaction was set off between countries that had formed alliances and were bound to defend each other if attacked.

When Austria-Hungary declared war on Serbia, Russia got involved in defending Serbia. And then Germany, seeing Russia mobilizing, declared war on Russia.

Sarah Taube was overwhelmed reading all this, and it was most confusing to her.

A week had gone by since Germany was at war with Russia. All the congregants had gathered in the synagogue for the Saturday morning service and were anxiously waiting for Rabbi Broide to finish his weekly sermon.

"In conclusion," he added, "many of you may have read in the newspapers that on the 30th of July, the Tsar instructed his military commanders to mobilize our armed forces and since then, Germany has declared war on Russia. We have to be strong and stand behind the choices our country makes, and we must be prepared to make many sacrifices.

"In the months to come, we will be asked to send our sons off to battle and perhaps to their death. May the Lord, our G-d watch over them, protect them, and bring them back safely to their loved ones."

The rabbi used a well though-out choice of words to describe what had happened that led to the outbreak of war. He did not want to convey his personal opinions of why Russia was drawn into the war in the first place because he did not want his words to be misconstrued.

On market day Thursday morning, Germany's declaration of war on Russia was barely mentioned but by early afternoon, there was a continuous buzz among the merchants, which lingered throughout the rest of the day.

Sarah Taube knew from previous readings in the Kovne newspaper there were disagreements between the German and Russian Governments. But war? She could not believe such a thing was happening.

One week later, on the 17th of August, Russia invaded East Prussia and hostilities on the Eastern Front began.

While the Western Front had reached a point where further action seemed impossible, in Eastern Europe the war continued. Russia's plans initially called for concurrent attacks on Austrian Galicia and German East Prussia.

In spite of the fact that Russia's primary push into Galicia was effective, German military leaders Ludendorff and Hindenburg, at the battle of Tannenberg and the Masurian Lakes, forced them back from East Prussia in August and September of 1914.

In Shavlan, rumors had spread that in several of the surrounding towns, representatives of the army had been sited along the countryside, picking up young men for conscription.

For many years, Sarah Taube and Charles avoided having their eldest son Yankel seen by the authorities in fear he would be placed on a list of eligible males who might be fated to enter the army one day. Now that the war had begun, she was concerned more than ever about his safety.

He had turned eighteen a few months ago and even as a young child, would spend hours in seclusion, devoting himself to academic pursuits. All of his time was committed to acquiring knowledge in as many subjects as possible in hopes of becoming a well-respected biblical scholar.

Today, because Yankel had finished his studies early, Mr. Koppel asked him to run an errand.

"You need to deliver a parcel to Count Simonis," he said, pointing to the suit hanging on a rod. "Take my horse and wagon and go to the Manor House. Mr. Sadunas, his servant, will be waiting for you.

"When you have finished, he will hand you an envelope with the payment. Thank him and come straight home. Be careful. Remember, Russia is looking for young men like you to help fight the Germans."

"Good afternoon," Yankel said politely when Mr. Sadunas greeted him at the door.

"We've been expecting you. Before you leave, the count wishes to try on the suit to make sure it fits properly."

Yankel was led into a large room adjacent to the drawing room and told to wait there. When Yankel stepped into the room, he found himself mesmerized by a portrait of an old man who appeared to be staring directly down at him. The only oil paintings he had ever seen were those in books and to see one in person completely captured his imagination.

When the count entered the room, he greeted Yankel, pointing to the painting hanging on the wall. "I see you have met my great-grandfather. They say I take after him."

"I do see a resemblance." After staring at the painting for a few moments, he said, "I've brought the suit you ordered from my father's partner. I understand, before I leave, you wish to try it on."

The count took the suit from Yankel's hands.

"This is exactly what I wanted," he replied, gazing at himself in the mirror, "and it fits perfectly. I see Mr. Koppel is a very fine tailor just as your father is. By the way, how is your father doing in uh... where was it he went?"

"Johannesburg, South Africa."

"Ah, yes. Johannesburg, South Africa."

"My father is doing well, thank you."

"Tell me, did he plan to move your family there?" the count asked, appearing unduly curious about the affairs of the Grazutis family.

"He did but due to the war, any plans he may have had were naturally put on hold."

"That's too bad, young man. I mean about the war occurring while your father was away. It looks as though all major decisions in our lives will have to be postponed until this crisis is resolved. Anyway, goodbye, and give your father my regards when next you write to him."

That afternoon, while Sarah Taube was shopping, she overheard one of the customers mentioning that several army recruiters were wandering around town, looking for able-bodied young men. Sarah Taube quickly ran home to warn Yankel. When Mr. Koppel told her he had sent Yankel on an errand, she was worried.

"He should have been back by now," she said, thinking the worse. "I must find him."

Mr. Koppel suggested she head toward the outer part of town in hopes of heading him off.

When Yankel came close to town, he grew thirsty and without thinking about the potential consequences of mixing with the locals, he pulled up at a nearby tavern. As soon as he entered the room, he knew he had made a mistake. Standing in front of a large wooden bar were two men in uniform, talking to the innkeeper.

They noticed Yankel right away.

"What's your name, age, address, and religious persuasion, young man?" one of the men asked, giving Yankel a cold stare.

Yankel became paralyzed with fear.

"Did you hear me?" the man said, addressing him loudly.

"Yes, sir," Yankel replied and proceeded to answer each of the questions asked of him, while the other man wrote down the information in a journal.

Then Yankel was handed a legal document and told to place his signature at the bottom.

"You are to report to Army Headquarters next Monday morning and if you do not report, you will face severe punishment."

Without saying another word, the men turned their backs on him and quickly marched out the door.

Yankel never intended to serve in the army. He felt no loyalty toward a Government that denied him equality and freedom so he left the inn, forgetting about his thirst, and headed back to town.

Sarah Taube, anxiously waiting near the roadside, caught sight of him.

When Yankel came closer, he pulled up hard on the horse's reins, causing the animal to come to an abrupt halt a few feet from Sarah Taube.

"*Mammeh, Mammeh.* Are you all right?" he called, leaping out of the wagon.

"I'm fine," she replied. "The horse startled me. You look terrible. Has something happened?"

Yankel embraced his mother and then told her what had taken place.

Sarah Taube could not believe what she had heard, thinking this was a bad dream. She felt she had to take responsibility for what had happened. She should have allowed Yankel to leave with Ruchel when she had the chance.

"Everything will be all right," she said and lovingly took hold of her son's hand. "Perhaps the war will soon be over and you won't have to serve in the army too long," she added, desiring to offer him a few words of comfort. Of course, she could not show how frightened for him she was.

Yankel spent Saturday morning in synagogue saying goodbye to the congregants and to the children he taught under the rabbi's supervision.

His mother had prepared a farewell dinner for him on Sunday evening and had invited Mr. Koppel, Rabbi Broide and his family, and Shaina and her family.

Yankel appeared to be in good spirits, despite the fact he would soon be entering a new chapter in his life, filled with uncertainty and danger.

After he performed the ritual for the washing of the hands and the blessing over the bread, Sarah Taube brought in a large platter of braised brisket with onions and carrots, a dish she usually made for Rosh Hashanah dinner, and placed it on the table.

"*Mammeh*, you've made my favorite," Yankel said, feasting his eyes on the table filled with food. He kissed his mother and thanked her for all she had done for him.

"Don't worry. The war can't last very long. I'll be home before you know it."

Early the following morning, Yankel left to meet the truck, which was to escort him and other draftees to the army-training center.

By this time, Russia was already three months into the war. With very little communication, except for the Yiddish papers, no one knew what was happening for sure. They only knew the war was being fought on the Eastern Front, beginning with Poland and advancing into Russian territory.

The following Thursday morning, while Sarah Taube was preparing to go to market, Mr. Koppel came into the kitchen.

He took her hand and sat her down. "I need to discuss an urgent matter with you."

Sarah Taube wondered what could be so pressing, requiring her immediate attention.

"What's wrong?" she asked, placing her bundle of baked goods on the table. "Are you sick?"

"No, Mrs. Grazutis. It's nothing like that. I must tell you, like Yankel, I've been inducted into the army. The recruiters came to my home late last night. Somehow, they had my name in their files. They questioned me and after a brief interview, I was instructed to report for training within the week. I'm sorry to have to leave you during these terrible times."

Sarah Taube rose from her chair and placed her hand on Mr. Koppel's shoulder. "It's not your fault. You have no choice. May G-d protect you and keep you safe."

That afternoon, while Sarah Taube was attending to customers at the market, she found out from some of the vendors that early in the war, Russia had invaded the German Empire's easternmost province. Almost one year later, the German army had inflicted devastating defeats on the Russian army and had occupied tens of thousands of square miles of Russian territory.

A vendor, who appeared to be knowledgeable, told her that as the Western Front settled into trench fighting, the German army on the Eastern Front was continuing to march further into Russian territory.

Recently, he learned from a soldier friend that German armies would soon be marching into many towns in Lithuania. This was very frightening news for Sarah Taube to hear. What would happen to the people once the Germans came into their towns and especially what would become of the Jews?

Shortly after the war began, Dimitri Bogdonovich was ordered by the Party to join the Russian army as an officer. The Party believed the war, which was very unpopular with the people, would lead to the revolution, and they knew they would need loyal Party members with military experience to help bring about and later preserve the revolution.

Dimitri was able to get a recommendation from a friend whose brother was a high-ranking officer in the Russian army, and in November 1914, he was commissioned as a captain and was assigned to a unit on the Eastern Front.

On a cold December evening, while returning from an officers' meeting, he noticed a soldier standing guard, leaning against a post, who appeared to be asleep. He approached the soldier and with a loud voice called out, “Attention.”

Yankel was startled at the sound of the officer’s voice and jumped to his feet.

“You know you could be shot for sleeping on guard duty,” Dimitri said in a harsh voice.

Yankel, seeing Dimitri’s insignia, knew he was in trouble.

“Yes, Sir, I know. But I’m so cold, and they did not feed my unit since yesterday morning.”

Dimitri, wondering why the soldier’s unit wasn’t being fed properly, saw he was with the Jewish company. Those Tsarist bastards, he thought. They keep the money instead of providing food for the Jewish soldiers. After the revolution, they will rot in hell. Dimitri told the soldier how to position his rifle to prevent him from falling asleep and walked away.

# Chapter 22 – Expulsion

## May 1915 – Kovne Guberniya, Russian Empire

The German Army marched into the Lithuanian towns of Libave and Rasayn—towns that were very close to Shavlan.

By order from the Russian Army Command, officials of the districts of Kovne Guberniya received the following telegram.

*All Jews living west of the line of Kovne, Yanove, Vilkomir, Rogeve, Ponevez, Posvol, Chelodz are to be evacuated by any means necessary. They are instructed to move to one of the following districts: Bakhmut, Marijupol and Slavianoserb districts of Ekaterinoslav Guberniya and Poltava, Gadiach, Zenkovo, Kobeliak, Konstanttinograd, Lokhvista, Luben, Myrhorod, Romen and Khorol district of Poltava Guberniya. With respect to the Jews living in territory currently under German occupation, this order must be carried out as soon as possible following the clearing of these places of enemy troops and the capture of them by our forces.*

On the 18th of May, Alexei Charkov, a member of the Board of Commissioners of the Kovne Regional Railroad Authority, said to his assistant:

"I have received a telegram from the High Command, stating all Jews from towns in the western part of Kovne Guberniya must be evacuated within twenty-four hours. Among the towns mentioned on the list is Shavlan. The train must pick up these Jews who will be waiting by the tracks, and they are to be dropped off at the Ekaterinoslav station in the Ukraine. We are to give this our highest priority."

"What is the reason the Jews are being deported?" the assistant asked.

"Because they have helped the Germans by supplying them with information," Charkov answered. "They can not be trusted. If I had my way, I would let them roam the countryside until they drop. Traitors, all of them. Anyway, we have our orders and have to obey them or else our heads will roll. So make the arrangements to have the proper number of railroad cars and boxcars available and map out a schedule to be followed by the engineer."

"The only train we have available is the one we assembled for the army to transport troops and supplies to the front," the assistant replied.

"I'm afraid that's the one we will have to use for the Jews," Charkov said. "We will put the men and boys in the boxcars and the women and children in the passenger cars."

Later that day, while Sarah Taube was preparing dinner, she heard loud banging on the front door. She was startled and ran to answer it. It was Shaina standing outside, panting as though a wild animal were after her.

"Hurry and let me in!" she yelled. "Have you not heard? Rabbi Broide wants all of us to gather at the synagogue?"

"Whatever for?" Sarah Taube asked, while untying her apron.

"I don't know. The rabbi never calls on us on a workday. Get your family and go quickly. When I've collected my children and sisters, I'll meet you there."

Within thirty-minutes, the entire Jewish community were assembled inside the sanctuary. It was the eve of Shavuos, the Festival of First Fruits, usually celebrated on the sixth day of the Hebrew month of Sivan, and the sanctuary was decorated with the greenery of spring.

The rabbi was standing on a platform at the head of the room, and next to him stood Mr. Kubilius and Mr. Vycas, the town administrator and police commissioner, respectively.

After observing his congregation for a few moments, the rabbi spoke.

"*Myne tay'er yiddisha menschen*—My dear Jewish people. Mr. Kubilius has informed me we are being deported from Shavlan for our own safety by order of the Army Command, and we must leave within the next twenty-four hours. This means all of us have to be out of here by sundown tomorrow evening and…"

"Any Jews," Mr. Vycas said, interrupting the rabbi, "remaining here will be punished according to wartime law, and if I do not carry out these orders, I will be dismissed from my post and put on trial."

"Mr. Kubilius," the rabbi continued, "has kindly provided horse-drawn wagons to take us to the railroad tracks south of Shavl. There, a train will pick us up and drop us off at our final destination, a Jewish community far away from the fighting. This district is called Ekaterinoslav Guberniya and is located approximately one thousand miles deep into the interior of Russia."

A buzz of murmuring voices immediately erupted.

The rabbi lifted his hands in front of the crowd and raised his voice. "Do not be afraid and, above all, do not panic. Arrangements have been made, and when we arrive in Ekaterinoslav, the authorities will make sure we are well taken care of. Now return to your homes my friends, pack a suitcase with only the essentials you will need for the trip and remember to take enough food to last you for several days. You must be ready outside your homes tomorrow morning by eight o'clock, so go and may the Almighty protect you."

Shortly after the meeting, several members of the congregation had gathered outside.

"Why are they making us leave our homes?" asked an elderly silver-haired woman. "My husband has died, and I have no children. Who is going to watch over me?"

A woman from the sisterhood tried to console her.

"Do not concern yourself," she said. "Rabbi Broide will be our guiding light, and he will keep us safe."

Another man spoke.

"This war should never have taken place. They have taken away our sons, they have taken away our homes and now they are taking away our dignity."

Mr. Zimmer, the shoemaker, made himself known. "We Jews are the scapegoats. Again, we are being punished for the wrongdoings of others. They are taking away our livelihood and moving us far away from our shtetl. The gentiles are happy to get rid of us and many of them hope we will never return. Today is a very sad day for the Jews of Shavlan."

Sarah Taube remained unflustered, mainly because she had to provide safety for her children and could not allow them to see how frightened she was.

As she began to pack, she placed into the suitcase clothing for the children and herself, non-perishable food for the long trip, a bar of soap, a small container of rose water, a blanket and the photograph of her family.

By this time, the suitcase was almost full, and lastly, she added her mother's brass candlesticks. No matter where she was, at least she would be able to light the Sabbath candles.

Where could she hide her great-grandmother's copper pot, two feathered pillows and the *Kiddush* cup she was given by Charles's aunt and uncle?

She remembered when she and Charles first moved into the house, a few of the floorboards were loose and had to be repaired. They both thought this would make a good hiding place so during the repairs, Charles secretly marked the boards. She got down on her hands and knees in hopes of finding the exact location of the wooden planks in question.

Once she found them, using a flat piece of iron, she lifted the planks to reveal a small area under the floor. And after gathering up the items she wanted to conceal, she lowered them into the hole. Then she reached for the wooden planks and carefully put them back.

A thought came to her. She still had time to compose letters to Charles and Ruchel and have one of Shaina's servants mail them. With envelopes in hand, she ran to Shaina's house.

"We think alike," Shaina said.

"What do you mean?"

Shaina flashed her letters in front of Sarah Taube's face.

"I've done the exact same thing. Hand me yours, and this evening I'll give them to Rasa. She is my most loyal employee, and I'm certain she will try her best to see that the letters are mailed.

"But now I must finish packing. Go home and care for your family. I'll see you tomorrow. *"Zay gezunt."* Be well.

Giving the house a complete going-over, Sarah Taube checked to make sure she had everything she could not leave behind, but there was something she had overlooked, Charles's sewing machine. I cannot worry about it now she thought, quickly putting it out of her mind.

The children were in the kitchen waiting anxiously for the holiday to begin.

"When can we start our celebration of *Shavuos, Mammeh*?" Chaya asked.

"Now," Sarah Taube replied, gathering her family around the table for the blessing.

Sarah Taube had prepared blintzes and sour cream for the *Shavuos* dinner and had baked a circular challah with a ladder design on top of the bread to commemorate the giving of the Torah at Mount Sinai.

"Tell us the story, *Mammeh*," Chaya asked, fidgeting in her chair.

"Yes, *Mammeh*," Fraida and Masha called out. "Tell us the story of *Shavuos*."

"All right, *myne kinder*. We observe *Shavuos* in honor of the day G-d gave the Torah to the entire Israelite nation that had gathered at Mount Sinai. On Passover, the Jewish people were freed from their enslavement to Pharaoh, and on this holiday they were given the Torah, thus becoming a nation committed to serving G-d."

Sarah Taube paused for a moment and looked at the children.

"Why do we eat dairy on *Shavuos*?" she asked.

"I know!" Chaya shouted, trying to swallow her food while she spoke. "Because when the Israelites reached their homes after receiving the Torah at Mount Sinai, they had little time to prepare a meat meal, so they put together a dairy meal."

"That's right *myne kind*," Sarah Taube replied, taking great pride in her daughter's knowledge of the subject.

"And who knows why we eat only two blintzes on *Shavuos*?"

"I know! I know!" Masha yelled, striking the palms of his hands together. "Because the two blintzes represent the two tablets of the Ten Commandments."

"Yes, *myne kind*," Sarah Taube said, a little surprised that he knew the answer.

Little Fraida was anxious to respond to a question like her brother and sister. A tear rolled down her cheek.

"Now it's Fraida's turn," Sarah Taube said, shushing the other children with a wave.

"Why is the synagogue decorated with greenery on *Shavuos*?"

"I know," answered Fraida. "Because Mount Sinai was a green mountain with trees and shrubs."

"You're right, my little one. I'm proud of all *myne kinder* today, and this tells me you are learning a lot from Rabbi Broide."

Sarah Taube knew she had to tell the children what was going to take place in the morning, and the events of that day would have a far-reaching effect on their lives. She thought about it carefully, deciding to make the trip sound more like an adventure. After all, they were still young and innocent, so why should they have to know what was going on in the world? Let them be children as long as they can, she thought. Sadly, they will soon learn about the evils of war.

That night, while the children were preparing for bed, Sarah Taube came into their room.

"*Myne kinder*," she said, untying her apron, "I know you found it strange seeing how everyone was acting after Rabbi Broide's talk."

"Yes, *Mammeh*," Chaya replied. "Tell us why the people were running around as if someone were chasing them?"

Masha and Fraida held their hand over their mouths and giggled.

"Tomorrow morning," Sarah Taube began, "we will leave Shavlan and be driven to the train tracks near Shavl, where we will board a long train and be taken to a place called Ekaterinoslav. Once we are there, a group of very nice people will pick us up and take us to a section of town where we will live for a while."

"Will anyone be there we know, *Mammeh*," Chaya asked.

"Of course, *myne kind*. Mrs. Shulman and her family, along with the entire Jewish community of Shavlan, will be coming with us."

"Hurray! Hurray!" Fraida and Masha yelled, clapping their hands together.

"We're going on a trip far away," Masha said with a silly grin on his face.

"And we're going to ride in a train," added little Fraida.

Sarah Taube's instincts were correct. It was a game to them, and they were eager to begin. She gave each child a kiss, pulled the edges of the blanket firmly under the mattress and wished them a good night blessed with sweet dreams.

Long before the clock struck seven the following morning, Sarah Taube was up. It was Wednesday, the 19th of May and the first day of *Shavuos*. After an hour, she woke the children, dressed them and gave them their breakfast.

"Chaya, take hold of Fraida's and Masha's hands," she said. "We have to leave now." She looked around one last time, grabbed her suitcase and headed out the door.

By this time, a crowd had gathered to watch the Jews being driven from their homes and, except for a few, not a tear was shed.

Within the hour the local police appeared, followed by a group of farmers driving horse-drawn wagons. Even the count had sent several of his workers to aid in transporting the Jews from the village.

Thirty minutes later, Mr. Kubilius arrived and began reading off a list of names. As each family's name was announced, they were told to sit in the assigned wagon.

After the last wagon moved out of sight, a stampede of villagers rushed toward the vacated Jewish homes, grabbing everything they could lay their hands on. Several of the locals decided to move in and occupy the empty dwellings while the police looked on, not lifting a finger to stop the looting and devastation occurring before their eyes.

The count was outraged when he saw what was happening. He owned all of the houses the Jews had lived in, and now others who had no right being there were occupying most of them. He knew he would not be getting rent from any of them and could do nothing about it since the authorities did not enforce the law, nor did the police do anything to quell the chaos. There was complete disorder and confusion in town that day.

The scenery of the rural countryside was beautiful. The temperature was warm and the cloudless sky was bright blue. Lovely violet and pink lilacs were in bloom along the side of the road and had a distinctive, pleasant fragrance that spread throughout the area. Scattered across the meadow were magnificent red and yellow tulips swaying back and forth, while a gentle breeze traveled through the air.

Sarah Taube was grateful this mass departure was occurring at this time of year. Fortunately, it was not during the dead of winter when they could be traveling through terrible snowstorms or life-threatening blizzards.

"When will we get to the train?" Chaya asked, grabbing onto the side of the wagon.

"We will be there soon, *myne kind*," Sarah Taube replied, holding on tightly to her suitcase.

The noon hour was approaching and the children were hungry.

"When can we eat, *Mammeh*?" Masha asked with an impatient look on his face.

Sarah Taube promptly reached into her suitcase and pulled out six slices of bread, along with three slices of cheese and made each a sandwich.

"Let's pretend we're having a picnic," she said, attempting to engage them in an activity. The children responded favorably. They began eating and laughing as though they did not have a care in the world. To them it was an event from which they derived enjoyment, which was all Sarah Taube could hope for.

Although she too was hungry, she chose to eat very little. She knew the food had to be rationed because she was not sure how long it would last, once they began their journey.

Three hours had passed, and they had arrived near Shavl. When the wagons lined up alongside the track, Rabbi Broide quickly jumped down.

"May I have your attention, please!" he shouted, in order to be heard over the crowd. "Everyone, when getting out of the wagon, remember to take your suitcases and all of your possessions! I'm not sure how long it will take for the train to arrive!"

The group did exactly what the rabbi asked, and within minutes, the drivers, without as much as a good-bye, turned their wagons around and headed back to town, while the Jews looked on in despair.

After a while, Rabbi Broide, the *rebbetsen*, and his two young sons walked over to Sarah Taube and her family. Sarah Taube could not help but notice one son was carrying a large bundle under his arm. Rabbi Broide saw Sarah Taube staring at the package.

"I've put my son in charge of the Torah Scrolls," he whispered.

"He will make sure they are protected until we can return them to their rightful place." Rabbi Broide was not going to leave them behind for the gentiles to desecrate.

While Sarah Taube stood by the railroad track, holding her youngest child in her arms, she wondered how she was going to cope with all the uncertainties that lie ahead.

"Sarah Taube! Sarah Taube! Make room for us!" a voice shouted.

She could see Shaina and her family heading toward her.

"Come over here!" she yelled, waving her hand.

Sarah Taube was happy to see that Shaina and her family had placed themselves close to her and her children. With no husbands to help them, it was comforting to know they had each other.

To make themselves comfortable, many of the adults either sat on their suitcases or stretched out on the grass. Young mothers held their babies tightly, while the older children kept busy playing games. And as a diversion to while away the long wait, the old men grouped together and prayed.

After some time, many of the people grew restless, wondering if the train would ever come. There was even talk of going back to the shtetl. Rabbi Broide begged them not to act hastily.

"We are instructed by the authorities to wait here!" he shouted. "We cannot go back to our homes! Please keep in mind this situation will soon change for the better!"

"The train is coming! The train is coming!" yelled a woman carrying a small child.

Rabbi Broide again faced the crowd.

"Please stand away from the railroad track! When the train comes to a stop, then you may line up!"

Within a few minutes, the train came roaring in. One could hear the brakes being applied, bringing it to a screeching halt. There were at least eighteen passenger cars and twelve boxcars pulled by a steam locomotive.

A tall, fat man, dressed in what looked like a worn out Russian uniform, appeared from the platform of the first passenger car.

"Hello to all of you!" he shouted. "My name is Egor Barosky, and I'm here to conduct an orderly transition of you Jews and to see that everything runs smoothly!"

After pausing for a moment, he reached into his briefcase and pulled out some papers. "When I call your name, gather your family, along with your belongings, and enter the car assigned to you! Women, children and the elderly will board the passenger cars! Men and young boys, age fifteen and over, will board the box cars at the end of the train!"

An old woman raised her hand. “Why are they putting our men and young boys in boxcars?” she asked.

Mr. Barosky gave her a sneer before he spoke.

“There are not enough passenger cars to accommodate all of you because we have to pick up more people along the way.”

Sarah Taube Grazutis and family!” he shouted, after running his finger down a long list of names.

Sarah Taube held on to Fraida with one hand, while clutching her suitcase with the other. “*Cum kinder*,” she said, motioning for Masha and Chaya to follow.

Shaina led the way with her family, and within the hour, all three hundred people had come aboard. The long journey was about to begin.

The cars were in poor condition. Large mounds of dirt were piled on the floor and many of the seats were torn. It looked as though they had been used for hauling cattle instead of human beings, but this did not bother the children. Never having been on a train, their cheeks were flushed with excitement, and after running back and forth and up and down the aisle for a while, they began to tire. It was time for them to have their supper and go to sleep.

Along the way, the train stopped several times to pick up Jews who were expelled from other shtetls, and each time the train stopped, the people were awakened by the noise, allowing no one to get a good night’s sleep.

The following morning, the train approached the Vilne Station where the old crew was being replaced with the next shift. Word had spread among the Jews of Vilne that there were evicted Jews from the Guberniya of Kovne on board, so the Jewish families from Vilne contributed as much food as they could spare.

The passengers were allowed to leave the train and gather up the provisions, which were so generously donated. Fortunately, their anxiety had been lifted, knowing there would be additional nourishment to sustain them for the remainder of the trip.

When the train continued to pass through the stations in the larger towns, Rabbi Broide noticed thousands of soldiers camped alongside the tracks and on the depot platforms. This gave him the impression that the Russian Army Command was more concerned about deporting the Jews, whom they considered collaborators with the Germans, instead of moving these badly needed soldiers and supplies to the front.

Later in the day, after everyone had finished their evening meal, some of the children grew restless. They were running up and down the aisles, uncontrolled by their mothers.

Mrs. Pinkus, a religious middle-aged woman, was fast asleep in one of the seats several rows in front of Sarah Taube and her family.

While a little boy was playing in the passageway, he spotted something that looked like a brown stuffed animal. Innocently, he grabbed hold of it and began tossing it up and down, playing with it as if it were a ball.

Mrs. Pinkus woke up because of all the noise the small child was making. Then she let out a scream.

"Stop him! Stop him!" she yelled. "He has my *shaytl.*" He has my wig. The little boy had lifted her wig right off of her head. The child became frightened and began running down the aisle, dangling the wig behind him.

Mrs. Pinkus started to run after him. By the time she caught up with him, she was breathing heavily. The boy ran into his mother's arms and began crying because he had no idea why this crazy woman was chasing him.

"Your son has taken my *shaytl* and should be spanked for being so bad!" Mrs. Pinkus yelled, trying to grab the wig away from the child's hand.

"I apologize," the mother said, handing her back the wig, "but my son is a child and was only being playful."

Mrs. Pinkus left in a huff, whispering under her breath, "The boy was very naughty and most certainly should have been spanked."

Wearily, another day was coming to an end as everyone settled in for the night.

The next afternoon, an announcement was made, commenting that the train would be stopping shortly at a junction in order to service the locomotive, and everyone would be able to get off to stretch their legs.

Rabbi Broide again took the opportunity to address his people.

"We are entering the third day of our trip, and you will be pleased to know we are almost at the end of our journey! The engineer has informed me that we will be arriving at the station in Ekaterinoslav within a few hours! When you hear the engineer sound the whistle, you'll know it will be time to exit the train, so gather up your belongings, take hold of your children and wait for further instructions from me!"

When Shaina heard the news, she got up from her seat and wrapped her arms around Sarah Taube.

"Thank G-d it's almost over," she cried. "I could not have stood it one more day."

"Neither could I," Sarah Taube replied. "With the stench of unwashed bodies and the screaming and yelling, my nerves could not have taken it much longer. Even the children were becoming unmanageable. I feel sorry for the women and children who had to sleep on the floor because the government did not provide enough cars for them. Let's hope and pray Ekaterinoslav will be a good place for us."

◄O►

When Dimitri was ordered by the Party to join the Russian army, he surprised himself by his ability to adapt to military life, and after a short time, he was transferred with his unit to a section of the Front, which was experiencing heavy Russian casualties.

One day, he was ordered to interrogate a group of German officers who had recently been captured. One of the German officers, he had learned, was the son of an extremely wealthy industrialist, and during his cross-examination, Dimitri became enraged at the officer's smug superiority. In a fit of rage, he shot the man at point-blank range right between the eyes.

In order to avoid the same fate after witnessing what had transpired with their fellow compatriot, the remaining German officers spoke out, divulging all of the German army's secret battle plans, and as a result, Dimitri was promoted to major and reassigned to the general's staff.

# Chapter 23 – Ekaterinoslav

## May 1915 - Ekaterinoslav, Ukraine, Russian Empire

When the train came to a stop, Rabbi Boride appeared.

"People of Shavlan! After your name is called, please move to the front of the platform!"

As soon as Sarah Taube and her family climbed down from the train, waiting wagons took them, along with others, to a Jewish Community Center set up as a temporary facility to house refugees. Upon their arrival, they were ushered into a large room with a high ceiling.

"May I please have your attention," a woman called out. "My name is Mrs. Ellis. I'm from the Jewish Society of Ekaterinoslav. I'm here to take down information about you and to find you a job and a place to live. Please step forward when your name is called."

When Sarah Taube's turn came, she answered the questions asked of her, stating she was a baker by trade.

"A baker," Mrs. Ellis said. "You have an excellent skill. I'll send your paperwork ahead to our Work Committee but in the meantime, I have assigned you and your family to Room 23. Bear in mind that this place will be a short-term location. Later, someone from the Work Committee will get in touch with you to arrange a meeting and go over your qualifications. Please give this form to Mr. Jaslow, the man seated outside. Do you have any questions?"

"No," answered Sarah Taube, "and thank you for your kind assistance."

"It's my pleasure and good luck," Mrs. Ellis replied, anxious to help the next family standing in line.

"What number are you?" a voice called. It was Shaina and her family waiting in the hallway.

"Number 23," Sarah Taube answered, happy to see a familiar

face.

"Good," Shaina replied. "Our room is a few doors away."

Mr. Jaslow, a middle-aged man wearing glasses, stepped forward.

"Welcome," he said. "I'll take you to your rooms, and after you've unpacked and rested, I'll give you a tour of the building. Please be aware, at seven o'clock this evening, an informative meeting for our new arrivals will be held in the main hall on the ground floor."

After going up a flight of stairs, Mr. Jaslow stopped in front of Room 23. He unlocked the door and stood aside to allow Sarah Taube and her family to enter. The room was small but it was neat and tidy. There were two beds with clean sheets and blankets and a washbasin in the corner.

"You'll find the bathroom at the end of the hall," he stated and handed the key to Sarah Taube. "I'll be back in a hour for your tour."

Sarah Taube looked at the children and smiled. "We'll be staying here for a while," she said, placing her suitcase on the floor. "Remember when I told you this was going to be an adventure? Has it been fun so far?"

Chaya looked at her brother and sister before she spoke. "Yes, *Mammeh* but this room is so small and what will we do here?"

"We'll only be here a short time, *myne kind.* After I find work, we'll be moving to a much better place. You'll see. Now rest for a while. After I finish unpacking, we'll go visit Shaina and her family."

Chaya wrinkled her nose. "Can we see Shaina and her family now?" she begged. "We're too excited to sleep."

"All right," Sarah Taube replied, realizing she felt the same way.

Shaina was happy to see that her friend was in such good spirits. She made a point of telling her about the modern bathroom in the hallway with toilets. "And there are sinks with hot and cold running water," she added. "It makes me realize how backward Shavlan is."

"This is a very big city," Sarah Taube replied. "No wonder everything is so modern compared to Shavlan."

An hour passed, and it was time for Mr. Jaslow's guided tour. By now, Sarah Taube, Shaina and their families were quite anxious to see the rest of the center.

Mr. Jaslow led the group down the steps to the first floor, pointing to the parlor off to the side of the main entrance. "Please note this room is only to be used when you have visitors and need privacy."

He took them through two double hung doors, which led to the community kitchen. "Here you can prepare your meals. As you can see, there's a wood-burning stove, a double sink and a cupboard full of dishes. This building is well equipped to provide shelter for more than fifty families and it's now full.

"Lastly, through the generous donations from the Jewish community, several of the Jewish charities have provided food for those who occupy this institution and platters are brought in daily. The only thing we ask of you is to be respectful of others who live here. Have a good evening, and I hope your stay will be a pleasant one."

That evening, as the clock struck seven, Sarah Taube and her family arrived for the scheduled meeting. A small group had already gathered. Once everyone was seated, Mrs. Ellis, who was standing at the front of the room, spoke. "Good evening, ladies and gentlemen. Welcome to Ekaterinoslav. I hope you have found your accommodations adequate. This meeting is to tell you a little about our city and to help answer your questions.

"Let me begin by telling you that Ekaterinoslav was founded in 1773 and named after the Russian Empress Catherine the Great. Fifteen years later, the Empress granted full citizenship to Jews in this region and because of this decree, the Jewish population increased rapidly.

"The Jewish merchants were very active in the growth of the city, and within a few years, thirty-five percent of the city's residents were Jews, owning close to a quarter of Ekaterinoslav's businesses. The town continued to grow. Now we have a population of more than 210,000, with Jews comprising around 38,000."

It was clear to Mrs. Ellis, from the whispering chatter she heard around the room, that no one had expected the city to have such a large Jewish population. She waited for the chatter to stop before she continued.

"Due to our large Jewish population, you'll be happy to know we have many synagogues spread throughout the city and several large Jewish communities who are willing to give you jobs and provide you with housing. Does anyone have any questions?"

One elderly man raised his hand.

"I ran a butcher shop in my town before the war. How can you provide for my livelihood?"

"You have asked a very good question. You will stay here until our Work Committee finds you a place in our community, hopefully doing similar work."

After taking several more questions, she reassured them there were good Jews in the city who were prepared to help.

A week later, while Sarah Taube was tending to the children, she heard someone at the door. When she answered, she saw a short, thinned-faced young man, dressed in a navy-blue suit, carrying a black briefcase.

"Hello, my name is Saul Lerner. I'm from the Work Committee. I believe you were told by Mrs. Ellis we would be contacting you to discuss your placement in our community."

"Yes, I've been expecting you," Sarah Taube replied, hopeful a job had been found for her.

"Can I get you a cup of tea before our meeting?" she asked.

"Just a glass of water, thank you."

He took off his jacket and put it on the seat next to him, placing his briefcase on the floor, under his seat. After taking a sip of water, he reached into his briefcase and pulled out a notebook.

"I've brought some good news. There's an opening for a baker, and you're being considered. But first, let me tell you about the position. Then you can decide if it's something you would be interested in.

"We've been communicating with a very nice woman named Fanny Bressler who has lived in Ekaterinoslav for many years. When her husband passed away last year, she found it difficult to run her bakery. She's looking for someone with baking experience who could help her with the day-to-day duties, both in preparing the baked goods and making sure the operation runs smoothly."

While Mr. Lerner continued to describe the qualifications, Sarah Taube's eyes lit up.

"I see you're interested," he observed.

"Yes, I am."

"I'm glad to hear it," he replied, pleased that perhaps he had found a well-qualified applicant. "I'll make an appointment for you, and when the arrangement is finalized, I'll let you know." He thanked her for the water and politely left.

Sarah Taube was excited and ran down the hall to tell Shaina the news.

"That's wonderful," she said, wrapping her arms around Sarah Taube. She suddenly let go and asked, "But why didn't he come and see me too?"

A few days later, Sarah Taube noticed a note sticking out through the crack at the bottom of the door. The note was from Mr. Lerner, stating he had arranged a meeting with Mrs. Bressler the following Wednesday at three o'clock in the afternoon. He included Mrs. Bressler's address, along with directions.

When the day of the meeting arrived, Sarah Taube was excited. After coming out of the public washroom with a towel wrapped around her head, she reached into her suitcase and pulled out a bottle of rose water.

Slowly, she combed the rose water through her long brown hair as she had done many times before, and, with a single motion, pulled her hair tightly into bun, neatly centering it on the back of her head, securing it with two straight pins.

"How do I look?" she asked Shaina who had come in to give her approval.

"Turn around slowly so I can inspect you from all sides. Everything looks good. Don't worry about the children. I'll take care of them. Now go to your appointment, *"zol zayn mit mazel."* Should be with luck.

The bakery was not far, and while Sarah Taube walked, she noticed many businesses on either side of the road.

As she stood outside the shop, looking into the beautifully decorated window, she paused for a moment before she entered. A tall, attractive woman appeared who looked to be in her early sixties. Sarah Taube noticed her body was slim, but her arms were quite muscular, a trait often found among bakers.

"You must be Mrs. Grazutis," the woman said. "I'm Fanny Bressler, the owner of this shop. I've been expecting you."

When Sarah Taube looked around, she noticed that the interior of the bakery was long and narrow. The room contained two glass display cases, a large wooden icebox, two cast iron wood-burning cook stoves, three baking tables, two hand mixers, and several wooden racks. It was the most up-to-date bakery she had ever seen.

"I was having my afternoon tea. Would you like to join me?"

"Yes, I would," Sarah Taube replied, gladly accepting the invitation.

"Please follow me," Mrs. Bressler said and led her through the shop and up a flight of stairs. "There are three rooms on this level," she pointed out. "This room is my parlor. I wanted a place where I could relax and receive guests when the bakery is closed. Come, sit on the sofa beside me."

The sofa was elegant with bright pink and yellow flowers resting on a cream colored background. Mrs. Bressler began to pour hot tea from a beautiful, white porcelain teapot into two matching teacups that were sitting on a silver tray on top of a small table. On the table she had placed two oval dessert plates, two forks, and two white linen napkins.

"Excuse me for a moment," she said and got up to leave. Within a short time she returned, carrying a platter filled with an assortment of pastries, a sugar bowl, and a silver container filled with fresh cream.

"Do you take cream and sugar?" she asked.

"Yes. I would like two sugars and a smidgen of cream," Sarah

Taube replied, quite impressed with the fineries displayed before her.

While they both sat, enjoying the refreshments, a pleasant and relaxed feeling came over them.

Later, after they finished eating and were feeling comfortable with each other, Mrs. Bressler asked, "Are you ready for our meeting, my dear?"

"Yes," Sarah Taube replied, wiping her mouth with a napkin.

"Let me tell you a little about myself," Mrs. Bressler began. "When my husband, Jacob was alive, I employed two young men as apprentice bakers. Jacob took care of the bookkeeping and deliveries, while my employees and I did the baking and selling. We had no children, so the bakery was our life.

"Last year, when my husband died, I was devastated. Also, around that time, both of my bakers were conscripted into the army. I tried running the business by myself, but I found it hard to keep my head above water with all the tasks to be done. Talk about trouble, I could not have asked for more, so that's why you're here today. I need someone I can rely on to help me run the bakery."

Mrs. Bressler turned her chair around and faced Sarah Taube.

"Now that you've heard my story, unfortunate as it is, please tell me about yourself. What experience have you had as a baker? I would also like to know a little about your life before the war."

Sarah Taube began by telling her of her mother's passing when she was a child, about her aunt and uncle raising her and that they too owned a bakery. And it was through them she had acquired all of her baking skills. She spoke about her marriage, her children and her husband's departure for South Africa in 1913.

"You mean your husband left you alone with the children?" Mrs. Bressler asked, raising her eyebrows.

"Well, he had had plans of opening his own business and sending for us but due to the war, his plans were interrupted."

"I see. Go on, my dear."

"There's not much more to tell. Shortly after the war broke out, we Jews were expelled from Shavlan and you know the rest. So here we are, along with others, driven from our homes."

Sarah Taube spoke simply and directly.

"I need this job," she said, trying not to sound as if she were begging. "I have a family who depend on me to make their lives as happy and meaningful as possible. If you think you would be satisfied with my work or at least want to give me a chance, I would appreciate it."

After digesting it all, Mrs. Bressler stood from her chair.

"I'm glad you want the position, and it sounds as if you could be a great help to me. But I need to delay my answer because I never make important decisions until I've thought it over for at least a day. I'll let Mr. Lerner know my decision by tomorrow afternoon. Thank you for your time."

Just before Sarah Taube left, Mrs. Bressler shook her warmly by the hand and whispered softly, "Now listen carefully. I want you to be very cautious when you go back to the center. It's late and there are many strange and perhaps dangerous people wandering about, especially with the war going on."

The interview had taken almost three hours, and it was six-thirty when Sarah Taube returned. When she came closer to her room, she could see Shaina standing nearby with her arms folded.

"I've been waiting for you. How long does an interview take? I was afraid something terrible had happened."

The following morning, Sarah Taube awoke early. She couldn't sleep, wondering about whether or not Mrs. Bressler had decided to hire her. After providing amusement for her family for most of the afternoon, she and her children returned to their room. By now, they were exhausted, so the children took a nap. Sarah Taube was about to doze off herself when she heard someone at the door.

"Mrs. Grazutis, I'm here with Mrs. Bressler. May we speak to you?"

Sarah Taube whispered, "My children are napping. Let's meet downstairs in the parlor."

At the beginning of the meeting, Mrs. Bressler sat, letting Mr. Lerner do the talking.

"Mrs. Bressler tells me she had a nice conversation with you and is impressed with your experience. She especially admires you for being such a strong and assertive young woman.

"About the employment. She is offering you a position, and since she lives alone, she would like to share her home with you and your family. Of course, it will be rent-free and..."

Before Mr. Lerner had a chance to continue, Mrs. Bressler interrupted.

"I will share the kitchen with you and your family, my dear. I want you to know the two rooms in the back, which are adequately furnished, will be occupied entirely by you and your children.

"With regard to the compensation, I'll give you a small weekly wage. As the business grows and you prove to be an asset to me, your pay will be increased accordingly."

A smile crossed Mrs. Bressler's face.

"What do you think of my proposal?"

Sarah Taube turned to Mrs. Bressler. "Thank you very much for your generous offer, and I gladly accept."

Then the two women reached for each other and embraced.

"This, I believe, seals the agreement," Mr. Lerner said, delighted with the outcome. "It's a verbal agreement between two honest and well-respected women, and it gives me great pleasure to have placed one more family into a fine home."

He wished them good luck and politely excused himself.

"Would you like to meet my little ones?" Sarah Taube asked.

"Of course," Mrs. Bressler replied.

"Come with me. I believe they should be up from their nap by now."

She took hold of Mrs. Bressler's arm and led her up the staircase to the second floor. When they approached Room 23, she could hear movement coming from inside.

Sarah Taube slowly opened the door and peeked in.

"I want you to meet Mrs. Bressler," she announced, motioning for the children to come closer. "We're going to live with this nice lady, and I'll be working in her bakery, just as I told you I once did with Aunt Lena. Please give Mrs. Bressler a nice welcome."

Chaya rose from her bed and politely said, "My sister, brother, and I are very happy to meet you."

Mrs. Bressler reached into her bag and pulled out three chocolate sweet cakes and handed one to each of them.

"What do you say?" Sarah Taube asked.

They all replied, *"A sheynem dank."* Thank you very much.

Sarah Taube, when hearing the children's response, was very pleased. She was certain they would say the right thing because she always taught them to be polite and respectful, especially to their elders.

"Your children have excellent manners, and I'm sure we will all get along fine. I'll send my driver at seven in the morning. Be sure to be on time. He has some early deliveries after he drops you off."

At seven o'clock the next morning, Mrs. Bressler's driver knocked at the door.

"We're ready," replied Sarah Taube, anxious to leave the premises. "*Cum kinder*," she called. "This nice man is taking us to our new home."

It was a typical June morning. The temperature was warm and a light rain began to fall, but it did not spoil the excitement seen on the children's faces.

While the horse trotted through the wide tree-lined streets of the business section, the city appeared to be flat. A few blocks into the ride, Mr. Primakov, the driver, pointed to an elegant synagogue.

"It's called The Golden Rose. We have several other synagogues scattered throughout the Jewish section, but this one is thought to be the most beautiful of them all."

After traveling a short distance, Sarah Taube noticed a large, brown wagon loaded with soldiers, and when she looked closer, she saw each had received some sort of injury. Two were lying on stretchers, while the rest had bandages either wrapped around their heads or around their arms and legs. Mr. Primakov said they were being taken to one of the local hospitals.

"The boys are coming back from the front with horrible wounds or sometimes even in pine boxes," he said. "It's the springtime of their lives. They should be enjoying themselves, not participating in a conflict that was not of their making. Our boys are dying at an alarming rate, both Jews and gentiles. When will this madness end?"

Sarah Taube agreed and was ready to tell him what she really thought of the war but not knowing him very long, she thought it would be wise to keep her opinions to herself.

She began thinking about her Yankel. In fact, one of the young men in the wagon could very well have been him. Her eyes began to fill with tears. She turned her head away so the children would not see her crying.

"Whoa!" Mr. Primakov shouted, as he pulled on the horse's reins. "We've here."

A large sign hung over the front door, "Fanny's Bakery Shop."

"Look at all the sweet cakes in the window," Fraida called out. "Is this where we're going to live, *Mammeh*?"

"Yes, *myne kind.* All of you may get down from the wagon and be careful not to dirty your shoes. I don't want you bringing mud into Mrs. Bressler's shop."

She thanked Mr. Primakov for dropping them off and wished him a good morning.

The warm comforting aroma of freshly baked breads wafted from the front door. When the door to the bakery opened, Mrs. Bressler greeted them with a smile and welcomed them into her home.

"I have some good news," she said. "I've arranged for the children to attend Hebrew school at the local synagogue.

"Beginning this Monday morning, at eight-thirty, a wagon will pick them up and bring them home at three o'clock in the afternoon. I'm sure they're anxious to continue with their education and make new friends.

"By the way, we have a large synagogue here in town, and it's only a few blocks away. You'll be happy to know our Rabbi Silver has invited your Rabbi Broide to teach Hebrew to the community's children. You must have passed the synagogue on your way here."

"Yes. Mr. Primakov pointed it out. It's wonderful how the community has accepted so many of our people from so many of the shtetls in Lithuania. Thank you for arranging the children's schooling. They're very eager to start, and they'll be happy to have our very own rabbi as their teacher."

"I think," Mrs. Bressler added, "since we'll be working together, we can be on a first name basis, so please call me Fanny. But the children, of course, will continue to call me, Mrs. Bressler.

"Now you can show your family your living quarters so they can familiarize themselves with their new surroundings. You'll have to go through the bakery to get there."

Sarah Taube led her family through the bakery, through the kitchen and into the first room at the far end of the house. This was Sarah Taube's room. It was exactly as Mrs. Bressler had described and was more than adequate for her needs.

Chaya looked around before she spoke.

"Where will we sleep, *Mammeh*?" she asked, seeing only one bed in the room.

"Don't worry, *myne kind*," Sarah Taube replied, asking the children to follow her as she led them to the room next to hers. "This will be your room," she said, noticing a sigh of relief on Chaya's face, realizing her daughter had thought they were all going to share the small bed in her room.

When Sarah Taube returned to the shop, Mrs. Bressler had already tied back the white-laced curtains covering the store front window. It was nine o'clock and Fanny's Bakery Shop was now open for business.

"Usually, my customers start coming at nine-thirty or ten, which gives me enough time to display my goods. By the way, the bagels will be ready to come out of the oven in a few minutes, so watch them carefully."

Mrs. Bressler had a reputation to uphold and told Sarah Taube she would rather throw out something than offer it for sale if it did not meet her standards.

As Fanny predicted, within thirty minutes, the first customers arrived. Fortunately, they came at intervals, which allowed Fanny plenty of time to discuss Sarah Taube's duties.

"I'm very strict about keeping proper records," she said, "and I never rush any job. My motto, "haste makes waste," is one I have lived by for many years. We do not want to squander our profits through negligence."

That afternoon, the shop closed early. It was Friday and time to prepare for the Sabbath. Sarah Taube thoroughly enjoyed her first day. She and Fanny had their own set of tasks, and each demonstrated a strong sense of duty.

A week later, Mr. Lerner visited Shaina to inform her that positions had been found for her and her sisters. The military was setting up an Army Training Base near the outskirts of town, and they were hiring civilians for various jobs. He said there would be three paid positions and would they be interested?

Shaina looked at her sisters and nodded.

"Yes," she said. "When can we start?"

"Wait," Mr. Lerner said, holding up his hand. "Don't you want to know about the jobs?"

"Of course." Shaina replied. "What do we have to do at this Army Training Base?"

"It will be a strenuous job. You and your sisters will have to prepare and serve three meals a day to a group of hungry young soldiers. I must emphasize, this will not be an easy task. Are you still interested?"

Shaina again looked at her sisters.

"What do you think?" she asked.

"We need to discuss it," one of them replied.

They left the room and after fifteen minutes, returned.

"It's an undignified position, but we have to find work, and we need to get out of this building and settle into the community. If this is all we're being offered, we accept. Perhaps we'll be able to find something later, which would be more to our liking."

Shaina thought for a moment.

"But where will we live?" she asked.

"I have good news. A highly respected couple has volunteered to give you lodging in their home. They are offering you and your family four rooms to live in, rent-free."

Shaina and her sisters took a deep breath.

"Thank you so much, Mr. Lerner," Shaina said.

"You need not thank me. It gives me great pleasure to find homes for you."

After Mr. Lerner left, Shaina and her sisters admitted they felt insulted. They were respectable townspeople from Shavlan, well-established business owners, and long time natives of Lithuania, who were being offered work well below their social and economic status.

It was humiliating for them but, given the recent events, they had no choice but to accept their fate. Things could be a lot worse. At least they had jobs and a place to live, provided by well meaning people. It was truly a blessing in disguise.

The war was not going well. By the end of June 1915, the Russian army suffered over one million casualties. The war was unpopular. Shortages were becoming more frequent and not a week went by without a workers' strike over unpaid wages or working conditions.

# Chapter 24 – Mrs. Bressler

## July 1915 – Ekaterinoslav, Ukraine, Russian Empire

As the weeks went on, Sarah Taube and her family had gotten used to their routine and quickly acclimated to their new surroundings. Even though they were displaced persons, they had no choice but to go about their daily activities, trying to get some normality into their lives.

Each evening after dinner, the children would settle down and either play games or study for the next day's lessons. Sarah Taube would clean up the kitchen and give them their baths, and, of course, they would want a bedtime story. She, tired as she was from her daily duties at the bakery, always gratified their wishes.

"Now *myne kinder*, what would you like to hear this evening?" she asked, hoping to gather up enough energy to last until the end of the tale.

"*Mammeh,* please tell us the one about the war and the soldier," Chaya said with a twinkle in her eye.

At first, Sarah Taube did not recognize her daughter's request. After a while, it came to her. It must be the one about the Grazutis' ancestors during the Patriotic War of 1812. She had not told the story for a very long time. In fact, only Chaya would have remembered it because the others were not even born when last she spoke of the old family legend.

The children jumped into bed, eagerly waiting for their mother to begin.

"Many years ago, another war, very similar to the one we're having now, was started by a man called Napoleon. Napoleon, who was from France, was a very famous general and had won many battles and after some time, decided to invade Russia.

"The Russians fought very hard to defend their country just as they are doing now fighting the Germans. While the French soldiers marched through Vilne, retreating from Moscow, they fought battles in towns nearby. And one of the towns they went through was near our home in Shavlan.

"On a cold winter day, a relative named Itzak Grazutis was outdoors chopping wood for the fireplace. When he looked around, he noticed a man, in uniform, lying on the ground. He was moaning quietly and appeared to be in a great deal of pain, so Itzak carried him into the house.

"Esta, his daughter, was frightened when she saw her father carrying what looked to her to be a wounded soldier. She asked her father what had happened, while she helped him place the injured man on the bed. Her father said he had found him lying nearby, and they needed to tend to his wounds."

"Did the soldier die?" Masha asked.

"No, *myne kind*," Sarah Taube replied. "Let me continue."

"Itzak could tell, by the young man's uniform, he was one of Napoleon's men. Earlier that day, he had heard rifle shots and cannons going off, and it was obvious to him fighting between the Russian and French soldiers were taking place close by.

"When the soldier awoke that evening, Esta was looking after his wounds. She brought him some broth and began spoon-feeding him. He was still very groggy and did not speak. After sitting up for a while, he dozed off and did not wake up until the following morning.

"After several days of constant care, the soldier got stronger. When he was able to speak, he thanked Esta and her father for taking care of him. He told them, as they had already suspected, he was in the French Army. He said the war was not going well and Napoleon's army was retreating, and many of his comrades were being killed and left by the roadside.

"Sometime during the retreat, he felt a sharp pain to his shoulder and a sudden blow to his head, and it was all he could remember until he woke up and found himself in a strange house. After thinking about what had happened, he grew very angry, realizing the men in his regiment had left him behind, not bothering to see if he were alive or dead."

"That's not right for the soldiers to leave the hurt man and go away," Fraida said in a sympathetic voice.

"*Mammeh*, please go on with the story," Masha called out.

"Now *kinder*, try not to interrupt.

"Just as the soldier stated, he could not remember anything after he was knocked out until he woke up and saw a beautiful young girl taking care of him."

"That beautiful young girl was Esta," Fraida said, again interrupting her mother.

"Yes, *myne kind*.

"The soldier told the family the war had become more violent and men were leaving their units and deserting at an alarming rate, and he knew if he returned to his regiment, he would be dead within a short time. So he made up his mind he was going to desert and asked if he could stay with Itzak and his daughter."

"*Mammeh*, what does desert mean," Masha asked.

Sarah Taube smiled at her son. "Desert means the soldier did not want to be in the army anymore and ran away.

"Itzak Grazutis, a very kind and gentle man, who thought all war was evil, agreed to let the soldier stay. The soldier, who was quite handsome, developed a deep affection for Esta, and Esta felt the same about him. Within a few months, he asked for her hand in marriage, and they lived happily for the rest of their lives.

"I want you to know, *myne kinder*, this story happened over one hundred years ago, and our family has handed it down over many generations. Whether it is true or not, I cannot say, but I think it's a very good story to tell. When you're married, you can pass the legend on to your children, and they can pass it on to theirs and so on."

"I love the story, and I will remember it always," Chaya said.

Masha did not say a word. Deep down, Sarah Taube could sense, although he did not want to admit it, he also was fond of the story.

"I'm glad you enjoyed hearing the family folk tale. Now my dear ones, you must go to sleep. Tomorrow is a school day." She tucked them in, wished them pleasant dreams and gave each her usual kiss and hug good night.

Fanny's Bakery was doing well now that Sarah Taube had been hired. Even though there was another bakery nearby, Fanny's customers were very loyal and patronized only her establishment.

Along with the bakery, Fanny owned several rental properties and was considered a fairly wealthy woman among her Jewish counterparts. When her husband died, she decided not to sell the properties because they would provide her with a good income, in addition to the bakery.

Because Fanny needed financial and legal advice in running her affairs, she hired Mr. Aaronson, an accountant, who was also an acquaintance of her late husband.

He, a short, partially balding man in his mid-sixties, came over every Sunday to go over the books and to prepare legal documents.

Sarah Taube could tell their relationship was amicable. Recently, she noticed he, a widower without children, was coming around more than usual. Fanny was oblivious of his presence and thought he was only coming in to have a cup of tea or to buy some pastries. He was, after all, a business associate of hers.

One warm day in August, while sitting in the park, Sarah Taube overhead two men talking about Mr. Aaronson. Obviously, they knew him and, even though she tried not to listen to their conversation, it was impossible for her not to hear what they were saying.

"Did you know, Mr. Aaronson is going to marry that rich woman, Mrs. Bressler very soon?" one of the gentleman said.

"No," answered the other man. "Isn't she the one who owns a bakery and some properties?"

"Yes, she's the one. I heard from someone at work that he has gotten himself into several bad investments, and he needs a good deal of money to help him get out of a sticky situation."

"Mrs. Bressler is a good catch," the other man said. "I hear she's loaded and probably would be willing to marry him just to have a man around."

Then the two men roared with laugher.

What was Sarah Taube to do? Should she tell Fanny what she had overheard? After giving it serious thought, she decided to say nothing for the time being. Hopefully, Fanny would realize Mr. Aaronson's advances toward her were suspicious, and the matter needed further looking into.

The following Sunday, Mr. Aaronson came by and presented Fanny with a bouquet of red roses and, after chatting for a while, invited her out to dinner. When Fanny returned, she asked Sarah Taube to join her in her parlor to share a cup of tea.

"Sarah Taube, I've experienced something rather strange this evening. Mr. Aaronson asked me to marry him. He said he had admired me for many years, and he could not control his feelings any longer."

"What did you say?" Sarah Taube asked, holding her breath in anticipation of the answer.

"At first, I was speechless. I thought to myself, why is he proposing to me? I told him I was surprised to hear his proposal and inquired if there was anything going on in his life I needed to know. After pausing for a few moments and feeling ashamed, he told me the truth. He said he had made some bad business deals and needed money to help him recoup his losses."

"So what did you say?" Sarah Taube asked again.

"I said, although I appreciated his help in the past, I could never marry him and his actions toward me were humiliating.

"If he had come right out and told me of his circumstances, perhaps I may have helped, but because he was totally dishonest with me, I could never forgive him. I made it clear, I didn't want to be involved in any further dealings with him. He stood there with his mouth open, so I left the restaurant, hailed a carriage, and returned home."

Sarah Taube did not have to ask any more questions. Fanny had handled the situation with considerable aplomb.

By now, Fanny and Sarah Taube had developed quite a close relationship. During their afternoon breaks, they would often discuss the latest rumors and unofficial information regarding the war. In reading the newspapers, it was difficult to determine what was true and what was not.

"Have you heard anything more about the war and how it's progressing?" Sarah Taube asked late one afternoon, over a glass of tea.

Fanny sat back in her chair and crossed her arms.

"It's difficult getting any news," she replied, offering Sarah Taube a tray full of pastries. "I haven't heard much at all. Have you heard anything?"

"Well, I did hear something last week," Sarah Taube said, choosing a slice of apple cake. "After services, Rabbi Broide told me he had heard that Russia had retreated into Galicia this past spring, and in August, the central powers had advanced into Poland's southern frontiers and seized Warsaw.

"His sources told him Russia was compelled to withdraw from Poland, and the German army now occupied the northern and western parts of Lithuania. You know what that means, don't you?"

"No. I'm not quite sure," Fanny replied. "All this talk about military maneuvers confuses me."

"Well, I'll tell you what it means. It means the Germans have occupied parts of Lithuania, and they are probably in my Shtetl, Shavlan. No wonder they wanted to get rid of the Jews."

Fanny put down her glass of tea. "You know, my dear, it turns out that you and the children are better off in Ekaterinoslav after all. Fate has strange ways of changing one's life, doesn't it?"

"You're right," replied Sarah Taube. "It certainly does."

"Did the rabbi have any more news?" Fanny asked.

"He didn't, but it doesn't look good for Russia."

"No, it doesn't. We should never have entered this war. It has spread so rapidly that now practically the whole world is involved. I hope it ends soon for everyone's sake."

Before Sarah Taube fell asleep that night, thoughts of her husband, Charles and daughter Ruchel kept gnawing away at her, and she wondered if her letters had ever gotten to them. A lot had changed in her life during the past few months and felt she was not the same woman she was before she and her family were uprooted from their home. Did Charles change too, she wondered, and if ever they were reunited, would their marriage survive?

With all the decisions she had to make without her husband, she realized she no longer needed a man to tell her what to do. She continued to hope Charles would not be successful in South Africa, and when he returned home, he would accept the idea of relocating the family to America.

She also thought about Ruchel. Was she as happy as she was when she first arrived in America?

# Chapter 25 – Rose

## August 1915 – Ellwood City, Pennsylvania, USA

Ellwood City, a small community, thirty miles northwest of Pittsburgh, was a typical town in America and had a fairly large number of Jewish Lithuanian inhabitants or Litvaks, a term Jews typically called each other who were from that area.

Charles's Aunt Hannah and Uncle Lazer had settled in the town and quickly adapted to their new environment. Charles' sister Freida had enrolled in the local night school. She learned English and received a good education, experiencing, first hand, the American way of life.

Aunt Freida had a steady boyfriend named Garson Rodner, whom she had met while attending night school. He was from a town near Shidleve and had left for America several years before her. They had recently become engaged and were planning to marry within the year.

Ruchel quickly adjusted to her new surroundings and, with Aunt Freida's assistance, enrolled in night school.

After a while, Ruchel changed her name to Rose, a more American name. She felt she needed to do this in order to more easily assimilate into American society. To avoid confusion by her family in Lithuania and South Africa, to them she still referred to herself as Ruchel.

Rose was worried about her family in Lithuania, especially with the war going on so close to Shavlan. She and her father continued to send letters, but they never received any in return, causing them much distress. She and her aunt would often go to meetings held by various Jewish organizations, where the main topic was the war and how it was affecting the Jewish population in Europe.

One Sunday morning, Rose, after she had finished eating breakfast, decided to take a stroll through the park. The day was warm and sunny and the park was crowded. After a while, she heard someone shouting her name. When she looked around, she saw Aunt Freida and Garson heading in her direction, accompanied by a young man.

"We would like you to meet someone," Garson said, pushing the stranger in front of her. "This is my friend, Herman Brason. Herman has been in the country for less than a month. Say hello to him."

"Glad to meet you," Rose said reluctantly.

This man was so shy that he began stammering over every other word. She was put in an awkward situation, and it was embarrassing for both of them. After making idle conversation, she excused herself and went home.

Aunt Freida and Garson were determined to find Rose a marriageable young man, but she did not want any part of it. She was going to find a husband all by herself. This she knew from the very first day she arrived in America.

That evening, during dinner, she made it perfectly clear to them.

"It's only a matter of time before it happens," she said, placing a spoonful of vegetables onto the plate in front of her. "I truly know in my heart, he's somewhere out there waiting for me to find him."

A week later, while Rose was attending a Jewish gathering, a nice looking young man with wavy brown hair sat down beside her, and she could see from the corner of her eye, he was looking in her direction. Being the outspoken young woman she had become, she turned toward him and began to speak.

"My name is Rose and what's your name?"

"My name William Krause. He immediately rose from his seat, shook hands with her, and sat back down.

"What brings you here today?" she inquired. "Are you looking for lost relatives in Europe?"

"No," he said smiling. "I've come with some friends. We're interested in learning about the war and the Jewish situation in Europe."

When Rose heard the sound of his voice, she could tell he was an American and, in her newly acquired language, told him about her family in Lithuania.

"I've lost touch with them for many months," she said.

A smile crossed William's face. "My cousin is an attorney. If you wish, I could speak to him about your situation."

Rose returned his smile. "I would appreciative it very much, and perhaps he can let me know how I can further pursue this matter?"

William was attracted to this beautiful young girl, and since she agreed to meet his cousin, it meant he had an excuse to see her again. Before they parted, he asked for her address and said he would get in touch with her.

After a few days, Rose received a note from him inviting her out to dinner the following Saturday and felt it was only proper to ask for her aunt and uncle's permission.

"You are a grown woman," Uncle Lazer said, sitting Rose down beside him, "and certainly old enough to make your own decisions. The only thing your aunt and I request of you is to have your young man call for you at the house so we may meet him. It's not considered respectable, even in America, for a gentleman not to call on a young lady at her home."

Almost immediately after the clock struck seven-thirty Saturday evening, the doorbell rang. William, who was carrying a bouquet of red roses, was greeted by Freida and led into the living room. Aunt Lena made the introductions and offered William a seat.

"Tell me, William," Uncle Lazer asked, "are you a native of Ellwood City?"

"Yes I am, sir. My family and I have lived here all of our lives."

Before the conversation went further, they could hear Rose coming down the stairs. As she entered the room, there was a certain glow about her, and William could not take his eyes off of her.

"Did you meet my family?" she asked.

"Yes, I did," he replied, handing her the roses. "Roses for my beautiful Rose," he said.

Rose blushed, not being used to American men and their informal manner.

Aunt Hannah took the flowers from Rose's hands. "I'll put them in a vase," she said, thinking Rose had found herself a very nice young man.

William reached for Rose's arm, escorting her into his automobile, and, as he took hold of the wheel with both hands, tried hard not to stare at her, while he drove away.

"I've eaten at a wonderful steakhouse that opened last month," he said, "but before I take you there, I'm curious to know if you keep kosher. If you do, we can go to a kosher restaurant nearby."

"My family keeps kosher. When I lived at home, I observed the Jewish dietary laws. Now that I live in America, I want to try all kinds of food."

"In that case, we'll go with my first choice," he replied, taking his eyes off the road for a brief moment.

The restaurant was elegant with a brass and crystal chandelier hanging from the ceiling, and while Rose listened to William speak, she felt as though she had always known him.

"All the food here is excellent," he said, pointing to the menu. "What would you like?"

"I'm not sure, but since you've eaten here before, why don't you choose for me?"

"I think you'll definitely like the house specialty, filet mignon. It's the tenderest cut of beef from the end of the tenderloin, and trust me when I say it literally melts in your mouth. I usually get a baked potato with sour cream and chives and a salad along with it. Is that agreeable with you?"

"Yes, but promise not to tell my family I have indulged in eating the meat of a non-kosher animal. They would most certainly neither approve nor understand."

William gently put his arm around her. "My family are second-generation Jews born in the United States, so they have already assimilated into the country's culture and adopted its customs and attitudes. Don't worry, your secret is safe with me."

After William placed their order, he moved his chair close to Rose and took hold of her hand. "Let me tell you what my cousin said regarding your family. He thinks the best way to get information would be for you to write our congressman, asking him to look into the matter through the proper channels.

"He suggested it would be beneficial if an attorney would write the letter on your behalf because that would carry more weight than if you were to do it yourself. He said he would be happy to represent you at no cost as a favor to me."

"That's very gracious of your cousin," Rose replied. "When can we meet?"

"I'll arrange a meeting for the three of us and let you know."

Their first date could not have gone better, William thought. After arriving back at Rose's house, he brought the car to a halt, switched off the engine and gently helped her out.

"Don't forget about our meeting," he reminded her, leaving her at the front door. "I'll let you know the time and place."

When Rose said good night to William, she thought, I could really settle down with this man. He's exactly what I've been looking for.

The following Monday, a note arrived from William, stating that a meeting had been arranged on Thursday evening at seven at a local coffee shop.

After arriving on Thursday, Rose saw William sitting at a corner table, accompanied by a man who looked to be in his mid-thirties.

He was tall and broad-shouldered with a rather kind-looking face, and, as she approached the table, he and William got up to greet her. William pulled a chair up for her to sit in and introduced his cousin, Michael.

"Would you like a cup of coffee before we start?" Michael asked.

"No thank you. I'm fine."

"In that case, let's get started. From what I understand, you haven't heard from your family in a very long time. As I told William, the first thing we should do is to contact the congressman from our district. I can write him, acting on your behalf, if that's all right with you?"

"Certainly," Rose replied.

Michael pulled out a notebook from his briefcase. "I'll need your family's name, address and when you last heard from them, so I may incorporate it into my letter."

After Rose related the particulars, Michael took a few moments to write down his thoughts.

"There, I'm finished. Let me read it to you."

*August 19, 1915*
*Congressman Henry Wilson Temple*
*U.S. House of Representatives*
*Pennsylvania's 24th Congressional District*
*Washington, D.C.*

*Dear Sir:*

*I have been engaged by Miss Rose Grazutis of Ellwood City, Pennsylvania who resides in that place and who is very desirous of information about her mother and siblings.*

*The name of my client's mother is Sarah Taube Grazutis, and she lives in the town of Shavlyany, District of Shavli, Kovno Guberniya, Russian Empire. Her last letter from her mother was dated the 26th of March 1914, and she has not heard from her since.*

*If you make inquiries about these people and inform me of the result, I will consider it a very great favor.*

*Yours very truly,*
*Michael J. Krause, Esquire*

Michael placed the letter and pen down on the table. "What do you think, Rose?" he asked.

Rose smiled the smile she used when she knew she was being given special attention. She liked the idea of William and his cousin taking such an interest in her.

“It sounds good,” she replied. “Thank you for taking the time from your busy schedule to help me.”

“Your perfectly welcome. My goodness, look at the time. I have a very busy day at the office tomorrow and need to head home to get some sleep.”

When William walked Rose up the steps to her house that evening, he asked, “Would you like to see a movie this Saturday?”

“Yes, I would like to very much,” Rose replied, handing him the keys to the front door.

Rose and William’s relationship had gotten off to a good start, and during the next few months, they were seeing each other on a regular basis.

One Sunday evening, while they were out to dinner, Rose realized she didn’t even know what William did for a living. Not wanting to appear nosy, she very tactfully asked if he liked his boss.

“Of course, I like my boss. He’s a very smart man.” Then William began to laugh.

Rose thought he was acting a bit strange.

“Let me explain,” he said, trying very hard to control his laughter. “I was waiting for you to ask what I did for a living, and I was going to tell you tonight.”

Rose looked at William. “What’s so funny?” she asked.

“I’m sorry for my odd reaction to your question. When I finish telling you what I do for a living, you’ll understand why I find it so amusing.

“When my father passed away a few years ago, I inherited a large produce and flower market. It’s a very popular place among the ladies. Forgive me for laughing when you asked if I liked my boss.”

“Now I understand why you found it so funny,” Rose replied, looking somewhat embarrassed.

Then they both began to laugh. William had made a small joke about liking his boss, and Rose finally caught on that he was the boss.

Several weeks later, William contacted Rose, letting her know that Michael would like to meet with them at the coffee shop on Thursday evening at seven.

“I have some encouraging news,” Michael said, when he greeted Rose and William. “Congressman Temple has sent a reply to my letter. He has written to Robert Lansing, the Secretary of State, giving him the information about your family.

“In his letter he states that Robert Lansing has sent two letters, one to the American Embassy in Petrograd and the other to Charles S. Wilson, the American Charge d’Affaires in Petrograd. In these letters, he's asking them to make the necessary inquiries and report back to him regarding their findings.

"You remember the incident concerning the Secretary of State, don't you, William? Lansing replaced William Jennings Bryan who resigned a few months ago over what he believed to be President Wilson's overly aggressive stance to the German sinking of the Lusitania."

"Yes, of course I do. As I recall, Secretary Bryan resigned in protest of President Wilson's allegedly hawkish approach to U.S. neutrality."

"That's right. By the way, I'm very pleased the State Department has gotten involved, but I suspect we may have to wait to hear any news because this next course of action will take quite some time to sort out, especially since there's a war going on.

Michael quickly looked at his watch. "If we're finished with our meeting, I need to leave. Tomorrow is Friday, and I have litigation early in the morning. I'll let you know when I hear more.

"Oh, by way, one more thing before I go. Have you read the latest article about what's been happening in Russia?"

"No, I haven't," William replied. "I've been busy at work, and I haven't had time to catch up with the news."

"It's been reported that Tsar Nicholas had taken over the command of the Russian armies because he was dissatisfied with their conduct of the war."

"I guess he thinks he can do a better job than his own military generals," William replied with a sneer.

"And my family," Rose added, glancing at William and Michael, "is caught up in all this chaos."

Over the next three months, Rose continued to see William. She was in love but wondered what William's intentions were. Even Aunt Hannah, Uncle Lazer, and Aunt Freida were curious to know where the relationship was going.

One evening, on their way back from a movie, William asked Rose if he could come in. While sitting on the sofa, he pulled her close and gave her a kiss. This was not his usual kiss, but a long and lingering one. He placed his hands around her waist and looked into her eyes. "Before I met you, I never realized how empty my life was. I've loved you from the moment we met, and I hope you feel the same about me. Will you make me the happiest man alive and do me the honor of becoming my wife?"

Rose smiled and, without even hesitating, replied, "yes, I will, sweetheart. You don't know how long I've been waiting to hear you say those words."

William thought for a moment. "There's one more thing I need to do before we make our engagement official."

"What do you mean?" Rose asked, looking somewhat confused.

"Since your parents aren't here to give their approval, I'll have to ask your aunt and uncle for their permission."

"Oh, your right. I didn't think of that. Come for dinner next Sunday at seven. I'll tell them you have something you wish to discuss with them."

"By the way," William added, "I've spoken to my mother about my intentions, and she can't wait to meet you. After I speak to your family, I'll arrange a meeting between the three of us."

It was Sunday, the 21st of November 1915, a very important day in Rose's life. Preparations were being made for the dinner, which was to be served that evening. Aunt Freida had invited Garson, thinking it would be a good opportunity for him to get acquainted with Rose's young man.

The front doorbell rang at one minute past seven. It seems William and Garson had arrived at the same time.

"Welcome, gentlemen," Aunt Hannah said, introducing the two of them. William handed Aunt Hannah a beautiful arrangement of cut flowers and thanked her for the invitation, while Garson, politely waiting his turn, gave her a bottle of very fine wine.

"What a lovely surprise," she said and led them into the parlor, motioning for them to sit on the large overstuffed sofa next to Uncle Lazer.

After a brief pause, Uncle Lazer got up from his seat and handed each a cup of punch, while Aunt Hannah passed around napkins and a silver tray filled with her tasty fried artichoke hearts.

"I think our guests have arrived," Aunt Freida announced, peering over the banister on the second floor.

"Yes, I hear them talking. I hope Aunt Hannah and Uncle Lazer are not giving away all of our secrets."

They both began to giggle like they were schoolgirls huddled in a corner. After a while, they made their entrance. William and Garson politely stood to acknowledge the young women's presence.

"Now that you girls are here," Aunt Hannah said, slightly perturbed that they had taken so long, "I can begin serving dinner."

After dessert, Aunt Hannah suggested they retire to the parlor.

Uncle Lazer turned to William. "I understand you wish to discuss something with us."

This was William's cue. He stood, facing Uncle Lazer and Aunt Hannah.

"From the first day I met your niece, I knew something important had occurred in my life. We both enjoy the same things, and when I'm with her, my heart fills with happiness. I love her and want to spend the rest of my life with her, so I'm asking your approval for her hand in marriage."

Uncle Lazer turned toward Rose. "Before your aunt and I give our answer, what have you to say regarding William's proposal?"

Rose suppressed her smile for a moment before she spoke. "I've been very lonely since leaving my family, but when I met William, my loneliness disappeared. I can honestly say, I truly love him and want to be his wife."

This was exactly what Aunt Hannah and Uncle Lazer wanted to hear, a declaration of love and commitment from the two of them. They looked at each other with smiling faces. "Then we give our consent," Uncle Lazer said. "Congratulations to the happy couple."

At that moment, William stood in front of Rose and got down on one knee. "My sweet Rose, I love you very much." He reached into his pocket and pulled out a small, red velvet box. "Will you give me the honor of becoming my wife?"

"I will," she said, holding out her left hand.

William carefully opened the box and took out a gold ring set with a single diamond and gently placed it on her finger. They both embraced and then a cry of Mazel Tov surrounded the room.

"William has made me very happy tonight," Rose said, while a teardrop fell from her cheek. "If only I knew my family were safe. This would make me the happiest girl in the world."

Aunt Hannah took hold of Rose's hand. "I'm certain you will see them again, my dear. We will pray for that day, *halevay*." It should only happen.

The next morning, after clearly composing the letter in her mind, Rose wrote to her father, telling him of her engagement. She asked him to please come to her wedding and escort her down the aisle.

Several days later, Rose received a note from William, stating that Michael had heard from Congressman Temple and to meet them at seven o'clock on Thursday evening at the usual place.

Although Rose was a few minutes early, William and Michael were already seated in the corner when she walked in.

"Would you like a cup of coffee," William asked, helping Rose off with her jacket.

"Yes, thank you," Rose replied, placing her purse on the table.

Michael stood from his chair. "William has told me the wonderful news. May I offer the two of you my heartfelt congratulations?"

"Thank you, Michael," Rose replied, giving William a smile.

"And may you find someone as wonderful as my Rose," William

said, "but I think I've gotten the last beautiful Rose ever made."

"What a sweet thing for you to say," Rose replied.

Michael, not a man to make small talk, sat down, reached into his briefcase, flicked it open, and pulled out one of three letters.

"Let's get down to why we're here today. I know you've been waiting patiently to learn about your family. Before I go any further, I'm going to read the communication I've received from Congressman Temple.

*November 27, 1915*
*Michael J. Krause, Esquire*
*75 East Avenue*
*Suite 105*
*Ellwood City, Pennsylvania*

*Dear Mr. Krause:*

*With regard to your letter dated August 19, 1915, the findings of the investigation by the American Charge d'Affaires in Petrograd of your client's inquiry, relating to the Grazutis family who resided in the town of Shavlyany, District of Shavli, Kovno Guberniya, Russian Empire state that, after an investigation, they have learned that the Jews in that area have been relocated by the Russian Government, and that their whereabouts are unknown.*

*Following, regarding this matter, are copies of the two letters my office has received, one from Charles S. Wilson, American Charge d'Affaires, Petrograd and the other from the Secretary of State, Robert Lansing.*

*Yours very truly,*
*Henry Wilson Temple*
*Congressman*
*24th Congressional District*

When Rose heard the news, she nearly spilled her coffee. She and William stared at each other, unable to believe what Michael had just read.

Michael looked at the two of them. "I must tell you that the other two letters contain the same information, so I won't waste your time reading them."

There was complete silence after Michael finished speaking. They knew no more than they knew before they began the inquiries.

Rose turned to Michael. "You mean to tell me after all the investigations, they could not find out any information about my family?" she asked, her voice quivering as she spoke.

Michael took hold of Rose's hand. "With the war going on and all the confusion and turmoil surrounding the countries involved, I'm sure it was difficult to find out anything about anyone who was caught up in it. We're lucky to have received a response at all."

Rose looked at Michael with tears in her eyes. "Thank you for all the time and support you've given me," she said, realizing he had done all he could.

"Don't be discouraged," Michael replied, trying to give Rose some encouragement. "Perhaps one day we'll be lucky enough to find out more."

William placed his arm around Rose's shoulder and wiped away her tears. "I'm very sorry, Rose. I only wish I could have helped in some way."

Then the three of them finished their coffee in less than a cheerful manner and sadly, the meeting came to an end.

# Chapter 26 – A Secret Place

## November 1915 – German Occupied Shavlan, Kovne Guberniya, Russian Empire

With the Germans advancing on the Eastern Front, Count Simonis' life had changed. Several months after the Jews were expelled, the Germans moved in and occupied most of Kovne Guberniya, including Shavlan.

They commandeered the Manor House and began using it as a command post. Count Simonis had no choice but to maintain a relationship with the German military, which allowed him to continue running his businesses with little or no interference. He, in order to protect his holdings, stayed on with his family and was forced to share one of the houses on the estate with several relatives.

This morning while the count walked the streets of Shavlan, it appeared to be haunted by the Jews who had once lived there. Many of the locals still occupied their houses, and unfortunately the police did nothing to restrain them. The count was angry and very impatient. He was not collecting rent from any of the squatters and could do nothing about it.

The entire town's economy was in ruins. No one realized the Expulsion Decree could have had such disastrous consequences. Every small business suffered. Where was the tailor shop, the bakery, the general store, the accountant, and the shoemaker? Gone!

Before the war, the count had had in his employment several educated Jews from the area—an accountant, two managers, and a few day-to-day administrators.

This arrangement worked out well for him because most of the gentile inhabitants were illiterate, and the only thing they could do was work the land. He leased his farmland to the farmhands who worked the soil and shared in the profits. However, without his Jewish staff and the Jewish business owners, Shavlan experienced economic disruption, as did many nearby towns.

---

During the war, Ekaterinoslav became extremely crowded with displaced persons. Today, another large group of expelled Jews arrived from Lithuania. They were either running from the Germans or being forced out of towns by their own countrymen. In either case, they were persecuted for no apparent reason other than being Jews.

Many of these newly arrived refugees were actual eyewitnesses to the conflict. They spoke of how the Germans, who had entered their towns, began looting randomly, breaking into private homes, warehouses and shops, stealing whatever they could find. And after their departure, mobs from nearby towns came and looted whatever the Germans had left behind.

As the Germans occupied more and more Russian territories, Nikolai Nikolaevich, the Tsar's commander-in-chief, had to come up with a reason for their defeats. This is when he set in motion the idea of blaming the Jews as colluders against Tsarist Russia.

Lies sprung up almost overnight about the Jews aiding the Germans by providing hiding places for them and alerting them to where the Russian forces were located.

These lies continued to spread among the Christian community, causing widespread anger and anti-Semitism throughout the entire Pale of Settlement. Jews could not believe such hatred could exist, especially at a time when they were fighting side by side with their countrymen.

The war was going so badly that in the fall of 1915, the incompetent Tsar Nicholas discharged Nikolai Nikolaevich as his commander-in-chief and made up his mind to take control of the Russian armies. This action was thought of as a symbolic gesture since his chief-of-staff still made all the major military decisions.

One cold winter evening, after the children had gone to sleep, Fanny called Sarah Taube into her apartment.

"Because we do not know from day to day how our lives will be affected by this war, I have something I want to show you. I think this is the right time to make you aware of this secret I've been keeping from you. I wanted to get to know you better and to see if you could be trusted. After knowing you for a while, my dear, I am thoroughly convinced I can trust you with my life."

Sarah Taube was curious. What could Fanny possibly be hiding from her, she thought. It sounded to her as if this secret was a matter of life and death?

"Come, Sarah Taube," Fanny said, taking her hand and leading her back downstairs. "Let's go into your bedroom."

Fanny got down on her hands and knees and, with a sharp tool, began to pry open some loose planks from the floor. This immediately reminded Sarah Taube of a similar idea she and Charles had had many years ago. However, the hole in the floor of her small wooden house was just that, a small space capable of hiding some small objects.

When Fanny removed the planks, Sarah Taube saw steep wooden stairs leading down to a room below the ground level of the house.

"Follow me," Fanny said and descended the stairs.

"This is a perfect hiding place," Sarah Taube said, looking at the dimensions of the room.

"Exactly," replied Fanny. "When my husband and I first built this house, we realized an underground room would be a perfect place to hide if ever we had to protect ourselves."

"You mean like a pogrom?" Sarah Taube asked.

"Yes, like a pogrom. So we had this hidden cellar built, and, I might add, we actually used it in 1905 when there was a pogrom that lasted for several days."

Sarah Taube shook her head in disbelief. "How did you manage to survive?"

"It was not a problem. When we heard the thundering horses of the Cossacks coming down the street, we gathered up food and water and stayed here until it was safe for us to leave. I truly believe it saved our lives. So my dear, remember well this secret of mine in case, G-d forbid, we may have to use it again."

Sarah Taube watched carefully, while Fanny positioned the flat pieces of timber back into their original place. The planks from under the floor were fitted with small hooks that could be moved back into place, so it would look as though nothing had been removed from the floor above.

"Now I need you to remove the planks and practice putting them back," Fanny said. "I want to make sure you can do it by yourself in case, for some reason, I'm not here."

After several tries, Sarah Taube got the procedure down perfectly.

"Excellent," Fanny said and then her face grew serious. "There's one last thing I want to emphasize. Please, under no circumstances should you tell this to anyone, not even the children. If and when the time comes for the room to be used, that will be the right time to divulge our secret and even then, only to your children. I hope you understand what I'm saying?"

"Yes, I fully understand," Sarah Taube said, nodding her head.

After Fanny and Sarah Taube climbed up from the space below and onto the first floor, they placed the planks back in their locations, and never spoke about the secret room again.

---

When Charles came home from work late one December evening, he noticed a letter sticking out from under the door. It was from Ruchel. He was so excited, he did not even have time to take off his jacket.

As he began reading, a smile came to him. He learned his first-born had become engaged and was soon to be married. She asked if he could come to the wedding. He wrote back, *"With the war going on, it would be too risky for me to take a ship overseas, and it saddens me not to be able to attend your special day."*

He asked if she had heard from her mother, and he worries every day about her and the children's safety. He wished Ruchel much happiness, and after sending his love, he folded the letter, placing it in an envelope, ready to be mailed the following morning.

Charles and Sadie had become good friends and spent a good deal of time together, with Sadie showing him interesting places to visit throughout the area. He admired her independence and enjoyed her company.

Chaim had become a successful businessman and began to deal in real estate, purchasing several rental properties. Charles was not involved in any of Chaim's financial dealings and was becoming less enchanted with South Africa.

While attending synagogue services, he would often listen to the men telling stories about those who had left to settle in other parts of the world, places he had never been like Argentina, Brazil, Mexico, Palestine, and Australia. This awakened in him again the desire to travel and rove about. It was like a disease that kept putting him in a repetitive loop, and he began to feel like part of his soul would die if he would not be able to cross the oceans to reach new lands.

---

One evening, while Sarah Taube was preparing the children for bed, she heard a gentle tap on the front door. To her surprise, it was Rabbi Broide. What was he doing visiting the shop at such a late hour, she wondered?

"Hello, Rabbi," she said, as she led him through the bakery and into the kitchen. "Is anything wrong?"

"No, everything is fine," he said. "Forgive me for calling at this late hour, but I need your help."

"My help?" Sarah Taube questioned, quickly inviting him to take a seat.

"Yes, your help. Please let me explain. I remember when you told me that it had been well over a year since Yankel was conscripted into the army, and you had not heard from him since. I pray, G-d willing, that he is well and will come home safely."

Sarah Taube glanced out the window for a moment and then at the rabbi. "Yes. My family and I miss him very much."

The rabbi scooted his chair close to her. "That brings me to the reason why I'm here. I have recently visited several young Jewish soldiers who have been hospitalized with injuries sustained fighting at the front. I wonder if you wouldn't mind accompanying me when next I visit them? I know you would want to do anything you can for them, just as you would want someone to help Yankel, if he were to be injured."

"Of course," Sarah Taube replied, saddened by what she had heard.

"I plan to go to the hospital this Sunday afternoon. Just to be there and talk with these young boys will boost their morale, and anything you can do to raise their spirits would be greatly appreciated. Will this Sunday at one be a good time?"

Sarah Taube didn't hesitate. "I'm sure it will. I'll ask Mrs. Bressler to watch the children."

"Wonderful. Goodness, I almost forgot. When my wife heard I was coming here, she asked me to pick up some pastry for tomorrow's breakfast. Can I still buy something or is it too late?"

"Rabbi," Sarah Taube said with a smile, "for you the shop is always open, and I recommend the apple strudel. It's one of Mrs. Bressler's specialties."

"Good. Wrap me up four pieces."

Sarah Taube led the rabbi into the shop. Reaching into the icebox, she carefully selected four pieces of the best looking strudel she could find and put them in a small, white box.

"What do I owe you?" he asked, pulling out a billfold from his coat pocket.

"Oh, no," Sarah Taube replied. "Put your money away. For you, there's no charge."

"Thank you," he said, gently placing the box of pastries under his arm, "and remember, I'll see you on Sunday at one."

That night, Sarah Taube had one of her recurring dreams. She dreamt she was wandering in a deep valley surrounded by beautiful rolling hills with a stream flowing through it. Avram and Gitka appeared with their arms outstretched as though they were seeking desperately to embrace her. She attempted to grab them but to no avail. The more she ran in their direction, the harder it was to catch them. Then the image of Yankel appeared.

"Yankel! Yankel!" she shouted. "What has become of you?"

Avram, Gitka, and Yankel took hold of each other's arms and began floating upward, like angels, toward the open cloudless sky.

"Avram! Gitka! Yankel!" she cried. "Come back! Come back!"

Each time, after one of these dreams, she would ask herself, why Yankel? She could understand Avram and Gitka being there. After all, they had departed this earth. But Yankel. Why Yankel?

Sarah Taube rose early the following morning. She told Fanny about the invitation Rabbi Broide had extended to her and asked if she could watch the children on Sunday.

"Of course, I can. Why don't you take the men some pastries?"

"You've read my mind," Sarah Taube replied. "I was just going to ask you about that."

"It's the least we can do for our young men, and by the way, when you're ready to go to the hospital, I'll have Mr. Primakov take you and bring you back. I don't want you walking the streets by yourself after dark."

On Sunday afternoon, as suggested by Fanny, Mr. Primakov dropped Sarah Taube off at the hospital. "Take your time," he said. "I'll be waiting here when you're ready to leave."

When Sarah Taube entered the front door of the hospital, she saw Rabbi Broide standing in the lobby. As soon as he saw her, he rushed over. "I can't begin to thank you for taking the time to come here this afternoon. I'm painfully aware that seeing these boys in their condition is something you could have done without."

"Don't give it a second thought, Rabbi. Like you said the other day, I would want my Yankel looked after if he were to be injured, and besides, I felt it was my moral obligation to come."

Rabbi Broide took her by the arm and led her through a brightly lit corridor and up a flight of stairs.

"I want to warn you," he said, stopping for a moment, "many of these men have been severely maimed, so please remember we're here to give them support and show them compassion."

Motioning for Sarah Taube to follow, the rabbi headed toward the end of a large room, stopping in front of three beds, which were curtained off from the rest of the area.

Occupying each of the beds was an injured young man. One had his right leg in traction, another, his head wrapped in bandages, and a third, a patch over his left eye.

"The three of you look much better than the last time I visited," Rabbi Broide said when he came closer. "I've brought you some company. This is Mrs. Grazutis, and she kindly agreed to join me this afternoon."

The men, while they introduced themselves, seemed to perk up the moment they saw her. Seeing a middle-aged woman standing before them somehow reminded them of the strong bond they felt for their mothers.

"Glad to meet you," Sarah Taube replied, giving each a warm smile. "I hope you boys are hungry. I've brought you an apple cake. It's from Fanny's Bakery where I work."

Sarah Taube plumped up their pillows, sliced up the cake, and began feeding them.

"Thank you. Thank you," they kept repeating over and over again. Rabbi Broide was pleased to see the men reacting so favorably toward her. She was exactly what they needed to lift their spirits, especially after the trauma they had gone through.

Once the men finished their food and felt more at ease with their company, they began to speak. They described in detail, their confrontations on the battlefield, and judging from what they said, the war was going to be a long and difficult conflict. As Sarah Taube listened, she was more convinced than ever that war was evil.

After spending an hour, and before she and the rabbi were about to leave, one of the soldiers motioned for them to come closer. They moved their chairs as close as possible to his bed. He spoke in a whisper.

"What I am about to tell you I know will surprise you, but you must know the truth about what is happening on the battlefield.

"It is well known," he began, "that there was much propaganda against us Jews early in the war. As the lies spread about us collaborating with the Germans, the hatred grew, and before long, even the generals were acting out their prejudices toward us.

"Throughout our last battles, we were ordered to be in the frontline for every attack. This was a direct order coming from the colonel in command. During a retreat, however, we were placed in the last row."

The soldier paused for a moment to clear his throat.

"This way," he continued, "we would be first to take fire from the advancing Germans. When this happened, of course, many of us fell. That's how I got a bullet to the leg. Fortunately for me, I was not left on the open field, as most were, to die like wounded beasts."

Rabbi Broide's face grew red. He could not believe his ears. He was well aware of false charges being placed on the Jewish people, but he could not understand why the High Command would take such criminal actions against Jews fighting to protect the mother country. The more he thought about what was going on during battle, the more he realized just how little he knew.

"What have they done to our people?" he asked, raising his voice, trying very hard to control his emotions. "They have driven us from our homes, humiliated us, and murdered us, and we still think we are part of this country."

Sarah Taube had never heard the rabbi speak with such bitterness. She began to think about her son Yankel. Hearing about the Jewish boys being sacrificed on the frontlines got her thinking. Was Yankel experiencing these same prejudices?

After a while, the doctors began making rounds, so Rabbi Broide said a short prayer and bid the men a warm farewell.

That evening, while enjoying a cup of tea, Sarah Taube told Fanny what she and the rabbi had learned that afternoon. Fanny was not surprised. There were rumors circulating throughout the Jewish community about that very subject, yet no one had ever heard it coming from a soldier who actually experienced that kind of savage behavior.

From time to time, Sarah Taube and Fanny would bring up the subject of war. They still could not find out much. According to the consensus of the majority of those living in the city, the war, under the direction of the Tsar, was not going well.

Recently, Sarah Taube had been questioning her beliefs. When the soldiers told her how they were being treated, she wondered why G-d was allowing this to happen.

She knew the Christians in Ekaterinoslav went to church to pray to G-d to protect their soldiers from the Germans. She thought surely, the Germans must be going to their churches to pray to G-d to protect their soldiers from the Russians.

"Is it the same G-d they both prayed to, and is it the same G-d we Jews pray to?" she asked herself and wondered which G-d she should pray to, to protect Yankel, Charles, and Ruchel?

# Chapter 27 – Under the Chuppah

## Sunday, January 2, 1916 – Ellwood City, Pennsylvania, USA

Today was Rose and William's wedding day. The wedding ceremony and reception was to take place in the home of William's mother, who had offered it to the happy couple when the date of the joyful occasion was first announced. All arrangements had been made weeks in advance, and the wedding was scheduled to take place at two o'clock in the afternoon.

As Rose lay resting, she heard someone calling her name.

"Rose, may I come in? It's Aunt Freida."

"Come in. I was just lying here thinking how lucky I am. I have the man I wanted, and I know I should be happy, but there's one thing that keeps wearing away at me."

"What's wrong, my dear?" Aunt Freida asked, moving her hand gently over her niece's face.

"*Mammeh* and my sisters and brothers are not here," Rose tearfully confessed. "I miss them so much, and I hope they're all well and safe, but I have doubts as to whether they're still alive."

Aunt Freida wiped the tears from her niece's eyes and tried to console her.

"Look at the bright side. You have your Uncle Aaron and his family who have come to support you, and you have Aunt Hannah, Uncle Lazer and me, standing beside you, giving you all our love."

While Aunt Freida helped Rose on with her gown, she noticed a heart-shaped locket hanging from a gold chain around her niece's neck.

"What a lovely locket," she said, taking a closer look. "Where did you get it?"

Rose unclasped the chain and slid the locket off into her hand, holding it up for Aunt Freida to see.

"My brother, Yankel gave it to me when I left for America. I wanted to wear it the day of my wedding, so I could feel his presence close to my heart."

"What a lovely thought," Aunt Freida replied, brushing away a tear drop from her own cheek. "I'm sure Yankel would be very proud of you today."

Rose continued to dress, and after a while, the doorbell rang.

"Hurry," Aunt Freida called. "The driver is here to take us to your future mother-in-law's house. Remember, the wedding is scheduled to begin at two."

Once they arrived, Mrs. Krause met them at the front door and led them into the study where the rabbi and the immediate family were waiting.

The rabbi looked around the room. "Now that everyone is here," he said, "let us begin."

After the *ketubah,* the Jewish prenuptial agreement, was read to the bride and groom and witnessed, the wedding ceremony began with the playing of the processional music. The guests stood from their seats.

Rose, with her long blond hair hanging loosely over her shoulders, gave William her warmest of smiles, and as their eyes met, a crosscurrent of electricity flowed between them. When the music stopped, the rabbi motioned for the guests to sit down.

After the ritual observances, the nuptial vows, the giving of the rings, and the breaking of the glass, the rabbi announced they were now husband and wife. He looked at them with a smile and said, "You may kiss the bride."

"I love you," William said and gave Rose a tender kiss on the lips.

"And I love you," Rose replied and gave him a kiss in return.

"Mazel Tov!" shouted the guests.

Rose could not believe the ceremony was over so quickly. American weddings were much different from the ones in the old country, she thought. Mostly, all of the age-old traditions were the same, but the speed with which they were conducted simply amazed her.

A receiving line was formed, which was considered proper etiquette, especially when more than fifty guests were present. Traditionally, the bride's parents would have headed the receiving line. Since they were not present, William's mother, who was officially the host, stood at the head of the line to be the first to greet the guests.

Rose and William were introduced and danced their first dance as

Mr. and Mrs. William Krause. Afterward, Rose's Uncle Aaron and the best man gave toasts to the happy couple. The evening continued with dining, dancing, and laughter.

After dinner, it was time to cut the cake. It was the most beautiful cake Rose had ever seen. She took the knife and William placed his right hand over hers and together they cut a piece from the front of the bottom tier and placed it on a plate. William took a small portion with his fork and gently fed it to Rose. Rose took a small bite and then fed the rest to William. It was a most tender moment performed by Rose and William and witnessed by the guests.

After saying their goodbyes, Rose and William changed into their "going away" clothes. William's car had already been packed with their suitcases, and all they needed to do was get into the automobile and drive away.

"Where are we spending the night?" Rose asked, snuggling her head into her husband's shoulder.

"I have a surprise for you," William replied softly. Where, in all of Pittsburgh, did you want to spend our first night together?"

"William. You mean you're going to make another one of my dreams come true? Is it the Hotel Schenley?"

"Yes, my darling. I knew how much you wanted to stay there and what could be better than spending our honeymoon night at the very same hotel where Lillian Russell spent hers."

Because of the motion of the automobile, Rose fell sleep. "Wake up," William said in a whisper. "We've almost there. Open your eyes. You don't want to miss any moment of this charming place."

When William's automobile came to a halt outside the hotel, a bellboy rushed forward to open the car door, and as they entered the lobby, Rose could not help noticing the interior. It was covered with marble, chandeliers, and Louis XV furniture.

The night manager congratulated them on their marriage, Rose was given a lovely bouquet of red roses, and, as was the wedding tradition in Pittsburgh, a beautiful tray of assorted cookies. After they were led to the elevator and taken to the Honeymoon Suite, the bellboy opened the door and brought in the luggage.

"That will be all," William said. He reached into his pocket and handed him a tip.

The suite was lovely. The front room featured a beautifully colored palette of rich salmon and tea rose. It had hardwood floors, expansive crown molding, tapestries, oversized lounge chairs, and elegant draperies.

The bedroom held a large feathered bed, layered with a rose printed silk taffeta bedspread. In addition, it contained a dressing table and a large chifforobe, along with a writing table and chair. In the bathroom stood a glass-enclosed tub and a double sink vanity with a large mirror.

This is the most beautiful place I've ever seen, Rose thought to herself.

Soft knocking was heard at the door.

"Come in," William said.

To Rose's surprise, a hotel waiter, dressed in a black tuxedo, rolled in a table decorated with Frette linens, white Bernardaud china, and sterling silver.

William turned to Rose. "Are you hungry? I think I've worked up quite an appetite."

Rose looked across the table. "William, you've thought of everything. I was so excited at the wedding, I didn't have time to eat a thing."

The meal began with a tomato basil soup with garlic croutons and moved on to crisp baby greens with aged vinaigrette, followed by herb roasted lamb chops, and lastly, orange blossom crème brulee.

"Is there anything else you wish, Sir?" the waiter asked.

"Rose, is there anything else you would like?"

"No, darling," she said, giving him a flirtatious smile. "I have everything I want." How attentive and considerate William was, Rose thought. She had not only chosen a handsome man but a very charming and thoughtful one as well.

"That will be all," William said, handing the waiter a sizeable tip.

Rose stood from her chair and walked unsteadily across the room.

"I've been standing in these high-heeled shoes for so long, I can hardly feel my feet," she said, looking a bit tired from the trip.

William sat her down on the bed and gently removed her shoes and stockings and began massaging her feet.

"Does that feel better?" he asked.

"Yes," she replied. "Don't stop. I think you have almost put me to sleep."

"Don't go to sleep yet," my darling," William whispered in her ear and began stroking her hair.

"You look beautiful," he said, carefully laying down beside her. They spent the next few minutes undressing each other. William felt her warm body against his. He touched her soft shoulders and kissed her slender neck.

"I'm the luckiest man in the world," he said. Their two bodies merged, and in that large feathered bed, they united as one.

It was a little after six o'clock the next morning as a hint of steely light began to show through the sheer draperies.

"Wake up, Rose," William whispered, giving each of her eyelids a warm kiss. "We have a train to catch this morning."

After traveling for most of the day, they had finally arrived at Pennsylvania Station in New York City. "Take us to the Algonquin Hotel at 59 West 44th Street," William said to the driver.

When they arrived at the hotel, Rose was so excited she could hardly speak. She remembered when she first arrived in New York, but she didn't expect her second trip would be as a married woman. Before they unpacked, William asked Rose to look inside the pocket of his jacket.

Rose smiled. "What's this," she asked, as she pulled out an envelope.

"Go ahead and open it," he replied.

"Al Jolson," she said excitedly. "You're taking me to see Al Jolson."

William nodded. "We were lucky. When I learned Al Jolson was in the musical, *Robinson Crusoe, Jr.* at the Winter Garden Theater, and since we were coming to New York for our honeymoon, I sent your uncle a note, asking him to get us tickets for this Thursday evening."

Rose took William's hand and kissed it. "You've thought of everything, sweetheart. Please don't ever change."

Rose and William spent the next day enjoying the sights. The time went by quickly, and it was Wednesday, the day they were to have dinner with Uncle Aaron and his family.

"Welcome, welcome, newlyweds," Aaron called out when Rose and William stepped out of the taxi. "Come in and make yourselves comfortable."

He pulled up a chair and sat down beside them. "Now tell me. What have you two love birds been up to in New York?"

A blush spread across Rose's face. She felt embarrassed.

"Oh, Aaron, leave them alone," Aunt Clara said, looking annoyed by Aaron's question.

Noticing that Rose felt uncomfortable and the look Clara had given him, Aaron quickly changed the subject.

"So tell me, still no word from your mother?"

"No. There isn't a day that goes by that I don't think about *Mammeh* and the children."

Aunt Clara turned and faced Rose. "It must be unsettling for you, not knowing where they are."

"Yes, it is. My heart is heavy with worry."

Uncle Aaron shook his head. "All we can hope for is that they are safe and well wherever they are."

"Amen to that," Aunt Clara said, rising from her chair. "Come, let's all go into the dining room. We can continue talking over dinner."

The rest of the evening was filled with good conversation and good food. Rose felt happy and at ease with Aaron and his family who had welcomed her into their lives.

As soon as they returned to their hotel room, Rose went into the bathroom to prepare for bed. After a while, which seemed like an eternity to William, Rose appeared wearing a white translucent negligee, one of several she had packed as part of her trousseau. She slowly got into bed and, of course, William eagerly followed.

"What shall we do tomorrow?" he asked, snuggling up close to her.

"Let's take it easy and do very little," Rose replied.

"You're probably right, my darling. We have a very busy evening tomorrow. We'll do a little sightseeing but nothing too exhausting. You look beautiful tonight," he said, staring at the outline of his bride's curvaceous body behind the filmy thin layer of white voile.

Rose turned to him and ran her fingers down the nap of his neck. They lay there, motionless, looking into each other eyes. William began to kiss Rose passionately. The more he kissed her, the more excited she became, and before long, an inner fire erupted in them that was so strong, they could not hold back.

"I wonder if you know how special you are in my life," William said, looking deeply into her eyes. Then the two kissed and fell asleep in each other's arms.

The following morning, after eating breakfast in the hotel restaurant, William hailed a taxi, and he and Rose were on their way to the Lower East Side.

"Drop us of at the corner of Allan and Hester Street," he told the driver.

"What will we do once we get there?" Rose asked.

"We can walk around the area and do some shopping, and later we can have lunch at Katz's Delicatessen."

It was a brisk winter morning as they walked through the streets of the Lower East Side. After a while, they found themselves on Orchard Street, a main shopping area. One could see many tenements with stores on the ground floor.

The smell of freshly baked bread coming from a nearby bakery reminded Rose of the smells that came from Aunt Lena's bakery. She saw pushcarts with their owners selling everything from pickles to pots and pans. It was apparent that the immigrants had brought with them their livelihoods from the old country.

William looked at his watch. "I'm hungry. Are we ready to go to Katz's for lunch?"

"Very well. I can't wait to taste the egg cream you've been raving about," Rose said jokingly.

After indulging in two of the restaurant's famous hot pastrami sandwiches, William ordered an egg cream.

"I beg your pardon," the waiter said, "We don't serve egg creams here. Katz's is a non-dairy restaurant and because egg creams are made with milk, we do not have it on our menu."

William lowered his head and then looked at Rose. He felt foolish in front of her. "I'm sorry to disappoint you, my darling. I should have known egg creams were not on the menu."

"It's all right," Rose replied. "Next time we're in New York, we'll have to go to Ratners. Since they serve only dairy, maybe we can get an egg cream then. I think we should head back to the hotel, though. We need to rest for a few hours. Remember, tonight we go to the theater."

Rose and William, not realizing how tired they were after all the walking they had done, laid down on the bed, and within minutes, they fell into a deep sleep. Some noise in the hallway had awakened them. They glanced at the clock and jumped out of bed. It was six o'clock, and they had less than an hour to get dressed and make it to the show on time.

"Take us to the Winter Garden Theater," William told the driver, "and hurry."

When they got to the theater, Rose noticed that the foyer was covered in gold and white marble, with hundreds of people milling around in gowns and handsome suits.

Because William wanted Rose's first experience at a show on Broadway to be a very memorable one, he asked Aaron to get the best seats in the house. And Uncle Aaron came through, getting seats a few rows in front of the orchestra.

When they took their places and the lights went down, William took Rose's hand and kissed it. And from then on the audience was held captive by the performance and personality of Al Jolson.

The following Sunday, an announcement of Rose and William's wedding appeared in the Ellwood City Ledger.

*Miss Rose Grazutis, niece of Miss Freida Grazutis, of Ellwood City, and William Krause, son of Mrs. Hattie Krause and the late Benjamin Krause, of this city, were united in marriage at the home of Mrs. Hattie Krause of Ellwood City on Sunday, January 2 at two o'clock in the afternoon.*

*The wedding was one of the prettiest home affairs to have taken place in this city and was attended by both local and out-of-town guests.*

*The bride, who was given in marriage by Hannah and Lazer Grazutis of Ellwood City, great aunt and uncle of the bride, was prettily attired in a gown of Ecru Embroidered lace. She carried a shower bouquet of calla lilies accented with roses, stephanotis, and eucalyptus. Attendants were Maid of Honor, Freida Grazutis, aunt of the bride, and best man, Michael Krause, cousin of the groom.*

The year 1916 passed, and the war continued with heavy casualties, especially on the Eastern Front. America remained neutral because most people were against getting involved in what they perceived to be a European war.

In Russia, the economy was tormented constantly by strikes in the factories and political unrest in the cities. The fabric of Russian society was falling apart. Russian soldiers were deserting—Russia's peasants were angry because they wanted land reform—Russia's workers were discontented because they wanted higher wages and better working conditions—and the Jews continued to be subjected to increasing anti-Semitism by the gentiles. All the Jews wanted were to be left alone and live out their lives in peace.

# Chapter 28 – World in Turmoil

## January 1917 – Ellwood City, Pennsylvania, USA

One Sunday afternoon, Rose asked William, "Where shall we go to celebrate our first anniversary?"

"Anywhere will be fine with me," he replied, taking one last sip of his morning coffee, "but I'm worried about leaving the business."

William had been working very hard in the shop, almost without breaks. His business had increased during the past year, and recently he had hired a salesman to ease his workload.

"We should go away for a long weekend," Rose suggested while gathering up the remainder of the breakfast dishes. "You need a break, and you've trained the new salesman so well that I'm sure he'll be able to manage without you for a few days. What about our going to New York? There, you'll be able to take it easy and enjoy the sites. And besides, remember the fun we had during our honeymoon last year?"

"You're right," William replied, realizing he needed to get away.

He thought for a moment. "I have an idea. Let's stay at the Knickerbocker Hotel. I've always wanted to stay there."

Arrangements were made, and within a few days, Rose and William were off to New York City.

In commemoration of their honeymoon night, William ordered room service, and they spent a quiet evening in comfort and relaxation.

"Wake up, William," Rose said, softly stroking his face. "You haven't forgotten that I wanted to have breakfast at my favorite restaurant, did you?"

"What restaurant?" William asked jokingly.

Rose's face crinkled in a smile. By now she knew when William was teasing her by the sound of his voice and the expression on his face. She reached over and tickled him under his chin.

"Stop! Stop! I give up," he yelled. "Of course I know where you want to go. I was just kidding with you."

"William, after being married to you for a year, don't you think I know when you're kidding?"

"Okay, Rose. You've found me out. Please, we need to hurry and go to Ratner's before they close." Rose's eyes opened wide. "Close. What do you mean?"

"See, you still don't know when I'm kidding," William replied, laughing under his breath.

Ratner's was a short ride from the hotel, and when Rose walked in, the owner immediately recognized her.

"Weren't you here a few years ago?" he asked, placing his hand on his chin. "Yes, now I know. Aaron Fineberg brought you here with his wife and daughter. As I recall, you had recently arrived from the old country. Your name was, ah, hum, Raizel, wasn't it?"

Rose stomped her feet. "No, it was Ruchel, but now I'm known as Rose."

"See, I never forget a face. A name, maybe but never a face. Come, I have a very nice table for you and your gentleman friend."

While Rose and William sat, Mr. Ratner continued to chatter.

Noticing they did not have a menu, he summoned for the waiter to bring one over.

After looking over the choices, Rose decided she wanted blintzes with sour cream and applesauce.

"Don't forget the onion rolls!" she added, remembering Uncle Aaron had ordered the exact same items when she last ate there.

"I'll have the same," William said, "and bring a pot of hot coffee."

William excused himself and in a short time returned.

After the food came, and they drank the last cup of coffee, the waiter brought over a large, round platter covered with a silver dome and placed it in front of Rose.

Rose could not believe her eyes. "Good heavens, what's this?" she asked.

William looked at Rose and smiled. "Make sure you close your eyes before you lift the dome."

When she opened her eyes, to her surprise, there in the middle of the plate stood a medium-sized Coca-Cola glass filled with some sort of liquid.

"What is it?" she repeated, baffled by what she was seeing.

William placed a straw in the glass and told her to take a sip.

"Now I know what it is," she said, her eyes gleaming with

excitement. "It's an egg cream, isn't it?"

"I cannot tell a lie," William replied. "Yes, it's an egg cream. I hope you like it."

When they finished their meal, Mr. Ratner thanked them for coming and hoped they would come back soon.

Because the day was cool and sunny, Rose and William decided to take a leisurely walk. As they headed north and turned left on 14th Street, across the way was a park called Union Square. It was a very striking park with magnificent statues scattered throughout the grounds, and standing not too far from the entrance was a most impressive equestrian statue of President George Washington.

After entering the park, they noticed a crowd had gathered nearby.

"I wonder what's going on?" William said, taking hold of Rose's arm. "It seems as though there's going to be some kind of entertainment. They've set up a platform."

Rose looked around. "William, ask someone. Maybe a famous person is going to be here."

William spotted a group of college boys standing nearby.

"Excuse, me," he said, tapping one on the shoulder. "What's happening? Why so many people?"

"Trotsky, the Russian revolutionist, is going to speak in a few minutes," the young man answered, adding that he was a student from CCNY.

"Tell me about this Trotsky," William asked, embarrassed he did not know who he was.

The student's face turned red. He was shocked at William's ignorance.

"He used to live in France but the French deported him to Spain," the student replied. "I've heard that the Spanish authorities didn't let him stay, so he came to the United States."

A man with a Russian accent chimed in.

"Have you read about him in the *Forward* recently?"

"No. Sorry I haven't," William replied.

"Well, Trotsky has written a few articles describing the conditions in Russia and the coming Socialist World Revolution. We can't wait to hear him speak."

William had recently read some newspaper reports about what was going on in Russia, but he did not want to talk about it in front of Rose.

Things were not going well for the Jews in that country. Since they had not heard from Rose's mother and the family in more than two years, they were afraid to think about what may have happened to them. In any case, William was interested in hearing what Trotsky had to say and finding out, first hand, his political views.

"Trotsky is going to speak soon," William said, pulling Rose closer to him to avoid her being pushed by some of the spectators. "We should hang around."

Rose was also interested in hearing from Trotsky, especially since her family was living in the midst of all the upheaval.

After a while, a heavily bearded man got up on the podium and in a deep Russian accent, began to speak.

"May I have your attention please? I am privileged today to introduce to you our honored guest, Leon Trotsky, a man who has a view of a better world for all us workers. Please give him a warm welcome."

A tremendous cheer from the crowd rang out.

Leon Trotsky, a beady-eyed, dark-haired short man, wearing eyeglasses, mustache, and a small pointed beard on his chin, stood in front of the crowd and after waiting for the cheers to quiet down, spoke.

"My fellow workers! I'm very happy to be here this morning, speaking to you on a subject very close to my heart. Many of you work in the garment industry only a few blocks from here. You do all the work but the bosses who own the sweatshops make all the money from your labor. In a socialist system, all of you, not the capitalists, would own the shops and share in the wealth you create."

Trotsky paused for a moment and wiped his forehead.

William could not believe what this odd-looking man was saying, and he especially could not believe that most of the people present that day were in agreement with him.

Trotsky continued to speak.

"Socialism is the next step in the evolution of human history. Socialism gives the workers social justice and economic freedom, while Capitalism enslaves the workers and enriches only the bosses. However, socialism will be possible only if you, the workers, unite to throw off the chains that bind you."

The people cheered and watched as Trotsky raised his fist in the air, waving it back and forth shouting: "Workers Unite to make the world for you and your children the utopia it can be!"

The crowd became hysterical. Trotsky had stirred them up to such a degree that he had to yell over them to make himself heard.

Off to the side, a small group of protestors had gathered, shouting various slogans against him.

"Stop spreading your evil socialist propaganda here!" they yelled. "Go back to Russia where you belong!"

The people became increasingly agitated, and the yelling and screaming got so loud that Trotsky could not go on. William could sense the event was about to turn ugly. He quickly pulled Rose toward him and whispered in her ear, "I've heard enough from this crazy man. I'm glad they finally shut him up. Let's hurry and leave."

"You're right, William. We certainly don't want to get caught up in this mob."

Then one of the protestors threw a large brick toward the stage, aiming it at Trotsky but it missed him by inches. Trotsky was immediately taken off the platform and ushered out of the park.

All hell broke out. Fighting erupted between the opposing groups. What was supposed to be a gathering of peaceful individuals, wanting to express their views, had turned into an unruly mob intent on causing violence.

Rose and William could not get out of the area fast enough, and when they finally left the square, they heard sirens.

"Here come the police," William said, taking hold of Rose's arm. "Now things will get back to normal, although they should have been patrolling the area from the beginning to make sure the demonstrations remained peaceful."

Rose and William continued to walk for several blocks. They grabbed a taxi and got off around Herald Square, walking along Broadway near 34th Street, heading toward Macy's.

It was getting close to lunchtime. "Where would you like to eat," William asked.

Rose thought for a while, and then her eyes lit up.

"I know," she said. "A few blocks back, while the taxi was passing through a busy street, I noticed a billboard displaying a curious advertisement. It said: You haven't lived until you've eaten at the automat. I want to eat at the automat."

"You mean you've never eaten at an automat?" William asked, giving her a strange look.

"Now William. I don't even know what an automat is, so what chance would I have had to eat in one?"

William looked at Rose and grinned. "You're in for a treat, darling. We'll go to Horn & Hardart. It's not too far from here."

"It looks like an ordinary cafeteria," Rose said, peeking through the window.

"This is a very special cafeteria," William replied. "The idea of putting coins into slots and pulling out prepared food from behind small glass windows will be quite an experience for you. Let's go inside."

Rose could hardly wait to try out this new method of getting food from a vending machine. She selected an item and inserted the required coins into a slot and pulled out from a glass compartment, her selection.

Quickly, an attendant, who was working behind the wall of the glass compartment, replaced the item. It was very interesting to see how the operation worked. The developers of the automat had it down to a system, and the system never failed, providing there were enough employees replacing the items as quickly as the customers were taking them out.

After Rose and William satisfied their hunger, they continued to explore the area. They were not used to doing so much walking, so the day's outing had tired them. It was time to return to the hotel to rest in preparation for the evening's activities.

"Wake up, Rose," William whispered, planting a soft kiss on her cheek. "Open your eyes. We have to get dressed. I have reservations for dinner at eight-thirty."

"Take us to the Reisenweber Café on Columbus Circle and 58th Street," William said to the driver.

They were led to a cozy table in a corner near the front of the room.

William explained to Rose that the café was originally a tavern in the mid-1800's. Since the Park Theater was located nearby and featured well known names in show business, it became an attraction and was frequented by theater stars.

"I can't wait to hear the music," Rose said, quickly looking around the room.

"By the way, about the music," William added, "I understand we're going to hear the Original Dixieland Jazz Band. It's a group of white musicians who started in New Orleans last year. They recently moved to New York and have become very popular among white audiences by playing Jazz music.

Shortly after Rose and William finished eating, the lights dimmed, and the master of ceremonies stood in front of the stage, asking for everyone's attention.

"It gives me great pleasure," he announced, "to introduce the Original Dixieland Jazz Band. They'll be providing music for your entertainment and dancing enjoyment. Please give them a warm welcome."

The band began playing one of the most requested tunes called "Tiger Rag."

Rose had never heard Dixieland before, and in no time, she could feel the beat from the top of her head to the tip of her toes as she tapped her feet to the rhythm of the music. The entire audience was literally tapping their feet on the floor and banging their hands on their tables.

"I love it," Rose replied, trying to control her enthusiasm. "How long have they been playing here?"

"Waiter!" William yelled, hoping to be heard over the noisy crowd, "how long has the band been playing at this café?"

"They've been here a little more than a month. Everyone loves their music. It's the latest rage, you know.

"I shouldn't be telling you this," he whispered, holding his hand over his mouth, "but Jimmy Durante is sitting at one of my tables in the back of the room. He came here to listen to the band.

"Don't say anything. He doesn't want to cause a commotion among the other guests. He wants to remain incognito though with his schnoz, it's going to be very difficult for him not to be found out."

Rose gave William a strange look. "Schnoz. What is a schnoz?"

"William laughed. "It's slang for nose. Durante is well known for his big nose."

Rose leaned her elbows on the table and spoke softly in William's ear.

"Tonight was one of the best times I've ever had. Thank you so much for making this evening such a memorable one."

---

In Johannesburg, Charles had become an avid reader of newspaper reports on the war on the Eastern Front.

He had no idea where his Sarala was, and he became more and more guilt-ridden because he felt he had abandoned her and the children.

The only pleasures he had in life was sightseeing outings with Sadie and the camaraderie the synagogue members offered him.

Late one evening, as he lay awake, his thoughts turned to Sarah Taube.

He wondered if she and the children were still alive and if so, were they living somewhere in Lithuania or had they moved elsewhere.

He asked himself, would she be wondering if he was still alive, living in in South Africa or had he moved elsewhere as well?

Finally, he thought about Ruchel and felt guilty that he could not get there for her wedding and share in her happiness.

# Chapter 29 – A New Republic

## February 1917 – Ekaterinoslav, Russian Empire

In February, Rabbi Silver, of the Golden Rose Synagogue, felt it would be beneficial to chair a weekly meeting with the rabbis from the local synagogues and those rabbis who were exiled from areas in Lithuania.

At these meetings, discussions would be held regarding problems facing the Jewish refugees from Lithuania, the war, and the political situation in Russia.

Rabbi Broide had learned during today's meeting that Germany had resumed unrestricted U-Boat warfare, and in early February, the United States had broken diplomatic ties with them.

In mid-March, Rabbi Broide also learned Tsar Nicholas II had abdicated the throne, ending the Romanov dynasty and the Russian Empire. As a result, the Russian Republic was created, allowing the members of the Duma, the legislative body, to set up a Provisional Government. Tsar Nicholas II and his family were then placed under house arrest.

The following week, at a meeting, Rabbi Silver said he believed because of America's entry into the war in April, it would herald a quick end to the turmoil.

Rabbi Silver was known to be a close follower of world events and spoke about the Zimmerman Telegram, which he felt gave rise to the Americans entering the war.

"It seems," he began, "this telegram was a diplomatic proposal from the German Empire to Mexico, urging them to make war against the United States. In return, they were offered the U.S. territories of Texas, New Mexico and Arizona. Fortunately, the British intercepted the Proposal before it got to Mexico and gave the information to the Americans."

◄○►

The German government was looking for ways to undermine Russia's war effort. After the abdication of the Tsar, they knew one way to do it would be to facilitate Lenin's return to Petrograd from exile in Switzerland.

◄○►

Dimitri Bogdonovich, having been wounded in battle, recovered and was honorably discharged from the army. His career had advanced in the Bolshevik Party and Lenin noted his accomplishments. The Party had informed him that Lenin had returned to Russia, hoping he could put an end to the war.

When Lenin arrived in Petrograd, he received a tremendous welcome. After several days of speech making, he came to a meeting held by the Party, and it was Dimitri's honor to introduce him.

Dimitri could feel his heart in his throat when he stood in front of the group. "My dear friends. I would like to present our great leader, Lenin, whom we have missed greatly, but now he's here again, ready to lead us. Let's give him a warm reception."

The crowd stood and clapped. The standing ovation went on for several minutes until Lenin finally raised his arms and signaled for them to sit down.

"Thank you my fellow Bolsheviks," he said, looking proudly around the room. "I've been waiting for this day for many years, but I must ask you to be patient. You'll know when it's time to take action."

Lenin went on to talk about the publications he wrote and what he expected would follow in the next few months. After the speech, he mingled with the crowd, and everyone tried to shake his hand and wish him good luck in the coming revolution.

In July of 1917, there was an unsuccessful attempt at an uprising against the Provisional Government, which had been planned when the Tsar renounced his throne, so Lenin again was forced into exile, this time going to Finland.

On the 6th of August, Aleksander Kerensky became Prime Minister of Russia. He believed Russia should continue the war against Germany, even though the Germans were pushing the Russian army further into their own territory.

The following month, German troops broke through the

northernmost end of the Eastern Front during the Riga offensive. Lenin believed that the time for radical change was now, so he sent a secret letter to the Executive Committee of the Bolshevik Party, ordering a violent uprising against the government.

In Ekaterinoslav, shortly after the Bolshevik Party took power in November of 1917, Rabbi Silver called an emergency meeting to discuss the current political situation. He told the rabbis what he thought would be the result of the Bolshevik revolution.

"As you know," he began, "Lenin, the head of the Bolshevik party, had his followers take over the Government buildings in Petrograd, dissolve the Duma, and essentially seize control of Russia. These people are followers of a man called Karl Marx who has come up with a terrible atheistic philosophy.

"I've since learned, they have begun taking over factories and businesses in other cities. The only advice I can give you to pass on to your congregations is to not voice their political opinions."

The rabbi paused and looked around.

"I'm afraid we have some bad times ahead of us."

The group realized they were looking at an uncertain future for themselves and their congregations because a government they disliked was now being replaced by one which could be even worse.

By now, everyone in Ekaterinoslav was feeling the strains of war and political upheaval. Mrs. Bressler was having difficulty getting flour, sugar, yeast, and eggs, and with her stock being depleted, she could not run her bakery properly.

Events in Russia were happening faster than anyone had expected. People in the communities were frightened, and they mainly stayed in their homes and would only come out to buy food and other necessities. That is, if they were able to get them.

Several months had passed since the Bolshevik Revolution of November 1917. The Bolsheviks had completely taken control of Petrograd and cities and villages throughout the former Russian Empire. By the 1st of February 1918, they had the Russian Constituent Assembly dissolved, announcing they were the new regime in Russia.

In each city, they imposed their political and economic system, which mandated government control of the means of production and distribution and prohibited ownership of private property.

Early one afternoon, while Sarah Taube and Chaya were tending to customers, a middle aged man and a young girl, who looked to be the same age as Chaya, came into the shop. Mrs. Bressler was not feeling well and was resting in her quarters.

"Hello," the gentleman said, politely tipping his hat. "My name is Zinovy Rosenbaum and this is my daughter Alisa."

Mr. Rosenbaum was a tall, distinguished looking-man, wearing half-moon spectacles, who exhibited a manner which seemed worthy of respect. His daughter, on the other hand, was short and dark-skinned with straight black hair and large brown eyes.

"It's my daughter's birthday tomorrow, and I was wondering if you have a cake for purchase?" he asked, giving a quick glance into the display case.

"Tomorrow is my birthday too," Chaya replied in a friendly manner. "I will be thirteen years old. How old will you be, Alisa?"

"I will be thirteen too," she said with her nose in the air, acting as though she were far superior to Chaya.

"We're so lucky to have the same birthday, aren't we?" Chaya said.

Alisa thought it very strange for this girl to carry on about them sharing the same birthday. After all, they did not even know each other.

"What's so lucky about that," she said, giving Chaya a cold stare. "I bet there are many people whom we don't even know that have our same birthday."

Chaya turned around and looked at her mother. She was almost going to say something hurtful, but Sarah Taube gave her a look as if to say, "leave it alone."

Chaya was smart enough to realize these people were customers, and even though Alisa seemed to act as though she were of a higher social standing, she had to keep her opinions to herself.

"About the cake, we do have one left," Sarah Taube replied. "It's an almond cake with white icing. Would you like to purchase it?"

Chaya was hoping that no one would claim the last cake so she could have it for herself to celebrate her own special day.

"I don't want to take the last cake from you," the gentleman said, feeling somewhat uneasy. "You probably would want it for your daughter."

Sarah Taube looked at him and smiled. "Don't worry. I'll bake another one this evening in time for my daughter's birthday tomorrow. Are you living here in Ekaterinoslav? I don't remember ever seeing you."

"No. I'm visiting my wife's uncle, Josef Brenski. My wife and my other two daughters are there with him now. Josef sent me here. He said you have the best bakery in the city."

"Where do you make your home?" Sarah Taube asked.

Mr. Rosenbaum waited for the last customer to leave. "I used to live in St. Petersburg," he replied in a low voice, "before they changed the name to Petrograd."

His daughter tugged at his arm.

"Father, tell her what those nasty Bolsheviks did to you and the others."

Mr. Rosenbaum gave his daughter a look.

"Please excuse my daughter. I'm afraid the Bolsheviks left a lasting impression on her. She will never forget what they did to me and to all the other business people who lived in Petrograd."

Sarah Taube listened very carefully while Mr. Rosenbaum began relating his story.

"I was a successful pharmacist in St. Petersburg and owned the building where the pharmacy stood. My family and I lived there for many years. When the Bolsheviks came into power, they confiscated my pharmacy and took everything I worked so hard for all of my life. They told me the "people" now owned it. Can you imagine that? The "people" now owned my pharmacy and my property."

Sarah Taube leaned over and placed her elbows on the counter.

"So what did you do?" she asked.

Mr. Rosenbaum looked at her, adjusting his glasses before he continued.

"In order to escape the situation, I decided to take my family to Crimea to live. I'm stopping off to visit my wife's family, and then I'll go on to my final destination."

Sarah Taube straightened up and shook her head.

"I can't believe they took your property and pharmacy away."

"Well, my dear lady, you do know what Lenin's slogan is, don't you?"

"No, I'm afraid not. We do not get much news here about what's happening in our country. We have to pick up information from people like you, plus whatever we can read in the local newspapers. We have our doubts as to whether we're being told the truth. So tell me, what is Lenin's slogan?"

"Peace, land, and bread!" Mr. Rosenbaum blurted out. "They wish to have peace with Germany, redistribute the land, and give bread to everyone."

Sarah Taube thought to herself, peace with Germany would bring Yankel home but redistributing the land was a concept she did not understand. However, bread for everyone was good since people in Ekaterinoslav did not have enough to eat. She wondered if Mr. Rosenbaum was telling the truth about the Bolsheviks taking away his business and property.

"We, in Ekaterinoslav, are allowed to keep our property and still own and run our establishments without any interference from the government. I cannot believe that something like that could ever happen here."

"Believe it," the gentleman said, pointing his finger at her. "It can happen here. My family and I were lucky to have left unharmed but others were not as fortunate.

"Someone I knew who owned a much larger pharmacy than I, objected loudly to the confiscation of his business, and the Bolsheviks came into his store and arrested him. He was never seen nor heard from again. Be aware, if it happened to me, it could happen to you, and when it happens to you, you'll know it's true."

"Believe it," his daughter cried out. "It's the truth. It will happen here just as it did in Petrograd."

Sarah Taube observed that his daughter was mature for her years and must have seen things that a child her age should never have seen.

She placed the cake into a white box and tied it with a decorative ribbon and handed the package to Mr. Rosenbaum, offering him and his daughter a pleasant visit with their relatives. He thanked her for her kindness, paid for the cake, and wished Chaya a happy birthday.

When he and his daughter headed toward the front door, he said, in a very calm voice, "Let us hope that a new government may be established, which will serve everyone's interest."

Sarah Taube remained silent for a few moments, thinking about what this man had said. Then she quickly glanced at the clock hanging on the wall, grabbed a letter sitting on the counter and said to Chaya, "Goodness, look at the time. I must go to the post office to mail my letter to Ruchel before the three o'clock collection. Look after the customers until I return."

Sarah Taube often had thoughts of Ruchel, hoping she was well and happy. This was one of many letters throughout the years she had mailed, but she never gave up hope that one day one of them would reach her daughter and she would get a response.

On her way to the post office, she passed the bank and noticed the doors were locked, and two armed men were standing outside. Why were guards standing outside and why were the doors locked, she wondered. The bank never closes this early. She had not yet learned how the Bolshevik Marxist ideology concerning private property translated into the confiscation of everyone's property, including her hard earned savings at the bank.

In March of 1918, during the weekly meeting of the rabbis, the impact of the current political situation was discussed.

Rabbi Silver stood at the head of the room and informed the rabbis he had learned that on the 16th of February of this year, twenty representatives of the Council of Lithuania had declared Lithuania an independent country.

He told the shtetl rabbis they would have to explain to their congregations why they can not go back to Lithuania now for two reasons.

One, it would be impossible to safely transverse through the fluid battle lines between the Reds and the Whites and two, if they made it to the border of Lithuania, which is now occupied by the German Army, they may be denied entry.

Rabbi Broide was saddened to have to tell his flock this unhappy news.

# Chapter 30 – Workers Paradise

## April 1918 – Ekaterinoslav, Soviet Russia

An officer of the Red Army announced late one afternoon as he entered Fanny's Bakery Shop, "I am the Commissar. I am in charge of this section of the city. My name is Dimitri Bogdonovich, but you will refer to me as Commissar Bogdonovich."

Both Fanny and Sarah Taube were taken by surprise. Who was this man and what did he want.

He was a handsome, middle-aged man and, at first sight, came across as being someone lacking in emotion. To Fanny, he projected an image of someone who could be cruel without ever thinking twice.

"Who runs this establishment?" he asked in a loud, sharp voice, striking his hand on the counter repeatedly.

Fanny had seen men like him before, and he reminded her of the Cossacks who came riding on their white horses in 1905, during one of the most devastating pogroms in Ekaterinoslav's history.

"I believe you're asking for me," Fanny replied, sounding very confident as she spoke. "I am the owner and this is my worker, Mrs. Grazutis."

Fanny called Sarah Taube her worker because she was familiar with the ideology of Lenin's new government, and by calling her a worker, she hoped that Sarah Taube would be accepted under the new regime and would be left alone by the Bolshcviks.

"Do you own any businesses or properties other than this one?" he asked, while backing Fanny into a corner.

"Yes, I do," she replied, looking directly into his eyes. "I own two apartment buildings."

"So you are a landlord as well," he said with a look of contempt.

"Yes, I am," she answered again, responding very proudly.

"What is your name, Mrs…? I did not hear you mention it."

"You did not ask for my name," was her curt reply, "but if you must know, my name is Fanny Bressler."

Their eyes met in a staredown that showed no signs of breaking. They continued to stare at each other until the commissar could no longer maintain eye contact and was forced to look away.

He reached into his folder and pulled out a proclamation and read aloud.

Attention All Citizens of the Former Russian Empire:

The following are the official directives issued by the Soviet Government:

*All power is to be passed to the Soviets of Workers', Soldiers' and Peasants' Deputies*

*All privately owned land is to be taken over*

*All Russian banks are to be transferred from private to state ownership*

*All personally owned bank accounts are to be frozen*

*All Church properties are to be seized*

*All foreign debts are to be invalidated*

*Control of all factories is to be turned over to the Soviets*

*Wages are to be secured at higher rates than during the war and a shorter, eight-hour workday is to be initiated*

When Fanny heard the proclamation, she became quite indignant. How dare these tyrants come into my shop and impose their far-left ideology on the people, she thought.

"Do you understand these demands?" he sneered.

Fanny pursed her lips and clenched her fists into tight balls. Try as she might, she could not contain herself. Within seconds she erupted like a volcano.

"No. I can't say I do," she said angrily. "I have worked very hard all of my life to get where I am today. You mean you intend to take it away from me and give it to someone who did not earn it or someone who thinks he deserves it more than I do? What has happened to the freedoms we once had under the Tsar? This new government cannot be the will of the people."

Fanny continued to ramble on, not realizing she was getting deeper in trouble with each sentence she spoke.

Sarah Taube remembered what Mr. Rosenbaum had said when he was in the shop last month. "Be aware, if it happened to me, it could happen to you, and when it happens to you, you will know it's true."

Those words had lingered in her mind, and it was now coming true for the people of Ekaterinoslav. She had to do something to warn Fanny she had better control her emotions, and this was not the time nor the place to sound off against the new regime.

"Fanny," she called out, interrupting her before she could say another word, "these changes are for the good of the people. We must obey the new decree and accept the new government for it is in our best interest."

"What is your name?" the commissar asked, taking notice of Sarah Taube's quick-witted intelligence.

"My name is Sarah Taube Grazutis and this is my daughter, Chaya," she replied, holding her breath, wondering what his reaction would be.

"You and I are going to get along just fine," he said as a smile transformed his grim face.

He summoned for two of the soldiers to come into the shop.

"Seize this woman!" he shouted, pointing in Fanny's direction. "She is an enemy of the people and must be re-educated."

The men grabbed Fanny by the arms and dragged her through the front door and onto a covered truck parked by the side of the road.

Chaya watched in disbelief while Mrs. Bressler was taken away.

"There is much work to be done," the commissar said thinking to himself, one more capitalist has been taken from society to avenge my sister, Gesya and my beloved Aleksandra.

He gave Sarah Taube a long stare before he continued.

"It seems in this area there are bourgeoisie who belong to the social class of capitalists and are unwilling to give back to the people what is rightfully theirs. These capitalists, who own most of society's wealth and means of production, have to be weeded out for the good of all mankind. There is no time to waste.

"I will return soon to discuss with you the new operation. In the meantime, go about your work as usual. You are a very smart woman. This I could see from the first moment I laid eyes on you. Remember, you will still be allowed to work here the same as all the other workers, but now it will belong to the people. Do you understand?"

He didn't wait for Sarah Taube's reply but instead, turned around and walked out.

When Commissar Bogdonovich left the bakery, he summoned the captain.

"Did you see what I have done here?" he asked, pointing in the direction of the shop.

"Yes, Commissar," the captain replied respectfully.

"I wanted to demonstrate to you how we turn a capitalist-owned business into an establishment run by the workers. I hope you took notice of how I accomplished this because you will have to do it from now on with every business in this district."

"*Mammeh,* what will they do to Mrs. Bressler?" Chaya asked late that afternoon. "We didn't even have time to say goodbye. Where did they take her?"

Sarah Taube put her arms around Chaya. "I don't know, *myne kind.* Let's hope she comes back to us soon."

Sarah Taube did not want to upset her daughter by telling her they probably would never see Mrs. Bressler again.

Night had fallen, and when Sarah Taube and Chaya closed the bakery, they made sure all the doors were shut and secured.

A strange silence came over the shop that night. Even though Sarah Taube did not agree with the new government's ideology and thought it was an unrealistic approach to solving Russia's problems, she had to keep her thoughts to herself, if she were to protect her family. She did not want to end up like Fanny.

Drastic changes were being made to the establishments throughout the business district, and if one spoke out against the new regime, they were arrested and never heard from again.

There were rumors circulating that those who were taken away were sent to Siberia. Sarah Taube often wondered if this was where they had taken Fanny, but she had no way of knowing.

One afternoon, while Sarah Taube was busy preparing a special order for one of her customers, she heard a familiar voice.

"Hello, Sarah Taube. I stopped by to see how you are."

Sarah Taube appeared from behind the display case.

"Shaina, I was thinking of you. How are you and your family?"

Shaina leaned over the counter. "Under the circumstances, we're fine. I heard about Mrs. Bressler. How are you managing without her?"

"Of course, we all miss her very much. Things are certainly not as they were. Some days I don't have enough flour to accommodate my customers' orders. It's supposed to be a worker's paradise. Well, if this is paradise, I wonder what hell is like? But enough about me. What's been happening at the military base since the takeover?"

"Nothing much has changed. The old Tsarist Army has left and been replaced by the Red Army. What does it matter to us what army it is? We obey the rules, show up each day, prepare the food, and dish it out. The only good thing about the job is we get to take home any leftovers, so fortunately our family is not starving. Even though food is scarce, they have to provide the military with nutritious meals.

After all, the men need to be healthy and strong when they go out to protect mother Russia."

Sarah Taube detected a bit of sarcasm in Shaina's voice, and luckily, there were no customers in the bakery.

"Shaina, you mustn't talk this way. It's dangerous to be so outspoken. Someone could misinterpret what you're saying and report you to the authorities."

"I know I should be quiet, but sometimes I get so angry, I can't help myself. When will this madness end?"

After a while, several customers came into the shop. Shaina grabbed her order, asked to give her love to the children, and quickly left.

Late that afternoon, while Sarah Taube was replenishing the empty display case with teacakes she had baked, Commissar Bogdonovich came into the shop.

"Hello, Comrade Grazutis. I've been craving Pryaniki, a Russian honey spice cookie. Why do you not have any on the shelf?"

"Sarah Taube looked across the counter at the commissar and folded her hands.

"These days, I find it difficult to get the supplies I need to bake my pies, cookies, and cakes, so I have to make due with the few ingredients I can still get. I have some Russian teacakes. They require very few ingredients. Would you like to sample a few?"

The commissar's enthusiasm lit up his face.

"But of course," he replied.

Sarah Taube placed several pieces on a dish and handed it to him.

"This is very good," he said, making a crunching sound with his teeth. "Wrap up the rest. I'll take them back to my headquarters and save them for later."

Sarah Taube wrapped up the remaining cakes. He did not offer to pay and she did not ask.

After staring at her for a while, it seemed as if he had something serious to discuss.

"Comrade," he said, looking around the shop to make sure there were no customers, "I think I can be of service to you."

Sarah Taube wondered what he was about to propose. I have to be careful with what I say, she thought, because I've already seen what happens to people who stand up to him.

"What do you have in mind?" she asked, leaning on the counter with her hand on her chin.

He moved slowly toward her. "I can make arrangements to supply you with all the ingredients you need in order to produce all the baked goods you want, but there's only one thing I want from you."

Again she thought, what could he possibly want from me in exchange.

"What do you have in mind?" she asked again.

He smiled and replied, "I must be supplied with as many desserts as I desire. But of course, along with this arrangement, I can offer you and your family protection if anything unforeseen were to happen."

Sarah Taube breathed a sigh of relief. She actually thought he was hinting at some kind of romantic relationship with her, and if he was, she did not know what she would say. She only knew that she would have to put her family's safety above her honor, if he were to suggest such a thing.

After hearing the commissar's proposal, she did not have to think twice. In order for her to make a living and especially since this man was offering to keep her and her family safe, it sounded like a good business arrangement and so she accepted his proposal.

As he passed her, with the box of pastries in his arms, he inhaled her scent, bent close and was about to kiss her, when she quickly stepped back. Without another word passing between them, he opened the front door of the shop and left.

Each week, a truck full of baking supplies would arrive. Communism was supposed to make everyone equal, she thought, yet some seemed to be more equal than others.

Her business began to flourish again, and she was given several workers to help ease her workload. Whenever the commissar came into the bakery, he would always ask for her.

"Good afternoon, Comrade Grazutis, and how are you today?"

"I'm very well, thank you, and what would you like to sample?"

"What do you suggest?" he asked as he came closer.

"You must try my mandelbrot," she suggested, pointing to the tray on the counter. "It's fresh out of the oven."

"I don't mind if I do," he said, giving her his usual stare.

She sliced off several pieces, placed them on a dish and handed it to him.

"This is delicious. I especially like the taste of almonds sprinkled throughout the cake. It tastes exactly like the *mandelbrot* my mother used to bake."

When Sarah Taube heard him say his mother baked *mandelbrot,* she was surprised. *Mandelbrot* was a dessert associated with Eastern European Jews. It was a Yiddish word, which meant almond bread. Was he Jewish, she thought. Her curiosity got the best of her.

"*Mandelbrot* is a Yiddish pastry. Why is it that your mother baked this particular dessert?"

"I thought you knew?" he said as he came closer. "I was once of the Jewish faith before I converted to Communism. There are over three hundred Jews who belong to the Bolshevik party. But of course, I do not believe in God. I am an atheist. However, I can still enjoy Jewish pastries, can't I?"

Not believe in G-d. An *apikoros*—an atheist. What kind of strange man was he? No wonder he displays a lack of moral principles.

She placed the rest of the *mandelbrot* in a box because she knew when the commissar liked one of her baked goods, he would take all of them, not leaving any for her customers. However, it was perfectly fine with her because as long as she was getting the supplies she needed, she had no reason to complain.

When Sarah Taube handed the commissar the package, a strange feeling came over him. It was the smell of her hair.

"What is that wonderful scent?" he asked, moving as close to her as possible.

"It's the rose water I comb through my hair each morning after its been washed," she replied, trying to distance herself from him.

That's why he was attracted to her, he realized. Sarah Taube uses the very same rose water as did his sister, Gesya and Aleksandra, the two loves of his life.

"You're not the type of woman a man gets tired of looking at," he said as his eyes met hers. He placed the box of *mandelbrot* down on the counter and took hold of her hand and kissed it.

She tried to pull her hand from his grasp, but he wouldn't let go. She tugged harder till his grasp broke. He had made an inappropriate gesture to her. She slowly walked across the room.

Commissar Bogdonovich, realizing he had acted improperly, gathered up his package and walked out.

That evening, after the children had gone to sleep, Sarah Taube looked into the mirror. Even though she was a woman of almost fifty, aside from a few gray hairs, she still retained many of her good looks, and she knew enough about life to know the commissar had been flirting with her.

Although he was an attractive and charismatic man, she hoped he understood she had no romantic interest in him, and the last thing she needed in her life was a relationship with an atheist. She was loyal to her husband and missed him more each day, longing to hear him call her his Sarala once again. No man could ever come between her and her *besherter*—fated one.

Three weeks had passed, and it was the day before Passover. Sarah Taube was getting ready to close the shop to prepare for the holiday. Unexpectedly, the door opened and there stood Commissar Bogdonovich, carrying three small packages.

"Good afternoon, Sarah Taube," he said, giving her his usual stare. "I'm glad I got here before you closed."

Sarah Taube did not remember telling him he could address her by her given name, but she wasn't going to draw attention to it. She still did not feel comfortable in his presence and correcting him would not have been a good idea.

"What brings you here?" she asked, trying not to look into his eyes. "You know I always close the shop early before a holiday."

"I'm sorry," he said as a slow grin passed across his face. "I was not aware of any holiday."

"Passover is tomorrow. You do remember Passover, don't you?"

"But of course. I thought I mentioned to you I was raised by a religious family. However, it's been a while since I've observed any Jewish holiday. Here Comrade," handing her the three packages. "These are gifts for your children."

As he watched her slowly walk toward him, he took notice of her long, black skirt making a rustling sound as it swayed about her legs.

Sarah Taube did not want to accept the gifts but was not going to offend him.

"Thank you, Commissar. It's very kind of you to think of them."

"Call me, Dimitri. I think we are good enough friends for us to be on a first name basis. Don't you agree?"

Sarah Taube looked away for a moment.

"May I suggest we keep our relationship during business hours strictly formal, but after the shop is closed, I would have no problem for us to address each other by our first name."

"You are a very smart woman. You have suggested a good solution. So Passover is tomorrow? I guess you'll be having a Seder? I remember as a child being very excited about this holiday. Will you be entertaining family for the ceremony?"

"No, there's only my children and me. We have no other family here."

"I too have no family. One can be very lonely without family."

The commissar was not very subtle about wanting to be invited to Sarah Taube's holiday festivities, but she was not going to have him sit at her Seder table. After all, he was a non-believer, an atheist.

"The bakery will be closed for the next week. Why don't you come this Sunday afternoon around two. You can give the children their presents then."

"I understand," he said, looking somewhat annoyed.

He walked to the front door, threw it open with a loud bang

against the wall and said, "See you this Sunday at two."

Whether or not to invite the commissar to her home socially was a difficult decision, but these were the times she was living in, and under the circumstances, she had no choice.

Sunday, after lunch, Sarah Taube told the children that Commissar Bogdonovich was coming for a visit and to be respectful. Chaya understood what her mother was saying.

She knew the commissar was a bad person, and her mother was only being nice to him because she had to, but it was different for Fraida and Masha. They were too young to realize what was happening. They saw Commissar Bogdonovich as a nice man who was being friendly.

A few minutes to two, several knocks were heard coming from the front door.

"Good afternoon, Sarah Taube," the commissar said.

"Hello, children. Come closer. I have gifts for you."

He handed the first gift to Fraida.

Fraida ripped off the paper and lifted the lid from the box.

"It's a doll," she said and began rocking it back and forth in her arms.

"I'm glad you like it," the commissar said, looking quite pleased that he had made a good choice.

One could see it was a very expensive doll with a hand-painted porcelain face and finely dressed in a traditional handmade Russian costume. Sarah Taube tried to hide her disgust. She had seen a similar doll carried by a child of one of her wealthier customers who had mysteriously vanished after the Bolsheviks entered the city.

"Who's next?" the commissar asked, motioning for Masha to come closer.

"Here, my little man," he said and handed him the second gift.

Masha held the box to his ear and began to shake it.

"It's rattling inside," he called out and began shaking it again.

"Come, Masha. Open it. Don't you want to know what's inside?" the commissar asked.

Masha plopped down on the floor and let out a scream.

"It's a toy soldier on a horse!" he yelled and began jumping around the room with the toy in his hands.

The commissar shook his head and roared with laughter.

"It's one of our Bolsheviks sitting on a white horse, leading the cavalry into battle."

"Who won the battle, Mr. Commissar?" Masha asked.

"You may call me Uncle Dimitri." He put his hands around Masha's waist and lifted him up with his legs dangling in the air.

"But of course, our Bolsheviks won the battle just as they win every battle," he replied, carefully placing Masha's feet down on the floor.

Sarah Taube was taking it all in, saying nothing, yet quite upset at seeing the gift the commissar had chosen for her son. This was one toy she did not think her son should be playing with. It reminded her of all the injured soldiers she saw when visiting the hospital, and it especially reminded her of Yankel, perhaps lying somewhere in a ditch. But she could not speak of the disgust she felt.

"What do you say, Masha?" she asked.

"Thank you, Uncle Dimitri."

The commissar's face swelled with joy. It gave him pleasure hearing Sarah Taube's son call him uncle.

"Did I leave anyone out?" the commissar asked, looking around the room.

"Yes, you left out Chaya!" Masha shouted, pointing his finger at his sister.

The commissar walked over to Chaya and placed the last gift in her hands.

When Chaya opened the box, she saw it was a miniature hand painted, wooden jewelry box.

"Thank you," she said, looking at the commissar with a vacant expression on her face.

Sarah Taube could not help but think to herself, "Which one of her customer's children once owned this beautiful piece of artwork."

Commissar Bogdonovich gathered the children around him.

"It would please me very much if all of you would call me Uncle Dimitri," he said, looking in Sarah Taube's direction.

Sarah Taube did not dare show her disgust. "*Kinder*, its time for you to take your presents into your room. Say goodbye to the commissar."

"Goodbye, Uncle Dimitri," Masha said. "Thank you for my toy soldier. I hope you will bring me another toy when you come again."

Commissar Bogdonovich laughed again, patting little Masha on the head.

"Goodbye, Uncle Dimitri," Fraida said and gave him a kiss on the cheek.

Sarah Taube could see that he was choking back tears. Fraida had brought out an emotion in him she had never seen before.

It was now Chaya's turn to say goodbye.

"Thank you for my gift, Commissar Bogdonovich. It was very kind of you to think of me."

One thing she definitely knew—she was not going to give him the satisfaction of calling him Uncle Dimitri. She remained in the kitchen and began putting away the rest of the dishes, which had been drying on the counter.

"So tell me, Sarah Taube, where is your husband?" I don't recall ever hearing you mentioning him."

Sarah Taube thought it was none of his business and tried desperately to ignore his question.

"Would you like a glass of hot tea?" she asked.

"Please, Sarah Taube, call me Dimitri."

"Of course, Dimitri."

"Yes," he answered. "That is exactly what I had in mind."

Sarah Taube felt her blush warm her cheeks as she filled the kettle with water from a small ceramic pitcher.

"Have you made any of your delicious pastries to serve with the tea?" he asked.

"Yes. I've baked my Aunt Lena's special Passover sponge cake. Would you like a slice?"

"But of course."

Within minutes, there was a white mist of water droplets in the air coming from the kettle.

"*Mammeh,* the water is boiling. Come and make the tea."

After finishing two slices of cake and swallowing the last mouthful of tea, he stood and stretched his legs.

"I've enjoyed spending the afternoon with you and your family," he said, gazing at his watch, "but I see I have overstayed my welcome." He took her hand and placed his on top of hers. "Thank you for a most pleasant evening." Then he swung his jacket over his shoulder and bid her goodnight.

Chaya walked over to her mother.

"*Mammeh,* why did that nasty man come here today?"

Sarah Taube put her hands around Chaya's face. "I thought I explained to you why we need him."

"Yes, *Mammeh,* but I still don't understand why he came here today, on our holiday?"

"Sit down, *myne kind.* You remember when the commissar arrested Mrs. Bressler?"

"Yes. I could never forget that day."

"Well, I brought it up because I want to stress to you how important it is for us to be on good terms with the commissar. He allows me to earn a living while running the bakery, and all he asks for in return is a few pastries. Without him, we would be starving. Now do you see why we have to accept him into our lives?"

Chaya thought for a moment. "Yes, but I will never call him

Uncle Dimitri."

The following week, early in the morning, Mrs. Goldman, a customer, came into the shop, looking as if she were about to explode.

"How could you bring yourself to entertain that barbarian!" she screamed.

It seems, even though it was none of her business, she recently found out from several neighbors that Sarah Taube had been entertaining the commissar in her home during the Passover holidays.

She called Sarah Taube all kinds of names and did not even give her a chance to explain why she did it. After shouting at length, she turned her back on Sarah Taube and left the shop in a huff.

When Dimitri came in the next day to get his usual box of sweets, he found Sarah Taube in low spirits. He noticed her eyes were red, and she obviously had been crying. He asked what had happened because he had never seen her this way.

Sarah Taube was upset and told him everything. When he asked for the woman's name, without ever thinking of the consequences, she went ahead and gave it to him.

A few weeks later, while Shaina was in the bakery, she told Sarah Taube about Mrs. Goldman's sudden disappearance. Everyone wondered what had become of her.

Sarah Taube felt ashamed. An ache started deep in her stomach. She turned away and her eyes welled up with tears.

"What's wrong?" Shaina asked, sitting her down on a nearby chair.

"I blame myself," she said and proceeded to tell Shaina what she had done. She was certain Dimitri had taken care of the situation the only way he knew how.

"You mustn't blame yourself," Shaina said, wrapping her arms tightly around her friend. "It's the times we're living in. The sin is on Dimitri and not on you."

As much as Shaina tried to console her, Sarah Taube would forever feel responsible for that poor woman's misfortune.

One warm July evening, when Sarah Taube was about to close the shop, one of her customers came running in.

"I have some terrible news," she said, clutching a newspaper in her hands.

"What has happened?" Sarah Taube asked.

"It says here on the front page that yesterday Tsar Nicholas and his family were executed. Who could have done such a thing?"

"Who do you think?" Sarah Taube replied. A sad look came over her. "It was the Bolsheviks or should I say, it was the Communists who did it." She thought to herself, will I ever be able to leave this horrible place?

Sarah Taube took the newspaper from her customer's hands and read further. The article also stated that on the 9th November 1918, Kaiser Wilheim, the German Emperor and King of Prussia, abdicated the throne and went into exile in the Netherlands. He was blamed by the German people for starting the war and was considered an ineffective leader by his army. This was just another sequence of events happening in the world, and Sarah Taube could hardly keep up with it.

# Chapter 31 – Change in Command

## November 1918 – Ekaterinoslav, Soviet Russia

The headline in the Russian newspaper this morning read, "WESTERN FRONT ARMISTICE."

Now that Germany had agreed to a cease-fire on the Western Front and the world war had ended, the exiled Jews from Shavlan again approached the rabbi, pleading for him to find a way for them to return to their shtetl.

At the next meeting of the rabbis, Rabbi Silver spoke. "While Germany is being forced to remove their army from Lithuania, the Soviets are instituting military action to take back Lithuania."

The rabbi lowered his head and then looked up. "I'm afraid returning to Lithuania at this time cannot happen because the Russian civil war still rages, and Lithuania is now a war zone."

Again Rabbi Broide had to tell his people there was still no way back to their shtetl.

Six months later, in April of 1919, while Sarah Taube was in the market purchasing some items she needed to make dinner, a few of the merchants told her they had heard talk about fierce fighting between the Red Army and the White Army. They said the White Army had succeeded in overpowering the Bolsheviks, and they were about to take command of Ekaterinoslav.

Those in the White Army were primarily made up of capitalists, aristocrats, business people, clergy, and Cossacks—loyal soldiers from the Old Imperial Army. They had voluntarily united, mainly in their opposition to Lenin's Bolshevik rule. Some wanted the monarchy to return, while others wanted a democratic government put in place.

Sarah Taube knew she had to get back to her family quickly,

especially since she heard that the White army was approaching with great speed. All of the vendors closed their stalls and headed back to their homes, as did Sarah Taube.

Chaya and her siblings began to worry, wondering why their mother had not yet returned. They heard gunfire coming from close by and became frightened, thinking something terrible had happened, and their mother was never coming home.

Sarah Taube would normally bring back whatever she was able to purchase at the market, and they would have a hot meal. It was already dark as the children huddled in a corner of the kitchen.

Masha was eating a large piece of bread he had hidden from them.

"Can we have some bread too?" Chaya asked.

Masha sat there, ignoring his sister and continued eating until all the bread was gone. He did not even offer them a small piece.

"Where did you get the bread?" Chaya asked.

"I took it from the bin in the shop?" Masha replied.

Chaya quickly went into the bakery and saw that the bin was empty. She hated to have to spy on her brother. After all, she was hungry too and understood why he was hiding the bread in the first place. Still, Masha's actions by not sharing, once again proved he was selfish by nature and would remain that way for the rest of his life.

"When is *Mammeh* coming home?" Fraida asked.

"Don't worry," Chaya replied. "She will be home soon."

Masha, on the other hand, was not concerned. He was sitting there with his belly full of bread. His hunger was satisfied, and it was all that mattered to him.

"Let me in. Let me in," Sarah Taube called from outside.

"*Mammeh*, where have you been?" Chaya asked, grabbing her mother's packages.

The first thing Sarah Taube did when she entered the house was to make sure the front door was securely locked and the shades were pulled down. Trying not to worry the children, she sat them down at the kitchen table and explained, as best she could, what had happened.

In less than an hour, she heard shouting coming from outside. Telling the children to stay in the kitchen, she cautiously crept back in the shop. As she peeked through the window, a group of soldiers on horses came galloping through the street. She knew immediately that these were the infamous Cossacks known for their unspeakable cruelties.

She quickly led Chaya, Fraida, and Masha into her bedroom and began to execute the plan she had carefully devised with Mrs. Bressler.

After lifting the floorboards, the children helped her carry food, a few candles, several pillows, and two blankets down the stairs. This was the first time they had seen the secret place, and they knew enough to follow their mother's guidance without question.

Sarah Taube went back up the steps and collected her mother's candlesticks and the family's photograph and again descended the steep steps, remembering to close the overhead boards just as Fanny had shown her. She made up a bed by arranging the pillows and blankets on the floor, preparing to settle down for the night.

After the children had fallen asleep, she heard a series of rifle shots and men and women yelling and screaming. Within minutes, she heard the sound of glass breaking and men walking, with heavy steps, through the front door of the bakery. They continued across the bakery floor, through the kitchen, and into her bedroom.

As they stomped around the room, opening and shutting drawers and cabinets, Sarah Taube was thankful she had brought down her mother's brass candlesticks. Aside from that, there was nothing of value for them to steal. Thank goodness the children were asleep, she thought. G-d in heaven was once again looking out for the Grazutis family.

After a while, Sarah Taube heard the men mumbling a few words, and then they left the bedroom, heading back toward the front of the shop. In less than a minute the front door slammed, followed by an eerie silence.

While Sarah Taube lay beside her children that evening, she continued to hear cries in the distance, but she had no way of knowing what was happening to the people of Ekaterinoslav and especially to the Jews. All she could think about was that her family was safe and would not be exposed to danger that night.

The following morning, while the children slept, Sarah Taube removed some of the planks from the ceiling and ascended the stairs. She moved slowly through the bakery toward the front window.

It was early in the morning and the streets were deserted. Where was the army? She still did not feel safe enough to come out of hiding, though it seemed clear to her the White Army had defeated the Bolsheviks and a new order was about to prevail.

After staying in the cellar for nearly three days, she decided to come up once more to have a look. She saw soldiers stationed along the business district, and people were walking about as if it were a normal workday. Before she turned to go back to the kitchen, an envelope under the front door caught her attention.

*My dear Sarah Taube,*

*Today, I stopped by your shop to inquire how you and your family fared during the events of the last three days. I was concerned about your being alone with your children. The Jewish community was holed up in their homes afraid to venture out while the fighting went on. The battle came to a close very quickly as the White Army tightened their hold on the city, forcing the Bolshevik Army out of Ekaterinoslav. Please let me know what has happened to you.*
*Rabbi Zev-Wolf Broide*

Sarah Taube felt the worst was over. The rabbi would not have asked for her to get in touch with him, if it were at all dangerous for her to do so. She opened the rest of the floorboards and asked the children to come up.

She was about to clean up the mess the soldiers had made when Rabbi Broide entered the shop.

"I couldn't find you anywhere yesterday. I thought something horrible had happened to you and the children. Where were you?"

Sarah Taube told him about Fanny's hiding place.

"Consider yourself lucky," he said. "Others have not been as fortunate. Some terrible things have befallen our people."

"What do you mean?" Sarah Taube asked.

"The General of the White Army allowed his Cossacks to enter the city and carry out a pogrom on us. They came through, looting, and burning many of the Jewish houses, and they also raped a number of women."

"How horrible," Sarah Taube replied thinking to herself, if it were not for Fanny, she would have been among those who were tortured. What would have become of her children?

"There's more," Rabbi Broide added.

"A Jewish colony called Trudoliubovka in the district of Ekaterinoslav was attacked by a group of partisan peasants. They went into Jewish houses and pulled everyone out into the street and forced the men into a barn and set it on fire. And as if that weren't enough, they raped all the young girls and women."

"Please, Rabbi, I don't want to hear anymore," Sarah Taube called out, holding her hands over her ears. "We have to get out of this country."

"That might be difficult now that the Whites have taken over," the rabbi replied.

"So there's no way out for us?" Sarah Taube asked as her face crinkled in a frown.

"I'm afraid not. We'll have to take a wait and see approach. Hopefully, the fighting will soon end, and then we can safely plan our trip back."

At first, there was disorder and confusion among the people but in less than a month, with the Whites now in control, things began to return to normal.

The Whites brought back some of the old ways the residents of Ekaterinoslav were used to. Businesses reopened but food was still scarce, and everything one needed to exist was very hard to come by. As each day passed, everyone wondered if and when the Reds would retake the city.

# Chapter 32 – Letter from Mammeh

## September 1919 – Ellwood City, Pennsylvania, USA

As William sat at the breakfast table, engrossed in an article in the *New York Times*, he quickly called for Rose to come into the kitchen. "I want to read something to you."

From the tone of his voice, Rose knew he had read something important. "What's happened?" she asked, wiping her hands with a dishtowel. "It sounds serious."

William began to read:

*The 14th of August 1919—In opposition to Lenin's Bolshevik rule, the White Army challenged the Bolsheviks by force, succeeding in overpowering them and taking command in the district of Ekaterinoslav, located on the west side of the Dnieper. Particular brutality was exercised on the Jewish colonies of this district. These areas, which were not affected very much by earlier pogroms, suffered heavily and..."*

William paused for a moment and then placed the newspaper in front of Rose. "Would you like to finish reading the article?" he asked.

Rose sank in her chair and let out a long sigh. "I don't want to," she cried. "Reading about the atrocities happening to the Jews in Europe upsets me. I think about my family. What must they be going through?"

William reached for Rose's hand. "I'm sorry. Please forgive me. I should never have read the article to you. It was not my intention to upset you."

"It's not your fault, William," Rose replied, attempting to calm down. "I'm well aware of what's been happening in Europe. I hear people talking."

William folded the newspaper, put it on the seat next to him, and placed his arms around her. "Come, it's a beautiful day. After breakfast, let's go out. We can stop and see your relatives. They haven't seen much of us lately."

Late that morning, after Rose had finished washing the breakfast dishes, the doorbell rang. It was Aunt Freida.

"I have some wonderful news," she said, "but first, sit down."

"What is it? Tell me," Rose asked.

"You'll never guess? This morning, my neighbor delivered a letter addressed to you. She got it by mistake. Brace yourself, Rose. It's from your mother."

Rose began to shake as she held the wrinkled envelope tightly in her hands.

"Open it," both William and Aunt Freida called out.

Carefully, she lifted the flap on the envelope and was able to grasp the folded piece of paper inside without tearing it. When she unfolded the letter, it was covered from top to bottom with words written in her mother's handwriting and, as tears rolled down her cheeks, she began to read aloud.

*1 February 1918*
*Myne tay'er tochter,*

*I have sent you many letters during the past three years but have not heard from you. I pray one of them will find their way. I hope you and the family are well. You must be wondering what has happened to us. The war has played a tragic part in our lives. Your brother, Yankel was conscripted into the Russian army in October of 1914. It has been over three and a half years, and I have not heard from him. I worry every day and pray G-d has kept him safe, and one day soon he will return to us.*

Rose removed the handkerchief from her dress pocket and wiped her eyes before she was able to continue.

*We were sent out of Shavlan by the Tsarist Government to a place called Ekaterinoslav on the 21 of May 1915. Don't worry. We are all well. All of us have lived through many unpleasant experiences but have managed to survive. When we see each other again, I will tell you all about it. Please let Tateh know we are safe and well, and I hope he is the same. Give him my address. I wait to hear from him. Here is the information you will need in order to respond.*

*Mrs. Sarah Taube Grazutis*
*700 Horbysta Street*
*C/O: Post Office*
*Ekaterinoslav, Guberniya Ukraine*
*Russia*

*Give my regards to the family. I anxiously await your reply.*
*Your loving Mammeh*

"After all these years," Rose said, "a letter from the past shows up. It's as if the letter had been hidden from us in some mysterious way and was waiting for a particular moment to be let out."

"I'm sure if the letter could speak, it would have quite a story to tell," Aunt Freida replied. "What an unexpected surprise and such good news."

"*Mammeh* and the children are safe and well. That's all I really wanted to know. I'll write *Mammeh* right away. I have lots to tell her. She doesn't even know I'm married."

All of a sudden, Rose let out a loud, piercing cry. "Wait a minute," she said. "*Mammeh* mentioned a place called Ekaterinoslav in her letter, didn't she? Wasn't that the city where the raids on the Jews took place?"

William glanced at the write-up a second time. "Yes, it's Ekaterinoslav," he said, underlining the sentence in pencil.

"My G-d!" Rose shouted. "It's the very same place where my mother and the children were exiled to. Now I'm really worried. Suppose they were among those families who were victimized during the pogrom?"

"I'm sure they're fine," Aunt Freida replied, trying to console her niece. "Sit down and answer her letter. I'm certain you'll hear from her soon."

Rose quickly reached into her box of stationery, pulled out a sheet of paper, and tried to pull herself together, before she jotted down her thoughts.

# Chapter 33 – The Reds Return

## September 1919 - Ekaterinoslav, Soviet Russia

The Red Army was intent on retaking Ekaterinoslav and had reorganized its forces to prepare for their next encounter with the Whites.

The ground fighting that ensued between the Whites and Reds was extremely fierce, but this time the Whites could not outfight their opponents. They failed to anticipate a full-scale attack and were not prepared. The Reds showed superior power and, consequently, the Whites were forced to retreat. Word had spread that the Bolsheviks had succeeded and soon would be occupying the city again.

Things were moving so fast that the residents of Ekaterinoslav did not have much time to prepare for the army's onslaught. There was great concern among the Jewish people as to whether the Bolshevik soldiers would conduct a pogrom against them. To be safe, they looked for the most secluded areas in their houses and locked the doors.

Sarah Taube knew exactly where she was going. She gathered her family together and sought refuge in Mrs. Bressler's secret hiding place.

Although the Red Army leaders did not sanction pogroms as did the White Army leaders, it could not stop some of the troops from carrying them out. When the Bolshevik high command found out who the troops were who were performing these acts of violence, they were court-martialed and put to death to prevent any additional outbursts.

The next morning, the Bolshevik army, completely drained of strength and energy, marched back into Ekaterinoslav, and fortunately for the Jews, there was not going to be a pogrom that day.

Many Bolsheviks who had left the city when the Whites took over returned to claim victory and reassert their powers over the people. It was not a good situation, and the Jews from Shavlan were now more determined than ever to return to their homeland.

Almost two months had passed since the Bolsheviks retook the city, and within a short time, Ekaterinoslav had returned to the way it was before the Whites had captured it.

"Hello, Comrade Grazutis," a voice called from across the room.

Sarah Taube did not hear the door open as she was engrossed in taking inventory of her stock. It had been dangerously depleted, and she was worried about how she was going to replenish it.

Again the voice called, "Hello, Comrade Grazutis."

Sarah Taube was startled at first. She looked up and saw Commissar Bogdonovich. It was as if her wish had come true. She was worried about where she was going to get the supplies she needed and there stood the only man capable of helping her.

"Commissar Bogdonovich," she said, giving him a pleasant smile. "I was not expecting you to return. Are you resuming your old post here in Ekaterinoslav?"

"But of course," he answered, staring at her as if he had never left. "They have reassigned me to the same department as before. I really love this city, and I'm happy to be able to meet with my old friends, especially you, Sarah Taube."

He again gave her a long stare, forcing her to lower her eyes and turn away. It took her several moments to speak.

"You have arrived just in time. With all the government changeovers, it has been difficult for me to obtain supplies. Now that you're back, perhaps we can return to our previous arrangement?"

"Comrade Grazutis. That is precisely why I'm here. I see your display case is void of many of the items I used to sample and love. I'm certain something can be worked out. Give me a few weeks to get settled, and I will see to it that you have everything you desire."

Dimitri moved close to Sarah Taube and flashed the warmest smile she ever saw.

"I've been away from you much too long," he said. "I'm not sure how to say this, but I hope you missed me as much as I've missed you."

Sarah Taube met his eyes and she blushed, pretending to disregard what he had said, but strangely, she liked him and liked the feeling of liking him. Was it because she was without a man for so long and yearned for some masculine attention in her life?

Dimitri waited patiently for a reply. She did not answer. They exchanged glances and within a few moments, he left.

Commissar Bogdonovich continued to make sure Sarah Taube was provided with the items she needed to run the bakery, and he was, as before, stopping by every few days to pick up his favorite sweets.

Late one October afternoon, Sarah Taube decided to go to the post office as she had done many times before. She never lost hope that the clerk would call her name and tell her a letter was waiting for her. Of course, in all the years she lived in Ekaterinoslav, not one letter had she received.

"Is there a letter for Sarah Taube Grazutis from America?" she asked when she approached the clerk. Without even waiting for an answer, she turned and began walking toward the front door.

"I was hoping you would show up today, Mrs. Grazutis," the clerk called out. "Yes, there is a post for you."

Sarah Taube changed directions quickly and headed back to the clerk's station. "Are you sure it's for me?" she asked, unwilling to believe her ears.

The clerk reexamined the envelope again. "I'm quite sure. It says Ellwood City, Pennsylvania in America, and it's addressed to Mrs. Sarah Taube Grazutis."

"I can't believe it," Sarah Taube said. "By some miracle, my prayers have been answered."

She quickly opened the envelope, carefully taking out the letter and with her hands shaking, began to read.

*September 30, 1919*
*My dearest Mammeh, Gitka, Chaya, Fraida and Masha,*

*After all these years of not knowing what had become of you and the children, I received a letter from you today dated 1 February 1918. I was so excited I could barely contain myself. I pray to G-d that you and the family are happy and well protected during these terrible times. I have been corresponding with Tateh and have written him about your whereabouts. Expect a letter from him soon.*

*I have some good news. I met a wonderful man named William whom I love very much. We got married on January 2, 1917 and live not too far from Aunt Freida, Aunt Hannah, and Uncle Lazer.*

Sarah Taube paused and then reread the last sentence.

"Dear G-d," she cried out. "My Ruchel is married!"

After a moment, she regained her composure and continued reading.

*Please write as soon as possible. The family and I are very anxious*

*to know what your life has been like since you left Shavlan.*
*All my love,*
*Ruchel*

This is why I felt I had to go to the post office today, she thought. *"Dos hartz hot mir gezogt."* My heart told me so.

Sarah Taube's hands were still shaking when she folded the letter, placed it inside her coat pocket, and rushed home to tell the children.

◄O►

Charles had come home from a very busy day at the shop. A letter was sticking out from under the door. It was from Ruchel in America. He could barely get his coat off and plopped himself down on the nearest chair.

In Ruchel's letter, she stated she was happy to have received a letter from her mother and the family. She wrote of Yankel's conscription into the army and of the family's expulsion in 1915 to Ekaterinoslav. Ruchel enclosed their address and asked that he write to them as soon as possible.

Charles was thankful to hear his Sarala and the children were safe. He thought of how he had disappointed her. He was trapped in South Africa at a time when she needed him, and he felt he had let her down.

A man does not leave his wife and family, gallivanting from place to place, in search of what? He did not know, and whatever it was he was looking for still remained a mystery. It was difficult for him to explain, even to himself. The only thing he knew was he had to return to Shavlan and hoped that Sarala and the children would forgive him.

The next day, Charles made an appointment with the local travel agent. He was told because of hostilities between Lithuania and Poland and Lithuania and the Soviet Union, it would be inadvisable for him to travel to Lithuania at this time. He would have to wait until the conflict was over before he could return.

That evening he wrote to Sarah Taube.

◄O►

It was three months into the new year. The birds were making melodious whistling and twittering sounds as they sat on the branches of the white birch trees outside the shop. Sarah Taube was taking a stroll when she again got the urge to drop by the post office.

"Mrs. Grazutis," the postal clerk called, "I have a letter for you. It's from a Charles Grazutis from South Africa."

At long last, a letter from Charles. She quickly read the letter and hurried home to share it with the children.

"Tell us what *Tateh* says, *Mammeh,*" they begged.

Sarah Taube pulled up a chair and made herself comfortable and began to read.

*My dearest Sarala,*

Sarah Taube stopped reading for a moment and tried to suppress her tears. It brought back memories of when Charles first called her Sarala, and she wondered if things could ever be the same between them. She was now able to stand on her own two feet and make decisions by herself. She had to face many difficulties in life, and despite those difficulties, she had evolved into a much stronger woman.

"Tell us what the letter says," Chaya urged, anxious to hear what her father wrote. Sarah Taube removed a handkerchief from her dress pocket and wiped her eyes.

"*Tateh* says he was very happy to have received a letter from Ruchel and to have learned we are well. He knows about Yankel, and he hopes G-d will look after him. He's planning to return to Shavlan, and he can't wait to see us. He sends his love."

"When will we see our father again," Chaya asked.

Sarah Taube held Chaya's face in her hands and replied, "I hope very soon, *myne kind*. I hope very soon."

It was July of 1920 and nearly a year since the Bolsheviks returned to the city. Some people were happy with the changes the Soviets had made for the "workers" while others had no choice but to accept the undesirable conditions the Soviets had imposed on them.

On this particular morning, when Rabbi Broide was about to leave for the synagogue, he could not help but notice the headlines on the front page of the newspaper.

PEACE BETWEEN SOVIET GOVERNMENT AND LITHUANIA

He could not believe his eyes. After more than two years of fighting between the Russian and Lithuanian armies, a settlement had finally been reached.

In addition, there was a clause in the peace agreement, stating that the Soviet government was obligated to transport to the Soviet border, at Soviet expense, all those Jews who proclaimed they were citizens of the Lithuanian Republic and were ready to return home.

This was exactly what the rabbi had hoped for. He could now begin discussions with the Soviet authorities because everything was spelled out. At last, the Jews of Shavlan could return to their homeland.

The following morning, he made an appointment to meet with the commissar.

"Congratulations," he said as he rose from behind his desk and shook hands with the rabbi. "Please have a seat. You don't act surprised. I'm guessing you've already heard?"

Rabbi Broide smiled. "Yes, Commissar. I read it in the newspaper yesterday."

"Excellent, and when headquarters notifies me how to handle this matter, I'll let you know.

"Oh, one last thing, Rabbi. Documents need to be prepared, which will allow your people to safely cross the border. I'll need the names of those who plan to leave."

That afternoon, Rabbi Broide arranged a meeting with his congregation. He told them what had transpired, and they needed to be ready to leave at a moment's notice.

A few weeks later, the commissar summoned the rabbi. "Come in. Please have a seat. I've received, from our foreign ministry, plans for moving you and your people out of the city and back to your homes."

Rabbi Broide moved his chair close to the commissar's desk. "I'm very eager to hear the details. However, I may have some questions."

"But of course. I understand your concerns. First, let me discuss our proposal. After you hear it, you may ask as many questions as you wish.

"Wagons will pick your people up in the park and drop them off at the train station. As they board, documentation will be handed to them, allowing them to pass through checkpoints. The train will then take them to the Polish border where they will get off.

"Rabbi," he said, leaning across from his desk, "I wish to make it perfectly clear. Once we drop your people off, we will have no further responsibilities. Since you are the rabbi and their leader, it will be up to you and the Jewish clergy, once you leave the Soviet Union, to make sure transportation is provided to allow you an easy way back to your town. We'll notify the rabbinical council in Poland with an estimated time of arrival."

The rabbi could not hold back his excitement. "Thank you. "Now that I've heard the plan, my questions have been answered."

"And remember," the commissar added when the rabbi got up to leave, "you and your people must be ready the moment you hear from me."

Slowly, the horses came to a stop in front of a weathered sign hanging outside a shabby wooden house. A tired, gray-haired man, lean, with sunken cheeks and white face, stepped out of the wagon. After waiting seven years, Charles Grazutis, who had aged far beyond his years, was home.

With sadness he glanced at the sign, but he could hardly make out the words. His thoughts went back to the first day he spent with his beloved wife in this very house and the jokes that were made regarding the wording of the sign.

How they laughed that wonderful day so many years ago. Tears began to roll down his face, and he longed to hear that laughter once again. Life was simple then but alas, those days were gone forever.

The front door of the shop was unlocked. "Hello," he called as he slowly entered. "Is anyone here?"

The walls threw back the echo of his voice, but the family he loved was nowhere to be found. He felt his life was empty and meaningless, and all he could do was wait and hope his Sarala and the children would soon return.

Late that afternoon, word had spread that one of the Jews had returned. "Hello, Mr. Grazutis," a voice from the past called. "It's Mr. Sadunas. Count Simonis has sent me. I've come to welcome you back."

Charles was happy to see a familiar face and gave him a small nod.

"Am I the only one who has returned?" he asked.

"Yes, I'm afraid so," Mr. Sadunas replied, shocked at seeing how Charles had aged. "I don't know if you were aware, but your family along with all the other Jews were expelled from Shavlan in May of 1915."

"Yes, I know, but I had expected my family to be here by now."

"Don't worry," Mr. Sadunas replied, giving Charles a firm pat on the back. "I'm certain your family will be returning soon."

"You're right," Charles said, staring at the empty room. "After all, I've waited all these years. I guess I can wait a little while longer."

That evening, Charles sat down on his empty bed and began to write a letter to the only woman he ever loved.

# Chapter 34 – Homeward Bound

## 2 August 1920 – Ekaterinoslav, Soviet Russia

Early this morning, Rabbi Broide received a note from Commissar Bogdonovich, asking him to come to his office.

The commissar rose from his desk, shook hands with the rabbi and motioned him toward a chair. "I have good news. Be ready in the park on Monday, the 9th of August at two o'clock in the afternoon. An official from the Communist Party will be there with wagons, ready to transport you and your people to the train station. One more thing. Do you have the list of names I asked for at our last meeting?"

"Yes, I have them right here," the rabbi replied, reaching into his folder.

"Good. I'll have my assistant draw up the documents and give them to you before you board the train."

"Thank you, Commissar for taking care of this matter so efficiently."

"Happy to have been able to help," the commissar said, wishing him good luck and a safe journey.

Rabbi Broide had no time to waste. There was a good possibility another challenge to the new government could be on its way, and they would be in the same predicament as before, with no way out of the country.

A few hours later, he called an emergency meeting. Once the Jews of Shavlan were told they needed to be ready on the 9th of the month, a clap of hands could be heard. At last, they were going home.

"Please listen carefully," the rabbi said, "to the following instructions in preparation of our departure. First, you are to take with you all official papers. Second, try to settle your affairs as best you can. Third, the day before we leave, pack your belongings and finally, bring enough food to sustain you and your family for at least two days.

"Please note," the rabbi added, "our trip back to Shavlan will not be as it was when we first came here. We will take a train from here to the Polish Border. When we get off, the local Jewish community will arrange for us to be taken by train to Lithuania."

There was muttering among the crowd. "Why can't we take a train directly to Lithuania?" an old man asked.

"Because the terms of the Peace Treaty between Lithuania and the Soviet Union requires that the Soviets only take us to the border," the rabbi replied.

"We came directly here. We should be able to go directly back!" another yelled.

Sarah Taube listened and thought, why are they complaining? They should be thankful they are going home.

There wasn't much for Sarah Taube to do except to count the days before their departure. For a brief moment, she thought about the bakery and wondered what would become of it.

*"Eich hob es in drerd."* The hell with it. "The bakery belongs to the people so let the people take care of it."

Late that afternoon, Sarah Taube received an unexpected visitor.

"Good evening, Comrade Grazutis," Commissar Bogdonovich said. "I've come to see if I can convince you to remain in our country. I know in a few days you and your family will be leaving. Please, Sarah Taube, what can I do to convince you to stay?"

A dozen thoughts flashed through her mind. Should she avoid telling him how she really felt or should she tell him the truth and hope he would accept her reply. A cold sweat broke out on her forehead. She had no idea her heart could beat that fast.

Then she spoke. "You've been very kind to me. I have a husband I have not seen in more than seven years. I have a son I have not heard from since the army took him from me, and my children have not seen their father since they were small."

"But why would you want to return to a place to be exploited by the Capitalists, while the rabbis fill your head with worthless talk? Stay here and help us bring about the workers' paradise. We are creating a new society, and soon we will take over the world. I want you to be part of it. Won't you reconsider?"

Sarah Taube thought for a moment, carefully choosing her words.

"I'm grateful, and I will always be indebted to you for what you have done for my children and me, but I cannot stay. I beg you to understand."

She would not dare tell him she had no desire to take part in this new society of his. She had already experienced a taste of the workers' paradise, and it was not the kind of world she wanted to live in.

"So there's nothing I can do or say to change your mind?" he asked.

"No, Dimitri," she answered, holding her breath momentarily in fear of his reaction. But instead, for the first time, she heard in his voice an expression of love and understanding.

"I have tried my best," he said, "but my best was not good enough. You are a virtuous and strong-willed woman. This is what I most admire about you."

Dimitri looked away for a moment. "You remind me very much of someone I knew and loved many years ago. She was a wonderful woman, intelligent, and full of life as you are, and she used the same rose water in her hair, as you do." Then his eyes filled with tears. Thinking of his beloved Aleksandra brought back memories he had kept pent-up in his heart.

Sarah Taube was surprised to hear him speak in such a personal way. He had not done so before and never had he mentioned a woman in his life. In fact, she was of the impression he was a man without feeling. To learn he had once loved someone made her think, perhaps early in his life, he had been a loving and caring man.

Realizing he had given out far too much information, Dimitri pulled himself together. "I'll be sad to see you go. I will never forget you. And perhaps, when you find yourself alone and your mind drifts back to the time you spent here, you will think kindly of me."

He reached for her hand and kissed it gently. They said their goodbyes, and as she slowly walked away, he could smell the scent of rose water permeating the air behind her.

One week later, at two o'clock in the afternoon, the former residents of Shavlan stood in the park, patiently waiting for the wagons to provide them an exit from the city.

Rabbi Broide was handed a stack of papers and told to keep them safe. Just as Moses had led his people out of bondage from Egypt and into the promised land, he was about to lead his people out of Russia and back to Shavlan.

The Jews were loaded onto the wagons, heading toward the railroad station, and in less than an hour, they had arrived. Everyone disembarked, standing quietly by the tracks, waiting for the train.

Before long, a little boy heard whistling from a distance.

"I hear the train!" he shouted. "I hear the train!"

Once the last person boarded, the train was on its way, heading North through the Ukraine, through White Russia, and on to the border of Poland.

While Rabbi Broide sat by the window looking out at the countryside, he was horrified. Where once there had been rich and productive land, now stood abandoned farms. Where once stood industrial factories spitting out black smoke, now stood silent factories with broken windows. It was a depressing sight, and he wondered what he would see when he reached Shavlan.

⊸O⊷

The next day, the train from Ekaterinoslav came to a stop. The Polish border could be seen over the horizon.

Rabbi Broide and his family were first in line.

"May I see your papers?" the inspector asked.

"Yes," Rabbi Broide replied and handed him the documents. After careful review, the guard approved his paperwork, authorizing him and his family to pass through the gate.

One by one, the others presented their documentation and, except for a few who were singled out for further questioning, were approved for entrance into the country.

Sarah Taube and her children were among those randomly pulled out of line. The guard kept interrogating Sarah Taube to the point where she felt she might be refused entry. By now, even those who were pulled out after her had been approved.

Sarah Taube noticed that the children were standing near the gate that led directly into Poland. While her papers were again being reviewed and unbeknownst to the guard, she quickly pushed them under the hinged barrier until they were on the Polish side of the roadblock. At least, she thought, if she were detained, the children would still be able to continue on to Shavlan.

After answering a few more questions, Sarah Taube was able to convince the guard she had a genuine reason for being there, and he stamped her document, allowing her to pass.

"I'm most grateful, sir," she said to the guard and quickly moved through the barrier. She took hold of her children and kissed each one, still not able to believe her luck.

"How will we get to the train now that we've crossed the border?" an old woman asked.

Emotions began to fly.

Rabbi Broide spoke.

"God will provide us a way," he said in an attempt to calm them.

After a short wait, a caravan of wagons appeared. The leader of the caravan, a middle-aged man with a long black beard, came forward.

"My name is Meyer Mendelsohn," he said greeting the rabbi. We were contacted by Rabbi Yehezkel Livshitz, the President of the Rabbinical Association of Poland. When he learned you and your people were leaving Russia, he organized a committee to assist you in your return to your shtetl.

"I am pleased to tell you, through the generosity of the local Jews, we have collected donations to help you out of a difficult situation. We have been assigned the task of taking you to the train station. Please be advised, you will be provided enough food and water to carry you through the duration of your trip.

"When you board the train to the Lithuanian Border, Lithuanian officials will come on board and check your papers. Once you have been approved, the train will continue to Kovne. Good luck and may you have a safe journey."

"Thank you for your help," Rabbi Broide replied, "and please thank your people."

When the train to Lithuania arrived, the people got on. By now, everyone was in a state of physical and mental fatigue. How much longer would they have to wait? How much more could they endure?

"Will we be there soon, *Mammeh*?" little Fraida asked, holding her mother's hand.

"Be patient, *myne kind.* We'll be there soon."

That afternoon, Rabbi Avraham Shapir, the Chief Rabbi of Kovne, was notified by Rabbi Livshitz, the President of the Rabbinical Association of Poland, giving him the approximate time the Jews of Shavlan would be arriving in his city. He added, he needed to make arrangements for their transportation to the railroad junction near Shavl, close to their homes in Shavlan. He immediately sent a telegram to Count Simonis, giving him the information and asking for his help.

Later that day, Rabbi Shapir received a telegram from the count, stating he was aware of the situation, and he would be happy to assist. He said the Jews would be picked up at the railroad junction near Shavl shortly after their arrival.

The count, after responding to the telegram, arranged a meeting with Mr. Kubilius and Mr. Vycas.

"You know how I've tried to get the intruders out of the Jews' houses," he said, pacing up and down the room with his hands behind his back. "You need to clear them out immediately now that the Jews are returning. We only have a little time, so you have to act quickly. I'll see to it that the farmers pick them up once they get off the train. This town has gone without these people much too long. We need them to open their businesses, and I need them to manage mine."

◄O►

When the people of Shavlan arrived at the Lithuanian Border, exactly as Mr. Mendelsohn stated, officials entered each car and asked for their documentation. Since they were already checked at the border of Poland, everyone's papers were in order. Their arrival in Shavlan was about to be realized.

◄O►

The warm, summer sun sparkled as the Jews of Shavlan got off the train at Kovne. They were overcome with emotion. It was still hard for them to believe they were stepping onto the free soil of their country.

According to reports, approximately one hundred and sixty thousand exiled Lithuanian Jews returned from the Soviet Union to the newly established country of Lithuania.

Rabbi Broide continued to lead, and even he wondered how they were going to get back to Shavlan. After several minutes, the rabbi saw a tall gentleman carrying a sign, "Representative of the Jews of Lithuania."

Rabbi Broide walked slowly over to him. "Are you looking for the Jews of Shavlan?" he asked.

"Yes, I am," the gentleman replied, reaching for a handshake.

"My name is Avraham Shapir, and I'm the Chief Rabbi here in Kovne. Rabbi Livshitz, the President of the Rabbinical Association in Poland, notified me you would be arriving today. He asked us to arrange to have all of you taken by train and dropped off south of Shavl, near Shavlan. Everything has been taken care of, and a train will be here within the hour. Count Simonis has already been notified, and he will arrange transportation from your drop off point back to your shtetl."

This joyful piece of news brought a smile to Rabbi Broide's face. "I want to thank you, Rabbi for those reassuring words."

Rabbi Shapir returned Rabbi Broide's smile and said, "May G-d bless you and keep your people safe."

During the trip from the Kovne Station to the junction near Shavl, Sarah Taube felt the emotions of the people building up in anticipation of returning to their homes after more than five years, and they wondered if and how their lives would change.

Sarah Taube also wondered how she would earn a living and provide for her family in this new Lithuania? Would her husband be waiting for her once she returned? Was life really going to be better than when she first left the country? These questions and many more kept repeating over and over again in her mind.

"We'll be arriving at our final destination in a few minutes!" the conductor called out as the train was approaching the tracks South of Shavl.

Rabbi Broide was already outside by the time everyone stepped out of the train. He once again addressed them.

*"Myne tay'er yiddisha menshen.* We must be patient and trust in G-d. He will take care of us and..."

After he finished speaking, he saw a caravan of horse-drawn wagons coming toward him.

Mr. Kubilius got off the lead wagon and approached the crowd.

After taking a deep breath, he pulled out a sheet of paper and read aloud.

*"Welcome, my friends. When you first left us, the Russian Empire ruled Lithuania, but now we have our independence and our sovereignty has been restored to us. It is an occasion for rejoicing, so now let us all forget the past. We must look to the future..."*

The Jews of Shavlan did not know what this man was talking about. They guessed, in his own peculiar way, he was apologizing for the town's insensitivity to their expulsion.

While Sarah Taube listened, she was more convinced than ever that she did not belong in this country. For him to stand there and expect them to forgive and forget all that had happened to them was beyond her understanding.

What a hypocrite he was, she thought. No one wanted to hear his sanctimonious talk. There were no cheers or shouts of joy among the Jews that day. All they wanted was to get back to their homes and begin anew the lives they had left behind.

As Sarah Taube and the children walked toward the wagons, she heard a loud cry.

"Sarala. Sarala. It's Charles."

When Sarah Taube first saw Charles, her heart sank. This cannot be my husband, she thought.

A long silence followed.

"Charles, is it really you?" she asked. A flood of memories came rushing back. His appearance was not that of the strong and energetic man she had last seen leaving her house. It seemed as though he had aged some thirty years. Charles reminded her of the old marble figurine Mrs. Bressler had displayed in her china cabinet, so worn it had chipped and turned gray.

Charles walked slowly toward her and embraced her with all the strength he could gather from his weakened body. "I missed you so much, my Sarala."

As soon as he called her his Sarala, thoughts came back of the happy days they spent together so many years ago. She wrapped her arms around his neck and gave him a kiss, and it was clear their love for each other had not diminished in the face of all they had gone through.

Charles attempted to hug the children but they pulled away.

This saddened Sarah Taube.

"*Kinder*, this is your *Tateh*," she explained, trying hard not to admonish them for being disrespectful.

Chaya, after studying her father's face, soon recognized him. She lovingly stretched out her arms calling, "*Tateh*, *Tateh*, I've missed you so much."

Charles got down on his knees. Chaya jumped into his arms and buried her head in his chest. "Don't ever leave us again, *Tateh*," she whispered in his ear.

Because Fraida and Masha were very young when their father left for Johannesburg, he looked vaguely familiar to them, but they kept their distance.

"Where are Avram and Gitka?" Charles asked, looking at the others standing nearby.

Sarah Taube was well aware that one day she would have to tell him what had happened and sadly, that day had come.

After they boarded the wagon, she began to explain the tragic circumstances involved in their deaths. When Charles heard the news, he was overcome with grief, and his eyes clouded with tears.

"I wish I had been there for you, Sarala," he said, taking hold of her hand.

"I didn't have the heart to write you," she replied, her voice shaking with every word. "I kept putting it off and when the war began, there was no time to think of anything else. Please forgive me."

"I understand, Sarala. You were under a great deal of pressure, but it's still a shock finding out this way."

Charles hesitated for a moment. "What about Yankel? In Ruchel's letter she wrote that Yankel was in the army, and you had not heard from him."

"Yes, it is true. I fear something awful has happened to him."

"I know, Sarala. Only last week I contacted the International Committee for Missing Persons. Hopefully, we'll get some answers."

While the wagon crossed the road, heading toward town, Sarah Taube spotted Shaina and her family.

"We're home at last!" Shaina shouted. "Isn't it wonderful being back?"

Sarah Taube gave a quick nod. She was certainly happy to have left Ekaterinoslav but to spend the rest of her life in this town was not the future she had in mind.

Dusk fell rapidly as the caravan traveled across the countryside and in the distance, one could see the crossroads at the bottom of the hill leading to town.

After a while, the wagon stopped in front of their house.

Sarah Taube noticed, like Charles had noticed, the beautiful sign they had displayed so proudly was no longer beautiful. It was old and broken and the letters were faded.

When the door opened and they walked in, the walls threw back the echoes of their footsteps. The light coming from outside gave notice to the peeling paint on the walls, and the beautiful lace curtain, which once adorned the window of the shop, had yellowed with age. Still, it felt good to be home. At last, the family was together again.

After Charles and Sarah Taube settled in, and the children were fed and put to bed, the two of them had a chance to discuss their plans for the future.

Charles filled his glass with tea and took a sip before he spoke.

"Count Simonis has been a good friend. He made sure our home was made decent enough for us to live in. The only thing missing is my sewing machine."

Sarah Taube sat back in her chair and folded her arms. "What do you want to do with your life now that you're back?"

Charles looked tired. His frame slouched forward in the chair and his hands began to shake. "All I know is I don't want to be a tailor. Are you surprised, Sarala?"

"Yes, I am. May I ask why?"

Charles sat quietly for a few moments. "I'm not sure why," he replied with a blank stare.

"Tell me Sarala, what do you want to do?"

What Sarah Taube really wanted to do was to make her lifelong dream come true. She wanted to leave Shavlan with her family and go to America. However, this was not the time to bring it up. She suspected Charles had not changed his mind or he would have suggested it in his letters. Besides, she didn't want to upset him, especially since he was obviously in poor health. Learning about the death of Avram and Gitka was shocking enough for him.

Sarah Taube stood from her chair. "I've been giving it a lot of thought. I'm thinking of opening a bakery."

Charles looked up at her and smiled. "If this is your wish, I see no problem with it. Tomorrow, we'll make plans to search for a location."

Then an idea came to her. "Would you like to help me run the bakery?"

"Yes," he replied as his eyes lit up and his hands stopped shaking.

After spending a short time with Charles, Sarah Taube could see he had changed. Where was the strong, self-determined man she had known in the past? She was beginning to wonder if the old Charles would ever return to her.

Within a few weeks, things were back to normal in the Grazutis household. The Jewish community had settled into their familiar routine and Jewish businesses were reopening. The count had rehired the Jews who once worked for him, and the vendors were once again at the local market selling their wares.

When Sarah Taube came home from the market one evening, she found Charles intently eyeing the old sign in front of the house.

"What are you doing out here," she asked. "It's getting late."

Charles remained silent, and then he grabbed hold of both sides of the sign's wooden base and, with all the strength he could gather, pulled them up and dropped them on the ground. He stood aside to allow Sarah Taube the satisfaction of being the first to see what he had done.

Sarah Taube stared at him, not sure what had caused this sudden display of violence until he got down on his knees, stared at the gaping hole, and shouted at the top of his voice, "Dear G-d, what have I accomplished in my life."

Sarah Taube's heart almost stopped beating. She walked across to her husband and kissed him gently. "Come inside," she said and took hold of his hand and helped him up the stairs. "I'll make you a glass of tea."

Charles quickly let go of her hand but only because he refused to allow her to help him up the stairs of their house.

Late one afternoon, Charles heard a firm rap on the front door.

"Hello, is anyone at home?"

Who could it possible be, Charles thought. He did not recognize the voice.

It was Mr. Koppel, looking very much different from when he had seen him last. His hair had turned grey, and he walked with a limp.

"Come in," Charles said, trying not to appear shocked at his appearance. "I wondered what had become of you. My wife told me you were conscripted into the army almost the same time as my Yankel."

"Yes," Mr. Koppel replied. "After the war, I returned to Shidleve and opened a tailor shop."

As Charles led Mr. Koppel into the small living area, Sarah Taube appeared.

"Good afternoon," she said, also taken aback by the way he looked. "This is an unexpected visit," she said, offering him a seat. "What brings you here?"

"Forgive me for calling so late in the afternoon. I need to speak with the two of you. It's about your son Yankel. I felt I must make this call as soon as possible, once I had gotten word you and your family had returned."

Mr. Koppel cleared his throat. "I'm afraid I have some bad news."

Sarah Taube's legs began to give way.

Charles quickly caught her and guided her to a nearby chair.

"Go on, Mr. Koppel," he said.

"I'm sorry to have to inform you that Yankel is no longer with us. May his soul be inscribed for a blessing?"

Sarah Taube's face grew pale.

An uneasy silence followed until Charles spoke. "How do you know this to be true?"

"Let me explain," Mr. Koppel replied.

"As I remember, Yankel was conscripted shortly before I was called up, and we both happened to be sent to the same training facility. After a month of military training, the two of us were placed in the same infantry battalion, and within days, we found ourselves deployed at the front in direct combat with the German army. Fierce fighting broke out. Our supply of ammunition and provisions were running low, and before long, the German soldiers were advancing. Our battalion was ordered to retreat. It was during our withdrawal when I heard the colonel give the order to place the Jewish unit behind our retreating line.

"Everyone was well aware that during battle if advancing, Jewish troops would be ordered to move up to the front but if retreating, they were ordered to move to the back. This way, in either case, we Jews would be the first to fall."

Sarah Taube sat bolt upright, stunned at what she was hearing. It was exactly the way the Jewish soldier had described when he spoke to the rabbi and her the day they visited the hospital in Ekaterinoslav, and it had happened to Yankel the exact same way. She could no longer listen. It was hard for her to accept that her son would never be coming home.

"What does this have to do with our Yankel?" Charles asked.

Mr. Koppel looked at Sarah Taube and then at Charles.

"Yankel and I were in that Jewish unit. When I looked behind me, I saw him within firing range of the Germans, and within minutes, he was hit and fell to the ground. I watched with straining eyes for the faintest stir, but nothing about him moved."

After hearing the news, both Sarah Taube and Charles were reduced to silence. There was nothing more to say.

Mr. Koppel glanced at his watch. "I must be going now. Please forgive me for bringing you such sad news."

As Mr. Koppel limped out of the house, Sarah Taube felt a little guilty. She did not even offer him a glass of tea.

When Sarah Taube climbed into bed that night, she couldn't get to sleep, thinking about Mr. Koppel's description of how Yankel had met his death. Now she knew why Yankel was always in her dreams, along with Gitka and Avram. G-d was trying to tell her something.

The following Sabbath, the Jews gathered in the synagogue to pay their last respects to the memory of Yankel Grazutis.

Rabbi Broide stood in front of his congregation and began his first sermon since returning to Shavlan.

"Welcome," he said, looking very solemn.

"After being driven out of Lithuania for over five years, thank goodness we have returned to a much better place than we left. At last, we have an independent Lithuania. Let us hope we will be able to live in a country where we will share in the rights granted to all Lithuanian citizens.

"Today, we say prayers for our dearly, departed Yankel Grazutis, son of Charles and Sarah Taube Grazutis, much loved brother of Ruchel, Chaya, Masha, Fraida and our dearly departed Avam and Gitka.

"Yankel had a bright future ahead of him. All he wanted was to study the Torah and one day become a biblical scholar. He did not want to go to war but when his country called on him, he went willingly."

Rabbi Broide stopped talking for a moment and looked around the room. "Yankel died in combat defending Tsarist Russia. However, he really died upholding the rights of all Jews to live in peace and harmony. May he live in our hearts forever. Now, let us pray."

# Chapter 35 – Family Conflict

## December 1920 – Ellwood City, Pennsylvania, USA

One morning while Rose was in the kitchen fixing breakfast, she called to William, "Can you get the mail, sweetheart? I'm busy."

"All right," he replied.

Within minutes, he returned.

"I have good news. It's a letter from your mother."

Rose ran into the living room, took the letter out of William's hand, and made herself confortable in her favorite chair.

"What does she have to say," William asked, peering over Rose's shoulder.

Rose began to read aloud.

*4 November 1920*
*Myne tay'er tochter un aidim,*

*We have at long last returned to Shavlan.*

*Ruchel, I want you to prepare yourself for what I am about to tell you. I have very sad news. Yankel will not be returning to us. We found out he was killed in action in 1915. Mr. Koppel, who served in his regiment, witnessed his tragic death.*

"Oh my G-d," Rose cried out as tears ran down her cheeks. *"Myne bruder is toyt."* My brother is dead.

"I'm so sorry," William said, pulling out his handkerchief to wipe her tears.

Her brother was gone and there was nothing more to say. She

pulled herself together and continued reading.

I have one more piece of sad news. Please forgive me for not telling you earlier. Gitka contracted diphtheria. She fought very hard but the disease was too much for her.

Again, Rose cried, "Oh my G-d, *myne shvester is toit.*" My sister is dead.

This was too much for Rose. She felt faint. The letter dropped to the floor.

"Don't read anymore," William urged.

"No, I'm fine," Rose replied.

After a few moments, William picked up the letter and handed it to her.

*It happened shortly after you left for America, and I did not have the heart to tell you. I waited so long to let you know that it became more difficult as the years went by. But now, Tateh convinced me it's time for you to know, as it would not be fair to keep it from you any longer. Please forgive me.*

*Now for some good news. I want to tell you Tateh and I have recently bought a bakery, and here is the big surprise. We purchased Aunt Lena's old shop. I plan to open it very soon.*

*I am still trying to convince Tateh we should join you and the family in America, but, despite my attempts, he still remains very much against it.*

*The children are well and send their love. We all hope you and William are in good health and happy. Give our regards to the family and write soon.*

*Your loving Mammeh and Tateh*

Within several months of being back in Shavlan, Sarah Taube had built up a nice business and was kept quite busy. Little by little, the Jewish population continued to decline. More and more were leaving for America and some were leaving for Palestine.

New changes in Lithuania's laws and regulations were being put into effect on a daily basis. In the past, Yiddish was allowed as a method of communication in Jewish businesses. But during this period of Lithuanian independence and national pride, a standard Lithuanian language was formed, and all businesses, including Jewish ones, were required to use it as their means of communication. All signs in Yiddish were restricted.

This new requirement was quite burdensome for most of the Jewish business owners since many of them, living in small shtetls, never learned or spoke any language other than Yiddish.

As time went on, more demands were made. Jewish schools were being forced to devote more time and education to Lithuanian culture, traditions, and language.

Although some Jewish educators fought against introducing these new demands into the classroom, most Jews realized, in order to be accepted into the new society, it was of vital importance they adhere to the new requirements.

In the months that followed, Sarah Taube was deeply concerned about what was happening in the country and thoughts of emigrating to America became uppermost in her mind once again.

---

The birds were sunning their wings, as they exposed themselves to the warm spring weather. Rose and William had finished eating breakfast.

"Rose, come into the parlor," William called, while he was enjoying a quiet morning reading the Sunday paper. "I'm reading an article I think will interest you."

"What is it, William?" she asked, untying her apron.

"It's about immigration in the United States and concerns President Harding has regarding too many people coming into the country."

Rose pulled up a chair.

"Go on, William. I'm listening."

"It says President Harding had sent Lillian Russell to Europe on a fact-finding mission to find out why there's such an increase in immigration. And after investigating, she recommended that a five-year moratorium be enacted. Last year, I remember reading that the President signed into law an Emergency Quota Act, limiting the number of immigrants entering the country."

Rose gave William a curious look. "Why is the government cracking down on immigrants now?"

"I'm not sure, but I had read many Americans fear that the large influx of immigrants will change American traditions and customs. What they really mean is they want to prevent more southern European Italians and eastern Europeans Jews from entering the country, so new laws are created to keep them out. It's another form of discrimination."

Rose stood and placed her hands on her hips.

"This does not sound good for *Mammeh*, *Tateh*, and the children. It sounds to me like our government is cracking down, and soon no one will be allowed to come here, thanks to our friend, Lillian Russell. Why he picked her as his emissary is beyond me. She's only an entertainer. What in the world does she know about such matters?"

"Well, she and the President have become close friends," William replied, placing the newspaper on the table. "Don't you remember when she campaigned for him, along with Al Jolson, Douglas Fairbanks, and Mary Pickford? Even Thomas Edison, Henry Ford, and Harvey Firestone gave their endorsements to his run for office."

"I can't believe Al Jolson is in with that bunch," Rose replied. "I guess he's lost touch with his Jewish roots."

"This situation sounds very serious. You had better write your mother. Time is running out, and they need to make arrangements to come here, or they may never get another opportunity."

While Rose sat by the window writing her letter, she wondered if she would ever see her family again.

With the approach of spring, Sarah Taube began to notice a change in Charles. He had grown so thin that even his clothes hung off him like flax on a spindle. He looked very tired so she refrained from asking his assistance in most things.

"Sarala, do you have any need for me today?" he asked, holding one of his religious books in his hand.

"No, Charles. You go and rest."

His cough had become more severe. He refused to seek medical help, and much to Sarah Taube's displeasure, he continued to smoke heavily. He was definitely in a state of depression, and there were times when his mind was beginning to fail him. Most days, she didn't have much to say to him and whenever she mentioned America, he would take a book and disappear into the bedroom.

Important matters had to be discussed with regard to their future, but he was not willing to listen. Even the children were beginning to complain. They were no longer babies and could sense the constant friction between their parents.

Sarah Taube realized that the discontent in the Grazutis family could no longer be overlooked. Decisions needed to be made and made quickly.

One Monday afternoon in the middle of April, Sarah Taube had just finished an order for her friend Shaina.

Shaina was doing well and was able to resume the operation of her business without much difficulty. This was mainly because she had left her employees in charge while she was gone, and they made sure her property was well protected. She owed them a debt of gratitude and made sure they were well rewarded for their efforts.

"Are you still looking to resettle in America," Shaina asked while picking up her purchase.

Sarah Taube stepped out from behind the display case.

"Yes. If only I can convince my husband to see it my way."

"I don't understand why you want to leave. Things are so much better than they were when we first lived here. We can move about freely, and soon we'll be given all the rights and privileges other Lithuanians enjoy."

Sarah Taube smiled, putting up her best defense. "For you, it's a big improvement. Your business is doing well, and you're content with the way things are. But for me, all I can see is more misery and unhappiness. Besides, I want to see Ruchel with my own eyes and meet her husband."

There was nothing more to say. Sarah Taube had reached a decision and was determined to carry it out.

The next afternoon, while taking inventory of her stock, she heard the bell over the front door jingle.

"Good afternoon, Mrs. Grazutis. You have a letter from America, and I believe it's from your daughter Ruchel. She lives in Ellwood City, Pennsylvania, doesn't she?"

Nothing much had changed from the way Mr. Stedman delivered the mail. He was still his usual nosy self.

After dinner that evening, Sarah Taube called the family together to read Ruchel's letter.

*May 8, 1922*
*Myne tay'er Mammeh un tay'er Tateh,*

*I hope this letter finds you in good health, and I'm happy you are settled in Shavlan. I have some disturbing news. William and I read that our President Harding is thinking about imposing new immigration laws, prohibiting certain people from coming into the United States.*

As Sarah Taube read, she sensed urgency in the letter.

*We encourage you and Tateh to look into leaving Lithuania as soon as possible. I fear the government will crack down on how many Jews they will allow into the country.*

Sarah Taube glanced at Charles to see his reaction. He was unmoved and said nothing.

Chaya looked at her mother. "*Mammeh*, this sounds very bad. Ruchel and her husband are telling us to leave as soon as possible. *Tateh,* you have to make arrangements quickly before it's too late."

"Yes, *Tateh*, we have to leave now," both Fraida and Masha said, hearing how upset their sister was.

Even the children were voicing their opinions. This was not the time to quarrel with Charles, Sarah Taube realized, especially in front of the children. It was obvious to her, he was unwilling to be involved in yet another argument about a subject which was distasteful to him.

Sarah Taube put the letter down on the table and looked up for a moment.

"Keep on reading, *Mammeh*" Chaya said. "What else does she say?"

Sarah Taube picked the letter up and continued.

*William and I are very happy. I love and miss you very much. Take good care of yourselves, and remember my warning. Please write soon with good news.*
*Love and kisses to all,*
*Ruchel and William*

Charles suddenly rose from his chair and disappeared into the bedroom, while the children watched with sad faces.

A strange and unaccustomed silence came over the room as Sarah Taube folded the letter and placed it back in the envelope. The children looked at her sadly and then disappeared in their rooms, and it was clear to her they were not looking forward to spending the rest of their lives in Shavlan.

Hardly a word passed between the Grazutis family over dinner that evening. The children knew because their father refused to discuss their present situation with their mother, it would have a disastrous effect on all of them.

The Juneberry shrubs William had planted last spring were in full bloom.

"You'll never guess," William said, glancing at the front page of the morning paper.

"Guess what?" Rose asked, while placing a plate full of scrambled eggs and toasted muffins in front of him.

"Lillian Russell has died," he replied, visibly shocked by the information.

"Really. What happened?"

"It says she suffered from complications of injuries sustained, while she was on a ship returning from a trip to Europe and listen to this. She was again on a fact-finding mission for the president."

"What was she doing in Europe this time?" Rose asked, pouring William a cup of coffee.

"Wait a minute. Let me read more. Oh, here it is. He asked her to find out why there's still an increase in immigration to this country. It says here, she died in her home two days ago."

"I didn't wish her any harm," Rose replied, "but I believe G-d punished her for conducting these investigations."

William put down the paper for a moment and then picked it up again. "This is very strange," he said, as he continued to read. "She was buried with full military honors. She must have done something good for the country but darn if I know what it was."

"Well, I guess she won't be going on any more fact-finding trips," Rose said sarcastically.

William took a sip of coffee and replied, "I'm sure though, it was a big loss to the theatrical industry. It's too bad we never got a chance to see her perform."

---

It was autumn and the Lithuanian countryside was ablaze with yellow and orange as the trees were beginning to shed their leaves. One could see the local farmers harvesting their crops and fruits in anticipation of a harsh winter.

Sarah Taube was preoccupied with the running of her business, and there was little time to think about anything else. Charles had become more of a loner with each passing day. He was no help to her, and as time went on, she grew more concerned about his general appearance and the state of his health.

They had very little to say to each other and when they finally did speak, the conversation was always about Sarah Taube's eagerness to move to America.

To avoid arguments, he would disappear into the bedroom and bury himself in his religious books and this would aggravate her even more. It was good she had the bakery because it was a means of escaping the unpleasant reality of what her life had become.

Late one afternoon when Sarah Taube was about to close the shop, Mrs. Bleekman came running in, full of excitement.

"I have some news for you," she said, untying her headscarf and placing it on the counter.

"I hope it's good news," Sarah Taube replied. "I certainly could use some good news."

"Well, it's good news for me, but I'm afraid you won't be happy."

"And what kind of news could make me so unhappy?"

"I'm leaving Shavlan, my dear. In fact, I'm leaving Lithuania. I'm going to America."

"America!" Sarah Taube shouted. "Why America? I thought you liked living here."

"Why America!" Mrs. Bleekman blurted out. "It's because I can't make a living here. There are no eligible young men left in this town. The only ones available are old widowers looking for beautiful young wives. The few young girls still around have turned up their noses at the prospect of marrying some *alter kocker*—old geezer. And even worse, some *alter kocker* with children."

Sarah Taube thought for a moment. "I didn't know you had family in America."

"But I do. My late husband, may he rest in peace, had a sister in Brooklyn, New York. Ever since we got back from Ekaterinoslav, I've been corresponding with her, and recently, she asked me to come and live with her."

Sarah Taube reached across the counter and took hold of Mrs. Bleekman's hand. "Then go," she said. "Now that you have the opportunity to leave, take advantage of it."

Sarah Taube wished her good luck and watched from the window, as she hastily disappeared down the rutted dirt road.

One evening, while doing the books, Sarah Taube noticed the figures from her receipts showed a decrease in profit over the past year. People were leaving to resettle elsewhere, thus there were fewer customers to patronize her bakery. With Charles not bringing in money and her income going down, it was getting harder for her to keep the business going.

It was ironic, she thought. Not long ago, she had a man who was strong and forceful and made all the decisions, but their roles had changed. Now she was the strong and forceful one and the decision-maker.

Even though she could no longer bear to look at Charles whom she had not spoken to for several days, late one night, while she and Charles were getting ready for bed, she thought it was a good time once again to bring up the forbidden topic.

"Have you had any recent thoughts about our leaving for America?" she asked.

Charles smiled and nodded his head the way people do when they aren't listening. He buried his head in his hands and didn't speak for some time. When he finally looked up, he said, "My mind has not changed, Sarala. I have made no secret about it all these years and nothing or no one can make me think differently."

Although Sarah Taube was aware Charles had given up all thoughts of making America his home, she still had to bring up the subject from time to time. She was waiting for that perfect moment when she would present him with a prepared list of reasons why they have to leave.

Nearly five months passed. Spring was here and the lilacs were in bloom. On this particular morning, the congregation had assembled in the synagogue not only to observe the Sabbath services but also to hear the rabbi deliver his usual heart-rending sermon before an important holiday.

"Good morning. I'm glad to see such happy faces gathered among you. In a few days we will celebrate Shavuos. This happy holiday is a poignant reminder of the passing of time. Many years have gone by since that sad day when we were about to pay tribute to this wonderful holiday. How could we forget that day? It was a harrowing experience for us, but we survived as our people have survived throughout the centuries. I have said many times, you have made me proud to have served as your rabbi."

He paused for a moment to clear his throat. "Sadly, I must tell you that on the 1st of June, of this year, I will no longer serve as the Rabbi of Shavlan."

A low murmur spread throughout the sanctuary. This news was unexpected. They were losing the one man who kept them together and guided them throughout the years of confusion and uncertainty.

With so many people, including rabbis, leaving Lithuania, the congregation knew it would be impossible to replace him. No one would want to move to their shtetl without a rabbi and before long, the Jewish population of Shavlan would disappear.

As soon as the whispering subsided, Rabbi Broide continued.

"I know this is a shock to you, and perhaps I should have spoken earlier. During the past months, I've been faced with a difficult choice. I had to decide whether to stay here and see if Shavlan would once more be filled with families or leave for another place, where I can be a religious leader and continue with my teachings.

"Several months ago, I was offered a position as Head Rabbi in a city called Baltimore in America. After careful deliberation with the *rebbetsen*, I have come to the conclusion it would be in the best interest of my family to accept the position, and I will be leaving on the 2nd of July.

"I will miss you and hope to hear from you throughout the coming years. Observe the holiday and enjoy the festivities, and may G-d continue to bless and keep you safe."

Most of the congregation did not fault the rabbi for his decision since Jews in many of the Lithuanian shtetls were doing the same thing. They had the right to leave the country and make a better life for themselves and their families. Rabbi Broide certainly had that same right. Who were they to judge?

That evening, after the children had gone to bed, Charles called Sarah Taube into the kitchen. He pulled out a cigarette, sat her down beside him, and poured her a glass of tea.

"This town is changing with each passing day," he said. "Now that our rabbi is leaving, our synagogue will soon cease to exist and the Jewish community here will disappear. So I've come to the conclusion, we must leave this shtetl and…"

Before Charles could finish his sentence, Sarah Taube spoke.

"At last you have come to your senses," she cried.

"Let me finish, Sarala. I've been looking into the possibility of moving to a large city."

A large city, Sarah Taube thought. What is he talking about?

"And what city might that be?" she asked.

"Keidan. That's the city I have in mind. Keidan is only thirty-two miles north of Kovne and has a population of over five hundred families, and they have a synagogue too. It would be a great place to bring up the children. The town has only one bakery so there would be room for you to open one of your own."

Sarah Taube at first was speechless. Then she realized this was the moment she was waiting for.

"Another city!" she shouted, her feet angrily tapping on the floor. "Why would I want to move to another city when I want to move out of this miserable country?

"Very soon, Keidan will be in the same position as Shavlan and then where will we go? Jews are not only leaving shtetls but they're leaving Europe.

"I believe we have not seen the end of our people's suffering. *Es vet bald kumen an andere milkhome*—Another war will soon come. And when that happens, we Jews will not be able to escape the hell which will be forced on us."

She paused for a few moments, waiting for Charles' reply. He looked away. This infuriated her even more. She began to pace back and forth, stomping her feet impatiently. Her face went livid, and right then and there she knew exactly what she needed to say.

"I'm taking the children and leaving for America!" she yelled. "If you wish, you can come with us but if not, you can stay here. So make up your mind."

This was something Charles thought he would never hear coming from his Sarala's lips. He was stunned. He had never seen her so angry and to give him an ultimatum, truly threw him off guard. It was as if he were hearing her for the first time. Either he goes with her and the children or he stays in Lithuania and lives out his life alone.

Thinking over seriously what his wife had just said, he lowered his head for a moment and took a deep breath. Then he spoke in a soft gentle voice that made you want to listen.

"I love you and need you very much, my Sarala. Even though I prefer to stay here, I will not be content living without you and the children. If it makes you happy moving to America, I will go. Write the family, and tell them I will get the documentation as quickly as possible. Next week, I'll go to Kovne and make the necessary arrangements."

Charles rose and almost stepped toward her but stopped in his tracks at the look on her face.

She could not avoid showing her anger. "You don't know how long I've waited to hear you say those words."

Sarah Taube felt as if a heavy load had been lifted from her shoulders. At last, she felt something positive in her life was about to happen.

The next day, during the afternoon, Mr. Stedman delivered a letter and, as luck would have it, it was from her brother, Aaron.

*May 2, 1923*

*My dear Sarah Taube,*

*I received a letter from Ruchel. She does not understand why you have not followed up on her urging you to leave the country. We're all aware our government will soon pass a law that will restrict people wanting to emigrate from Eastern European countries. This would be you and your family.*

*The only way you'll be able to come into the United States is to have a relative who is a citizen vouch for you. So I have undertaken the responsibility of acting as your sponsor. I'll fill out the proper papers and when it is approved, I'll mail them to you so you can present them to the authorities at Ellis Island.*

*In this envelope I have taken the liberty of sending you a money order, which will cover passage for you, Charles and the children. You'll have to make the arrangements through the steamship company in Kovne and purchase your tickets there. There is enough money for two third-class cabins.*

*You must take care of this quickly. This is the best place for you and the family. Take advantage of it now, while you can.*

*Your loving brother,*

*Aaron*

# Chapter 36 – Intellectual Discussion

## July 1923 – Shavlan, Republic of Lithuania

Sarah Taube and Charles rose early this morning. They were finally going to close on the sale of the bakery. A very nice couple, the Lachmans, had agreed to purchase the shop.

Charles and Sarah Taube had very little time to put their affairs in order. Arrangements were made for them to leave and be in Bremen, Germany in time for their ship's departure on the 22nd of August.

Sarah Taube and the children were happy to be leaving Shavlan after so many years of thinking it would never happen. Charles did not express feelings one-way or the other and went along with whatever decisions Sarah Taube made. He was not a well man, but he seemed at peace with himself.

A week before the ship was to sail, the long awaited day had arrived. The Grazutis family was leaving for Bremen, Germany to board the ship called the *America*.

Sarah Taube put the last item into the suitcase, making sure her mother's candlesticks and copper pot were tightly packed away. The family photograph was placed in her carrying bag, along with the documents needed for the trip.

May I come in," a voice called from outside the shop. "It's Shaina."

"Come in" Sarah Taube said, offering her a chair. "I was sitting here thinking about you and how long we've known each other."

"Quite a long time," Shaina replied, "and we've lived through many hardships. We're good friends. I wish for your life to be full of happiness, and may you always be in G-d's favor and protection."

Sarah Taube put her arms around her. "Yes, we have gone through a lot," she said, "but because of those hardships, we have become much stronger women. It's a bittersweet moment for me. I too wish you all the best, and I will always hold you dear to my heart."

The two women cried and then embraced. No goodbyes needed to be said as Shaina walked out the door.

With sadness in her heart, Sarah Taube went to the window and watched while her best friend headed down the street, disappearing out of her life forever.

Sarah Taube knew the moment she stepped on board the *America* at Bremen that she was embarking on a journey she had been dreaming and preparing for most of her life.

As she watched the dock recede, a small bird flew overhead and landed at her feet. The bird looked up at her as if to say, "Now you are as free as I am."

One evening, while Sarah Taube and her family were finishing their dinner, a young couple with a little boy around two years old asked if they could join them.

"We're the Macklins," the man said, placing the small child in a chair next to him. "My name is Boris. This is my wife, Anna and our son, Mikhail. How are you enjoying the ship?"

Sarah Taube took a sip of tea and introduced herself.

"My name is Sarah Taube Grazutis, and yes, I'm enjoying the ship very much."

After exchanging pleasantries, the gentleman asked where she was from.

"I'm from Shavlan, a small shtetl in Lithuania and where are you from?"

He scooted his chair close to her and replied, "We are from Petrograd in the Soviet Union."

"So you're from Petrograd?"

This poor family must have fled the country not wanting to remain under Soviet rule, Sarah Taube thought, and after spending over two years living under the Soviets in Ekaterinoslav, she certainly could sympathize with them.

"You must be happy to have gotten out of that country?" she asked. "It's terrible that the people have to live under such conditions."

"How would you know?" Boris questioned, giving her a rapid inspection with his eyes. "I'm sure you would agree, the people are much better off now than they were under the Tsar."

"How would I know?" she replied angrily. "I've lived under the

Tsar's rule and under the Bolsheviks' rule. I was there when the White Army took control and when the Red Army marched in and reclaimed control. I was there during the Russian Revolution, and I was there during the Russian Civil War. I was there and witnessed it all. The people are much better off, you say. This could not be further from the truth."

"My dear woman, I'm afraid I must disagree with you."

"Tell me, why did you leave if living there was so wonderful?" she asked.

"We had to leave. My wife was a pediatrician, and I was an official of the Communist Party. My job was to re-educate the people to our way of thinking.

"After living in Petrograd for several years, it was decided by the Party to transfer my wife to another place hundreds of miles away. We were told it was for the good of the people, but I was to remain in Petrograd.

"We had already a son, Mikhail, and she was to take him with her. We decided we did not want to be separated, so we made arrangements to be secretly smuggled out of the country."

Sarah Taube could not believe her ears. She stood with her hands on her hips, trying hard to regain her composure.

"You mean if the Communist government makes a decision affecting your personal life and if you don't like that decision, it's all right for you and your family to go against them. But others have to abide by the rules the Communists set forth. Is this what you're telling me?"

Sarah Taube waited to hear his answer but he did not reply, and it was obvious to her he was feeling quite uncomfortable.

In Ekaterinoslav, she had similar talks with people of his sort and knew it was useless to carry on an intelligent conversation with them. Case in point was Dimitri Bogdonovich. These people were stuck in a particular mind-set and nothing she could say or do would ever change their way of thinking.

After a few moments, the man picked up his son, took hold of his wife's hand, and politely excused himself.

As the family left the dining salon, Sarah Taube noticed that Mr. Macklin was dressed in a well-tailored, wool suit and his wife wore a silk dress with lace trimming. They were a lot better dressed than the other immigrants on board the ship.

"I see that the Bolsheviks made sure their party members were well dressed, even though the workers wore rags," she muttered under her breath.

Sarah Taube failed to make the connection that when she was

living in Ekaterinoslav, didn't the commissar provide her with a means of making a living, while others starved?

The following morning, Charles, while having breakfast with his family, felt the urge to have a cigarette. Sarah Taube did not approve of him smoking and wished he would stop. She immediately recognized the look on his face and knew he was going for a smoke.

As he exhaled, he leaned over the railing of the *America* and saw the water rushing by the side of the ship. A sudden intense feeling came over him. Just as the water was rushing by so had his life, realizing his ambition to become a success had vanished before his very eyes.

When Sarah Taube saw Charles heading for the stairs, she was concerned. She left Chaya in charge of Fraida and Masha and rushed to the upper deck.

As soon as she saw Charles leaning over the railing, a wave of panic came over her. With a slight tremble in her voice, she said, "Don't even think about it."

Charles looked out across the ocean and for a time did not speak.

It was Sarah Taube who finally broke the silence.

"Charles, come away from there. Let's go for a walk around the deck."

Charles turned his head in her direction and slowly walked over to her. He took her in his arms and said, "Sarala, you know I would never do anything to make you unhappy." Sarah Taube seemed satisfied with his reply.

The next two weeks seemed like eternity to Sarah Taube, and today the tiring long-awaited trip was coming to an end. The Captain announced that the ship would be coming into the New York Harbor in twenty minutes and if anyone wanted to see the Statue of Liberty, they should do so now.

"*Cum kinder*," Sarah Taube said, taking hold of little Fraida's hand. "I have waited practically all my life to see this beautiful lady, and I want you to see her too."

By now, the deck was overflowing with eager spectators and the statue was within sight. Some people were knelling down in prayer, while others were wiping tears from their eyes. How lovely she was, standing tall, holding a book of laws in one hand and a torch in the other.

"*Mammeh,*" Fraida asked, "why are the people crying?"

"We express our emotions in many different ways, *myne kind.* Look at the wild birds flying in the sky. Do you hear them singing?"

"Yes, *Mammeh.* The birds are happy they are free."

"Of course they are. Just as the birds are free, so are the people who will soon be leaving the ship. This is what the Statue of Liberty represents to all immigrants."

"You mean just like us?" Fraida asked in her sweet voice.

"Yes, *myne kind.* Just like us."

Once the Statue of Liberty passed, there was nothing more to see until the ship pulled into the dock.

After the first and second class passengers disembarked, those in third class were ready to leave the ship and board a ferry to take them to Ellis Island, the entry point for immigrants to the U.S.

With their tickets pinned to their clothing and their documents in hand, the Grazutis family entered the main building and waited behind two long lines. Doctors stood on either side of the line, spot-checking each person for any obvious physical or mental defects and if any appeared, they were noted. Happily, the first part of the inspection was completed by the Grazutis family without a problem.

Then they went on to the second part of the examination, the physical, including the test for trachoma. After the doctors probed their bodies, looking for any sign of illness and tested them for signs of trachoma, it was determined they were fit and able to move on.

Now the final test was about to begin, the asking of the twenty-nine questions. Sarah Taube had reviewed the questions with her family over and over again during their time on board the ship.

While they stood in line, waiting their turn, Sarah Taube witnessed exactly how one could totally mess up their answers and get into trouble with the authorities.

One woman was asked how many sons she had in America. She told them she had two sons, and on the Manifest, it stated she had only one. The more she spoke, the worse it got and before she knew it, they had pulled her out of the line for further questioning.

Before long, Charles, Sarah Taube and the children were called by the inspector to step forward. "Good afternoon," he said as a smile reshaped his stern face. "May I see your papers?"

"Yes," Charles answered politely.

The inspector, with an interpreter at his side and referring to the ship's Manifest, began asking Charles questions. At first, Charles answered without difficulty. However, when the questions got more complicated, Charles hesitated, thus appearing to the examiner to be unsure of himself.

It became obvious to Sarah Taube that Charles could not continue. If he should give even one wrong answer, he could be found unsuitable for admittance and subjected to deportation. She had to do something quickly.

"I beg your pardon," she said. "Would it be all right for me to answer the remaining questions?"

"Come closer," the inspector replied.

Luckily, he was in a good mood and agreed. Sarah Taube finished the remainder of the questions without a problem.

"You and your children have been approved," he said, stamping the word "Admitted" beside their names on the Manifest, "but your husband will need further questioning. Please step aside."

Sarah Taube observed a notation written beside Charles's name, stating there were suspicions of him having senility, which could affect his ability to earn a living. He was pulled over to one side and taken into a small windowless room behind the inspection's station.

"*Mammeh*," Chaya whispered as not to alarm her sister and brother, "why did they take *Tateh* into that room?"

"Don't worry, *myne kind*," her mother replied, wrapping her arms around her daughter. "He will be out soon."

Sarah Taube did not want to upset the children but she was worried. What if he were denied entry? She could not allow him to return to Lithuania alone. She knew he could not survive without her.

The children sat on a nearby bench with their eyes fixed steadily at the closed door, wondering what was happening to their father.

After a while, the door to the room opened, and when Charles came out, a smile appeared on his face for the first time since the journey began.

Sarah Taube rushed to his side. "What happened in there?" she asked, realizing that his smile might be a good thing.

Charles took her into his arms, the way he used to when they were first married. "Don't worry, my Sarala," he said, kissing her gently. "They asked me more questions and when they were satisfied my memory was not impaired, they stamped the Manifest, "Admitted". The inspector said my family and I were free to pass through the gate. He shook my hand and welcomed me to America."

Sarah Taube breathed a sigh of relief. She had thought the worst. G-d in heaven was truly looking out for the Grazutis family that day.

"Pardon me," Sarah Taube said, when she approached an officer standing nearby. "My family and I have just been admitted to America. I am to meet my brother. Where do I go?"

"Oh, you're looking for the New York Room, madam," he replied, pointing to the appropriate stairway.

"Thank you, sir," she said just before she made her way with her family down the stairs and through the front door of a large yellow room with wooden benches.

A smartly dressed man with silver-gray hair, wearing a black coat and pinstripe trousers, stepped forward.

When he came closer, his eyes lit up and a smile passed his face.

"Sarah Taube, Sarah Taube," he called.

"Aaron, Aaron," she cried.

"Aha," he said with a twinkle in his eye. "I knew it was you, *myne tay'er shvester.* I knew it was you."

They ran into each other's arms. Tears flowed down Sarah Taube's face.

"I've dreamt of this day for so long, *myne tay'er bruder.*"

Aaron took out a crisp, white handkerchief from his coat pocket, and as he gently wiped the tears from his sister's face, he murmured softly, "You're home at last, my dear sister. You're home at last."

# Epilogue

Leah and Morris Levitt

Leah and Morris Levitt left Shavlan in 1909 and settled in Baltimore where Morris began working for his cousin as a cashier in a grocery store. He continued to work there for many years. They were able to save money and buy a small row house in the downtown section of the city.

When Sarah Taube and her family came to Baltimore in 1923, they stayed with Leah and Morris until they were able to buy a row house nearby with the money Charles had saved in South Africa.

Aunt Leah lived until she was seventy-five years old. Uncle Morris died a few years later at the age of eighty.

Mrs. Bleekman

In 1923, Mrs. Bleekman left for America. She moved in with her sister-in-law in Brooklyn, New York and adjusted very quickly to her new life. She joined the sisterhood at the local synagogue and made many wonderful friendships.

Before long, she found herself once again trying to bring together a *shidduch* between various single or divorced people. It was not any different from in the old country. People still wanted to meet their ***bashert***, even if it was through a matchmaker.

After a few successful matches, her reputation began to soar. In a short period of time, she had built up an extensive dossier of singles, widows, widowers and divorcees and began to offer meetings in her home between selected parties, charging small fees for her services.

As her reputation grew, so did her clientele, and before long she had many successes in putting together *shidduchs*. Word traveled fast in the community.

Not only was she a successful matchmaker, but she also became a very successful businesswoman. She formed a company and called it "Mrs. Bleekman's Matchmaking Service." In fact, one could say she had created one of the first dating services in American history.

Her company flourished for many years and from it she became a very wealthy woman. She never remarried but enjoyed seeing others joined in matrimony. She continued her matchmaking business until she was well into her eighties. After suffering a stroke, she sold her business and, in 1943, moved to Florida and lived there until her death in 1950.

Aaron and Clara Fineberg

Aaron and Clara lived in their brownstone in New York City for the remainder of their lives. Although Sarah Taube resided in Baltimore, she and her brother remained very close and kept in touch throughout the years. Aaron passed away in 1948. His wife Clara lived for several more years, enjoying her daughter Tessie and her two grandchildren.

Chaim Gluckman

Chaim Gluckman remained in Johannesburg, South Africa, and opened several more tailor shops throughout the area. After several years he met a woman who had emigrated from his hometown, Shidleve. They married and had two sons. His business thrived and after his death, his two sons ran his shops. Today, the shops still exist and are known as Chaim Gluckman and Sons.

Bessie and Bernard Meyers

Bessie and Bernard Meyers went on with their lives living in the East End of London. Bernard always wanted to emigrate to Palestine but his dream never came true. Bessie could not bring herself to move there. She had gotten used to her life in London, and the change would have been too dramatic for her.

Bernard continued to work until his retirement in 1950. Even though he worked very hard, he could never improve his status in life. They both continued to live in the East End of London until their deaths. Bessie died in 1953 and Bernard, in 1955.

After college, their son Leonard married and left for America, settling in Walnut Hills, California. While on vacation in 1989, the author visited Leonard who was then living in Los Angeles.

Mrs. Jacobs

Mrs. Jacobs emigrated to America in 1923 and went to live with her sister in the Bronx, New York. With Mrs. Jacobs' experience as a caterer, she started a catering business in New York. Starting out on a very small scale, doing private parties and group luncheons, her reputation grew and her clientele increased greatly.

She began doing upscale weddings and bar mitzvahs, hiring more staff to accommodate the demands of her customers, and went on to become one of the most sought-after caterers in The Bronx.

After running her catering business for over twenty years, she decided it was time to enjoy the remainder of her life, and so she sold the business and began traveling throughout the United States.

She did volunteer work at the local food bank, which fulfilled a need in her to help the less fortunate. In 1955, after a short illness, she passed away.

Freida and Garson Rodner

Freida and Garson Rodner, along with their three children, continued to live in Ellwood City. In 1930, Garson was offered a partnership by a friend who was opening a large printing shop in Los Angeles, California. It was an opportunity he could not pass up.

After many years of running a successful printing business, Garson and his partner decided it was time to sell. They had built it up to be one of the most lucrative companies in the area and had many offers. The business was sold and Garson retired.

Garson lived to be ninety years old and passed away in 1980, while Freida lived another five years.

In 1989, the author and her husband visited Los Angeles and met, for the first time, Freida and Garson's children Sarah, Dorothy and Leonard. Sarah talked about her experiences with Rose and the other members of the Grazutis family.

Shaina Shulman

Shaina Shulman, her son and daughter, along with her sisters, remained in Shavlan and continued to operate the General Store.

Her daughter, Rifka was married in Shavlan and in 1929 emigrated with her husband to Johannesburg, South Africa, where she raised a daughter named Nessa.

Caught up in the Second World War, on October 2, 1941, Shaina's sisters and her son, along with other relatives and all remaining Jews of Shavlan, were taken by the Nazis, aided by the Lithuanians, and marched to Zagare Town Park, where they were murdered.

Rifka's daughter, Nessa, grew into a lovely young woman and

fulfilled her life long dream of becoming a physician. After graduating from medical school, she met and married another physician and set up practice. In 1970, they moved to the United States and settled in a suburb outside of Washington, D.C.

As fate would have it, Shaina's granddaughter, Nessa and Sarah Taube's granddaughter, Eunice, the author, met many years later while they were both searching for information on their ancestral town, Shavlan. When Nessa and Eunice learned they both had ancestors who once lived in the same shtetl in Lithuania, they were overcome with emotion. It was almost impossible to believe this could happen and yet it did. To use the Yiddish word, it must have been ***beshert.***

Count Simonis

Count Simonis lived in Siaulenai (Shavlan) until 1939, when the Russians took over Lithuania.

One evening while his loyal servant, Mr. Sadunas, was in town, Mr. Vycas, the police commissioner, approached him and informed him he would soon be in charge of running the count's affairs. He secretly told him there was an order issued for the count and his family's arrest, and they were to be sent to Siberia. The count was considered bourgeois and a capitalist, and his wealth needed to be taken away from him and given to the working class.

When hearing this news, Mr. Sadunas immediately told the count. The count, not having much time, quickly arranged for him and his family to be smuggled out of the country.

He relocated to a small farm town in Germany where, because of his agricultural experience, he managed the agricultural production on a farm owned by a small landowner.

After World War II, the count and his family emigrated to the United States and settled in Chicago, Illinois, which had a very large Lithuanian population. The count was quite elderly by this time and lived for another five years, dying at the age of ninety-two.

Vytas Simonis

After finishing his schooling in Switzerland in 1918, Vytas returned to Siaulenai (Shavlan), where he took over many responsibilities of running his father's estate, and in 1927, he married and had a son named Mykolas.

In 1939 he, his family and his parents, in order to avoid arrest and deportation to Siberia, escaped to Germany. Five years after the end of World War II, the family emigrated to the United States and settled in Chicago, Illinois.

Vytas's son Mykolas was twenty-one years old when he emigrated to Chicago with his family. At an early age he developed a passion for drawing and painting and attended the Art Institute of Chicago where, in 1956, he received his M.F.A. He spent most of his time teaching in various colleges. He also loved illustrating books and later became interested in designing bookplates.

In later years, he went back to Siaulenai in order to reclaim his grandfather's estate, and after many years of litigation, he was awarded his ancestor's property. However, due to rigid laws and regulations, he found he could not do as he pleased with the estate and decided to give it back to the Lithuanians.

Sarah Taube's granddaughter Eunice, while doing research for this book, happened to come in contact with Vytas's son, Mykolas, and through him she learned a great deal about his grandfather, Count Simonis, and the shtetl of her ancestors; and she will be forever indebted to him.

Mrs. Rubin

Mrs. Rubin remained in Shavlan and continued to assist women in childbirth. In her home she set aside a special room where women would come for periodic examinations during their pregnancies, and many times she would perform deliveries on the premises, especially if the patient was from another shtetl.

She continued her practice up until 1941, when the Nazis took control of Lithuania. According to the town's official records, she and the remaining Jews were rounded up by the Nazis and on October 2, 1941, aided by the Lithuanians, marched to Zagare Town Park where they were massacred.

David Schoenberg

Madeleine Solvey

David Schoenberg settled in Johannesburg, South Africa. He frequently came in contact with Madeleine Solvey, who continued to run her establishment for several more years. Everyone in town was well aware, however, of the kind of hotel she ran. The genteel residents of the area considered her to be a woman of low morals.

On occasion, she would run into Mr. Schoenberg, and would often confess to him how unhappy she was with her life. A romance soon developed between them and in 1920 they married. Mr. Schoenberg wanted to make an honest woman of her, and so he convinced her to close down her House of Pleasure and turned it into a legitimate hotel.

Although it took several years, Madeleine was finally accepted as a respectable member of the community, mainly because of Mr. Schoenberg's influence. They raised two well-mannered children and lived a very happy and productive life.

Madeleine continued to operate the hotel until she became ill. She passed away in 1955, while David lived another ten years. Their children took over the hotel and operate it to this very day. The hotel still goes by the name of Hotel Victoria.

Raisa Brodsky

Raisa, after being deported by the immigration authorities, returned to Bialystok, Russia. It was determined, as the doctors at Ellis Island had suspected, she did, indeed, have tuberculosis. Although, at that time, there were no cures for the disease, there were various treatments which had a healing effect. It was suggested she go to a sanatorium where she could receive a regime of rest and good nutrition.

Raisa did not have the finances to go to a sanatorium, but when her fiancé discovered the reason why she was deported, he sent her money so she could get the proper treatment. He loved her very much and still had hopes of her joining him in America.

After almost a year at the sanatorium, her condition worsened. Within six months, Raisa was dead, and Raisa's family notified Alfred about her passing.

It was a very sad story about two young lovers who wanted to begin a new life together in a new country, but as fate would have it, it was not to be.

Feige Rowin

Feige Rowin was met by her fiancé, Jordan, at the famous Kissing Post at Ellis Island. After gathering up Feige's belongings, Jordan and she took the ferry to Manhattan, where he had a small apartment not too far from the garment district.

Jordan was interested in becoming a well-known dress designer, but he knew he had to start at the bottom and work his way up the ladder. He was lucky to get a job working as an assistant designer at one of the large dress factories in Manhattan, and after a few months, he and Feige married.

Because of Feige's beautiful figure and good looks, Jordan managed to get her a job modeling high fashion clothing and within two years, she became one of the top models in New York. Through hard work and perseverance, Jordan's dream came true. He became one of New York's top fashion designers, creating costumes for the motion picture industry and Broadway Theater.

Alisa Rosenbaum

As a young girl, Alisa developed a love for the liberal arts and showed a good deal of promise by writing screenplays and novels. After graduating from Petrograd State University in 1924, she studied Screen Arts for a year at the State Technicum.

In 1926, she applied for a visa to visit relatives in America, and one of the relatives owned a movie theatre, where she was able to watch many films. The movies fascinated her and because she had expectations of becoming a screenwriter, she moved to Hollywood to fulfill her dream.

It was very difficult for her to survive once she got to Hollywood, but she was lucky to meet director Cecil B. DeMille, who gave her a job as an extra in one of his movies and from there she became a junior screenwriter.

While on a set, she met her future husband, Frank O'Connor, a promising young actor and they were married in 1929. Several years later she became an American citizen. She missed her family very much and tried many times to bring them to the United States, but they could never get authorization to leave Russia.

Alisa Rosenbaum went on to become a very successful writer, and her two most notable novels were The Fountainhead, and Atlas Shrugged. Her professional name was Ayn Rand. She remained married to her husband until he died in 1979 and followed him in death the 6th of March 1982.

Dimitri Bogdonovich

Dimitri Bogdonovich continued to serve as an administrator in Ekaterinoslav. He did an excellent job for the Party, and his career progressed with more important assignments which he executed diligently. As he became more popular, he came under the close scrutiny of Stalin. In his insane jealousy of anyone who could threaten his position as Dictator, Stalin developed a plan to arrange to have Dimitri guarded by special agents of the secret police. Then Stalin, a few months later, instructed Beria, the head of the secret police, to have Dimitri assassinated.

The following day according to Pravda:

*Yesterday, Dimitri Bogdonovich, a trusted and loyal member of the Party, was assassinated by a mentally deranged Jew named Abraham Klamensky. In spite of the efforts of our beloved leader, Joseph Stalin, to protect Dimitri Bogdonovich by around-the-clock police security, the assassin was able to shoot the victim in the head two times as he left his apartment yesterday morning.*

Rabbi Zev-Wolf Broide

On July 1, 1923, Rabbi Broide and his family emigrated to America where they took up residence in the south side of Baltimore, Maryland.

The Synagogue, Beth Hamedrosh Hagodol, was located on South High Street. The area had been a long-established Jewish community, and Rabbi Broide was very happy to be part of it. The congregation welcomed him just as his flock from Shavlan had done so many years before.

The Synagogue, in 1936, moved to a new location, at 2041 East Baltimore Street.

Five years after Ida (Chaya) Grazutis was married, she and her husband bought their first house on East Baltimore Street directly across from Rabbi Broide's Synagogue.

Rabbi Broide taught Ida's children Hebrew just as he had taught Ida's brother Yankel years before in the shtetl of Shavlan. He remained the rabbi there until 1945, when he retired. He continued to be active in the Jewish community until his death in 1955.

Masha Grazutis

After arriving in Baltimore with his family in 1923, he changed his name to Morris. He attended school and learned English, and at the age of eighteen, he enrolled in a trade school to become a barber.

Shortly afterwards, his mother Sarah Taube, acting as a matchmaker, arranged for him to be introduced to Eva, a young American born woman she knew through friends. After they married, Morris bought a barbershop in East Baltimore and had three children.

Morris' personality remained the same. He continued to work as a barber and in 1984, passed away.

Fraida Grazutis

Fraida changed her name to Freida shortly after arriving in America. She was enrolled in the public school system and graduated at the age of eighteen.

A year later, she met her future husband, Sam, another Jewish immigrant and was married in 1929. Her first child, a son, was named after his grandfather, Charles. She went on to have two more children.

Later on in life, Sam became ill, and Freida nursed him until his death in December 1969. Freida lived for ten more years.

Chaya Grazutis

Chaya changed her name to Ida shortly after arriving in Baltimore. She went to night school to learn English. She was a good seamstress and got a job working in a pajama factory.

Several years later, while riding on a streetcar, Ida's mother, Sarah Taube, met a young man named Joseph whom she had been introduced to a few years back. She mentioned to him she had an unmarried daughter and arranged a meeting between the two of them. It seemed Sarah Taube had learned a great deal from Mrs. Bleekman, the matchmaker as she herself was matchmaking, although she did not realize it at the time.

Ida and Joseph were married in 1930 and within five years they had two children, a son named Charles, who was also named after his grandfather Charles and a daughter named Eunice.

Joseph bought a grocery store in 1948, and Ida helped him in the business. After several years, they bought a row house in the northwest section of town. Joseph purchased an automobile and continued to travel to and from work.

In 1961 Eunice married and had two daughters, Cynthia and Deborah. Joseph and Ida sold the store in 1962 and retired. They enjoyed their retirement years and especially spending time with their grandchildren. Joseph died in 1969 while Ida lived to age eighty-eight, passing away in 1993.

Rose and William Krause

When Sarah Taube and the family moved to America in 1923, Rose was no longer happy living in Ellwood City, Pennsylvania. She wanted to relocate close to her mother and family in Baltimore. William sold his business, and he and Rose moved to Baltimore where he opened another Fruit and Flower Shop.

In 1962, it was discovered William had cancer and after a short illness, he passed away that same year. Rose moved to the Levindale Home for the Aged in Baltimore a few years later.

After two months, Rose met a very nice couple who had been living in the home for several years and they became very good friends. After the gentleman's wife passed away, Rose received an offer of marriage from him.

Rose consulted with her sisters, Ida and Freida before she accepted the gentleman's proposal. This was the first time in the history of the home two residents wanted to join in matrimony. A special Board of Directors meeting was called to decide what to do about this unusual situation.

After considerable discussions, they decided to allow the marriage. After all, who were they to stand in the way of two lonely people trying to find a bit of happiness during the twilight years of their lives. Ida and her husband agreed to have the wedding at their home and invited all the relatives to witness the ceremony.

The management of the home prepared a large room located in the East Wing of the building, where they spent their remaining years, sharing each other's company.

Rose had been suffering with arthritis for quite some time, and it was beginning to take a toll on her body. In 1978, she became totally incapacitated and in the spring of 1979 she passed away.

Charles Grazutis

Charles' health began to decline shortly after he arrived in America. Sarah Taube took very good care of him but he was growing worse. In 1926, he became ill. When he saw a doctor, it was discovered he had throat cancer. The disease was in its last stages, and within six months, he was dead.

Sarah Taube Grazutis

After meeting with her brother in the New York Room at Ellis Island, Sarah Taube and her family boarded the train for Baltimore where Aunt Leah and Uncle Morris were awaiting their arrival.

Within a short time, Sarah Taube and Charles had purchased a home, and in order to bring money into the house, she operated a stall in a local market a few blocks away.

After her children were married, Sarah Taube remained in her home until it became difficult for her to manage her affairs. In 1946, she developed diabetes, which required insulin shots. She was seventy-eight years old and at this time in her life, decided it would be best for her if she moved into a nursing home where she could be given proper care. She did not want to burden her children and felt this was the right thing to do.

Sarah Taube enjoyed her grandchildren very much, and they loved her dearly. She was very smart and kind. All the grandchildren called her *Bubbe*.

Eunice, Ida's daughter, as a teenager, would often visit her grandmother, accompanied by her girlfriend Marilyn. One Sunday morning while visiting her grandmother, Eunice noticed a bottle of rose water sitting on a chest of drawers. She observed her grandmother combing rose water through her long gray hair, and, with a single motion, she pulled her hair tightly into a bun, neatly centering it on the back of her head, securing it with two straight pins.

Eunice was very curious about the life her grandmother had led in the old country and would ask her many questions. "What happened to you during the First World War? How did you survive during your exile to Ekaterinoslav? How did you cope while witnessing the demise of the Russian Empire?"

After attending Eunice's high school graduation in 1955, sadly, Sarah Taube fell ill and died at the age of eight-eight.

As a result of the stories her grandmother recounted, Eunice became interested in the genealogy of the Grazutis family, and in 1996, after visiting her maternal ancestor's home in Shavlan, she began to work on Sarah Taube's story.

Recently, while Eunice was shopping at a nearby bath and body shop, she came across a display of rose water. She quickly opened a sample bottle and took a deep whiff. It took only a moment for the image of her grandmother to appear, combing the fragrance through her long silky hair.

At that moment, all the memories of her *Bubbe* came rushing back and a warm feeling came over her. She had to buy a bottle of the rose water so whenever she needed to feel her grandmother's presence, she could take a deep whiff and let out a long sigh, wishing for days gone by.

Shavlan

On JewishGen's website, the author developed a webpage on Shavlan, which may be of interest to those reading this novel.

JewishGen is a free website, featuring databases, research tools, and other resources to help those doing Jewish ancestry research. Simply log on to https://kehilalinks.jewishgen.org and click on Lithuania and then click on Siaulenai (Shavlan).

# Photos

**Photo of Sarah Taube's mother's brass candlesticks and her great-grandmother's copper pot handed down to her by her Aunt Lena in May of 1888.**

Photo of Shavlan Synagogue as it looked at the time Sara Taube lived there. Courtesy of Lituanus, Lithuanian Quarterly Journal of Arts and Sciences, Volume 27, No. 3 - Fall 1981.

Photo of the Bimah in the Shavlan Synagogue. Courtesy of Lituanus, Lithuanian Quarterly Journal of Arts and Sciences, Volume 27, No. 3 - Fall 1981.

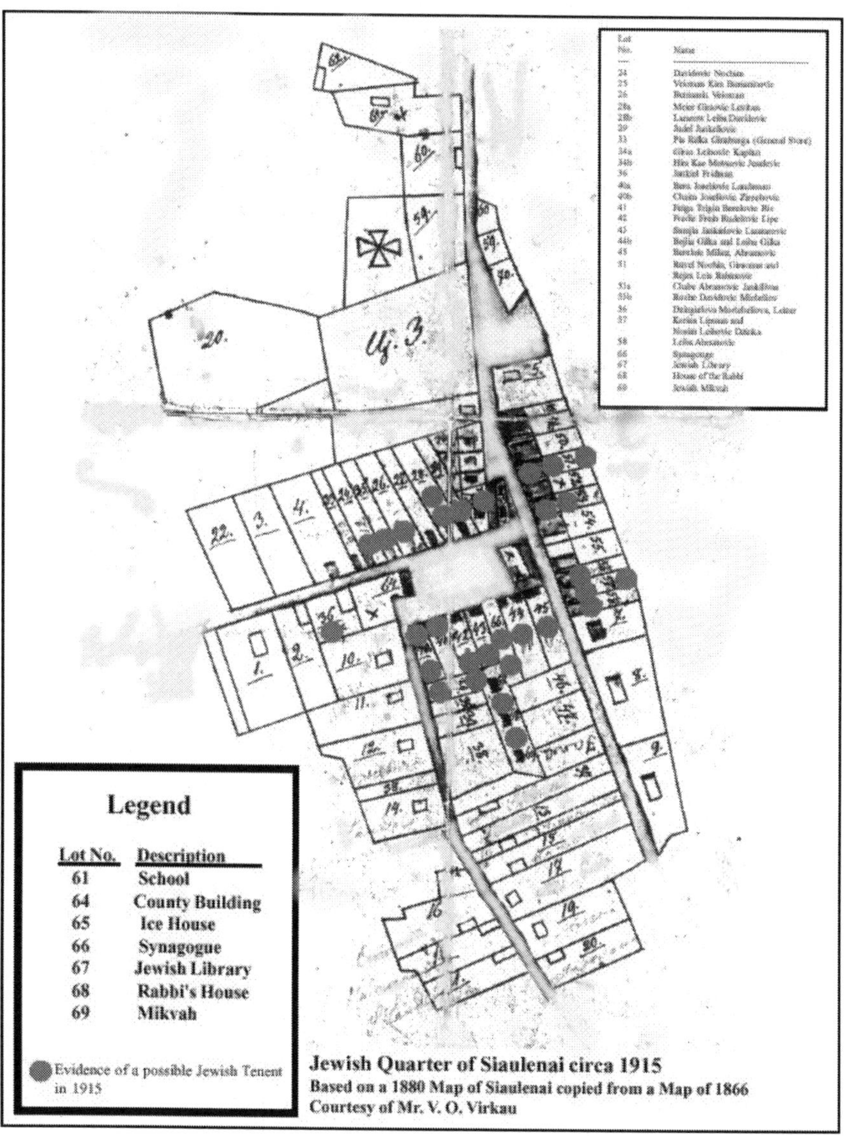


Jewish Quarter of Shavlan circa 1915. Courtesy of Mr. V. O. Virkau.

Photo taken of Chaya Grazutis (Sarah Taube's daughter and the author's mother) in June 1923 before she left for America.

**Photo of Rose (Ruchel) Krause circa 1923.**

# EUNICE E. BLECKER

# Historical Notes

Early in the 12th century, Duke Mandauga of Lithuania needed help improving his country's economic status. He sent representatives into Western Europe, mostly France and along the towns of the Rhineland in Germany, to entice Jews to emigrate to his country with the promise of religious freedom.

Life for the Jews in Western Europe was very hard, subjecting them to many restrictions and religious persecution; so because of the Duke's willingness to bring them to his country and allow them to practice their religion freely, many of them took him up on his offer and left their homes. This accounts for many Jews in the Pale of Settlement having German surnames. Yiddish, spoken by these Jews, evolved as a German dialect written with Hebrew script. The Jews who settled in smaller towns referred to their villages as shtetls.

The town of Siaulenai, referred to by the Jewish inhabitants as Shavlan, was first mentioned in the mid-fifteenth century as being part of an estate and Manor House owned by Andrius Semeta.

As per family history, in the 14th century, because of his bravery, Andrius Semeta was granted a large piece of land located in the Samogitia duchy/eldership of Lithuania. He was also granted a family Coat of Arms, which was a crest of a swan on an azure background as well as a short-handle scythe on gold.

Through the generations, the land was handed down to the Semeta descendants. Those who inherited land through their ancestors were recognized by law as an advantaged class and were considered a member of nobility.

Shortly after the death of the last Semeta landowner, his wife remarried and the property was parceled off between her and other relatives. Because all property in Shavlan was considered rental properties, Jews and non-Jews were required to pay rent to the owners for the houses they lived in.

The Jews of Shavlan earned their livelihood as small business owners such as shoemakers, tailors, butchers, and storekeepers, and they also worked the land, producing fruits and vegetables.

Not too far from the marketplace was an old wooden synagogue dating as far back as 1650.

In 1765, the town had approximately 33 Jewish homes with 160 Jewish inhabitants.

Under the Tsarist regime, Siaulenai was known in Russian as Шавлян. It may also be listed on historical documents as Shavlan, Shavlyan, Shavlyany, or Szawlany.

After Lithuania regained independence from Russia in 1918, inhabitants were free to purchase the lots or pay rent. Some did and some did not according to their circumstances.

In 1915, the population of Shavlan was approximately 1000 people, 50% of which were Jewish. In 1923, the Jewish population had decreased to about 200 due to emigration.

The author has used the Gregorian calendar for all dates used in this novel.

During the time frame in which events take place in the novel, names of towns and cities in the Russian Empire were changed. Yiddish names of places differed from the Russian or Lithuanian names. However, the Yiddish names remained constant throughout the history referred to in this story.

After the start of World War 1, the Tsarist government, believing the name sounded too German, changed the name of St. Petersburg to Petrograd.

A chart of alternate names, for your reference, appears on the next page, showing the cities and towns, their Yiddish, Russian and Lithuanian names.

Note: For those who are interested in finding out more about Shavlan, you are invited to go to the JewishGen website at: https://kehilalinks.jewishgen.org and click on Lithuania and then click on Siaulenai (Shavlan).

Bibliography/Resources:

Excerpts taken from the Lithuanian Encyclopedia, sundry articles in the Lithuanian press and from a monograph "Siaulenai", a book of 204 pages comprised of various topics and many authors, published in Vilnius in 2004.

# Location Names

| YIDDISH | RUSSIAN | LITHUANIAN |
|---|---|---|
| Kiev | Kiev | Kiev |
| Kovne | Kovno | Kaunas |
| Mozir | Mozyr | Mozyr |
| Shavl | Shavli | Siauliai |
| Shavlan | Szawlany | Siaulenai |
| Shirvint | Shirvinty | Sirvintos |
| Vilkomir | Vilkomir | Ukmerge |
| Vilne | Vilna | Vilnius |
| Yekaterinoslav | Ekaterinoslav | Ekaterinoslav |

# Acknowledgments

I will be forever indebted to the following people for their contributions to this book.

First and foremost to my husband, Herb, my first and final reader, who helped shape my thoughts, raised fruitful objections, provided me with the historical background I needed to tell this story, and assisted in the editing and formatting of the manuscript. Thank you for giving me all of your support and encouragement and for being my constant source of inspiration. Without you, the telling of this story might never have come to pass.

Next, I would like to thank Professor Philip Goldberg for his professional advice and assistance in editing my manuscript. I thank him for his expertise, useful critiques and willingness to give his time.

To my daughter Cynde, I would like to offer my special thanks for reviewing my final draft and aiding in the editing. Thank you for your critical and helpful comments.

Lastly, a special word of gratitude to Susan Weinstein who, during the early stages of my novel, read, edited and commented on several chapters. Thank you for your thoughtfulness in volunteering to read and make comments.

EUNICE E. BLECKER

# About the Author

Eunice Blecker was born, raised and educated in Baltimore, Maryland. She worked full time as treasurer for an engineering software company while raising two daughters. Fascinated by the stories her grandmother told about the life she led in the old country, Eunice was inspired to tell her story.

In 1996, after she and her husband, Herb visited her ancestral town, Shavlan, she wrote an article "To Walk Their Walk" published in Mishpacha, Volume 17, No 1 - Winter 1997, a quarterly publication of The Jewish Genealogy Society of Greater Washington.

Eunice lives in Potomac, Maryland with her husband, Herb and two Siamese cats, Chloe and Lacy.

Please visit the author's website at www.Shavlan.com.

# SHAVLAN

Made in the USA
Middletown, DE
17 October 2021